this much is true

Books by *Katherine Owen*

Truth In Lies Series

This Much Is True, Book 1

The Truth About Air & Water, Book 2

untitled, Book 3, 2015 release

Standalone Novels

Seeing Julia

When I See You

Not To Us

Katherine Owen

The Writing Works Group

Seattle

this much is true

a novel

This book is a work of fiction. Names, characters, businesses, organizations, places, events, and incidents are all a product of the author's imagination or are used fictitiously. Any resemblance to actual persons, living or dead, events, or locales is entirely coincidental.

ISBN: 978-0-9835707-69
eISBN: 978-0-9835707-76

Text design by The Writing Works Group
Cover design by The Writing Works Group

PHOTOS:

The Writing Works Group

Book Design - Cover & Interior

PHOTOS:
© Geber86 | Sexy Male Model
© Yuliya Yafimik | Beauty portrait of beautiful brunette girl in the studio
© vasst | Female standing against grey wall
© Beto Chagas | Baseball Player pitching a ball
©Doodkoalex | Beautiful Dancer on black Dreamstime

Printed in the United States of America

First Edition

DEDICATION

THIS BOOK IS DEDICATED TO MY daughter Lauren, who has stuck with me throughout the premise and ongoing (sometimes, never-ending) development of this particular story line from the beginning. All I ask for in return is that she no longer steals my character names for her pets. It's distracting.

Katherine Owen

PART 1 — FALLING

OUBT THOU THE STARS ARE FIRE;
DOUBT THAT THE SUN DOTH MOVE;

DOUBT TRUTH TO BE A LIAR;

BUT NEVER DOUBT I LOVE.

~ William Shakespeare
(Hamlet, 1.2.123-6)

CHAPTER ONE

Tally · If I die young

WE'RE DRIVING.

We're driving and arguing.

These are our two favorite pastimes these last days; it seems.

I've lost her already; I just fail to register its absolute permanence.

I'm driving actually. We're arguing, and it's raining. I make my way over from 280 to the 101 because I am more familiar with the freeway that takes us from the swankiest neighborhood called Sea Cliff back home. And I'm driving because Holly is too hyped up from her secret rendezvous with Rob Thorn; and I am too pissed off at her after waiting in the car for two hours while she met up with him in this stupid clandestine effort to prove her love to him because of their big fight just yesterday. And it's Valentine's Day. What couple in their right mind breaks up the day before Valentine's Day? *Rob and Holly.* So today has to be make up day.

I'm driving. And I'm pissed.

We're arguing.

And it's raining.

"You know what your problem is?" Holly asks.

"My problem is Rob Thorn," I retort, which is definitely unkind and borderline bitchy.

Holly shakes her head at me in sudden fury. I'm not sure she expected an answer from me quite so readily, or that one in particular, but she launches into a long lecture. About *me*. Apparently, I sleep around with way too many guys for her liking. *This*—according to my twin's thou-shalt-never-disappoint-mom-and-dad quest for perfection—is my problem. This wielding of moral judgment is a recent development for my twin. Holly slept around plenty, too, before she and Rob Thorn got together. She goes on and on about me being selfish and not caring about anyone else. She manages to deliver a low blow when she accuses me of only caring about ballet and what Allaire Tremblay thinks. I wince because it's so true.

"Ballet is my life. Allaire Tremblay is the best ballet teacher on the West Coast, and we are lucky to have her," I say and shoot her a dirty look. Holly used to care about ballet, too. *Used to.* Now all she cares about is Rob Thorn. It's Rob this and Rob that; I'm so tired of it. Regardless, I just let her talk and try to concentrate on the freeway while Holly just goes off on me. I basically tune her out. Yes, I allow Holly to talk for a long while about my shortcomings and my rebellious lifestyle that constantly upsets Mom and Dad. I let her talk and talk and talk. Finally, I say in true Tally Landon style with a distinctive measure of vehemence for pure effect, "Oh, fuck off, Holly!"

That shuts her up for a good three minutes. Dear Holly doesn't like it when I resort to using the f-word. I can't help it most of the time. That word fits just about every situation there is in life, at least to my way of thinking. I glare in her general direction and then concentrate more fully on the rain that's pounding at my old car's windshield. It reminds me of latex paint that's been carelessly splashed against a wall. Or better, it's like all the splashed blood that's everywhere in that Stephen King movie *Carrie*. My sister always refuses to watch it with me. Holly doesn't like to be scared whereas I tend to use it as a strategy as part of my constant battle to be unafraid and conquer my biggest fears, which come in threes: falling, failing, and losing.

The wipers rage on high, but they aren't making any difference in visibility whatsoever. I can barely spot the cars in front of us now, and it's getting dark—darker than when we first started out from Sea Cliff, where the irritating boyfriend, the one and only Rob Thorn, resides. He lives a long forty miles up the road from Palo Alto High School so why he still attends school at Paly doesn't make any sense to me or anyone else, except Holly. Oh, yes, the inevitable answer to that question sits right next to me. *Holly.* I glance over at my twin and smile ever so slightly because it's hard to stay mad at her.

Everybody loves Holly.

Me, most of all.

The traffic is worse than usual, even for a Sunday, and we're late. Mom's probably wondering where we are. Our best friend Marla is probably doing the same.

I sent her an overjoyed text earlier, briefly filling her in on the big fight Holly had with Rob the night before. However, I haven't gotten a chance to send a follow-up text beyond the one about the frantic drive up north to Rob's, and now I have to backtrack and report the dismal update that the two lovebirds are apparently back together.

Sure, life at Paly contains angst just about every day. We're seniors in high school, four months from graduating, and about to embark on the greatest time of our lives according to pretty much everyone. Yet my sister seems to be in a huge rush to make things permanent with Rob Thorn, and I really don't understand this at all.

She's been without her own car for two weeks for some vague punishment our parents meted out on her for carelessly bashing in the passenger side door of her Jetta at some strip mall. With her car indisposed at the auto body shop—getting the dent fixed as well as a new paint job because, in the end, Mom and Dad felt bad for her, like always—I drove her to Sea Cliff against my better judgment, as in all things related to Rob Thorn. I drove because, although Holly takes good care of her things—including her car at almost a meticulous level of attachment—my boat of a car was the only form of transportation available. I sure as hell wasn't going to let her drive my car after she wrecked her own. I love my Mercedes. My dad bought it for me at an auction two years ago. Unlike Holly's sporty Jetta, I think my old car exudes uniqueness and style. It's bad-ass, like me. I smile over at Holly again because I let her criticisms roll off of me like rainwater and don't really listen all that closely. Holly is Holly. I am most definitely me. I'm not going to change, and we both know it, and I let her know this now.

"I like my life and the way I conduct it. Ballet is all there is because it's the most important thing. To me. And, you know that." We're done fighting. I know this when I get a glimpse of her infamous happy smile. "Sorry for the f-word slip."

"It just makes you sound so vulgar, sis." Holly tucks her hair behind one ear and glances over at me.

God, she is an angel.

"It makes me *hot.*" I laugh as I exaggerate the word, so does Holly. "Besides, guys love it when I scream it out loud at the height of their…you know… climax."

"You have no problem with the word *fuck* but you turn three different shades of pink at the word *climax*. You are an enigma."

"Don't tell anyone." I glance over at her and grin wickedly. "I just want to be like you," I say in a sugar-sweet tone.

"God forbid. Nobody would recognize you. All those guys," she says with a little sigh and rolls her eyes. "I don't know how you keep up."

"That's what birth control is for, baby."

We both laugh and promptly drop the subject of my promiscuity and ever-changing list of guys and chance encounters. I need to concentrate on the road anyway. Traffic suddenly slows way down and is quickly piling up in front of us. I take my foot off the gas and brake a little to slow down the old sedan even more just as the rain becomes more intense, as if that is at all possible. I worry about flash flooding because the freeway lanes have begun to fill up with rainwater, and it feels like we're driving on a river more than a freeway.

I wonder about Rob Thorn and Holly. *Again.* What does she see in him, anyway? Why the hell did we have to drive all the way out there from Atherton, so she could express her undying love for that guy? Why do I put up with this? I should have said no. But, no, I didn't. Because it's Valentine's Day, and she was too scared to drive by herself all the way to Sea Cliff and back at almost nighttime because she openly admits that she isn't as good at driving as I am. On this, we do agree.

Although Holly has been all but screaming at me for the past half hour, apparently her tirade at me is over. I served as enough of an emotional outlet for all that pent-up angst she had for the amazing Rob Thorn, which has now mysteriously vanished. She gets this secret smile and closes her eyes and leans back against the headrest. Apparently, they worked out their differences.

"We worked everything out, and we're back together," she says.

"What do you *see* in him anyway?" I ask again for what feels like the hundredth time in the past year and a half. My unhappiness with the Rob Thorn situation is well-known but, I can never let it go completely.

She opens her eyes and looks over at me with an almost fanatical look. I take a brief moment from looking at the road and gaze into those green eyes of hers that effectively reflect their incredible sameness back at me. She openly laughs and flips her hair back from her sweaty but still beautiful *I-just-had-the-best-sex-of-my-life* face in her always endearing Holly Landon way. I roll my eyes at her and begin to extol the benefits that carefree sex, and no entangling emotional attachments have to offer while she continues to babble on about Rob and this summer and how great everything is going to be.

Her over joyous expression clearly tells me that I'm not going to win this debate today on carefree sex and no emotional attachments with guys so I refocus my efforts on locating the white dashed line indicating our lane, which keeps disappearing, and attempt to see farther down the road up ahead of us. The freeway signs indicate we are still fifteen miles from home, but I calculate that at a steady pace of forty miles an hour, slower than usual, because I'm somewhat responsibly compensating my speed for the inclement weather just like most of the cars that surround us. "We'll be there in fifteen minutes," I say to Holly.

"Tally, I love him," she says with a contented sigh. She pauses for a full minute and looks over at me intently. "Look. We're getting married. *We are,*" she says at my incredulous look. "Soon. We're getting married. It's all planned out."

My twin gets this secret smile while I openly groan and search for the right words to stop this nonsense. But I know that smile. It's the same one I get after every ballet performance, after every first place title I've been awarded, after every standing ovation that follows those hard-won performances. It's all powerful—that smile. I start to return it, but then I remember Rob Thorn—this nemesis that has constantly plagued my life for the past year and a half and has effectively taken Holly away from me.

"You're crazy," I say harshly. "You can't *love him*. You just can't. We have plans. Besides, you have your whole life ahead of you."

"I do. I have my whole life ahead of me, and Rob is a part of that. He's the plan."

It's then that I take a singular, crucial moment to look past her and see the black flash of this over-sized four-wheel-drive SUV as it splashes water everywhere in its erratic path right next to us. It must be doing seventy-five and readily speeds past my slow-moving car. Then the SUV clips my front bumper, suddenly swerves, and proceeds to hydroplane directly into our lane facing the wrong way on the freeway.

Like a personal affront to the oncoming horror, the rearview mirror warning flashes through my mind. *Objects in the mirror are closer than they appear.* I get an unexpected glimpse into our future in that split second. It happens so fast that I don't even make a sound.

Holly's dark hair lights up with all this sudden bright whiteness like there's a halo around her head. She truly looks like an angel for that singular moment. It's clear to me then, even before time alters everything else forever, that I really am the bad twin, have always been the bad twin, and will need to try much harder to be more like Holly.

Then time stalls out and comes to a full stop.

Crash landing.

❦

I come to with this impossibly cold water running down my face, spilling through this unexplainable jagged crack in my precious sunroof. *This will cost a fortune to fix.* My chest feels like I've been hit with a hammer in multiple places. I feel incredibly broken and eye the culprit—the steering wheel—with true contempt as I gasp and attempt to force air into my lungs.

There's this vague whimpering sound right next to me. Blood runs down my forehead and into my eyes. It becomes almost impossible to see. In a daze, I swipe away at the wetness, irritated by this ridiculous spider web that

I somehow have walked into. This doesn't make sense. *Where is the spider?* My eyes sting, but I can see a bit better; and I stare at the unexplainable mixture of blood and rain on my left hand, which just sort of dangles there. *Where is the pain? Why doesn't this hurt?*

I become aware of Holly then. Long dark wet bloody strands of her hair are plastered against the side of my face. She's wedged up against my right shoulder. I try to push her away because her body has mine pinned hard against the driver's door. She moans at my touch. I vaguely wonder why she's so close to me because she was all the way across the bench seat just seconds before, yakking away about Rob Thorn. She's making all these weird, gurgling sounds as if she's drowning. I look around for the water that must have caused this. *Where are we? Why does my chest hurt so much?* I brush her hair back from my face as well as hers and try to assess the situation because somebody needs to forge ahead for some kind of control. Holly's face and neck gush with all this blood. "Holly. Holly. Holly!" Each time it becomes more urgent. After a minute, she opens her eyes and looks over at me with this dazed expression. I think she's smiling, but then dark blood flows up from her mouth. Her beautiful white teeth get this garish look. "Holly?"

"Tally," she whispers and then starts to choke. "Get. Out. Go!"

"Holly?"

"Go. Tally. Go. Now."

I do what I am told. *For once.* I feel bad about our fight earlier, so the least I can do is listen to her and go for some help because God knows we need help. So in one rote unpracticed move, I undo the door handle and slide unceremoniously down to the wet pavement below. From behind me, I hear Holly scream. "Run. Run, Tally!" I vaguely note these blue and yellow flames that now lick at her legs from beneath the crushed dashboard of my car. "Run," she says again. Her look conveys that there will be no argument about this. I don't want to give her one. There has been enough arguing between us today.

"Love you, Holly," I call out as I crawl away from the car. For some reason, my legs refuse to cooperate. I can't stand up. I drag my body along the wet concrete on my forearms. I keep telling myself I can do this. Then, these strong arms lift me skyward. The rain endlessly pelts my face and my uncooperative limbs. It drenches my clothes while this intense pulsing pain comes out of nowhere and becomes almost unbearable all at once over my entire body. It's difficult to breathe, and I fight for every breath. I frantically scan the crowd that has suddenly gathered along the stopped freeway and search for any sign of Holly. *Is someone helping Holly?*

"Need. Help," I say to the stranger who carries me.

We run—this stranger and me. *He runs*. His baseball jacket and jeans are already soaked by the heavy rain. His dark black hair is plastered against one side of his face. He wears a Stanford Cardinal baseball cap backward at a jaunty, cool-guy angle. I keep thinking his dry-cleaning bill is going to be astronomical in order to get all that blood out of his clothes.

"I was driving. We were arguing. It's become our favorite pastime. We argue over Rob Thorn and my overuse of the word *fuck* all the time."

He looks down at me in surprise. Then, he just looks sad. I start to ask him why but then there's a thundering explosion from right behind us. He shields my face and runs faster. After a few moments more, he automatically turns, still holding me in his arms. The two of us helplessly watch this raging inferno engulf what's left of my car as well as the black SUV forever welded to it. The flames rise high into the air. There are the faintest screams for a few precious seconds, and the gathering crowd cries out in this unified song of terror. I focus on those screams, despite the hypnotic chorus all around. "My sister. She's an angel," I say in this toneless voice I don't really recognize as the screams die away. I point to my car—the raging inferno that was my car. My wrist dangles at an odd angle and there's so much blood. *It's everywhere.* "My sister."

"Oh God. No," the stranger says.

"There is no God, Elvis," I whisper.

And then there's nothing. Mercifully, the blackness takes me.

Months later, I still hear Holly's screams in my head in just about every moment I'm awake. No need to write horror; I live it.

CHAPTER TWO

Linc ~ There was this girl

"THERE WAS THIS GIRL. SHE WOULD have been brought in a few hours ago? She was in a car accident with her sister. Her sister…she didn't…make it." I swallow hard as I'm all too familiar with how to damp down this kind of painful loss for myself, even though empathy attempts to wrestle with me now. I'm still shaken by what transpired on the 101 just three hours ago. It was horrific for everyone there but especially for the girl I swooped up in my arms and ran away with from the inferno. The image of her beautiful devastated face and haunting emerald green eyes stay with me.

The woman behind the information desk has this long mane of silver hair that's gathered up in this huge gold clip and neatly pulled back from her surprisingly unlined face. I notice the fashionable style because my mom used to wear her hair that way, whenever my mom had a big interview with one of the entertainment shows or a big spread with Harper's or Vogue. Cara Sanderson Presley said it made her feel young and fresh and put together. This woman looks like the same kind of regal queen as my mother as she sits there behind this huge computer monitor that makes it difficult to fully see her.

This lady stares at me with her mouth half-open, as if she's trying to place me but isn't quite sure yet. For my part, I pull my baseball cap forward because the last thing I need is someone to recognize me, *although that might help with the situation.* Seconds later, I decide to take off my cap and hold it in my hands and give her my best *I-need-your-help* look, complete with a charming smile. "There's this girl. She has raven-black hair; well, it's more the color of dark ground espresso, I guess. It's long? She was in a car accident about three hours ago. And I was just wondering…"

"We can't give out information about our patients, young man. And aren't you that baseball player? The one the major leagues are clamoring to sign?

Baseball pitcher. What's your name? A President's name. Something Presley. I remember it because I remember it was Elvis's last name. The singer? Surely you know his songs. Young people these days not remembering Elvis Presley is just a crime. We watch American Idol sometimes, and I keep hoping one year they'll feature his songs because if you really want to know who could sing and dance—well, it had to be Elvis Presley. Well, it's a good way to remember your last name in any case. I'm sure you get that all the time."

"All the time."

"My husband would be thrilled at meeting you. I am, too, of course, but… well, I'm not much for baseball anymore." She sighs. "We used to go all the time, but now it's just so darned expensive. Our son will splurge for tickets every once in a while, and he takes *Dickie*—that's my husband Richard, actually; but everyone's called him Dickie since…well, since we met in the eleventh grade fifty years ago." Her cheeks are flushed, and even her scalp that peaks through her thinning silver hair is tinged a faint pink.

I swoop in when she gives me a chance to speak. "My name is Lincoln Presley. Yes, I'm actually playing on the Stanford Cardinal baseball team again this year. First game next week. Now it's practice pretty much all the time."

"Oh. Well, good luck—although I personally think you should stay in school."

"Yes, ma'am. I'll finish up at Stanford this June. And the sports reporters are covering the stuff with major-league baseball's interest in me. I can't really comment about that. My publicist would have my head if I did." Kimberley would be so proud. I actually try to smile. "My dad's Davis Presley. He played for the Giants. Maybe your husband remembers him."

"Oh, my goodness, yes. Your father is Davis Presley? Then your mom was Cara Sanderson? I remember when she up and married Davis Presley. I loved her films. I'm so sorry she died."

She makes this sympathetic clucking sound while I hold my breath and strive for composure by hanging my head to hide my face before it betrays all these emotions that I don't usually give into when people mention my mom.

"I don't…I don't talk about my mom. I'm sorry."

There's this awkward silence. She folds her hands into her lap and mumbles an apology and manages to look disappointed at the same time. *In me?*

I'm a little taken aback that even this woman demands I talk about my mother. I have to tell myself to forget it, even though I feel bad for a brief moment like I always do. I let the moment pass because, even though it's been eight years, I still hold on tight to the notion that I don't talk about my mom or my brother Elliott to *anyone*, least of all a stranger. My feelings about their loss are mine, and I don't tell anyone how I feel about that. I sigh deeply and start again. "I'm looking for this girl. There was this girl. She was in a car accident, and I was just wondering if you had any way of looking up her information. I'd like to know if she's okay. Her sister…" My voice shakes. The woman's blue eyes alight on mine. She looks sympathetic again. "Her sister didn't make it. I didn't get her name."

"Mr. Presley, I'd like to help you—I *really* would—but I can't give out information about the patients."

"What's the information desk for, then?" I ask gently and flash her one of my most charming smiles as a last-ditch effort to disarm her enough to help me anyway.

"Oh, you know." She gets this little smile. "We tell people how to find their way around. And when people *know* the patient's name, we look up the room number for them and direct them from there. That kind of thing. I'm just a volunteer three days a week. It helps pass the time."

"I'm sure it does." I sigh again and fidget with the baseball cap in my hand.

The woman eyes me closer. "Were you there at the accident? It sounds like it was awful. It's all over the news, and that girl—the other twin—she was too young to die such a horrible death. How sad. I just feel so sorry for the family. He's one of the best…here." Her eyes get teary. "But there was just nothing he could do. It was too late for his daughter." She studies me for a few long seconds, clearly aware of the small tidbit of information she's just given to me. "You really need to get the blood of out your clothes before it completely dries; otherwise, it will never come out. She's not going to want to see you like this. You'll scare her and remind her of the terrible tragedy she's just been through. Poor girl."

"I don't think I'll be wearing these again."

"Why don't you sign for a nice bouquet of flowers with the gift shop? I can make sure they get delivered. I can't give you the room number, but I can deliver it after you leave."

This seems the best I'll be able to do. Charm isn't working today, and my inexplicable quest for pursuing this whole thing begins to weigh upon me. There's nothing I could have done. I did all I could, and clearly it wasn't nearly enough. I push off the counter and head toward the gift shop.

Within minutes, I pick out white roses and baby's breath, and a nice little blue and white vase that I think my mother would have liked. I add a small teddy bear to my purchase as an afterthought once I reach the counter.

I manage to spend a little over $120 on a girl whose name I don't know and probably never will in less than ten minutes. And it still feels like it's not nearly enough. But I have to do something. I lay out my Visa card, and the cashier runs it through with a slightly dazed smile.

Ten minutes later, I'm placing a nice little cardboard box containing the vase of flowers complete with a white ribbon tied around it—because pink seemed inappropriate, and red seemed too morbid—and the little teddy bear tucked in next to it back on Mrs. Trinity's desk. Times ahead were going to be rough for this girl, and giving her some flowers is the least I can do.

Mrs. Trinity beams at me. Women really do like it when you do exactly what they've told you to do. It never ceases to amaze me even under these surreal circumstances.

I can't even explain why I'm here. Why I felt compelled to check three hospitals in the general vicinity of San Francisco and basically got the same answers from the same kind of helpful women at each information desk I went to. This is the first one who suggested the flowers, so I know I am, at least, in the right place this time. I flash her a little smile and give her a slight wave, and she nods with approval at my gifts.

"She'll be better tomorrow. Tonight, she's just resting. Tomorrow, she'll wake up and wonder where her sister is for a few minutes before she remembers." The woman's lips tremble as she says this. "It's very kind of you to do this. I must say, I'm impressed. Now, if you just stay in school, Mr. Presley, and finish up at Stanford before you chase the money and that huge contract for baseball, you'll really make me and your wonderful mother in Heaven both proud."

Audacious. My smile falters a little because she's mentioned my mom again and Heaven in the same sentence.

She waves her index finger at me. "Get those clothes washed. I'll be here again tomorrow. Look for me then, and maybe she'll be well enough to ask me about the flowers and who sent them, and I'll tell her. Oh, you need to sign the card."

She slides the little white card that the cashier placed in with the flowers over to me. *Thinking of You* is printed in black script across the top of the card. I'm not sure it's the best thing to say, but it's better than the other card choice that said *With Sympathy*.

I hate those cards.

I write:
Thinking of you. This much is true,
Elvis

For some reason, the anonymity with the name Elvis seems appropriate. She probably won't even remember that she called me by that name at the accident. I can't be here tomorrow. I *won't* be here tomorrow. I'll be on my way to L.A. to see my dad. I don't volunteer this bit of news to Mrs. Trinity because, for some reason, providing her with that easy excuse and garnering her general disapproval is too much. Truthfully, the idea of seeing the girl from the accident again scares the hell out of me because there was something about her that captivated me at a soul level. Somehow, I think this woman would pick up on that. The truth is this: I can't afford any kind of distraction, not even for the beautiful broken girl with the amazing green eyes and long dark hair lying in a bed somewhere in this hospital.

My one and only focus is baseball. That's the way it's been for almost ten years, and every call from my dad about the upcoming season and major league baseball's June draft serve as constant reminders of that singular focus and commitment to this one and only thing allowed in my life—baseball.

CHAPTER THREE

THE AIR IS DIFFERENT. I CANNOT breathe, and a part of me doesn't really want to anymore. We spent the first seventeen years of our lives together and shared everything from our looks to our clothes to our innermost thoughts.

But then, one day, it was over.
And no one prepares you for that.
No one.

The church where the funeral was held had been packed. And now, at the cemetery, the entire student body of Palo Alto High School (Paly to the initiated) has come. It's a chilly day—this third Saturday in February. Even the promise of spring has made an auspicious retreat. The wind blows off San Francisco Bay as if in conspired commemoration to coincide and dominate the funeral of one Holly Elizabeth Landon. This fierce wind is both cruel and cold; it sears the skin. Its own grief is palpable and felt to the very bone of all the mourners who attend this last event for Holly. God has let there be sun and blue sky; but few bother to look up. No. Most are caught in the foggy haze of nothingness and left to wonder how this kind of tragedy could happen to someone so young and so full of life.

How can she be gone forever?

I feel Holly's loss at such a potent level that my mother has slipped me another one of her Valium. Yes. Pills at regular intervals have been dispensed to keep me functioning among the living. For once, my mother and I agree that pills are the only thing that can potentially save us.

And, for once, I do as I'm told.

I swallow this. I drink that. I wear this. I stand here. I do this. I say that. Rote memorization serves me well in these dark days.

If Holly were here, I would have suggested sneaking away by now. I would have proffered up a pack of my favorite cigarettes, while Holly would have waxed on about the hazards of smoking between every toke she took with me. The thought makes me almost laugh, and I dully acknowledge its inappropriateness at my sister's funeral, even as a fresh round of heartbreak surges across my mid-section and threatens to tear me in half.

I am only half a person now. My better half lies in a casket slightly suspended aboveground, while everyone awaits my reaction and takes turns saying something meaningful about her. I've declined to participate in this social commemoration of the already clearly dead in this way.

What a debacle. What a sham. They do it for themselves—to cleanse themselves in some way—for not being able to do anything to save her in the first place or bring her back from the dead now.

Ignoring the swirling paranoia that flows freely with all eyes upon me—the remaining twin—I slyly glance sideways at Marla.

"Are you okay?" she whispers in that sympathetic all-knowing way of hers.

I focus on her long enough to slightly move my head up and down in answer. Marla is my best friend. Always has been. The three of us had been inseparable even though Marla was more like me—edgy, rebellious, and competitive. Marla loved my sister Holly as much as I did; however, she had always been closer to me. Holly knew this. She accepted it. She loved us both. I close my eyes and sway, remembering when Holly first noticed this. "Marla likes me well enough, but she *loves* you. You have some kind of mind meld thing going with each other. That's okay. I love you both." I remember not answering her, just giving her a nonchalant shrug as acquiescence and recalling her gap-toothed grin. I open my eyes and stare at the black-clad crowd. We must have been seven or so when Holly said this. *She always knew.*

Now, I stand here gazing out at Holly's white casket and curse the sun, the blue sky, God, fire, rain, black SUVs of any kind, and Rob Thorn. The last one stands forlorn in a far corner. He's dressed in an ill-fitting dark suit.

He hasn't said a word. We share in this oppressive silence, but that's all I'll give him. I glare in his general direction and crazily blame him for this catastrophic event that has upended and changed my life forever. If he hadn't insisted upon Holly coming over to prove her fucking love to him; none of this would have happened. If it hadn't been raining. If it hadn't been Valentine's Day; but a different day. If I hadn't just filled up the gas tank of my old Mercedes sedan. If God had cared at all about Holly and me, none of this would have happened.

A sheen of wetness shines on Rob's face. It takes me another full minute to realize he's crying.

Go ahead and cry, you bastard. You did this.

Why did she have to love you? Why?

We all want to know the answer to that.

From some faraway place in my mind, I calculate the ineffectiveness of the Valium against grief and make a promise to myself to take another as soon as we return from the cemetery.

The turnout is grand.

Spectacular.

I stare at the crowd in fascination. My drugged state makes me feel loopy and ungrounded. I am like a helium balloon all set to float up and away just as soon as they release me. My parents stand on either side of me and hold onto my hands effectively holding me down. This is how I am able to stay here—tethered to them both in my newest role as the dutiful daughter, however incongruent that might be, instead of floating up and away to Holly in heaven. The brilliant daughter? The perfect one has gotten away. The good one? She's been incinerated into obliteration. All they're left with is me—the rebellious one—and Tommy. At eight years old, my little brother understands less of all of this than I do. But I can feel his fear—in losing Holly. Everyone loved Holly best. And now there's just me—the lesser part of the twin set— this prize of little consolation.

What a disappointment for us all.

And no matter what these well-wishers and the priest will insist upon saying—in concerted shrill, I might add—just know that telling me that Holly lives on in our hearts doesn't resonate as true with me because, in my heart, I can't feel anything. There's nothing there. It's empty.

I'm empty. I can't feel her there. Not yet. A big part of me wonders whether I will ever feel my twin again. This thought alone just about breaks me.

A part of me is now missing. I fear its permanence. I am only half of a person without Holly. Can half of a person survive?

"Ashes to ashes. Dust to dust." The priest's words mill their way into my head poking at me like shards of broken glass, effectively cutting away at my psyche with every sweetly bestowed utterance. A lone tear rolls down my face but my parents clasp my hands so tight from each side that I can't even reach up to wipe it away. I can't even cry properly. And I can't feel Holly. That terrifies me most of all.

It's been sixty-four days to the day. I still wear a cast on my wrist and although my ribs are almost healed they still ache with too much movement. *I ignore the pain—all of it.* Instead, I rise early before I hear the stirring of my mom and dad or Tommy. My parents were up late, whispering in that quiet way of theirs that's been prevalent since Holly's death. Last night, I heard my mom's muffled cries again and my dad's gentle tone as he tried to soothe her.

Now, I shiver at the memory as I don leotard and tights and pull on a pair of cast-off navy sweats that Holly left in my room all those days ago. The faint smell of her assails my senses. I start to shake, wipe at my eyes, and gasp for breath. Grief arrives in such unexpected ways and moments. I can't decipher if it's the remembering that is more painful or if the incessant worry of not remembering everything about her that might be worse.

One of my new greatest fears these days? That I'll forget what she looks like, unless I check a mirror. Desperate to escape the morbidity of home life, I've decided to embrace my normal routine again for a Saturday—dance class. I run a comb through my hair and tug at it hard with my good hand and hope to at least re-channel some of the pain when I think of Holly and carefully re-wrap my three broken ribs with the heavy ace bandage my dad got from the hospital staff.

After a few minutes, I put my hair up in a familiar ponytail, but I don't bother with the painstaking Bobby pins to clasp up the strays. *Screw Madame Tremblay.* I'm not pinning my hair back the way my ballet teacher will insist upon as soon as she sees me. Today I just want to dance. *Forget the hair.* I grab my ballet bag that contains two pairs of shoes and an extra leotard and retreat from the bedroom without looking back. Reminders of Holly are everywhere. A silver hair band she liked—that she must have cast off in one of those last days—remains on the hall table like a permanent memento. Her favorite lipstick still sits in the brass key tray by the foyer. A stack of sympathy cards are rubber-banded together there, too; but no one among us is brave enough to open them and read them.

The house remains still, even as I noisily take the stairs two at a time. Intent on escaping this tomb for the majority of the day, I stop only long enough to write on the message board: "Saturday 4/18 Gone to class. Then to Marla's. Back at 6:00 p.m. or so. T."

This is probably the most direct communication the three of us have had since the accident. Holly would think it is funny that she died on Valentine's Day. She would laugh at the thought of haunting all of us in this way, as the colors—red, pink, and white—and valentines and flowers and happiness and love and, basically, anything good left in the world serve as constant reminders of her loss.

I try to conjure up her face or even the faint echo of her laugh, but I can't feel her. That scares me even more. I could always feel Holly. Now, I can't feel anything.

I shake myself from this sad reverie. I'm still holding the dry-erase marker in mid-air although the note is finished. I have no idea how long I've been standing here. Time stands still like that every so often. I cannot explain it, and I've quit trying. A glance at my watch tells me I'm running ten minutes behind now.

My stomach growls and I temper its excitement with a glass of water and a few vitamins. *Breakfast is served.* I can count on one hand the things I've eaten in the past few months. *Since.* Normally, my diet regimen is closely monitored after the bout with an eating disorder just last year, but since a decade of sorrow has moved in permanently on all of us, thoughts of what Tally has or hasn't eaten no longer registers with importance of any kind for any of us. Plus, I've judiciously erased all the voice mails from my counselor who I'm supposed to be seeing every week. The idea of discussing my eating disorder carries no significant weight in my psyche any longer and seems to have slipped my parents' minds as well.

Grief counseling prevails these days. At least, there is a discussion of this. Yet, even the medical doctor among us—*my father*—doesn't have the stomach for a single session. My mother will only go if my father attends. My father will only go if I attend. No one wants to even consider Tommy attending since he remains the most normal among us these days. We should all take cues from the eight-year-old. My mother won't go. So, the circle begins and ends there. And, there are no grief counseling sessions for the Landon family. We are in this implied standoff, and we all wallow in the loss of Holly. None of us can really breathe, though not one of us will openly admit this to anyone else, least of all, ourselves.

***

The bus ride gets me to the dance studio a miraculous eight minutes early. I quietly slip inside and discover Allaire Tremblay dancing alone. She dances to Tchaikovsky's *Swan Lake* from Act II, seemingly unaware that class is scheduled to start soon. She's oblivious to her captivated audience of one, unaware that her star student—the silent voyeur—watches. *Me.*

Her legs move freely, so sinewy and taunt. Only her face belies her youth, although she gracefully moves across the floor with such enviable confidence and fluidity that she remains unsurpassed as the best dancer I've ever seen. She would seem to be a girl of twenty, not a woman approaching forty. With angst and fascination, I gaze at her from behind the marble pillar at the far end just out of sight of the gigantic mirrors that grace all four walls of the dance studio and normally provide Allaire Tremblay with an uncanny view of all that goes on in her renowned dance studio. The music echoes and seemingly pulses with her movements. Tremblay continues to perform at a high level. She artfully executes the most complicated steps in this pivotal scene with enviable ease. She is not so much a part of the dance as the epitome of it, serving as the very definition of both perfection and beauty. Her mastery of the intricate movements from the strength of her leg as it lifts into a perfect arabesque to the endless execution of the tortuous foutes is not lost on me. Taxing, difficult. Tremblay makes it look easy. Envy washes over me as if perfectly timed to coincide with the knowable sadness that still follows me around like a chronic flu.

Will I ever be as good as Tremblay? Admiration and hate for the accomplished principal ballerina course through me at an astonishing rate as if these two feelings have been synchronized with my heart beat.

Even as a teacher, Tremblay's demand for perfection prevails. The woman has zero tolerance for laziness, tardiness, or absence—no matter how profound, no matter how gut-wrenching, no matter how devastating. She expects and demands her students to be here.

And, I've been gone for nine weeks.

Even as I entered the premises, I experienced a good dose of trepidation that has now developed into downright palpable fear as to what she will say to me when she sees me. Tremblay expects her students to be ready to go at precisely nine in the morning on weekends and four in the afternoon three times a week, at a minimum. Seven days a week, if you're serious.

I have been serious for the past seven years, up until two months ago.

I'm almost catatonic—suddenly impaled by certain grief and this appreciable unease at having displeased her with my continual absence these past weeks—these now threaten to overtake my weakened psyche. Apprehension tears through me but a small part of me still besieged by the endless sorrow is prepared to do ferocious battle with the unexpected cold front that is so clearly Allaire Tremblay. This numb part of me that has almost brought me to my knees even now, on this day, just another day like yesterday, and the day before that one, which always has me silently asking: *Why am I still here?* As if anyone would answer or know of one possible reason for this.

Holly is dead. The thought assails me yet again.

I'm stolen from the respite of this almost dreamlike state in watching Tremblay's impromptu performance and plunged into harsh reality by grief again. It feels like a punch to the gut. Well, what I imagine that would feel like. The assailant is grief. The aggressor is fear. A double dose. Only the pillar

I still hide behind provides me with solace. I tightly grip the cold marble and lean further into it, suddenly engulfed in this strange fervent hope of finding some kind of relief from all of it for a just a little while longer.

My movements, unchecked, disturb the prima ballerina's concentration. Tremblay stops dancing and glances my way. She purses her lips, intimating deep tumultuous thoughts, and gets this disdainful look. She will be both judge and jury of my fate.

"Talia," she says. "I didn't see you there. Don't dawdle. Are you ready to go? We only have two hours today before the next class. Come. Come."

So this is how it is going to go.

"What are you waiting for?" she asks.

I struggle to put one foot in front of the other and meet her halfway across the room. I have to will my body to move any further into the room and conquer my fears and the devastation of grief at the same time.

"What are you waiting for?" she asks again with a more derisive tone.

I'm waiting for Holly.

I want to say this, but I wouldn't dare.

At one point, Allaire Tremblay held the title as the world's most premier prima ballerina; and, almost ten years later, she takes pride in her ability to teach and create champions even here in San Francisco that is still so far away from the seductive offerings of New York City and the School of American Ballet.

Yet she can help me get there from here.

And, getting there?

It's all I have left to live for.

Tremblay bites at her lower lip with notable impatience at my slow cautious approach, but she refrains from saying anything more although she stonily glares at my hair. I remain ever defiant and willfully take my designated place at the front of the class. One glance in the long mirror directly in front of me practically undoes my resolve as I stare at the physical replica of my dead sister. After a prolonged moment, I save myself by looking away and catch Marla's encouraging smile in the side mirror to my left as she scurries into place and barely avoids being cast as the prime example of a late arrival. No one wants to star in that role.

I incline my head in her direction but don't attempt to smile. We're all just trying to power through it. There's a vacant spot where Holly normally stood. The class remains subdued while the last of the girls takes their places in the back row. All of us seemingly stare at the empty spot and must think of Holly, until somewhat mercifully Madame Tremblay starts the music signaling the beginning of class.

Ballet is all about the mastery of repetition and a continual quest for perfection. Somehow, that works for me, even now. I can take in the air again as I dance. I can breathe again. My movements are fairly fluid and almost graceful. I ignore the protest my ribs made. I've healed enough. I suck it up and concentrate on perfecting the movements. My legs go higher and higher. Perfection is imminent and holds such a worthy promise for me. And, for the next few hours, I can actually feel myself acquiesce to the possibilities of living without Holly by fully embracing and accepting the almost impossible demands of ballet. It won't replace my twin, but it's all I have left. Ballet is all that remains of me.

⁓⊙⋅⊙⋅⊙⁓

Madame Tremblay waits by the door after class and touches my forearm in earnest. It's an unexpected gesture. The woman is as cold as a dead fish, a critical instructor, and nobody's friend. Her golden-brown eyes gaze into mine reflecting such a dissimilar color, I'm somewhat disconcerted. Even so, I spy the sadness in hers, surely they mirror mine. I involuntarily step back from her upon seeing this, somewhat afraid of how it reflects upon me. "Talia, you did well today."

"Thank you, Madame."

It seems to pain her to speak. I can see the rush of sympathy before she actually utters the words. I brace myself for them, but still they assault me as she says the obligatory, "I'm so sorry about Holly."

I stiffen my upper torso and steel myself against the abrasiveness of these familiar words but like an arrow just glancing off of my beating heart, I feel the briefest of acute pain. I chase the grief away before it can get all the way inside of me. "Thank you, Madame," I say in rote.

She nods. Her eyes crinkle at the corners. I'm taken aback by the slight smile upon her lips. Normally, her mouth portrays this taut straight dark-red line upon her otherwise impeccable ivory face or even more often a downward frown because nothing is ever right or perfect enough for Tremblay. I can't quite hide my surprise at her smile. However, incongruent it might be. My mouth drops open.

"You've done well. You and Marla. You're both ready."

She motions towards Marla, who's made a point of staying a good twenty-five feet from us so as not to disturb our conversation or even more likely not to get drawn into it at all. Nobody likes to talk to Tremblay. It generally means you weren't up to standard or were not going to make the cut for an upcoming performance.

Again, she motions Marla forward.

We wait.

Tremblay sighs like a school girl and looks directly at us both. "SAB was pleased with your performances last summer. They're considering inviting you back for September. There's been a change of plans, and I've arranged for the two of you to help out with the summer program this year. Delora and Laurent have decided to leave New York for a while. Try things out here on the West Coast." She pauses for effect it seems. "In any case, I'm officially the new director at the School of American Ballet, and I've chosen the two of you to come with me to be my quasi assistants and star students at the school. We've made an exception for the two of you to attend classes. I've spoken briefly to your parents about possible accommodations and tuition. Both sets of parents were extremely pleased with your accomplishments, and I made sure that they understood the opportunities the two of you are being given. I only asked that I be able to tell you personally so as to not have any misconceptions about what this is and isn't."

She smiles wide but joy doesn't reach her eyes. "There are no favorites. You'll have to work very hard to earn and keep your place at the school. I'll demand more and expect more from both of you." She makes a point of searching out both our faces with her direct, penetrating gaze. "In any case, I leave in a couple of weeks, and once you graduate; you'll both soon follow. Now, let me be perfectly clear; you earned this shot at the big time not because of me but because of your immense talent. Both of you. Talia. Marla."

This is high praise from Allaire Tremblay. Her sponsorship of us will mean everything, both in returning to one of the most prestigious ballet schools in the country but also in the launch of our dance careers within the next six months and possibly being given a chance at the internships with New York City Ballet. It's not supposed to work this way, but it does. She breathes deep, automatically commanding our attention again. "This is your chance, your best opportunity."

She pauses for so long, I'm not convinced she has anything else to say. Then she adds, "Don't screw it up."

"Wow," I manage to finally say.

"Thank you so much, Madame Tremblay." Marla grins and makes a few joyful squeals next to me. In jubilation, she grabs the older woman's hand. We hold our collective breaths, while Tremblay gets an exasperated look and withdraws her hand from Marla's grasp.

"Marla, you earned the spot with your hard work. This has nothing to do with me. *Really.* I'm just going to be the director at the school. Delora and I go way back so when she came up with the idea of trading places and *lives,* basically, for a while, well, it sounded like a good plan. You and Talia are the best dancers I have. You both did well last summer at SAB. It's a natural choice—with or without me being involved." She laughs ever so slightly. "Any questions?"

"My parents really want me to consider Stanford, what with Holly—"

"A good school," Tremblay says with an almost imperceptible shrug of her bony shoulders, and then she shakes her head side-to-side. "But Talia. You're a dancer. You have *talent*. Immense talent you should make the most of. You both do. You, too, Marla, if you could keep your mouth off of a boy's long enough and better dedicate yourself."

Marla protests at the teacher's accurate assessment of her love life, which makes me almost laugh because it's hard to argue with that particular truth. I exchange a slight knowing look with Tremblay, who smiles widely and actually laughs. She waves her hand in a dismissive way at both of us. I'm still reminded of a black widow spider but attempt to smile back and push my general distrust of her way down. I shiver, and wince at the movement even as my sore ribs silently protest. I've overdone it on this day.

"Okay. Yes. I want to train with you and return to New York." I look over at Marla, and she's nodding a more enthusiastically than me. "We both do. We want the chance of a lifetime. We won't let you down."

Tremblay laughs again while Marla and I exchange these surprised glances. It appears she's as pleased with herself as much as she is with the two of us. "Good. We will start tomorrow then. After school, every day, until we leave for New York mid-June. I don't want to leave anything to chance. It's your commitment to the program that I'm counting on from both of you."

I envision my father writing a gigantic check to Tremblay to pay for all these extra lessons, the apartment back east, and the tuition itself at SAB. I imagine his grief-stricken face as he blankly hands me the check while he vainly searches mine for any sign of Holly.

Holly I can never be.

We all know that.

But I continue to try.

CHAPTER FOUR

Tally's Conundrum

THE INCESSANT PUBLIC GAZING FOLLOWS ME down the hall as if they're watching an accused witch march off to a wooden stake for burning. We're studying the Salem Witch Trials in U.S. History, so I'm sure that's why I'm feeling this particular persecution with such potency. I keep my head down and allow my eyes to study the various patterns in the linoleum as I make my way past all these jostling students and sympathetic stares. *Nobody wants to be the dead twin's sister. Nobody wants to be brought down by this tragic story. Including me.*

"Tally." Marla's voice reaches for me from the other end of the hallway. I skirt past a couple of additional voyeurs who mumble their words at me as I slash my way through the last of the fervent bodies of Paly high-schoolers.

"Hey," I say when I reach her locker. Marla's presence represents a certain sanctuary, however temporary, and I almost smile.

"Hey," she says with meaning, scrutinizing me closely. "How are you holding up?"

It's been more than three months since the funeral, long after the debacle in the Caribbean with my parents and Tommy, where we did a lot of pretending that everything was normal even though it clearly wasn't. We holed up in a five-star hotel room and blithely watched the ocean waves from our hotel suite most of the time, and no one said a word. Although after three days of this imposed confinement with what was left of my family, I did sneak off into the streets of St. Thomas and found a brief respite in the arms of one of the handsome locals. He didn't know a word of English, and that suited me just fine. He seemed to like the fact that I chain-smoked one cigarette after another after we'd done the deed in all various ways possible at least a half-dozen times and I didn't ask for money. Apparently, this was a refreshing change for him as well. At least, that's what I was able to put together through his various hand gestures and his excited Spanish. He seemed to like the fact that I didn't ask for anything except sex and silence.

But the risk factor to both my body and soul was patently high, and I almost lost it with him completely at one point. The shock of what I'd done with a complete stranger in a foreign country resonated with me on an ever deeper almost visceral level. And, as much as I'd felt something, however lascivious it was, fucking a foreigner—a complete stranger from a different culture—both pleased and shamed me on some incalculable, twisted level of my psyche. After that, I made a promise to myself—to do better, to be good. The harsh truth was far simpler. He made me feel *something*. Good or bad. I wasn't sure; but I was disturbed by all this contemplative thought. Enough so, that when we returned home, I was intent on changing my ways. I was intent upon becoming the good daughter my parents so desperately needed. I would serve as Holly's replacement in the only way I knew how: I would become more like her, at least for the foreseeable future, and effectively eschew my defiant and deviant ways for fucking a stranger—a foreign one at that. I'd be more careful. I'd be good.

Even so, here at Paly, despite my rather stealthy and unspectacular return to school and maintaining a somewhat earnest intent upon being more like Holly and focusing solely upon ballet, I've been unable to completely avoid the piercing spotlight. You would think after a long while that people would forget all about my sad circumstances—sans sister; but no, you would be wrong. A proverbial slow season of inevitable relationship breakups this spring keeps Holly's fiery demise firmly planted into the hearts and minds of Paly's student body and continues to hold their unwelcome attention upon me— sole survivor Tally—the victim's sister. With Holly's tragic end still reigning as the top newsflash for the year, I serve as the unwilling entertainment—fodder for the social headlines—starring in the lead role as the dead sister's twin.

And I hear the whispers. The fervent gossip is everywhere around me.

Did you *see* her? How do you think she *does* it? Have you *seen* her mom? I hear her mom's *drinking* again, and her dad works all the time at the hospital. It must be hard on them all, losing Holly like that. I don't know what I'd do. She looks *so sad*. Do you think we should *say* something? Or, do you think she *wants* to be left alone? Have you *seen* Rob Thorn? I hear he's thinking of *transferring*. It's probably hard on the guy *seeing* his dead girlfriend's face every day in the form of Tally Landon's.

I do hear you, you know.
I hear it all.

This is not attention that I am seeking. This is not a story I want to star in; but, apparently, I don't have a choice in the matter. I'm counting the final hours that will lead me to the safe haven that only graduation can promise—a permanent respite from the self-serving gossip. A permanent break from high school is just what I need.

"There's a party tonight—a kind of welcome-summer-lets-celebrate party." Marla pauses for a moment, letting her announcement sink in. "At Charlie's," she adds in that breathless way of hers.

I glance at her sideways and grimace. "As in Charlie Masterson? As in the Charlie from two years ago? That one?"

"Don't start."

"He broke your heart. Who's starting anything? The question is. Why do *you* want to finish it with him?"

She shrugs in a weak imitation of nonchalance. "Apparently, he's changed." She tries to smile but the corners of her mouth tremble and betray her futile attempt at bravado.

I roll my eyes and sigh. "Uh huh. He's between girlfriends and wants to hook up with a previous one. Let me guess; finals are done at UCLA, and he's home for the summer."

My cynicism hails from the last two years of Marla's never-ending mental anguish over Charlie Masterson. He managed to break her heart and for that—even though she was only sixteen at the time and couldn't possibly know what she wanted in a guy, in a first love, no doubt—*he sucked,* in my mind. *Big time. Still does.*

Marla ignores my mocking tone. "His cousin will be there. The baseball player. I told Charlie I'd bring a friend. I want to set you two up." She smiles wider as if she's discovered a new magic trick and is just waiting to show me.

"No."

"His cousin and you as a setup is a great idea."

"Because?" I swirl my finger in mid-air forming a question mark.

She laughs. "Because you need to get out and let off some steam." Marla leans in closer. "Have some *fun.* Break the rules again. Tally, you need to get laid."

"Probably so," I say tartly. "But that is not an option that I'm willing to take on at this particular moment in time." I frown and recall my last questionable hook-up in St. Thomas all those weeks ago. I never told Marla about that one; I didn't need the lecture. "I just don't feel anything right now. I think it needs to be that way…to survive this."

Marla allows for a long protracted silence. We both still struggle with the firm grip that grief over Holly manages to keep a hold on us both.

"Besides, I hate baseball, and I won't know anybody else at this party." I brush back my hair, hoping for nonchalance, and start emptying my locker out. *Graduation can't come soon enough.*

"That's the best part. It will be all these people that Charlie knows. No one from Paly. Older guys. Older crowd. College guys. You could lose yourself a little. Lose your story." Marla frowns. "*Come with me.* I want…I need…to see Charlie."

"Why? He's just going to hurt you again. And he drives too fast. There's really no point in getting attached to someone who drives too fast, now is there?"

She glares at me. Her eyes are a lighter green than mine more like a dusty sage-green, but they darken when she's mad. My morbidity has that kind of effect on people. I blow air out of my mouth and sidestep the guilt for a few minutes in saying something so cruel like this aloud. We've talked about Charlie Masterson's driving skills before. I try to diffuse the bomb of this particular discussion by saying, "Why don't you go out with a guy who drives a Volvo or something?" I don't know why that idea popped into my head, and then I spy Rob Thorn as he slowly saunters past us. Marla looks clearly disenchanted with my attitude. *What else is new? Everybody is.* "Sorry," I tack on. "I shouldn't have said that about Charlie's driving. I'm such a bitch. I'm sorry."

Marla sighs. "Why do you have to be so cynical? Maybe Charlie wants to see me *for me* this time. Maybe he's grown up. Maybe he doesn't drive as fast anymore."

"That's a lot of maybes."

"He's been away at UCLA for three years. That can change a person, you know. *College.*"

"You think *college* changes people, Marla? That's what you're going with here?" I briefly glance over at Rob Thorn, who is eight lockers away from us. He's eavesdropping on our conversation and has this solicitous look. I glare at him and turn my attention back to my best friend.

"I want to see him. *I do,*" she says when I roll my eyes again. "It's been long enough, and we have our own plans for New York after graduation. I wish Tremblay didn't commit us to the two workshop performances right off the bat after we get there, but what do I know? I want a chance to say good-bye to him one last time." She sweeps her hand around, encompassing the expansive hallway, and gets this determined look. "But most of all, you're my best friend, and you *have* to come with me. It's an unwritten rule." She laughs and squeezes my arm. "Come on. Come with me. I *need* you to be there with me. I have to see him. I want to."

"I have pointe class tonight. So do you."

Allaire Tremblay could not care less that it's Friday night before the long Memorial Day weekend. She expects us to be there; and, since her influence is pivotal to our return to SAB and New York by the middle of June, I am beholden to making Tremblay's class. *Marla? Not so much.* I can tell by the unwavering look upon her face that I will be going with her to Charlie Masterson's party, too. I suppose it's possible that Marla is absolutely right and maybe what I really need to do is get good and drunk *and* laid. These particular pastimes have become so absent from my life since the middle of February that I've forgotten how to have fun. The respite in the Caribbean just led me to question myself and my motives.

I've been busy keeping it together for my parents and Tommy serving as the perfect daughter and big sister. All this good behavior is warranted, especially since my parents reluctantly agreed to let me go to New York with Tremblay and Marla again this summer. It may lead to a winter term with SAB if things go the way they're supposed to and may lead straight to the New York City Ballet internship if miracles ever happen for me again. Yet we're all still broken and swamped with so much grief over Holly that there appears to be no way out of it for any of us. My family still walks around the house in a sad stupor. We barely talk. We never have dinner together anymore. Memorial Day weekend is unplanned, unprepared, and unwelcome at the Landons. My mother has effectively shunned all the neighbors' good intentions. She doesn't leave the house anymore. The only thing that changes is the level line on the vodka bottle that I started marking off weeks ago. My parents probably think I don't notice, but I do.

This truth is I don't know who I really am at this point. I used to do things—fun things. I'd attend parties every so often, drink frilly drinks and do shots, and have random sex with reckless abandon with guys who were willing, while all the while maintaining a clear, dedicated focus on my ballet career at all times. I was rebellious Tally. I did what I wanted while Holly followed the rules and willingly played the part of the perfect daughter. Look where that got her? Now with me serving in that role, my personal sacrifice hasn't even been noticed by my parents. It hasn't changed anything. My family still slowly decays right in front of me. My parents are under a great deal of stress. I see their pain every time I look at them. We all seem to be falling apart in slow motion.

So does being perfect really change anything? Would we all be better off if I just stopped trying to be perfect and was just myself? These thoughts come in on me swiftly. Have I been doing it all wrong? Is the secret to surviving the loss of Holly just trying to feel something and be myself again?

I spin the dial on my lock on the locker, which is located right next to Marla's, and try not to look over at Holly's on the other side. Some brilliant wonder on the student council thought it would be a good idea to make Holly's locker into some kind of shrine. There are cards and dead flowers and unlit candles (because the district has a strict policy against actually lighting them) strewn about. There's a Tinker Bell balloon that's begun to lose its helium. *Dead. Like Holly.* 'We miss you' it says in a black script. It limps up and down with every student who passes by stirring the lifeless air all around it. I shiver. *Who's going to clean all this up?* I'm pulled from my concentrated study of Holly's shrine back to reality when Marla puts her arm around my shoulders and vies for my undivided attention.

"*After* pointe class. I'll come over and pick you up. I've got a few things you can borrow."

"This just gets better and better."

Marla rolls her eyes at my obvious reluctance and closely scrutinizes my standard attire of black jeans and matching T-shirt. "*Please.*"

I sigh heavily after another ten seconds of her *please, please, please* plead. "All right. I'll find something of Holly's to wear, and you can pick me up a little after eight."

"Good. That'll give me time to re-do your make-up."

"What makes you think my make-up will need to be re-done?"

"We need to look older, more sophisticated. The über-talented ballet girl isn't going to cut it tonight." Marla laughs. "These guys are older. Remember?"

"Right." I check my dance gym bag and ensure I have an extra pair of toe shoes and zip up my bag. "You're not coming to pointe class. Are you?"

"Nah. I want to shave my legs for Charlie." This pink flush stains her cheeks and she starts to giggle. Marla flips her long blond hair over her shoulder and gets this dreamy look.

I still don't understand why Charlie Masterson let her go. Marla's mother is from Sicily; she's a retired fashion model. The girl inherited every one of her mother's gorgeous genes, including the European olive skin tone, golden blond hair, and these amazing green eyes complete with the long, lean perfect body. *Charlie Masterson is a jerk. A big one.* I frown and begin to worry all over again about Marla getting hurt by him. "Are you sure…about seeing Charlie again?"

"I'm sure. It'll be okay. New York is our future." She catches her lower lip between her teeth. "It's closure more than anything," she says with a slight shrug.

Closure, my ass.

"Tremblay isn't going to be happy with you," I finally say.

"I can still drop you off for class so you don't have to take the bus. Can you cover for me?"

"I'm good and I'll cover for you with Tremblay." Her wistfulness has captured my attention. *The girl is seriously excited to see Charlie again.* It's troubling on too many levels to count. I've spent many a night handing this girl tissues, while she cried her eyes out over Charlie Masterson, and lamented about who he was dating, who he took to prom, and why they broke up. He effectively cut Marla out of his life like a toy he'd outgrown. My intolerance—for a guy like this—overflows; it's at an all-time high, especially now. I get even more anxious about this party and worry about Marla even more. "I just don't think this is a good idea…to see Charlie again," I say as one last-ditch effort at talking her out of this.

"Maybe not." She lifts her perfect chin and looks at me in defiance—the look that says *I'm-doing-what-I-want.* I know that look because I have one, too. "But in a matter of weeks, we'll be back in New York. And I'll see Devon again."

Devon St. Claire was one of the few decent guys we'd met in New York. He and Marla hit it off right away. I liked Devon. He was nice enough, worthy enough of Marla. He genuinely liked her and seemed to appreciate Marla's goodness. He was a young hot shot on Wall Street in a time when everything had been soaring and then crashing, but he seemed to survive all the turbulence and stayed grounded and true to Marla. Still, there was something missing from their relationship and the guy wielded too much control. Something was missing in that relationship. Maybe it's the simple blissful smile on Marla's face that I plainly see right now. She gushes on about seeing Charlie again, and how he sent her a text along with a little heart next to her name.

"Well, a heart next to your name is everything, now isn't it?" I press my lips together to keep myself from saying more but can't help myself. "Devon may be worse than Charlie. Sorry," I add when she glares at me.

"I thought you *liked* Devon."

"Well, the guy can do shots with his eyes closed, but that doesn't make him right for you. He drives a Porsche for Christ's sake."

"A death trap for sure." Marla's sarcasm is not lost on me.

I shrug. Helpless. Found out. No one understands my worst fears these days. That much is clear.

Marla starts to laughs. "Maybe I should date a forest ranger."

"Maybe."

"Or a cowboy. With a horse! Is that safe enough for you?"

"Probably." I hang my head, so she won't see my sudden tears.

What the hell is wrong with me?

I swipe at my eyes and turn away from her.

"I've never seen you get this excited over Devon—*not* that I'm endorsing Charlie Masterson here."

"Yeah. I got that. Message received, loud and clear." I force myself to smile as I look over at her. "Look, Charlie is a thing of the past, but—as I have so cleverly pointed out—it is important to have *closure*. Closure. That's all it is," Marla says with a little sigh.

I turn away from her again, slam my locker shut, and give the lock a few extra spins. Marla looks like she's in love every time she talks about Charlie. With Devon, I never see the happiness seep out quite like this. All of this will require further study on my part. Obviously, I'm going to have to go to Masterson's party if only to protect Marla from herself. Finally, I steal a look at her. She has the twisted-up pout going.

"*Fine*. I'll cover for you and go to the party as your wingman." She laughs outright at the *Top Gun* reference. At first, I catch myself, but then I actually laugh because it proves hard to resist Marla's contagious charm. "Maybe you're right. Maybe all we need to do tonight is break a few rules to get back into a rhythm. *Closure* like you said. I'll do the baseball player, and you do Charlie and get closure."

I look up and see Rob Thorn still watching us. He looks envious and sad at the same time.

"That's what I'm thinking." Marla's hazel eyes flash with excitement. She tells me good-bye, leans in and hugs me, and then flounces off toward the exit doors.

Rob Thorn watches her walk off down the hall for as long as I do. We turn back at the same time and just stare at each other. I think we're both remembering Holly in that moment. I manage to turn away first.

Marla's happy. Marla's in love with love while I'm instantly reminded of Holly and how she used to look like that whenever she was in love. But loving someone that much? Letting them in like that and losing all your power to them? That's the one thing I could never allow to happen to me. The idea of caring that much about someone else scares me, especially now.

Look what happens when you love someone that much and then lose them? I can't lose anyone else. I just can't.

Rob Thorn walks past me and gives me one last wistful look before he saunters out the same exit doors as Marla. I soon follow, prepared for public transportation on an almost reverent level, yet I still find myself watching him walk over his car.

To what else? A Volvo.

I shake my head and almost smile at the irony of it all. However, I do say *yes* to him when he offers me a ride.

There has been nothing but shared stony silence for the entire twenty-minute drive from Paly High to Tremblay's dance studio. I made the mistake of asking Rob if he knew the way to Tremblay's, forgetting that he used to take Holly there all the time. I think the question almost made him cry. I've kept up the vigilance for not speaking because seeing Rob Thorn cry reminds me of the funeral when I first saw this aberration. And for some reason—ninety-six days since that said tragedy—is not nearly long enough from seeing that particular emotional rendition from Rob Thorn all over again.

It is with unspoken relief that we both start to breathe freely when he pulls up in front of the dance studio. He turns in his seat and gazes at me while I try not to notice the unshed tears on his dark-brown lashes. I'm sure looking at me takes a certain amount of fortitude, and I'm not sure how long he'll be able to hang on to that.

"So," he says as if we've carried on this whole conversation the entire time. "You're going to Masterson's party?"

"Looks like it."

"Be careful, Tally."

"I'm always careful."

"I mean it. There's going to be a lot of older guys there. And they're there for one thing only."

"Well, I'm sure we'll all be there for the same thing then."

"Just be careful, Tally."

"Rob," I say softly. "I'm not Holly. I fu...*screw* who I want."

"Right."

If a single word can carry the entire weighty emotion of disappointment, then Rob Thorn has achieved this goal. *He'll make a great father someday.* "Sorry, I...I shouldn't have said that." I bite at my lower lip.

"But you did. And you're right. You're not Holly. Can never be. No one can." His voice catches.

"Sorry."

"Thanks for the ride." I slide out the passenger side and lean back into the open door. "Thanks for the ride," I repeat myself for some unknowable reason.

"Do you think you'll ever be able to drive again?"

"No."

"How do you *know?*"

"I don't want to. I'll be in New York without a car. Just stuff I know about myself, I guess." I stare at him hard in a hope to look bitchy enough to somewhat end this conversation.

"I got into NYU," he says in sudden earnest. "I start this summer."

He gives me the implied *maybe I'll-see-you-around-Manhattan* hopeful look.

I must shut this down. "Anxious to get to New York, I see."

"No. Anxious to get through college, get it over with."

He gets this expectant look, as if I'm already supposed to know this. All I can do is shake my head in endless wonder because he is so different from every other guy Holly went out with. He is hot, but not. Kind of cool, but not. Kind of awesome, but not. *A conundrum.* I'm staring at him, and he starts to smile. It's crooked. It's weird. *He's weird.* He drives a Volvo. His dad has more money than God, and he drives *a Volvo.* It's a losing proposition for him socially; and he doesn't even care. He is Wonderland. Johnny Depp. Sawyer from *Lost.* The dead Kurt Cobain. He's wearing a black Nirvana T-shirt. *How did I fail to notice this before?*

"Tally? Tally?"

Apparently, he's said my name quite a few times. "Thanks for the ride," I say again.

"Maybe I'll see you tonight?"

It's a question looking for an answer. His face gets hopeful, and I feel this insane impassioned need to crush it *right now.*

"I don't think so. Look, I have plans." I wave my right hand toward the red front doors of Tremblay's dance studio. "One focus. One goal. I don't have…" He's biting his lip, and it's distracting as hell and in a sexy way, which is weird and downright incestuous. *He was Holly's boyfriend.* "I don't do relationships of any kind. I'm in. I'm out. Everybody wins." I flash him my award-winning smile. My best stage smile.

"Right."

There's that word again; and the emotive disappointment from him is even more real this time and duly noted by me, whether I like it or not. *What the hell is wrong with me?*

"Right. Right. *Right,*" he says with more intensity each time.

"Thank you for the ride." I hesitate. *Me. Tally Landon, hesitating? No. No fucking way.* "We're not…we're not friends, *Thorn.* I just think we should be honest *here* about *that.*"

"Holly?" he asks gently, just as I'm about to close the car door all the way.

My fury knows no bounds at that salutation for my dead twin. "What did you just say? I'm…*Tally.* You are so…*messed up!*"

Now he looks mortified at having spoken Holly's name aloud, as if he'll be struck down by lightning for saying it. Or God. Or both. "Sorry. Sorry. Right."

Oh, my God. Will the remorse from his mortal wounds ever stop? Ever?

My anger quickly dissipates, and I'm left with this overriding uncanny need to comfort him. It's sixty-five degrees out. It's a perfectly sunny day and yet this Arctic chill seemingly passes through me as if Holly is visiting my psyche from the great beyond. *Console him. Don't kill him this way.*

I glance at his car radio clock. *Shit. I'm late on top of everything else. Tremblay is going to kill me.*

"I'm late." Rob's face goes white. Every word I utter just makes it worse for both of us. "For class? I'm sorry? Thanks for the ride? I've got to go?"

I slam the car door because there just isn't anything else I can say to him that will make this any better. But then I stand on the curb and watch him slowly drive away and give him this little silly wave. If he looks in his side mirror, he'll see me pathetically waving. His silver Volvo merges with the traffic, and he disappears into the mass of thirty or so cars after a few minutes. I can finally breathe again.

What the hell was that?

Yet I am the one who is about to cry as I slowly ascend the stairs and stumble into Tremblay's pointe class exactly ten minutes late. She glares at me. *Naturally.* I just wave her off and take my time putting on my toe shoes. *What the hell is wrong with me?*

And what is going on with Rob Thorn? Why do I care? When will my life ever be normal? Why do I have to feel these extreme almost debilitating rounds of emotion every waking minute of every flipping day? Why? Somebody please tell me why.

CHAPTER FIVE

Linc ~ The Valentine's Day girl

EMERGING FROM THE SANCTUARY OF MY aunt and uncle's guest house, I move somewhat stealthily through their kitchen side door. I'm assailed by the strong odors of cheap beer and overcooked pizza. Smoke fills the air as if someone has forgotten to rescue it from the oven soon enough. I do a quick survey of the kitchen and see Charlie cutting up the rescued pizza and serving it up on a cookie sheet. He gives me the thumbs-up and turns to talk to some blond girl, who is helping him with this party-host detail. The noise level is already at the awesome-party stage; and I rapidly count at least eighty people. Uncle Chad and Aunt Gina picked a fine time to be gone for the evening and leave their only son in charge.

The music blares, and the general feeling of high-level party chaos prevails and completed by the hundreds of sparkling Christmas lights that must have strung up in a hurry for this event. The only thing this party needs to complete the ultimate party theme is a Piñata. Then, I spy one in the fair corner of the great room where some girl, who wears an overly tight T-shirt and a loosely-tied blindfold around her head, drunkenly swings a Nerf bat at the pink and blue paper-*mâché* donkey. *Charlie does know how to entertain, or break all the rules, equally.*

I help myself to a bottled imported beer from the refrigerator and consciously avoid the keg that is set up on the far end of the black granite counter-top of Aunt Gina's normally pristine gourmet kitchen. I didn't want to come, but Charlie insisted that I swing by and celebrate the long weekend since I was around. My baseball team has a curfew, but my dad took care of things with the coaching staff that basically allows me to forgo those installed rules that apply to everybody else but me. I had the coach's grudgingly-given permission to stay at my aunt and uncle's house, away from campus, and avoid the check-in routine. I was covered, like always, because of who my dad is.

Meanwhile, my dad is already headed back to L.A. His work is done. He set things up with my sports agent in terms of which teams are expected to be at my game tomorrow against Oregon State. We lost today, and I will pitch tomorrow. So, yes, technically, I shouldn't even be here; but the meeting with my agent and my dad and talk about the upcoming draft left me on edge. So I took off, after dropping those two off at the airport bound for LAX and promptly left after the Cardinal team meeting and ended up here. Charlie mentioned inviting a few friends over since it was a long weekend, but this has turned into a full-blown party.

I recognize a number of people from Paly from years before, and I do what I can to avoid direct conversation and just incline my head in their general direction; even so, that anti-social move only takes me so far. After being drawn into the fifth conversation about me and baseball and my big-time draft rumors, I install myself against the farthest wall and keep to the shadows and privately cajole myself for being here at all. I begin to plan my exit, so I can avoid any further encounters with old high school classmates and fan-girls looking for a good time with an almost-famous baseball player. Mindless sex with a stranger isn't hard to find when you're an athlete and even less so when you're on the verge of fame because everybody wants a piece of that action. God knows I used to play into that, too; but the free-sex-no-strings-attached lifestyle catches up to you. As it turns out, everybody wants a piece of you or that action. You can't really trust anybody to want you for you. They always want more. Now, I abide by strict rules of not getting involved with anyone—at least not often and never permanently—because there's too much on the line with me and baseball these days. It used to be that saying yes to every invitation offered was a whole lot easier than saying no. Sometimes, it's still that way. But now? The only thing that matters to me is baseball and keeping my dad happy. And we're so close. *I'm* so close, as my dad constantly reminds me.

So here I am, imbibing in a few beers and trying to appear normal and avoid all the supposed fan-girls, if at all possible; and then, there she is—the girl from Valentine's Day. I'm just staring at her—the raven-haired girl across the room—remembering Valentine's Day and the horrible circumstances under which we first met and immediately having trouble remembering all my set rules for not getting involved with anyone. Ever.

At one point, I catch her green-eyed gaze, and she looks right through me. I actually shiver at the unspoken admission that she doesn't remember me at all. I find myself suffering with this crushing disappointment as if I've been hit squarely in the chest by a baseball. What dumb luck is it that she's shown up at this party, and that she doesn't even remember me?

She surveys the room with a disdainful look and takes one long, slow pull of her drink from a red plastic cup. I watch her slender throat move up and down as she swallows. My body reacts to all of her in a single instant.

Man, I want her bad. Just like that. At the very least, I want to know her name before I leave here tonight.

I watch her for so long that I can tell when the vodka-spiked punch actually hits her system. She sways ever so slightly now and leans further up against the far wall as if that alone is the only thing still holding her up.

My conscience surges with guilt that I should have gone over to her sooner, but still directs me toward her before I actually think about what I'm doing. I'm not sure where this urgent need to protect her comes from. Perhaps I'm spurred on by a few of these guys partying it up right next to her that seem to have taken notice of the swaying, dark-haired girl at about the same time I start to make my way across to her. Still, I'm determined to be the one that saves her *again,* even if she doesn't remember me from the first time we met more than three months ago on Valentine's Day.

CHAPTER SIX

Tally ~ It is true, if you want to, you can be someone else

I T IS TRUE THAT, WHEN A girl wants to look more like twenty than seventeen, her best friend can apply liner and dark shadow to her eyelids and black mascara to her lashes and achieve sophistication, however contrived. It is not true that, when a girl wears a miracle bra that she is ever a size C instead of a B, however illusionary. There's no miracle there. It's just my secret, but it is mine to keep or share.

The truth is I look older and decidedly sexy because I'm wearing Holly's designer clothes and boots and pose like a New York fashion model by the punchbowl. These things bring about the desired effect. I feel older, sophisticated, and sexy.

The rebel is back. It feels good—different, somehow—but good.

It is sometimes true that a girl can become someone else with the simplest of changes.

༺━━━━●━━━━༻

I wouldn't be here if my twin sister hadn't died. My mom would have probably grilled me about this party, and I wouldn't have been able to come up with a reason so easily as to why I needed to spend the night at Marla's. I think my parents were secretly relieved at getting a night off from the pretense of having to act like everything is okay when it clearly isn't. Normally, I'd have to combat questions, provide enough details, and employ a few innocent lies about my intended plans and whereabouts, but with Holly dead now and my parents all but absent even when present, tonight they didn't even remember to ask where I was going.

My father buries himself in his work—performing miracle surgeries. He's intent on saving everyone else since he couldn't save Holly. My mother nurses her grief in constant seclusion—the master bedroom door rarely opens—where she takes this necessary solace in silence and these little white pills that make her numb, bestowing her lovely face with a constant faraway look. She is twice removed from all of us, it seems. She's definitely farthest away from me. She gave me a backhand wave as she trudged her way back up the stairs to her bedroom while my dad kissed my forehead and reached the front door first and raced to open it as I was about to leave. He told me to text them later before bed. I'd just nodded and promised to check in at some point and beat a hasty retreat to Marla's car, completely undone by his long-sought-after affection but unable to properly respond when he finally gave it to me.

Yes; it's true. Adam and Tessa Landon are unaware of Charlie Masterson's Memorial Day weekend party. They're hardly aware it's a three-day weekend or that Memorial Day is Monday, or that I graduate in ten days and leave for New York in seventeen. It's been more than three months since Holly's death, but it feels like yesterday. The grief is just as palpable in our house. The day we came home from Holly's funeral still feels like the worst. We just sat there for hours and stared into space without saying a single word to each other. We seemed to wait for the darkness to descend outside like it had so effectively penetrated the inside of all of us. The pain is just as raw and visceral now as it was then for me, for my family, for all of us.

It doesn't matter. Upon this, my parents and I agree; none of it matters anymore.

I imbibe in some alcohol-laced concoction because my sister isn't alive to say, 'let's go,' and my parents are too grief-stricken to notice or see me at all these days.

Meanwhile, Marla is full of laughter. Contrived or otherwise, I still wonder where it comes from. I can only watch as she wanders off with some more-than-casually-interested guy with a promise to be right back.

Her intention to make Charlie Masterson jealous seems to be working. I note the golden guy flinch unconsciously as she drapes herself all over this other guy. A platitude, no doubt. I almost feel sorry for Charlie. He's become a somewhat innocent bystander in all of this drama and unable to take his eyes off of Marla since we arrived over an hour ago. Marla's first mission is accomplished. Charlie Masterson is definitely taking notice of her every move and is undeniably paying dearly for his previous transgressions and cavalier ways with Marla's heart.

Good. On some level, this seems good, right?

Untethered from Marla, for the moment, I must admit I carry a modicum of resentment for my best friend. It's there for just a split second, where I feel this irrepressible bitterness because Marla Stone can still laugh. So easily. She loved Holly, probably as much as I do…*did*…but she can still laugh so easily. Marla stills sees the good in the world, instead of all the oppressive nothingness that I so clearly see. For just a brief second, I resent her for it—for being happy, for being able to laugh, for being able to breathe.

And then it's gone. Indifference takes its place and I openly welcome the respite that comes with feeling nothing at all while Marla waves to me one last time as she seductively makes her way up the stairs with the casually interested guy in tow. Charlie Masterson soon follows them. I can only imagine what's unfolding upstairs with those three. I roll my eyes and seek out a new form of entertainment. Alone among strangers, I lean against the far wall, finish off my third drink (make a mental note that I should stop and definitely count all these sugary calories), and yet valiantly start in on a fourth. All my mother's party rules—about a maximum of two drinks and avoiding the punch at all costs at any party—slip away from me.

That last afternoon together, we'd talked for hours, sometimes laughing at each other as we conducted this lively debate about our plans after graduation and how Rob did or did not fit into those long-held plans. Then, rain and a black SUV changed everything good about my life in a mere fifteen seconds. "Run, Tally. Run."

She's gone. Gone forever. So sudden, so tragic, so sorry. Everyone's so sorry. Everyone's still so sorry.

It is true.

Grief changes you.

You're different, not the same.

So you play the game, Seuss-like.

I ignore the sympathetic stares of the partygoers as word begins to circulate through the crowd about who I am and what happened to my twin. As a momentary distraction from the debilitating sympathy swirling its way toward me, I subtly nod and help myself to yet another round of this bewildering but delicious punch. *Nobody wants to talk about Holly. I know that.* No one wants to be reminded of my sister's tragic ending. I wish it didn't plague me so much of the time, either. Silly me. I thought being among strangers would change the outcome. Apparently not.

Holly and I used to play a game where we would pretend to be each other. We did this whenever we were feeling out of our depth. We could fool just about anyone—even Marla. With the aid of the red punch and a desperate need to feel normal again on some knowable level, I decide to be Holly the rest of the night. I throw my shoulders back, toss my hair in that *fare-thee-well-princess-way* of hers and adroitly smile, mimicking my twin's infectious enthusiasm for life. Everybody loved Holly. Just adopting my twin's persona makes me feel a little better. I quietly laugh to myself enjoying this secret amusement and imagine Holly being right there cheering me on. "That's it, Tally. Have some fun."

Another interested guy tops off my glass with more of the red bubbling punch. This one is definitely older with a striking resemblance to the iconic said host of this party.

In need of a distraction from Marla's love situation, I profusely thank this latest interested guy for the top-off. I'm overzealous. I check myself and strive for nonchalance with him, strive for the sophistication bestowed upon me by my dead sister's designer clothes, Marla's application of flawless make-up, and the general personification of Holly's lively personality I've managed to perfect over the years. We make idle chatter about the holidays, the break from school, the lame red punch, and the limited food offerings—the opened chip bags haphazardly strewn about. I attempt to keep a keen eye on Marla, who has returned from upstairs, and now gyrates to some love song with the same more-than-casually-interested guy from before, while Charlie watches her like a self-appointed chaperon intent on saving her virtue.

The effects of spiked punch begin to descend upon me. I again glance over at covetous actions of Charlie Masterson, who is now having a heated discussion with my best friend on the other side of the room, gesturing this way and that towards the more-than-casually-interested first guy, who gyrates on the dance floor by himself.

I start towards Marla, but she waves me off. Unsure of what I should be doing, I find myself in the middle of the dance floor. *Alone.* To hide my embarrassment at being caught up alone in the middle of the room, I pretend to take an ever-increasing interest in the sparkling lights that someone has meticulously trailed along the ceiling's edge. A little glazed now, the lights shimmer at me; I swill my drink in salutation. The interested guy from earlier stands in front of me again.

Tall. Dark. Handsome.

He is the cliché for sex on a stick, but he's kept me company during the past half-hour. I brazenly take in this male-model look he has going on with his dark-brown wavy hair and his devastating, too-white smile and his tall lean body. *Sure. Okay. Bring it on.*

"I'm Linc," he says during a respite from the loud music.

"As in President Abraham—"

"Not funny." He sighs and shakes his head side-to-side and gets this disconcerted look. "Lincoln Presley."

"Elvis is in the building then," I deadpan.

He looks taken aback now. "What did you say?"

"I *said…*" I lose my train of thought because he is stunning—so good-looking, in fact—that these warning bells seem to go off in my head. I shake it to try to shut them off. "Never mind." His look is weirding me out as if I know him from somewhere. "You remember," I say softly. "*Elvis?*"

"I remember," he says slowly and gets this expectant look. "Do you *remember?*"

I'm just staring at him open-mouthed. "No. My mom loved him when she was a teenager. I like a few of his songs…" My voice trails off because he looks disappointed by my answer, and I'm not sure why.

"Don't you remember?" he asks again.

"Remember what?" I look at him blankly and then break his gaze and start toward the punch bowl for a fifth round.

He takes the glass from my hand and then hands me bottled water. "Drink this. That stuff has Everclear in it. You shouldn't have any more of that unless you're going for anesthetization."

"Gallant. How noble of you," I say with as much sarcasm as I can. Then I shake off his concerned hand on my arm, uncap the bottled water, and drink it down. "Happy now?"

He nods slowly and eventually smiles and then proceeds to take me in from head-to-toe in one long, practiced, seductive move. *Smooth.* I laugh because he's so blatant about his interest in me now.

"How are you?" he asks when the music stops playing for a few welcome seconds.

Odd.

An odd thing to ask of a stranger.

"I'm fine." I give him a bewildered *what-the-hell-are-you-asking-me-that-for?* look.

He leans in. "*Who* are you?"

"Oh." I half-smile. "Holly," I say with an airy wave of my right hand. The lie comes so easily to my lips that I surprise myself with the ease in which I tell it.

It is true, when you want to, you can be someone else. Seuss-like.

"Let's dance, *Holly.*"

I don't know why I say yes to him. I don't dance at parties. I save that for my training, usually, but there's something about him that has me gyrating out on the dance floor, getting bolder with every song they play. All kinds of things are being communicated between us, the least of which is this overriding uninhibited sexual attraction for one another.

We both know where this is going.

His eyes light up and crinkle at the corners as he notably watches me while I ratchet up my dance moves to a rather risqué level, by the time we're through the fifth song. We have a bit of an audience now as the party people begin to gather and lasciviously watch us move without inhibition across the dance floor. The alcohol buzz being carried through my system feels like water being passed along a fire line that is way too late to actually fight the intense blaze with. I'm buzzed, more than a little drunk, and definitely emboldened.

After another song, I strip off my outer black sweater and toss it toward Marla, who catches it one-handed and grins suggestively back at me. Now, she's saying something to Charlie. The two of them lean closer together in order to be heard over the music. They talk intently now. Her ex-boyfriend doesn't even glance in my direction because he only has eyes for Marla.

Meanwhile, my dance partner and I show the partying crowd just how provocative dancing together can be. The music pulses. I welcome the numbness that descends upon me even as I gasp a little for breath at the frenetic pace of the movements. My ribs begin to throb in painful protest. I brush up against him a couple of times, and he twirls me around. His eyes never leave my face; and I smile a little, enjoying the unexpected freedom from sorrow. I'm enamored by the idea of just being in the moment and nowhere else. It's been a long while since I felt this free.

The rebellious side of me seems to have been shaken from her slumber. Then, someone decides to mess with my newfound rhythm because the very next song is a slow one with some singer crooning about love and loss. I start to walk off the makeshift dance floor when Lincoln Presley grabs my hand and pulls me into his chest. I can feel his fast heart rate as it pulses through his shirt directly against my cheekbone. He pulls me in closer. His membership as part of the male human species serves as a dead giveaway of his physical attraction for me. I look up at him, a little disconcerted by this and the sudden intensity I see in his eyes. He nuzzles my neck with his chin.

"Sorry." He laughs a little. "What can I say? You're *seriously* attractive."

"Seriously." I kind of push away from him but he holds me tighter to him.

My body resists him for a few seconds and then reluctantly molds to his. I allow myself to enjoy the closeness of him while my mind indulges in all kinds of fantasies. I'm unleashed. He is the sexiest guy I've ever met. He makes all the others before him seem like boys. I guess they were.

He traces my lips with his fingertip. "What are you thinking about?" he asks.

"Boys to men."

"Ah…the band? Was that one of their songs?"

"No. I don't think so." I smile because he's so misinterpreted my secret thoughts. I almost laugh, and he's looking at me even more intently.

Somewhere along the way, the music has stopped; but we're still swaying to all these secret musical notes that apparently only the two of us can hear.

"Do you want to get out of here?" He gets this shy, hopeful look.

I laugh a little because, *yes, I do want to get out of here with him,* and he's quite charming with this innocent *I've-never-done-this-before* kind of look on his face. "I want to get out of here."

The music starts up again, louder now. He smiles and shouts something to Charlie the party host, who briefly nods and absently waves a hand in our general direction. I manage to give a little secret hand wave to Marla to text me later with the plan. We always have a plan. She lifts an eyebrow, takes a long practiced look at my conquest, and covertly assesses his worthiness as a hook-up. She finally gives me the subtle finger-lift of approval.

Linc leans in and whispers, "This way. Follow me."

He clasps my hand in his and hauls me out of the party in an experienced two-minute drill.

This is going to be fun.

As I follow him out, I swear I hear Holly's contrived whisper asking me, "are you sure?' I nod my head in an attempt to dispel my mind's eternal quest for hearing her voice just one more time.

"I'm sure," I say as the cool summer breeze stirs my hair and lifts his at the nape of his neck. Linc glances back when he hears me say this, and he smiles.

CHAPTER SEVEN

Tally — (sure thing

INC PULLS ME ALONG THROUGH THE back door of the kitchen and
then directly across the expansive lawn toward a nicely trimmed
hedge. He lithely climbs up the few steps that lead to a charming stone guest
house located in the back of the Masterson's gigantic property. He produces
keys, unlocks the door, and steps aside, allowing me to pass through first.

"My place. When I'm here. They let me stay here whenever I want," he
says by way of explanation.

He still grasps my hand, keeping me steady. His smile is strangely reassuring.
Like I need reassurance. His light seems to chase away the shadows that have
plagued me all these months. It's true; the darkness actually diminishes within
his illuminating presence.

We enter a large great room. The walls are painted white with dark accents
all around while high wood beams stretch across the ceiling in a crisscross
pattern. There's a large stone fireplace at one end that matches the exterior
of the house and a kitchen is located at the other end. It's charming. Cozy. I
like it. It feels like a home. He hits a couple of switches, and lights come on
and then automatically dim to a pre-programmed ambiance while the gas
fireplace roars to life. *Instant seduction scene.*

He leads me down a long hallway where we enter the master bedroom. The
door latches behind him and I pretend not to notice the sudden intention for
confinement. *This is what I came for.*

I do a full circle in the center of his bedroom and look over at him
somewhat quizzically, while he just stands there and manages to look a little
unsure of himself.

Surprisingly.

"My place. I stay here. When I can." He pauses.

"I said that already. My aunt and uncle let me stay here. I'm at Stanford. My parents used to live here a long time ago, but they moved to L.A. and then…my dad still lives there." He gets this twisted-up smile. "I'm not sure why I felt the need to explain all of that." He shakes his head and gets this rueful smile. "There's a restroom right there." He points to another door to my left.

My mind clicks with swift understanding at all he's just said. "Lincoln Presley." He nods. "You're Charlie Masterson's cousin? The baseball player?"

He nods. What are the odds that I would run into the very guy Marla wanted me to meet? I kind of laugh; I'm somewhat awestruck by the guy's attractiveness and my whimsical ability to recall his talent, even though I seriously hate baseball. *One word I would use to describe it? Boring.* I put this sudden clarity to realizing who he is down to the acute but overwhelming effects of the party punch. He gives me a definitive smile as I disappear into his bathroom.

Minutes later, I emerge equipped with knowledge for his favorite cologne—Armani. His shaving preferences—a razor. "The art of shaving?" I tease.

Linc laughs. "My college roommate got me hooked on that. It really does work."

I make a point of touching his face as I stroll past him to get a better look at his bookshelf. "Smooth."

The thrill of him begins to work its way through me. All at once, I'm thankful Marla picked out the black lace leggings with the red mini for me to wear. Thankful for my sister's black leather boots—calfskin, silky soft, and practically reaching my thighs. Thankful, I shaved my legs and permanently borrowed my sister's Dolce & Gabbana "The One" perfume and lightly sprayed it all over. The scent is now faint, but it's still there. I'm thankful for it all because here is this baseball player from Stanford—Lincoln Presley—and he will expect these things. I wave my free hand toward his bedroom wall of self-achievement and look straight at him. "Famous."

He shrugs.

Modest.

His unassuming look almost undoes my bravado. I turn away and resume the impromptu tour of his room, examining his baseball trophies and covertly studying his photographs. Linc runs the bases. Linc makes the winning pitch. Linc holds a gold trophy high over his head. His winning smile flashes from all the photographs. All his achievements.

Always the winner.

I turn around and consciously assess the real one before me. He's slightly built, surprisingly, but he's tall and lean and incredibly attractive. In an attempt to still play it cool with him, I again study all the newspaper clippings someone has proudly framed of the guy. The headlines proclaim his fast ball is his specialty, and he holds the number-one spot as lead pitcher on athletic scholarship at Stanford. According to the sports world, Major League Baseball has been circling and assessing him for some time and may soon call upon Lincoln Presley—the superstar—to further explore and exploit his talent.

A scholarship. Ten trophies. Five blue ribbons. Two reds. Four gold medals.

I touch each one as if receiving benediction for doing so and trail my fingers over one of his winning medals. It hangs from a gold ribbon like a talisman. I slip it over my head.

"You've collected a lot of trophies already, Lincoln Presley."

"It's not about the trophies. It's about winning. At least, that's what my dad says." He sounds apologetic as if he wishes things could be different.

"We must be perfect for the parents." He studies my face for a long moment. He gets this look of regret and slowly nods with some kind of shared recognition. "At least, we have to try," I say with a little grimace.

"Yes, we have to try," he says back to me.

It's true that I shoulder perfection in every way possible for my parents now. They depend on me to be perfect. They *need* me to be perfect. I shudder all at once tired of the shackles and their expectations that I be the fun, smart, and accomplished daughter—that I *be Holly for* them. The burdens are heavy. The expectations are high. Yet, the grief threatens, and surges ever higher, poised to engulf all of me.

Perfect. The only thing I'm just about perfect at is ballet. Someday everyone is bound to figure that out.

I force myself to smile like Holly would and glance over at Linc because we share this quest to be perfect.

He gets this sexy smile. I incline my head in acquiescence because I know where this is going. I'm ready for the respite from the pain I still carry, and I instinctively know Lincoln Presley can take it from me for a little while.

He comes over and puts his arms around my neck and pulls me close. I breathe in his cologne while he trails his mouth along my neck again. He leans in and kisses me and lifts me up off the floor and then starts to hold my body above his, but I move out of his hands quickly and involuntarily moan at the instant pain.

"Sorry," I say, forcibly breaking the moment. "Normally that move would send me over the edge, but I broke three ribs three months ago and if I let you lift me like that I'll be screaming for all the wrong reasons." I shake my head in embarrassment and kind of laugh. "Sorry, I didn't mean to kill the mood like that."

"Let me see." He moves to lift up my shirt and spies the heavy ace bandage wrapped tight around my mid-section. The black lace Wonderbra does little to camouflage the hideous beige bandage, and it's decidedly so not sexy. "I've got this miracle salve that works wonders on aching muscles and broken ribs. I broke a rib a few years ago, miscalculating a steal for third." He looks straight at me. "It hurt like hell for months, but this stuff works wonders, like I said." He gets this thoughtful expression and then disappears into his bathroom. He soon returns and holds up this little green jar.

"What is it? Or do I even want to know?"

"No, probably not," he says with a laugh. "But it works. Do they hurt right now?"

I nod and bite at my lower lip. "Probably shouldn't have shown off so much on the dance floor. They're raging in protest right now. It's hard to even breathe."

"And I thought that was my special kind of magic making it so hard for you to breathe."

I laugh a little. "You're weird, Elvis," I say airily. "You're seriously weird." He looks taken aback. I start to laugh again and realize that it actually feels strange to be laughing, to be curiously happy for no reason at all. I stop myself and look at him more intently. "No one's ever called you weird before, have they?"

"No." He gets this little smile. "I've been called lots of things. With a name like Lincoln Presley, the imaginations of kids from seven on are pretty ruthless and know no boundaries. But, Elvis? You call me *Elvis*...all the time...since we first met." He looks at me intently as if I should have figured this out by now. "*Why?*" he asks.

Why.

Why?

"Why," I say slowly. "I don't know. No reason. You have dark hair, blue eyes. Do you sing?"

He gets this slight smile and bites at his lower lip but concentrates fully on the task at hand. I'm suddenly shy as he directs me to lift my arms and then deftly strips off my black lace blouse and slowly undoes the final wrapping of the ace bandage around my ribcage. My ribs have been tightly wrapped for the past fourteen hours. Their inevitable release from the ace bandage is accompanied by this deep visceral pain—the price to be paid for seductive dancing and a rigorous pointe class done all in the same day. "God. I overdid it. *Oooohhhh.* That hurts something...*fierce.*"

"Are you..." He pauses. "Are you, like, trying to stop yourself from swearing? Because of me?" He laughs. "Because I can completely handle it."

His mocking makes me almost laugh, but that makes it hurt worse.

"Shit. Don't make me laugh, Elvis." My eyes fill up with tears. "Damn. It's incredibly *fucking* painful."

"That's more like it. I love a girl who can swear like a truck-driver."

He dabs his fingers in the salve and moves toward the front of my chest and starts rubbing it in. I wince, prepared for an onslaught of pain; but there is none. Yet, surprisingly, I experience this general embarrassment at the size of my breasts, which have been unceremoniously unmasked for him in this unexpected clinical way. Which is strange, in and of itself, because I—Tally Landon, as I like to think of myself in the third person at inopportune yet completely mortifying times like this—have never suffered from a single moment of embarrassment or regret over my small breasts until this particular moment. "It's the price to pay for fame," Holly used to say. I mutter these very words to him now.

Linc stops what he's doing and looks at me. "It's the price to pay for fame," he says back to me. "What's that in reference to?"

I don't say anything. I point to them. He nods with sudden understanding and keeps rubbing the medicinal stuff into my ribcage like nothing has changed between us.

"What a way to kill the moment," I say looking away from him. I intently study the fame wall again. *What the hell is wrong with me? I need to plan my exit. He probably thinks I'm the biggest loser.*

"You think the size of your breasts kills the mood for me?" He takes my right hand and moves it over him. I feel his erection through his jeans.

"Oh."

He pulls me up to a sitting position on the bed. *Not what I was expecting.*

"Raise your arms."

I do, dutifully. He re-wraps my rib cage, sans Wonderbra. He pulls the lace blouse back over my head and straightens my clothes as if he's dressing a doll. I start to feel disappointment, but then he gently pushes me back to the bed and kisses me while being careful not to lean too heavily into me. He raises his head from exploring my neck for a moment and looks at me quizzically; making his intentions clear once again.

His seductive move plays extreme havoc with these dormant notions of what love could be like. I'm not sure if it's the effects of the laced punch from earlier or his magnetic attraction or his amazing physical presence, but I have to secretly admit that no one has ever made me feel quite this way. *Undone. In want of more. Need. I need this. Him.*

I smile up at him as he looms over me. *I want this. I want to be with him.* Being with him is exactly what I want to do because Holly isn't here anymore, and my parents are too besieged by grief to care properly. It's just me now. But tonight, I don't want to be alone. I want to be with him. I want to be with someone, who is still alive and makes me that way again, too. *Because it doesn't matter. None of it matters anymore.*

"How old are you?" Linc asks suddenly. "*Really.*"

"Old enough." I look at him in defiance. "How old are you?"

"I'm definitely old enough." He shakes his head side-to-side at my answer. "I'm twenty-two, almost twenty-three. October." He hesitates.

He doesn't believe me. It fuels me.

"Twenty." My seventeen-year-old lips curve into a slight smile as I tell this lie. In a little over eight hundred and two days, this will be true.

Satisfied with my answer, Linc plays with my hair, traces my jaw line, and then my lips. He trails kisses across the tops of my breasts and doesn't care about their size. I can feel myself dissolving away. I savor the building intimacy with this stranger, but not. This super god, so designated in the sports world, is here with me. Lincoln Presley's reputation for athletic stardom and dating every hot girl is somewhat legendary. At Paly. In the papers. I heard things. I read them, just like everyone else. I can handle it, handle him *handily;* I decide.

"You're on the pill…right?"

A solicitous question. "Of course I'm on the pill, Elvis," I joke. "Every twenty-year-old girl in America is on the pill. It's practically handed out along with your college course list."

He looks suspicious at my flippant answer while I silently count backwards. How many days has it been since I took one of those birth control pills? Two? Maybe three at the most. Does it matter? Yes. Think, Tally.

The lies have just built upon one another. One follows the other like connected dots on a road map; but this path leads me to him, and I can't stop now. Not yet. I hold my breath and take quick inventory one by one of the lies I've told him. Name. Age. Birth control. *What am I doing? Why am I doing it?*

He shakes his head. Then he walks over to his night stand, blithely opens the drawer, and holds up a foil packet in triumph. I take in air and slowly exhale with relief and nod with approval of his Cracker Jack prize. When it comes to contraception, I'm normally better prepared than this—but then nothing is normal anymore.

"Oh, good. Yes, let's use that, too." Then my nerves get the better of me and begin to take over. I'm shaking. *What the hell is wrong with me? This is standard operating procedure.* I attempt to affect a casual air, slip off his bed and out of his arms, and resume my innocuous tour of his room. The top two rows are filled with books. I finger each one and read the names aloud. "Shakespeare, Hemingway, Cheever? Have you read any of these?"

"No. I'm pre-med at Stanford, but the major leagues are interested. The draft is coming up. We'll see what happens with baseball soon enough," he says, looking a little uneasy.

"Stanford. Nice. My dad went there. He's a doctor—a surgeon. They'd like me to consider Stanford, but I like NYU…" I shrug with nonchalance and have to hope he won't ask me anymore and wonder why I brought all this up to him in the first place. I've sent in registration papers for NYU, but I won't have time to go there. *But isn't that what a twenty-year-old would be doing? Going to college?* Desperate at my over-sharing ways, I switch topics. "Dad saves a lot people—most of them anyway." I turn, look at Linc, and frown. I'm momentarily stopped by all these thoughts of Holly that unexpectedly come rushing back at me in saying this. *We can't save everyone, now can we?* "Is that what you want to do? Save a lot of people?" I can't keep the sadness out of my voice.

"Saving people is the ultimate," he says with this disquiet. His grey-blue eyes darken, and he gets this intense look.

I'm not completely sure what I've done or said to upset him as much as I have myself. I automatically step back from him, intent on fighting the demons plaguing me from the inside alone. Our unsteady breaths begin to match up, and I look at him in growing bewilderment.

"I don't need saving."

"No one said you did."

"Really? No one said anything to you at the party? Marla didn't talk up my particular assets? Lay the Landon girl because she fucking *needs* it."

"Who's Marla?"

Oh shit.

"I'm Holly and definitely not the one you want to get involved with." I start toward the door. For some unknowable reason, he scares me. I feel out of control. This whole scene has become too much, and all I want to do now is leave. Then I remember my bag. I put it on his bed at one point. I close my eyes for a second, willing myself to get it together. I turn around and face him. "My bag. I need it. It's got my stuff."

He's just staring at me—wary, of course—because I'm sure I sound like a flipping lunatic.

"Stay. I'm scared, too, because baseball is my sole focus." Then, he shakes his head and gets this apologetic look. "Med school is a plan B. I'm trying to finish early with an undergraduate degree in biology, but it doesn't really matter. My dad is intent on me having me play in the Majors…Baseball is my sole focus. If all goes according to the plan, I'll get drafted in the first or second round, play in some minor league working up to triple-A ball and eventually make my way up to Major League Baseball in the next couple of years. *Baseball.* That's all there is. That's the way it has to be."

He gives me this quizzical look as if to ensure I've heard all he's said. Then he slowly appraises me just like before. It's disconcerting as if I'm auditioning for some kind of part. He shakes his head and slowly smiles. "We should go."

"We should go," I echo his words, defiantly lift my chin, and look right at him. "Most definitely."

He doesn't say anything for a few minutes. He seems to be wrestling with indecision. Frustrated by his silence, I turn and start toward the door again.

"You're an incredible dancer," he says from behind me. "But you *know* that."

I glance back at him again with a little smile and then turn to face him more fully. "I've been told…I have talent. I'm expected to be the next Polina Semionova." I smile wide and laugh at his confused face. "And you don't even know who that is." He gets this sexy half-smile and shakes his head side-to-side, looking apologetic. I nod and flip my hand toward him. "That's *big*, like Major League Baseball kind of big, Elvis." I shake my head at him. "Look, I don't want anything from you."

He looks relieved at what I've said and I battle this distinct feeling of crushing disappointment at seeing it. "And you shouldn't expect anything from me, either," I say more unkindly than I intended.

Now he looks surprisingly disconcerted by what I've just said. I take a step back from him because, for some reason, I'm on edge again. As a counterbalance for feeling so mysteriously out of control, I put my hands on my hips and breathe out, daring him to come closer, daring him not to.

I hesitate and weigh my options—*leave or stay.*

I'm not really sure what I'm doing here any longer. Seducing guys is normally the easy part. I get what I want. They get what they want. We move on. One night together, here or there; sometimes not often, a party or two afterward together; and then there is the inevitable ending. Because nobody gets that I have dance class. *All the time.* That I don't ever have a night off. That I don't eat often. That I rarely drink. That I do little else but dance and train.

Sure. People admire the dedication but then they resent it. *And me.*

So. There are no promises. No phone calls. No texts. No birthday cards. No love notes. No flowers. No dates. No prom. There is only dance class and training; and rehearsals and performances. A decade of those. A decade of life on a stage or in a class. Five picture albums capture every performing moment and every starring role I've ever had, but little else, because there has been nothing else in all that time. Because when you've got the talent you have to constantly train for it and perfect it in order to reach and remain at the top—the most exceptional level of high achievement. *Always.*

Surely, the baseball player knows this.

It was easier to conduct these superficial encounters in New York last summer. Marla and I soon discovered after our arrival there that everyone was on their way to being someone else. The superficiality of it all was not lost on anyone in that town; there, everyone seemed to know that relationships were deal-breakers on the way to fame and fortune. *Surely, Lincoln Presley knows this, too.* Because who has time for such a distraction? The rules—in perfecting a God-given talent and ultimately seeking fame—are known, followed, and kept. Things are casual, however physical, and definitely noncommittal. *The way things are.*

Even so, here in Palo Alto's hometown sphere, the moral considerations for casual sex and no commitments have become strangely confusing. I'm caught between who I was before Holly died and who I am now. *Is there a difference?*

The old Tally needed casual sex; wanted it, in fact. I was noncommittal, detached and uninvolved. That's all I asked for and needed. *Then.*

And now? I steadfastly hold on to the belief that there can be no commitments of any kind beyond ballet because I don't want any complications. I still say *no* to: most phone calls, to most texts, to most movies, to most parties, to all school dances, to all Friday-night football games, to all prom and dinner dates. What's the point of going to dinner with someone who is just going to end up questioning why I don't *ever* eat anything?

Complications.

I don't need them. I don't want them.

I am so right about this.

"Would you like to go out sometime? Not this weekend." He shakes his head side-to-side and looks hopeful. "I fly out to Tempe, Arizona tomorrow, after my game. And then we have Regionals next weekend, but I know this great Italian place we could go to sometime and maybe we could catch a movie or something afterward."

It takes a full minute to comprehend what he's just asked me. I take a step back and eye him in disbelief. "Are you asking me *out*? On a *date*? To *dinner* and *a movie*?" I'm incredulous that he's somehow guessed at my most recent and truly errant thoughts.

"That's about the safest thing I can think of…to do…with you." He half-smiles and looks a little dazed and unsure of himself at the same time.

"The safest thing?" I wave my hand around his bedroom. "I don't *do* dinner or go to movies. And this is a strange conversation to be having *here* in your *bedroom*."

"How about now? Did you eat dinner?" He moves swiftly past me, opens the door, and starts down the hallway.

"No." I follow him more out of curiosity than anything wondering why we're talking about a future date and dinner.

"Did you want to go back? To the party?" he asks, turning back to me briefly.

I don't answer. No. I just slowly trail after him and watch him make his way to the kitchen.

"*Yes.*" I finally say, with this discernible, petulant whine. "I want to go back to the party." I cross my arms across my chest, but he essentially ignores what I've said and keeps on walking. "I don't eat, actually," I say airily.

True.

He turns back to me again, shakes his head, and gets this secret smile as if I just presented him with the ultimate challenge. *And maybe I have.*

"Bring it, Elvis."

He laughs.

***

This sure thing has taken an odd turn. All I can do is helplessly watch as he places a saucepan on one of the burners he's lit, deftly gathers a few things from his Viking refrigerator, wields a knife across a red bell pepper and white onion, and eventually adds it all to the pan.

Soon, the sizzling sound of vegetable sautéing in cooking oil dominates the space between us. He's humming and seems to concentrate on the food preparation rather intently and generally won't look at me. Intrigued by his surprising culinary efforts, I take the opportunity to study him, while he chops up raw chicken and adds it to the mixture. He drizzles in some balsamic vinegar from a fancy green bottle and minces up garlic and throws that into the saucepan as well.

Within twenty minutes, the food smells delicious, and I secretly acknowledge that I'm starving, and he's cooking me dinner, and I like that about him, and it's this unexpected, incredible turn-on. *Whoa, Tally, slow down. It's dinner, not a date. Focus. Breathe.*

"Can I ask you something?" He looks straight at me from across the granite countertop, where I sit precariously perched on one of the kitchen stools. His smile gets wider because he's caught me openly staring at him. I blush. "Has anyone ever cooked for you?"

I cannot think up a lie fast enough. I'm trapped into responding, undone by the honesty I see in his face as he awaits my answer. I haven't even begun to contemplate why it's important to him. "No one has ever cooked for me. Usually…we do the deed, and I'm on my way."

"Do the deed?" He gets this lopsided grin. *It's charming.*

"You know what I mean." My face gets uncharacteristically hot. *What is going on with me?*

"Do I? Is that what they say in Palo Alto these days? *Do the deed?*"

I can't tell if he's teasing or not. I'm not sure that it matters. The room's suddenly become electrically charged with a lot of things being left unsaid between us and a lot of things that will never be said.

"Elvis," I finally say, breathing softly. "I'm pretty much *a sure thing*…if you don't piss me off," I add, wagging my finger at him.

He laughs at the reference, playfully bites at my pointed finger but otherwise ignores my answer. *Again.*

Still, I manage a seductive smile because I'm rather enjoying this unpredictable cat-and-mouse game we're playing. I gracefully slide off the chair and make my way around to the edge of the counter toward him, while he's busy placing the sautéed chicken onto two gold ceramic plates using professional-looking, chef-style tongs as if we're at Tamarine or something. The dishes remind me of the ones my mom had in college. They're like a throwback to the eighties.

He hands me a fork and directs me back to my chair. His arm rests across my shoulders for an instant, and he gently pushes me down into the seat. "Eat," he commands.

He goes around to the other side of the counter again—away from me—and holds his plate in one hand and eats with the other. He forks his food into his mouth slowly as if he's in dire need of judicious concentration. He seems conflicted and looks away from me as if lost in his own thoughts for a few minutes.

I must admit I'm a little confused by this whole scene. By what I've said and the way he's ignored what I've said. *Me. Sure thing. Let's do this. The deed. You and me.* I guess I haven't said that explicitly enough; and now I'm not sure where this is going, and I'm caught off balance.

I push my food around the plate and ponder my next move.

Should I go?

Or, should I stay?

He nudges my hand and then produces an empty wine glass and starts filling it with Perrier water. The green bottle is a dead giveaway.

"No wine?" I ask in confusion.

"I think that spiked punch did you in."

"That's what you think? So...what? The food is to *sober* me up?" I try not to sound personally offended, but I am. "I don't need a babysitter."

"I didn't say you did. It's just...if things lead to something else; I want you to be awake for it." His smile takes my breath and the propensity for a withering comeback line to what he's just implied whooshes away from me. And so I shift my shoulders in response and Marla's borrowed blouse, which is a size too big for me, slips off to one side, as if on cue. It's an unexpected sexy move; and I let it go, although I notice Linc is taking it all in. He stares at me intently but looks a little self-conscious when I catch him doing it. I hold my breath in response and then slowly smile in triumph because I have his complete attention now. But then, he sets his cleaned plate aside on the granite counter-top and examines mine with apparent disappointment. He's frowning, which makes me uneasy.

"Eat something." He sounds a little irritated with me, so I force myself to take three bites in quick succession.

"Hmmm...it's good."

It really is good, and I try to hide my surprise that he has these extraordinary culinary skills as well as being this guy with these off-the-charts good looks. My stomach gurgles a bit, and I can't quite decide if it's really because I'm starving or his company. I take another two bites and then force myself to push the plate aside. The willpower comes from years of disciplined practice; plus, I have a newfound incentive to finish up. I'm intrigued by whatever this notorious baseball player has planned for me next. I guzzle the Perrier and wipe at my mouth with my fingers. He's watching me closely as I finish. Unnerved by his intense scrutiny, I clasp my hands in my lap and look up at him with this coquettish *did-I-please-you-sire?* look.

He bursts out laughing. Eventually, I do, too.

The tension between us eases for a few minutes while I help him clean up the kitchen and thank him profusely for the food. He gets this bemused look as he reaches into the freezer and holds up two York peppermint patties and then begins to thoughtfully unwrap the foil.

"I love these things. I allow myself two a week," Linc says as he hands me one.

"I'll just take a bite of yours. I don't need one of my own. I'm in the middle of training so I can't..." I grimace because I'm telling him way too much.

"Training for what?"

"Ballet. It's boxer training, really. Well, the diet for it anyway." I nibble at an edge of the York patty and hand it back to him.

"Boxer's Diet. The one where you lean out?" He shakes his head.

"That's too severe. You'll strip more muscle than you should. What do you weigh one hundred and two on a good day? You're too thin as it is, Holly."

"I know what I'm doing. We do it all the time. Off and on. It works."

I've inadvertently entered into this strange conversation with him, and if he's paying attention to it at all and what I've said before, I'm giving up way too much information. All the lies I've already told him could start to unravel if he puts it all together.

He takes a bite out of the York dessert and closes his eyes a moment, clearly enjoying the simple pleasure of it all. I consciously lick my lips and begin to savor the mint candy taste, while all these uncontrollable salacious thoughts about him race through my mind as I covertly watch him.

Then he's staring at me again, and I'm staring back.

We both know where this is going.

It's not like I haven't done this before. I have. With too many guys by some girls' counts. It's just this time seems different, note-worthy. I'm unsure of myself, and my twin sister isn't here to tell me how everything is going to be okay, that everything happens for a reason; that love can be as real as the sex can be. I straighten up, square off my shoulders, affect a dancer's stance, and seemingly look for a spot in front of me as if I can plan for the jump and time it to the music suddenly playing inside my head. Ballet is my life. Ballet is what I know. Ballet is all I have left. *Run, Tally. Run.* My vision blurs, and the room goes dark. *I can't breathe. Ballet is all I have left.*

It's as if I'm readying for a performance but there's this whimpering sound filling the room. It proves to be a distraction for both of us. Linc has this strange look upon his face. The sound gets louder, and it takes another long moment to realize it's me who is making it.

He's there within seconds. He holds me to his chest, strokes my back, and tells me that everything is going to be okay. I attempt to take in air and vaguely note I can't breathe and tell him this. Somehow, he knows what to do for me. He undoes the clips in my hair and runs his fingers through it. The intimacy of his actions moves me on some deep level that I'm incapable of understanding at the moment. I just know that I don't want him to stop, and I tell him this between these staggered gasps for air. The room gets smaller and smaller as I struggle to get air into my lungs. He leads me over to the sofa, and I sort of collapse on top of him while my limbs refuse to cooperate and move in any synchronous way at all. I couldn't stand again even if I wanted to. The world seems to be fading away in all different directions at the same time. My neck pulses in time to my heaving chest, which goes up and down in this staccato, jerky rhythm. I struggle with all these competing convulsions and try to take in air. All the while, Linc holds on to me.

"Not sure. What's happening? To me." I gasp between breaths. Embarrassed now as I seem to spin even further out of control, I close my eyes in an attempt to ward off this attack. All these incongruent thoughts hurtle towards me. *What is his game? Is this part of the Good Samaritan act? Comfort the Landon girl? She needs saving. What is wrong with me?*

Eventually, I tell myself to just focus on breathing, and I think I hear Linc tell me this, too. "*Holly*," he says with true concern. "It's going to be okay." He's said my sister's name with such believable reverence that I actually accept that I'm Holly for a few interminable seconds. My breathing returns to normal, and the uncanny filmy dark recedes.

The alcohol must have rushed through my system at an accelerated rate and been spurred on by this emotional outburst that has literally overtaken me despite reinforcements of food and kindness—or maybe because of them.

I haven't cried since my sister's funeral, but I do now.

They are these slow-motion tears. '*Hot fudge tears*' Holly used to call them. The kind that trail down your face in an uncontrollable stream, like the hot fudge sauce that endlessly drips over the sides of a sundae cup at Dairy Queen. "*Tears of heartbreak*," Marla called them once, after she and Charlie broke up the first time. My tears seem to be a combination of long-held grief and this tremendous relief at actually being able to breathe again. However, remnants of panic still swirl. I take an unsteady breath and dully note I've smeared this guy's silky grey shirt with Marla's black, long-lash mascara. This unsightly charcoal stain trails across the front of it now.

"Your shirt."

"It's okay."

"No...I..." Words desert me. I can't speak. I can't explain what just happened.

He gently strokes my face and tells me it's going to be okay.

All I can do is nod a couple of times and focus on the farthest point in the room away from him just past his shoulders. I do what I can at all costs to avoid looking directly at him. *Breathe.* I just keep telling myself that. Only my uncontrollable sniffling and unsteady jagged breaths every minute or so serve to break up this pall of silence that has overtaken the room. Inevitably, mortification rolls its way toward me. *I've just lost it in front of a complete stranger.*

"I think that was a panic attack," Linc says into the quiet after a few minutes. "You okay?"

I nod, still unsure of my ability to speak coherently. After a long while, I steal a covert glance at him. Now he leans against the back of the sofa with his eyes closed. One of his hands is still wrapped up in the strands of my hair like a rope he's been holding on to—a safety line, perhaps. I half-smile at the irony. *Who is saving who in this scenario? What is wrong with me? What just happened?*

He opens his eyes at my somewhat involuntary movements and tugs at my hair and pulls me toward him. He gently kisses my forehead. His lips travel down the side of my face and then reach the sensitive spot at my neck. I practically melt at his subtle seduction at a soul level, while my body heats up under his careful ministrations. *Oh, God. Why is he doing this to me?*

"We used to have a ranch when I was about eight years old," he says so softly that I strain to hear him. "My dad liked to train wild horses. He always said it just takes patience and time, and that you don't tame a horse as much as you come to understand it."

"Am I the wild horse in this scenario?" I ask faintly. My pulse races out of control. I bury my face into the dampness of his shirt thoroughly embarrassed by my unusual emotional breakdown. I catch my breath and hold it and will myself to pull it together.

"I'm not sure," he says. "But you definitely need saving."

"Does that line work with all the girls you bring here?"

"I don't bring girls here."

"Oh." I slide out of his arms and stand up, intent on achieving balance on a physical level as well as an emotional one because for some inexplicable reason I already know that it's vital to initiate some kind of distance from this guy. He scares me on some deep cosmic level because I like him *too much* already, and, as it is, I have more than enough fears to battle on a daily basis. "I should go."

"What if you didn't? Go?" Linc pauses for a full minute and seems to just draw me in with his kind face.

He's good-looking. At a detrimental level. The kind of guy you would be seen in public with and most girls would cattily be saying: "Why *her*? Why did he choose *her*?" I catch my lower lip between my teeth, embarrassed at the calculating assumptions I've made about him in such a short amount of time. We've gone from the prospect of a one-night stand to a relationship. The first I often employ, and the second I will never entertain. *Ever.*

It dawns on me that I've been staring at him again. His eyes are incredible, and I get lost in them again because there's a part of me that clearly wants to jump into the alluring deep end with him and another part of me that uncharacteristically hesitates mightily. *I can't look away from him.* It's disconcerting and enthralling at the same time. I take in air in the faint hope of clearing away all these wayward thoughts of him. Then I absently wipe at my face with an embarrassed hand wave in the next.

I'm supposed to be Holly—perfect and sweet, *not Tally*—bitchy and on edge. *What am I doing here?* And I *cried* in front of him. I haven't cried since the day we buried Holly.

"I should go." I attempt to smile and extend my arm around the great room. "*Really*. This has been…illuminating.

He raises an eyebrow, surprised by my exceptional vocabulary, perhaps. *Me, too.*

He reaches for my hand and pulls me to him. I experience this inevitable solace as his arms go around me and hold me there.

"Don't go, Holly," he whispers.

And then he kisses me.

So I stay because when a girl wants to be someone else, she can be.

He strips off the calfskin boots one at a time and then helps me shimmy out of my skirt. Slowly—with purpose—he fingers the lace top and gets this secret smile. His touch sends an electric thrill all the way through me. He explores the inner layers of my lingerie and slides his hand inside the waistband and then travels further down. Obviously, he's seduced lovers before. We both have, and yet I hold my breath and willingly fall back with him to the bed and put my arms around his neck and pull him to me because *I need this. I do.*

He leans down and kisses my neck while he explores my body more urgently and the sensation of being set on fire from within flares all over again.

"I want you." His words whip against my neck and accelerate my heart rate.

Our movements co-mingle like the old-fashioned lava lamp on his night stand. Green wax yields to the warm blue water. We're lit up and changed by the heat and perform this ritualistic dance. I laugh at these crazy thoughts and Linc laughs, too, pleased he can please me, I suppose.

Lincoln Presley is a god. His star power illuminates my skin with light and sets fire to the rest of me. He whispers the name '*Holly*' into the crook of my neck and trails kisses there, too, while I openly experience all this secret regret for not telling him my real name and lying about my age.

It is true that *no* is not a viable answer to his question: "*Do you want this?*" Because I do.

Want this? I *need* this. I do.

Years ago, Ms. Kenner, my health education teacher, said sex should not be taken lightly. When I was a seventh grader, I wondered how it was to be taken, and, by ninth grade, I knew. Lightly was not a word that ever came to mind when it came to sex. Yet there's something more significant, more substantial, and more absolute with Linc; he's different from all the rest. I relish the unexpected liberation, although I know I'm being reckless and wasteful at the same time. I'm like a bird on fantastical flight. I soar above it all and revel in the unique experience of Lincoln Presley. *Sex is not to be taken lightly. No. Not lightly at all. Not with him.*

Linc tells me how much he wants me. I giggle and remind him we could have done this before dinner. I treasure his easy laugh as his exploring hand parts the space between my thighs. My resistance of him evaporates as I become water being splashed onto a hot surface and all but disappear.

I'm the one who told my parents she was gone when the state patrolman let me borrow his cell phone. "There's been…an accident. In my car. Accident. An explosion. A fire. She's. Gone." I'm the one who sat and held hands with the medic and first learned there was nothing I could have done and that Holly was gone, gone long before any of them had arrived on scene. I knew this. I saw what happened, but it is true that I didn't believe him.

It is true that I haven't really cried until tonight. It is not true that I don't care. It is not true that I'm over it, over *Holly*.

I am coping. This is me coping.

Intense thrumming brings me back. I look up at Linc and wrap my legs tighter around his waist and grip his shoulders. This guy's amazing body overtakes mine. It's real, not imagined. His concentrated efforts have a purpose. It is true that I could say *no* to the baseball star who's now intent on going all the way again, because he believes I'm twenty and old enough, believes I'm Holly, and believes I've got the birth control covered. But then, it becomes close to impossible to actually say *no* when the word morphs into an ecstatic moan of *why not?* It is not true that if a girl is given a choice, she will actually make one. The obscure line between *yes* and *no* disappears like an etch-a-sketch drawing that once shaken will be gone forever.

This baseball star from Stanford is swift and fantastic. He is both adept and gifted. He's the magician and masters the only magic I believe to be left in the world. I need his magic or I just might drift away.

I bask in the astonishing thought that I am with him. *With him.* Liquid fire burns through me. I struggle to breathe. He is steel. I am the magnet that holds him here. I am here. He's here most definitely. He's alive. I must be, too.

It is not true that fizzy holiday punch mixed with 100 proof vodka and champagne lessen the need for feeling something—anything at all, but the unexpected escape from grief proves to be true. I cry out and strive for control at the same time as we climax together. I'm suspended somewhere in between surprise and wonder as he moves inside me in a steady rhythm now.

His breath stirs my hair. He's so close that I can feel his heart beat. It answers mine.

Closeness erases the many secrets still held between us although the important ones remain. No longer strangers, we venture to a secret place where just the two of us exist. This connection of continuity seems to contain a degree of permanence, but that's further up ahead.

This is just a girl's dream.

"You'll know when it's love," Holly once said. "It'll mean something. It'll mean *everything*." I envision my sister's last dazed smile, now so permanently lost.

She died quickly. There was very little pain.

They lie.

I can't get the image of my charred Mercedes sedan out of my mind. My parents couldn't bear to see it, but I couldn't look away. Someone had to be there while the firemen culled through the ashes for the last of Holly's remains. I remember their faces, dazed with ultimate horror. All their faces conveyed the unanswerable question: Why does a girl so young die so tragically? Burned beyond recognition. I remember cringing at first, then gasping for air. All these panic attacks later. Triggers unknown. Just that image in my head that never really goes away and her dying screams—the constancy of her last dying sounds that reverberate through all of me. Because yes; it's an unbelievable sight when your sister dies at the scene. And, you hear it. It's the worst horror film. Only it's real. It happened right in front of me.

Linc traces my lips. "Are you okay?" He searches my face and looks anxious.

"I'm okay. I'm fine."

It is true that I lie. It is true that I have become very good at it. "Are you okay?" my parents still ask me every day. "Are you okay?" Marla asks every time she sees me. "Are you okay?" my teachers ask as I walk down the hallways. "I'm fine," I always say.

It's been months. Who wouldn't be fine? Is it true it doesn't matter? Or is it true because it does?

His radiance reaches for me. It brings me back. He catches a single tear with his index finger as it trails down my face and surprises me once again with his compassion. "Holly, where were you just now?"

After a long pause, I gaze up at him and smile because he brought me back. "Nowhere."

Lies told in a carefree tone with lips parted in a practiced smile are often believed.

"You're so beautiful," Linc says. "Your eyes. They're this amazing green—not hazel exactly or just plain green—they're always changing. They're mesmerizing. You're so…beautiful." He lingers near my face with his own. "Has anyone ever told you that?"

My sister. My sister always told me that. Holly would say, "Tally, you're so beautiful," and then she'd laugh. Her laugh was like the melody of a song. Holly made everything magical. *But now she's gone, and I'm still here—half-here, anyway.* I look away from him and attempt to combat the sadness at losing Holly. *Get it together.*

He fingers my chin and turns my face toward his. He gazes at me curiously in the dim light.

"Holly." He breathes my sister's name into the pulse at my neck. I shudder at his passion and my lies.

For a moment, I hesitate beneath him and hold my breath and wonder about the truth. The amazing joy of being with him starts to seep away while remorse for all the lies I've told him threatens to take over. *No.* I draw a deep breath. Determined to outrun both the newfound guilt and the ever-present sadness, I smile up at him. It's harder now, but I'm intent on staying within the realm of this newfound wonder—this amazing nirvana I've discovered with him—for a little while longer.

Playful, I pull away from him in one moment and straddle him in the next. Evocative, I finger his medal ribbon. It sways between my breasts and still radiates warmth from our combined body heat. I lean in and dangle the medal near his face. He kisses my fingertips and slips the ribbon from my neck and casts it aside.

I'll serve as one of his trophies. This is a girl's dream.

"Holly," he breathes my sister's name again.

Holly smiles.

It's true, when you want to, you can be someone else.

<hr>

I wake up in a panic, unused to the complete darkness inside the room and unsure of exactly where I am. It takes a full minute to realize that I'm not alone as I begin to hear the steady breaths of the sleeping baseball player beside me.

My head pounds. It's clear that drinking the champagne late last night while we watched some old movie, combined with the red punch from earlier, was not a good idea. Despite the delicious food, Linc prepared and served to me early on in the evening, my head aches. I slip from his arms and work my way out of the twisted bed sheets.

I acknowledge my nakedness in a clinical kind of way to keep myself from completely freaking out about breaking my first golden rule—never stay over at a guy's place. I go in search of my clothes and a much-needed bottle of Advil.

Linc turns in his sleep. I pause mid-step across the room from him and wait. I only move again when I hear his steady breathing. *This walk of shame definitely needs to be done alone.*

I quietly close the bathroom door just off of his bedroom, fumble for the light switch, and silently wince at both the bright light stabbing my eyes and my mascara-streaked face gazing back at me from the mirror. *Accusing. I should not be here.* I should have left with Marla when I got her text a couple of hours ago. She and Charlie had a major fight, and she went home without me because I was nowhere to be found. She felt bad for leaving me since she'd driven me here but didn't quite know what she should do. So much for being her wingman. Now I am in need of one. My parents are still under the impression that I'm staying at Marla's. At least I have that particular misdirection going for me. Even so, at three in the morning, all the lying I've been doing really makes me uneasy.

Linc called me *Holly* at several euphoric junctures. I should have just come clean with that particular omission and told him my real name. Now it's too late.

It's finished.

We're done.

I'm out of here. After performing a mini sponge-bath of sorts by using a fresh bar of lavender soap I found in one of the drawers, that I'm pretty sure Charlie's mom must have picked out, I feel reasonably put back together. I slip on the black leotard and long skirt I happen to have in my bag since I was supposed to be at Marla's. We have plans to leave directly from her place for an early dance class with Tremblay in the morning. A five-minute make-up job reestablishes a semblance of order with my face. I finger-comb my hair, turn out the light, and wait another self-designated two minutes while telling myself to keep it together before embarking on the walk of shame through his dark house. Intent on not disturbing the guy and making my way back home the long ten blocks without saying good-bye, I stoop to pick up my discarded boots off his great room floor just as the lights are turned on. *Shit.*

"Going somewhere?" Linc asks.

"Geez, you scared me." My heart races, different from the panic attack, but the same kind of surge of adrenaline swarms me.

"Sorry." He smiles and seems perfectly comfortable standing there buck-naked and partially aroused.

Apparently, he's just waiting for me. I ruefully smile. I can't help it. *He is fun.* We had a fantastic encounter—a nice memorable connection—he and I. On a scale of one to ten, I would give it a firm nine without any hesitation whatsoever. If I hadn't been so needy and could have more fully concentrated on all he was offering, it probably would have topped out at a ten. I can unequivocally say that he is the best lay I've ever had. And, if lovers were classified in the dictionary by prowess and style points, Lincoln Presley's photograph would certainly come up first on that particular search. I bite at my lip to stop all these provoking thoughts from taking me over completely.

"I have an early class," I say with a nervous wave. *Lame, but it's true.* He gets this dubious look as if he doesn't quite believe me. "Don't you have practice or something?"

"Not at three in the morning. I don't play until this afternoon. Another twelve hours." He crosses his arms. It proves more distracting. "What kind of class?"

I sweep my arm across the room. "Dance class."

"This early in the morning," he deadpans. "On a Saturday?"

He doesn't believe me.

For some reason, this bothers me. Yes, I've lied about virtually everything else but the fact that he doesn't believe me when I say I have a ballet class is what pisses me off. "Tremblay doesn't care that it's a long weekend." I don't make an effort to hide my annoyance.

"Who's Tremblay?"

"Allaire Tremblay is one of the best ballet teachers in San Francisco. She was a principal ballerina at the New York City Ballet for more than ten years. She's going to help ensure we get into the School of American Ballet full-time and with NYC Ballet after that. *That's* who she is." I've said too much, and I bite at my lower lip again to keep myself from saying more. But then, I wait and hold my breath because for some unfathomable reason, it's important to me to know what he thinks of ballet. *And me.*

"Ballet." He nods and slowly runs his hands through his wavy hair. "It's important to you?"

I reward him with a knowing look. "It's everything."

He winces. We share this look of understanding. "So what's it like? Ballet, I mean. There's lots of training. Do you do the shoes?"

"The shoes? You mean *toe shoes? Of course.*" I practically snort with derision at his lack of knowledge.

"Show me. Show me what you can do."

He extends his arm across the room. I take in the hard wood floors and gauge the location of the furniture strewn about the room, including the heavy coffee table in front of the sofa. Within fifteen seconds, he's moving it out of the way; and I'm laughing at the spectacle of him moving the furniture in his current naked state. He hears me laugh and turns back towards me and looks a little disconcerted. "You're naked. Moving furniture at three in the morning. It's kind of funny."

"Is it?" Now he smiles mischievously and comes over to me and grabs my hand and pulls me into the somewhat cleared space of the room. "Show me," he says again. "Show me how you do ballet. I've already experienced all your other moves. Show me what you do on stage."

I blush at his carnal reference. The guy is seriously attractive. I'm still attracted to him, because, for some reason, the hardening of my emotional heart has not quite set in yet, like it normally does.

I sigh with pretended exasperation and blithely sit down on the edge of the sofa and search through my bag for a pair of toe shoes. It's standard fare in any dancer's bag. You don't go anywhere without them. I slide some on and begin to tie up the ribbons on the right one. He regards me carefully even as I watch him casually slip into a pair of black sweats and a black T-shirt while I'm getting ready. His not being naked anymore is strangely disappointing on this remote emotional level that I allow myself to feel. I finish with the ribbons on the second shoe and pretend nonchalance as I stand in front of him prepared to perform just the basic steps.

"Hey," he chides. "Warm up first. I mean I know you're fairly warmed up from tonight's earlier escapades, but don't pull a muscle or aggravate your sore ribs trying to show off right away."

"Right."

I incline my head and start doing a number of warm-up stretches. I slowly smile, having decided to teach him a real lesson, show him what I can do since he obviously doesn't seem to be taking my ability to dance all that seriously. I start out nice and slow. I stretch this way and that showing off my agility in ways that seem to surprise and also arouse him. He sits there with his mouth half-open and gets this enthralled interested look on his face at my prowess. I smile to myself, enjoying the exhibitionist part of this little game with him.

Normally, this is the easiest part of my day. I perform warm-up stretches at almost a rote level, but with an audience, it's different and even sensual in ways that I've only just become aware of. I feel powerful. I can sense his growing libido stirring as he straightens his shoulders and looks at me more intently as I do a couple of the more difficult moves, including arabesques and a few running jumps across the floor and back. With Linc being a professional athlete, I imagine he has a better appreciation for the degree of difficulty involved in performing these moves than most people do.

"Music?" he asks. "You should have music. What do you like to listen to?"

I stop and stare at him for a long moment. "I can dance to anything."

"I guess I already knew that." He dips his head in that charming way of his before striding over to his entertainment system, which takes up an entire wall of his great room.

He surprises me with one of Kelly Clarkson songs, *Already Gone*. An interesting choice. Haunting but seductive.

After a few minutes, I forget about my captive audience and move solely with the music. I do an arabesque and another and then incorporate fouettes— these whip-like rapid foot movements which are some of the most difficult to perform. Tremblay has been intent on both Marla and me mastering them. We spent all year perfecting these for a performance of Swan Lake that we did last summer. The competition had been brutal but Marla and I were the standouts in that class. And now, with the plan already in motion to return to SAB, it appears Tremblay was right to train us so hard. We'll probably tour the country and possibly even Europe sometime next spring if all goes according to our plan, and we make it into NYC Ballet. This is the plan. Our plan. Marla and me. *Holly.*

Our plan.

The three of us in New York that was the plan.

But plans change, don't they?

I miss a step in the routine and lose my count. I stop—suddenly unsure of my surroundings and still woozy from the last traces of alcohol and something else. Perhaps, the theatrics with Linc earlier and definitely the lack of a good night's sleep with all the foreplay and play between the two of us is wreaking havoc on me now. Maybe, the lies. All of it seems to be crashing in on me.

It's three-thirty in the morning. What am I doing here? What am I doing?

Linc stands in front of me now. He has this purposeful almost untamed look as he reaches out and then deftly lifts me high up over his head again being careful to avoid my ribcage. He holds me lower, intimately. I'm caught up in the moment with him and the exhilaration that comes with the dizzying height. I gaze into his eyes from up above. He doesn't even seem to strain with the lift. He studies my face as I extend my arms out to the sides like a child playing airplane with a parent.

"You're incredible. Where did you come from?" Linc gingerly puts me back down. I land on my feet but grasp his shoulders for want of certain balance. "You're one of a kind."

"No. I'm not." I blush under the intensity of his powerful gaze. His words 'you're one of a kind' cut across me like a slow tear in the fiber of my very being. *I was part of a pair; but now Holly's gone. And it's all different.*

It's lonely and empty, and I've been battling this harsh truth for months. And yet this painful reality still continues to lurch its way below the surface of my consciousness, confirming the only truth I still know to be true: this profound ache and this almost unbearable loneliness that will probably always be there inside of me at the loss of Holly.

I miss Holly. I miss my twin.

There's nothing anyone can do about that. Spending the sexiest night ever in my life with an amazing guy like Lincoln Presley is not going to change that one life-altering truth. *Holly is gone. Gone forever.*

I turn away from him in order to hide my face for a moment in a desperate attempt to regain my composure. He seems to sense I need a minute or two alone.

The music stops. I automatically lift my head and covertly study him as he stands there just watching me from across the room looking a little less certain as to what to do. "You know what I think?" he finally asks.

I'm out of sorts, reeling from the discovery of this personal truth about myself, but he waits for my answer. "What?" I finally ask and manage to hold my breath at the same time.

"I think you should *stay*. Whatever it is…" He gets this knowing look like he already knows my pain, which is weird because I haven't talked to him about the accident. I don't remember much of it. I try not to remember anything about that day. He starts again. "Wherever it is you need to be…can wait. Right now, I want you here with me. Can you stay? Will you…*stay?*"

I suppose it's the way he asks that has me vacillating with my plan for a hasty retreat from his home. I stand there—assailed by equal doses of loss and guilt. All these jumbled thoughts swirl around me as I contemplate all the lies I've told him tonight and just as swiftly along comes the realization that I still have this surprising profound attraction for him and that a big part of me doesn't want to walk away from him quite yet. The fact that I still hold this unfathomable attraction for him is disturbing on too many levels for me to assimilate at this particular moment but I do manage to shake my head side-to-side. "No," I say without much conviction.

Here's the truth: I am the female version of a heartbreaker. The one that everyone says is too dedicated to ballet, too self-involved to ever care about anyone else besides herself. I'm the rebel. The bad twin. I am Tally—the loner, the party of one. The love and leave 'em prototype. Heartless. That is me. I have no time for romance, flowers, or relationships. I like one-night stands with plenty of sex and no promises of a future. I like the lies I tell. I'm comfortable in telling them…most of the time. This is me. Okay, maybe, this is me acting out, but I like it like this. I have been this way since I was fifteen.

Only the stakes have gotten higher. The love game has become so much more complex. Sometimes, it's even dangerous. I shiver at the thought of the foreign stranger in the Caribbean. I can't remember his name. I was with him for a few nights, and I can't even recall his face or remember his name. Shame seeps in with the admission, but then some sense of self-preservation rolls in behind it. *Play the game, Tally.* Everyone who plays it with me knows the rules. We know exactly how the game is to be played. I don't stay overnight. I don't cuddle. I let them into the physical part of me, and then I let them out. That's it. That's all there is. *This*—whatever *this* is—has to stop. This is a dead-end road that I am unwilling to go down.

I ready myself to give this very speech to him aloud, but I make the mistake of looking at him. Lincoln Presley has this expectant look. He looks hopeful as if I will not hurt him. *Don't look at me like that. Don't make this into something more than it was. It was sex. Nothing more. Nothing less.*

And yet.

It's not the physical aspect of him that seems to be luring me in now. No. It's the sincerity written all over his face. It's the memory of his unexpected kindness that he's shown me in the darkest times of this night. It's the underlying truth of him that has me feeling this forceful need to reach out to him, even while, deep inside; I begin to panic. I need to leave—*to escape,* really. *Now.*

And yet.

I step toward him instead, but even as I do this, my mind rattles off all these self-preserving commands: *Just walk out the door. Walk away, Tally.*

And yet.

He extends his hand towards mine. My fingers find his.

I close my eyes to escape the allure of him, but instead it draws me in closer. I'm compelled to move further into his arms by some unknowable force.

"Stay," he whispers against the side of my face. He kisses my right cheek and then leans the other way and trails his lips along the sensitive spot at my throat.

This? This is seduction at its finest.

My heart races out of control and this whole part of me gives way.

"Stay with me."

"No." I don't sound convincing. I sound weak and out of control. "I should go."

"I know. But what's the worst that could happen?" He laughs a little against the side of my face. "What's the worst that could happen? *Holly*...stay with me. What are you so afraid of?"

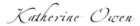

"Falling. Failing. Losing. Those are the big three. They're practically interchangeable and apply to every aspect of my life."

He pulls me tighter into his arms. "Me, too," he says, breathing the words into my hair. "Stay with me for a while. *Please*. You make me feel unafraid."

"I do?" I look up at him in surprise and study his face for a long while.

"*Yes*. Please stay."

I'm overwhelmed by his honesty and the deep-seated fears we share. I bury my face into the base of his neck and feel his pulse against my lips. I ignore the rising guilt that tries to attack me from all sides in realizing he doesn't even know my real name.

The truth is simple. He moves me. He makes me feel something. He makes me believe in the good of life again and that alone proves too much to resist. *So, I stay.*

CHAPTER EIGHT

Linc ~ Thank you, Elvis

SHE LEFT A NOTE. I CHASTISE myself for expecting more from her. Still, I trace her seductive handwriting and ponder the three simple words she's written: *Thank you, Elvis.*

For a few minutes, I begin to wonder if she remembers me from the day of the accident. But then I decide, *no*, probably not. It's just the crazy connection she made between me and my last name. It's strange though that she would call me that.

Some small part of me begins to wonder exactly what I was supposed to believe is true about this girl. She's this enigma to me. An enigma, I'm intent on getting to know better because I still don't have a clue about her—except maybe her name now. *Holly.* I want to see her again.

I spend an inordinate amount of time in the shower recalling every aspect of her—about how vulnerable she was at times yet, at the same time, how closed off emotionally she seemed to be. She was uncomfortable when I tried to reach out to her, even at her most vulnerable point. She seemed to acknowledge our amazing connection but remained unaffected by it. Her dedication to ballet was obvious. It was when she seemed to come alive and was more open with me last night in sharing her greatest fears, which surprisingly mimic mine. Even when we were going at it for a third time, I noticed how distant she seemed, unattached and unmoved by it all; but then I'd looked into her beautiful eyes and glimpsed her sadness. All I could think of was to try to reach her and take the pain from her, if only for a little while. It's what I've wanted to do since the first time I saw her. I still feel this urgent need to protect her somehow from the torment of grief because I know what it can do. There were more than a few times I almost confessed to knowing about the accident, of having been the one who carried her away from the car just before it exploded, of knowing about the loss of her sister. Even now, I feel a little guilty for not having been more forthcoming with her about who I was in relation to her and the accident. At one point, I asked her more about how she'd broken her ribs in the first place, but she effectively shut me down about that. The truth is it doesn't matter. I *know*. And, this girl had me hooked the first time I looked into her eyes three months ago. I am way out of my depth with this girl *Holly. Way out.*

Last night, I kept thinking as I watched her dance and saw her face change with a cascade of emotions from sadness to serenity that I could reach her somehow. I could *save her* even though she'd mocked me earlier about doing this very thing. I couldn't help but notice the dark shadows beneath her make-up after she'd washed it all off in the middle of night. After disappearing for a long ten minutes, she'd slipped back into my bed, but her absence had been long enough that I'd begun to wonder if she'd gone, left me, actually. That was the first time I experienced the unfamiliar ache at the possibility of her leaving. Loss, a long-held fear, I know well. It beat like a drum inside of me even then.

It's true—even though she'd stayed—some part of me already recognized how deeply affected I would be by her absence. The loss of her. It was more than a premonition even then. After her prolonged absence behind the bathroom door and this building fear that she was already gone, she'd quietly reappeared. I pretended to be asleep just so I could continue my covert study of her. I wanted to savor the essence of her, in all aspects, without her paranoid questioning of why I would be doing such a thing. She was elusive, like a rare butterfly I was unable to fully capture. I listened intently for her low sighs as she drifted off. I was somehow lulled into this absurd wishful thinking that she would stay, that I could keep her here. Maybe forever. Eventually, fatigue overtook me, too; even though I fought to stay awake so I wouldn't miss a single stolen moment with her. The familiar chants lulled me to sleep. *I have a game. I need sleep. All there is…is baseball.*

Yet, in the light of day, at half past eight, all I have left of her is this note. *Her fucking note.* A note that doesn't tell me anything and simply thanks me. *Thanks me.* She didn't even sign her name. For some reason, this bothers me on a whole separate level. I stand still for a long time, holding the note, and let it all sink in. Her leaving is almost palpable like a gale-force wind that's rolled into my life in the span of a single evening and left behind all this incalculable destruction, both inside and out. Yes, the tempest has passed, but the air around me feels different. I can hardly breathe. Nothing is the same without her. As the lone survivor of her particular storm, I begin to wonder just exactly what I'm supposed to do now.

It's only later, after wandering listlessly around the guest house for another hour, after I eventually resign myself to the unenviable task of cleaning everything up and throwing away the empty champagne bottle we shared; after I wash the wine glass smudged with her lipstick; after I purposefully pick up and look through each and every one of the DVDs she touched and so casually left in a forsaken heap stacked precariously at the edge of the great room rug so clearly forgotten by her, which seemingly represents this wry reflection of myself that even I can admit to; it's only after I pushed the heavy furniture pieces back into place and, in essence, effectively erase all genuine evidence of her incredible presence from the night before; yes, only after all of that, do I realize I have absolutely no way to get in touch with her.

I'm practically paralyzed with equal doses of disappointment and despair at the cruelty of this one indelible fact. Yes, this hits me hard because I *want* to see her again, *need* to see her again; and yet, I have no way to get in touch with her. I begin to wonder if that was her intention with me all along.

I race out of the guest house with an urgent need to locate Charlie. He'll know what to do. He'll have more insight as to who this Holly is because of her friend. *What was her name?* It started with an "M" or an "N". *What did she say the friend's name was?* Breathing hard from my jaunt across the massive lawn—a rather intense sprint from the guest house to my aunt and uncle's palatial palace, I let myself in through the side door of the Masterson's kitchen, bend over, grasp my thighs, and try to catch my breath.

Aunt Gina is busy at the counter stirring some kind of batter. She looks up at my hasty entrance and smiles.

"Hey, Linc. I was just going to come get you. Your dad called. I guess the Angels are sending a scout to your game tomorrow. He wants you to call him." She makes a funny face and starts to laugh. "Sorry. Let's start again. Good morning, handsome nephew. Happy Saturday. Have you had breakfast? Pancakes?" She points to her mixing bowl.

"Good morning. No breakfast. I was up late." I hide my flushed face from her, but I see her get this mildly curious expression. She's obviously cognizant of a sleep-over taking place at her guest house. To avoid further scrutiny, I busy myself with swiping whipped cream from one of the mixing bowls laid out on the counter and try to ignore her sudden interest. It looks like I'll be missing another one of her fabulous dinners this weekend. "Have you seen Charlie?" I ask, trying to appear casual and disinterested.

"No. I thought he was with you last night." She gets this impish look, purses her lips, and makes this judgmental clucking sound that only a mother or close aunt can make. "I thought the two of you were together last night at the guest house after the big party. I saw someone head out from there about three hours ago. Around six? When I was making coffee. I couldn't sleep."

"Which way? The person you saw. Which way did she go?" I don't quite hide my desperation. My adorable aunt seems to notice it, too. She cocks her head to one side and studies my face intently.

"She headed east," Gina says softly. "She was very pretty. Does *she* have a name?"

"Holly. Her name is Holly." I try not to sound too forlorn, but I don't think she's fooled.

"Does she have plans?"

"For this weekend?" I get this wan half-smile and shake my head side-to-side. "I don't know." I glance out the kitchen window toward the path that leads from the guest house to the house in an attempt to put my aunt off from the conversation and somehow see if I can conjure up my mystery girl just by wishful thinking.

"For the rest of her life?" Gina asks.

I look over at my aunt, unable to completely hide this hollowed-out, just excavated feeling because that's how I feel whenever I think about this girl or her damn note. "I don't know."

"Wow," Aunt Gina says as she takes a step back and looks me over. "She's the one, huh?"

"I don't know," I answer numbly. This helpless feeling stays with me. I am way out of my depth with this girl already. I can feel it. *Not good.*

"Who's the one?" Charlie saunters into the kitchen and grabs a bag of chips and loudly crunches down on his ready-made breakfast with his usual charm. He hugs his mom and replicates the whipped cream trick in swiping at the creamy foam, just like I did.

"The girl Linc met last night."

"Who was it?" Charlie asks with indifference. After opening the refrigerator, he pours himself a tall glass of milk and quickly gulps it down and looks over at me and then his mom. "What?"

"She said her name was Holly," I say slowly.

"Holly." Charlie looks disconcerted for a few seconds. "I didn't see her. Or *you*. For quite a long time." He gets this wicked grin. "I had to clean up the whole mess without you, Prez." He gives me a somewhat exasperated look.

"Not my party," I say with a shrug. "Sorry."

"That's okay. Marla helped me clean up. Well, for a while—"

"Marla. Is that the girl you were with?" I ask.

"Not just any girl," Charlie says, giving me this thunderous look.

He seems to get more uneasy as his mother begins to take an interest in our little exchange. Charlie sets the bag of chips down slowly as if vying for more time. Then he slides his hands deep into the front pockets of his jeans and develops a keen interest in the kitchen floor, tracing the tile's intricate pattern with his shoe.

"What *girl?*" Aunt Gina stops what she's doing and looks over at the two of us intently. Then, as if to better ensure she has his full attention, she goes over and lightly taps Charlie's shoulder with one of her wooden spoons. A fait de complete. It's the Aunt Gina *I-will-not-be-left-out-of-this-conversation* move.

Surprisingly, Charlie hangs his head and avoids looking at her. "I saw Marla last night," he finally admits.

"Marla. *The* Marla? The one from Paly a few years ago?" Gina asks in surprise. "Charles Michael Masterson, I will not stand by and watch you break that girl's heart for a second time."

"Mom, it's not like that. Marla knows how things are."

"I can't believe we're even having this conversation. That she came here, and you would—"

"Would what? *Nothing happened.* We *talked.* It was good to see her again. Same-old Marla. Same-old issues. Same-old fight at the end." Charlie gets this dazed expression, and then he looks decidedly unhappy. "She has her plans. I have mine. We're very clear about those."

"What about her friend? What do you know about her?" My words come out in a rush before I can stop myself from asking.

Charlie looks uneasy. "I don't know all of her friends—anymore. It's been a few years since we were together. Maybe it was Marla's friend Holly? But that would be weird because I thought she was still with Rob Thorn. They got together right before Marla and I broke up toward the end of my senior year. You…met a girl named *Holly?*"

"She said her name was Holly," I say.

"Marla's a senior at Paly, and she was in New York all last summer, I guess she still hangs out with—"

"*Paly*…as in our former high school?" I ask. *Holy shit.* This sick feeling becomes more insistent inside.

"Marla's a couple of years younger than me. We started going out when I was a senior, and she was a sophomore." He glances over at his mom. "She's just about to graduate. In a few weeks, in fact." He gets this look of defiance, but it doesn't last long because his mother eyes him intently.

"You served *minors* at your little party last night, Charles?"

Charlie hangs his head. *There's no place to hide with that one.*

"It appears I did."

"Do you like your life? The way you can come and go as you please around here? Getting your fine education at UCLA? Charlie, do you have any idea what would happen to you or your father and I, if a minor who'd been drinking—partying at our house—was then injured or killed on their way home because you just wanted to have a little fun?"

"I messed up, Mom."

"No doubt about that," she says sadly.

"Her friend is at Paly, too?" I choke on the words as well as the implications become somewhat clear here. It's been five years since I attended Palo Alto High School. The math is pretty easy to do. I run my hands through my hair, as if this would somehow change his answer, while anxiety runs unchecked through all of me now. *This is unbelievable. Is it possible that I've just gotten duped by a girl still in high school, and she'd had the gall to leave me a thank-you note?* No wonder she did that. She probably thought it was fucking funny. She's a girl—still *in high school*—still capable and willing to do childish things like that. Sleep with the college guy. Tell all her friends.

Aunt Gina eyes me closely now, while I struggle for composure.

"High school girls are a little out of your league at this point, Lincoln Davis Presley," Aunt Gina says. "And your dad would not be pleased."

I nod into the growing silence while she frowns with notable disapproval in my general direction. I wince because my morning is just getting worse.

"I'm not necessarily worried about either of those girls," she says after a few minutes. "But the two of you? *Way* out of your league…and *trouble,* I might add. For both of you. Equally."

"No lecture needed on that front, Mom." Charlie glances over at me. He seems desperate to change the topic of discussion and get his mom to focus on something else—*anything else.* "You don't look so good, Prez."

Charlie has called me *Prez* since we were about seven or eight. He is about the only one I allow to call me that. Nicknames aren't my thing. I don't like them. This definitely came about from the constant teasing I experienced as a first-grader tagged with the double duty of a weird first name like Lincoln and a famous last name like Presley. Little kids had a field day with that two-pronged wonder, and my stigma with my names set in fairly early. Yet *her* nicknaming me *Elvis* didn't exactly bother me. *I liked it. I liked her.* She called me *Elvis.* I close my eyes, remembering her smile. It was a thing of beauty, her smile—like one of life's unexpected wonders. It's right up there with pitching the perfect game or reaching the summit of Kilimanjaro—which I did three years ago—or falling in love for the first time—which I swore I would never allow myself to do—but I am pretty sure that this is exactly how you'd feel as if it was just the most beautiful and unexpected thing to ever happen to you. *Elvis.* She'd called me Elvis all night long. I usually hated it when people unwittingly associated me with the famous singer, but the girl from last night had said it with affection. I didn't mind being her amusement for the evening—or forever, if I'm being honest. *What is wrong with me?*

On some twisted level, I even cherish her note. Now, I feel for it in the back of my jean's pocket, where I'd put it before making my run to the main house, just wanting to make sure it's still there. And yet some distant part of me begins to feel the inevitable disenchantment with all of this—with *her.* It's growing steadier inside because, even though this girl had been calling me Elvis from the moment we met, she obviously doesn't remember me saving her, and I can't decide if I'm more wounded by that fact or her thank-you note or now learning she lied to me about how old she was in the first place. If Holly is still in high school, and I am almost twenty-three, and she clearly isn't, it's done. It's over. *Wow.* The thank-you note holds a whole new meaning and a completely different kind of innuendo. Was she making fun of me the whole time, going from laughing to crying to laughing again and getting under my skin in all these different, almost-permanent ways, while her intention all along was to dupe the baseball player from Stanford by lying about her age because she was still in high school?

Defeat sets in, because, if she's still in high school like Charlie's ex, the situation is impossible. It isn't going to happen. *Nada. Done.* I am so done with it. Anger begins to filter its way through, eclipsing past the shock I felt for the last few minutes at the idea that she's still in high school. I have to admit that this girl *Holly* is a true mindfuck, both literally as well as figuratively. I shake my head side-to-side with this growing sense of distrust. Granted, she is a beautiful girl, unlike anyone I'd ever known, with her long, dark hair and those incredible green eyes and that unforgettable dancer's body. She is off the charts in every way. This girl's the true kaleidoscope for me because she's edgy and fun and complicated. This girl's clearly an original. She's unique in every way I can possibly think of and could certainly be classified as completely amazing. Deep down, I can't ever imagine getting tired of looking at her or hearing her speak or just listening to her breathe.

Yet, regardless of how much my instincts tell me that she probably needs saving—she's worth saving, in fact, more than any other girl I've ever been with—it can't happen with her again. *I have too much at stake.*

My rising baseball career. My genuine reputation. My general well-being.

My mind begins to race with all these incomplete thoughts. *Is she a minor? What are the age limits for sex with a minor in the state of California? What if she isn't even eighteen?* If my dad ever found out I'd been with someone who is still in high school…well, there'd be hell to pay. *I got off easy. I'm lucky.*

I don't feel lucky. Right now, I feel like shit even though I may have gotten off easy. I can turn this thing around right now by not seeing her again. No, being with her won't happen again. Not with this girl. Not in this town. After today, I'll be gone—back to Stanford and baseball that will take us up and down the West Coast for NCAA Regionals. It can't happen soon enough. The sooner, the better.

"You okay?" Charlie asks me again.

"I'm…fine." These were Holly's same exact words from the night before. She lied about her age. What else did she lie to me about? I remember her looking up at me with this faraway look, and I'd felt the sadness in her. Then she smiled at me and saw only me, or so it seemed. Of course, I knew what could make her so unhappy. At the time, I was determined to be the one that helped her forget…about the accident and the loss of her sister—for a little while. I shake my head again to clear all these racing thoughts of this amazing girl because I have to stop thinking about her. I have to stop. *I have to.* This won't happen with her again.

"Marla always did her own thing. She still does." Charlie gets this uneasy half-smile and looks bleak as he glances over at his mom. "She's pretty independent with all that stuff. It's better that way for both of us. I'm not sure who she hangs out with anymore." Charlie hangs his head again and avoids looking at either one of us. It is an obvious indication that the subject is now closed. "I'm sorry about the party. It won't happen again."

"I know. I think you understand the consequences." She glides toward the open doorway that leads to the living room. "Just promise me that you won't allow under-age drinking here again. I don't want to worry your dad."

"I promise." Charlie sighs. "Anyway, Mom, do you need us to go to the store before Linc and I head to his game, or what? Dad says you do."

"Yes. I have a list. I need pies. Cherry, if you can find it."

Aunt Gina looks a little concerned as she hands Charlie three twenties for the store. She glances over at me with a quizzical look. "Everything okay?"

I nod and attempt to follow their back and forth banter as a way to put my mind at ease about the girl from last night, but it's not working.

"How come Linc doesn't get a ration about a girl?" Charlie asks while he heads for the side kitchen door and grabs his car keys from the wooden rack.

"Because Linc treats women better than you do, Charlie."

"Not true. I treat them fine, and Linc's not perfect when it comes to women. Are you, Linc?" Charlie shoots me a knowing glance and wickedly smiles. I remain silent, shrug into my leather jacket, and hope my aunt doesn't pursue this line of questioning. Dipping my head, I avoid looking directly at her.

"Baseball is easier," I say, hoping to end the conversation.

There have been a few escapades over the past few years in L.A. involving some noteworthy girls from UCLA on my infrequent visits to Charlie's place by the beach the last couple of times. Yes, there have been questionable moments for Charlie and me with a few hook-ups gone wild. These didn't bode well for either one of us or our reputations about treating women better than most of the guys we hang out with. We've always held onto those hellish secrets just between us. I am a little taken aback that Charlie would be so cavalier and bring them up in front of his mom now. Other than last night with Holly, I haven't hooked up with a girl in a long while, since Nika Vostrikova from my stats class last year at Stanford. Nika still shows up at most of my games, but she surrounds herself with various friends—usually guys—at all times. I've been too busy with baseball this past season to take a break and actually breathe and have a little fun. Until last night. With Holly. Disappointment seeps into me. I ache all over.

Too much alcohol? *Not really.*

Too much sex? *Is that possible?*

Too much emotional entanglement? *Most definitely.*

"I can't win with women—you or Marla," Charlie is saying. He holds up his hands in protest.

"Not true," Gina says with a gentle knowing smile. "I love you. Marla must still have feelings for you, too, since she came to see you again after all that went on between the two of you." Aunt Gina gets this somewhat serious look as she gazes affectionately at her son. "Give it some time, okay?"

"And, for the record," Charlie says and pauses for a moment and then sighs. "She turned me down. When I said I wanted to get back together? Marla said, '*no way.*'"

At Charlie's revelation, Gina goes over and embraces him even though he's a good six inches taller than she is.

"If it's meant to be, it will work itself out somehow. Love always does," she says. "Right now? You need to concentrate on graduating and getting into med school, right? Marla will figure things out for herself soon enough. Time will do that. Nobody has the world figured out at eighteen—not even at twenty-one. Trust me."

"She's not even going to be here. She's going back to New York."

"She'll come back."

Charlie looks at his mom with newfound doubt. He shakes his head side-to-side. "She says she won't be coming back."

"Trust me. I know what I'm talking about. Besides, you're at UCLA. If she's in New York, why does that even matter?" Gina asks with a little laugh.

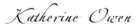

"Palo Alto is a whole lot *safer* place for her to be."

"You mean because your friends here can keep an eye on her and respect your off-limits edict?"

"Something like that." Charlie sounds defeated. It gets my attention.

"An eighteen-year-old girl does not know what she wants, even if she insists she does. Time and experience change those things—the ones that matter, anyway. *They do*. Believe me, I know."

"Marla seems to know *exactly* what she wants. I just don't fit into her plans," Charlie mutters.

With that somewhat hopeless observation, he puts on a baseball cap and heads out the door before his mom can reach him with the damp kitchen towel she flips towards his backside in jest. We all laugh. I'm thankful for the distraction. I pull on a baseball cap like Charlie's and promise my aunt that we'll do our best to locate a cherry pie for her and follow him out the door.

CHAPTER NINE

Tally Spell

HE MADE ME FEEL SOMETHING. DIFFERENT than all the other guys I've been with. *Better. Worse.* I slide out of bed, head to the bathroom, and turn the water on as hot as I can stand it. I lean against the shower wall and allow the spray to blast away at my head. *I can't think about him. I have class. I have to focus.*

I have to keep Marla at bay about last night; somehow, that resonates with me as important. I wash my hair and make good use of the ten minutes of self-talk, and the solace that only a hot shower can bring.

Within a half-hour, I'm dressed and downstairs putting hot tea in a to-go cup. My little brother Tommy eyes me from the kitchen table, where he's busy shoveling milk and cereal into his mouth at a steady, recognizable boyish pace. I pause, practically in mid-flight at leaving, and smile over at him. He's a miniature replica of our dad with these dazzling blue eyes and golden-blond hair that hasn't been cut in a long while. I'm not the only one forgotten in the Landon household these days. My little brother epitomizes the look of unintentional neglect. He sports a wrinkled green-and-white-striped rugby shirt and blue jeans that look like they've missed the laundry cycle a few too many times.

Guilt squeezes my heart. I haven't made a lot of time for Tommy. I've been keeping myself from emotionally drowning at Paly with the constant stares and sympathy over Holly, taking Tremblay's ballet classes with even more ardent intensity, and maintaining an avid focus on packing up my life for the big move to New York in a matter of weeks.

His face scrunches up as he looks up at me. A mixture of disappointment and sadness crosses his features. I know he misses Holly. I would bet every time he looks at me; he's reminded of her.

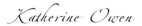

"What are you doing up so early?" I ask as I finish prepping my tea and anxiously check the bus schedule. I've got twelve minutes to get to my stop. I need to leave in two. I twist the cap on tea mug and open it and blow on it and take sip.

"I've got baseball practice at ten." He looks at me closely. "Dad is taking me to the Stanford game this afternoon. Lincoln Presley's pitching." Tommy is a Cardinal fan since Dad went to school there. How could I have forgotten that my little brother, even at eight-years-old, has a boy's devotion for Stanford and baseball and their star pitcher?

I promptly choke on my tea and look over at him. "You know who Lincoln Presley is?" I try to sound casual, but it comes out decidedly anxious instead. *Shit.*

Tommy rolls his eyes. The extent of his world begins and ends with baseball, until hockey season and then football.

"Do *I* know who Lincoln Presley is? He's only the best pitcher the Cardinal have, and the Angels and the Giants want him *bad.* Do *you* know him?"

My face gets red. This overriding need to impress my little brother wins out for some inexplicable reason. "I met him last night. We…spent some time together. He's nice." I turn away, preparing to leave, not wanting to get into a deep conversation about Lincoln Presley with the youngest member of my family.

"What?" I turn back to face Tommy and discover this look of pure amazement on my brother's face. "Where?"

"At a…party…" I shrug. "His cousin is Charlie Masterson? Marla used to date Charlie. The Mastersons live about twelve blocks from here. *Anyway.* He's nice." I recap my tea ensuring the drinking slot is closed. "So, he's good at baseball, huh?"

Tommy snorts. My lack of knowledge about baseball has him shaking his head in utter amazement that I don't already know this. "He's *really* good, Tally. *Really good.* Dad likes him, too."

"Well, if Dad likes him, and you like him, then he must be good. The Landon men have given Linc their finest endorsement. He must be mighty fine," I tease and then laugh.

He grins. "Are you going to see him again?" Tommy gets this wistful look and holds up his baseball as well as his favorite glove.

"No. No. I'm definitely not going to be seeing him again."

This inexplicable feeling of disappointment comes over me in just admitting that I won't be seeing him again. This strange sense of loss assails me from all sides. *Shit. No. Don't think about him.* I smile uncertain at my little brother.

"Maybe you should come with us to the baseball game. You could see him again and ask him to sign my ball and my glove." Tommy gets this charming, hopeful look.

"Maybe. We'll see."

"'We'll see,' means *no*." He screws up his face and gets this disappointed look.

"I've got *class*. I'll *think* about it. Okay?" I head toward the side door. "Tell Mom and Dad, I'll be back around noon."

Tommy still looks disappointed. "Say you'll come. Come on. It'll be fun. Dad has an extra ticket. Mom's not going." He inclines his head toward the direction of our parents' master bedroom upstairs where my mother has been holed up for months. I nod into the silence, swayed by guilt over our mother's continual absence from our lives and not wanting to be the one to disappoint Tommy, as well as experiencing this inexplicable desire to see Lincoln Presley again.

"Okay. I'll try to be back in time so all three of us can go to the game. Okay?"

The things we do for love. The question is who am I doing it for? Tommy? Or myself? I don't want to answer that particular question because, deep down, I know the answer isn't about one little kid's wish for his hero's autograph. I can't examine that too closely because that's the most disturbing thought of all.

CHAPTER TEN

Linc~ Soul taken

CHARLIE GUNS HIS JEEP AND WE roar out of the driveway. Eventually, he looks over at me with a sheepish grin. "Sorry about that. Gina's still crazy about Marla, but it's more complicated than that." He looks uneasy. "And I don't want to talk about it."

With that, he shifts the Jeep into high gear, and we speed toward the freeway without exchanging another word. We are both brooding over girl trouble but neither one of us are willing to talk about it. Instead, we focus on finding a grocery store.

Tired, pissed, out of my normal span of control, I sink further down into the passenger seat and pull the front of my baseball cap over my face and shield my eyes from Charlie's close inspection. I've become somewhat resigned to the fact that Charlie isn't going to help me locate this mystery girl, if only to read her the riot act for lying to me about her age. No. Charlie is being evasive about this ex-girlfriend Marla for some other reason. While driving around Palo Alto's various strip malls in search of cherry pie, I bring up the taboo topic of Marla twice and both times Charlie effectively shuts me down.

"What's with you and this girl Marla?" I ask for a third time now.

"She's everything, and that's the fucking problem." Charlie hesitates and seems to stall for time. He takes a deep breath and parks the Jeep at some foodie place off Middlefield Road and stomps toward the entrance without a backward glance at me. I eventually follow.

The girl in the bakery is more than happy to sell the pies to us. She knows Charlie and even seems to recognize me, although I haven't set foot in Palo Alto High School in five years. I basically ignore the bakery girl because I'm caught in the riptide of gloom in thinking about Holly again. I note Charlie picks up the slack and flirts with the bakery girl. *Stacy.* She'd introduced herself to me and held my hand for five seconds too long. I'd mumbled, "Nice to meet you." I still don't regret the insincerity that was so distinct in my tone. *Who gives a shit?* I have a thank-you note from a minor to show for my charm and effort and scoring ability in the hook-up department. The last thing I need is another local girl—from a bakery, no less—who clearly wants my number and some of my time and attention and probably even more than that. *More.*

All I still see in my mind is Holly's face, even though I already know I should be focused upon someone far less complicated. I need to stick with girls who are less intense and don't leave me reeling this way over a damn thank-you note the next day. I don't need a girl who's left me without any way of getting in touch with her again.

Maybe I just want the chance to tell her off. I need to stay focused on empty selfish girls. Girls, like Nika, the brilliant Russian girl in my stats class from last year. She's smart and wicked and fun. Nika doesn't need to be entertained. Hell, we don't even date. We hook up occasionally when it's not baseball season. She's gone to my games. Usually she brings some guy along with her. I've seen her. She waves. I wave back. The emotional connection between us is non-existent. Nika does what she wants. I do what I want. I throw a baseball at least six months out of the year, and most girls don't like to put up with that kind of dedication in the long run, but Nika seems to get that. Understand it. Accept it. She doesn't demand anything from me. I don't demand or expect anything of her. That's the way it works. And it *does* work. That's the kind of girl I need to be seeing, not these Holly's of the world, who blow through and cause me to lose all my concentration.

I dial Nika's cell number. It goes straight to voice mail. I hang up without leaving a message, already knowing she'll call or text me back within the hour or so. That's the way Nika is—predictable, smart, wicked, and fun. Nika is easy, not complicated, like Holly, who's managed to fuck with me mind, body, and soul. *Shit.* My cell phone buzzes. Nika's sent a text. *"See you at the game."* Momentary relief courses through me. *Concentrate on Nika.* Yet I still envision Holly's face.

For needed distraction, I glance over at Charlie. He's busy asking this Stacy about people the two of them know at Paly. He seems to have worked his way up to the topic of Marla. He kind of frowns when he says Marla's name and seems to hold his breath at the same time. I know that out-of-control, out-of-depth feeling.

The girl doesn't seem fooled by his questioning. She gets this secret smile. Her brown eyes glint a little as she takes in all of Charlie, and her glance strays to his mid-section where it remains as she blatantly stares. *Jesus, she's checking him out right here in the store like I'm not even five feet away.* I turn away in disgust, but vague curiosity has me turning back around a few minutes later as their conversation filters my way.

"She was gone all summer. She and Tally. New York? They did pretty well. I'm sure she told you that." Stacy eyes him warily, making it obvious whose side she came down on over Marla and Charlie's apparent break-up. "She has a boyfriend back East, you know." She glances over at me and smiles and then turns her attention back to Charlie, who doesn't quite hide the jealous rage that travels across his face. His eyes narrow, and he stares hard at Stacy. "Devon something," she says. Her eyes dart back-and-forth between me and Charlie. "He's some big Wall Street hotshot."

Charlie seems to do his best to hide his surprise, but I know he's agitated because he bites at his lower lip. He slowly nods and then tries to smile. He glances over at me with this look of misery apparently in search of some help with Stacy. I subtly nod at him, but I'm not too sure what he wants me to do or say.

"Right. Devon. She mentioned him," Charlie says abruptly.

"Uh-huh. Well, things have been a little down around school since her twin was killed in that weird car accident in the middle of March. Poor Rob Thorn. They'd been going out—hot and heavy. For what? Like two years? And then she up and dies. It's so sad."

"Wait," Charlie says and suddenly grabs Stacy's hand. "What?"

"Tally's twin. You remember her, don't you?" she asks, incredulous, and then shakes her head in disbelief.

"Of course, I remember…" Charlie mutters.

He briefly closes his eyes and seems to be experiencing this kind of shock. Then, he anxiously glances over at me to see if I'd heard what Stacy just said. I stare at him hard having missed most of the conversation and slowly shake my head.

"Yeah," she says, leaning into Charlie.

I have to strain to hear her now.

"Rumor has it that the mom has basically flipped out. At school, Tally seems okay. I mean she was always the rebel, but now she just seems kind of lost. It's just so sad. Anyway, Marla has her hands full with all of that, and those two are intent on getting back to New York as soon as they can. They leave in something like a week after graduation."

She glances up at Charlie with renewed interest. "But you know ballet is all those two care about." Stacy gazes at Charlie and licks her lips in this obvious *I'm-up-for-it* way.

Charlie seems dazed by Stacy's sudden interest and apparent about-face in terms of her loyalty to Marla. He vaguely follows her hand movements and barely smiles when she fingers his rolled-up shirt sleeves and touches his chest in a none-too-subtle, provocative way. Her message is obvious to both of us: *I'm here; I'm available. Pick me.*

"Whoa." Charlie finally says, shaking his head and stepping back away from Stacy. "Yeah, well, we're working on it—getting back together; I mean," he says to Stacy quietly.

I try to smile, not actually able to put together the whole conversation since I don't know all these people, but I'm intent on asking Charlie about it as soon as we reach the car. I've only heard parts of the conversation so it doesn't make any sense to me, but I have this sick feeling in the pit of my stomach as I look at Charlie's face. He's upset about something from their conversation.

"Really? Even with this Devon from New York on the scene?" Stacy asks, looking a little deflated by Charlie's pronouncement. She frowns. "You and Marla again? Can Silicon Valley handle those kind of explosive fireworks?"

"Funny," Charlie says with indifference. "Come on, Linc. Let's go. See you around, Stacy."

<hr>

Charlie backs the jeep out of the parking lot and floors it for about ten blocks and then hastily parks the car in an empty parking lot and gets out. He runs through this open field at a high rate of speed all the way to other side, as if he is outrunning someone or something before he turns back and slowly makes his way back to the car.

I get out and make my way over to him. We meet up mid-field.

He's crying. Not softly. *Hard.* The tears just stream down his face like he's been shaken to the core of his being.

"What the hell is going on?" I grip his forearm, but he angrily shakes it off. He wipes at his eyes and shields his face from me, so I won't see. He's inconsolable. I'm almost afraid to know why.

"I need a minute." He gasps for breath. "Maybe a year." He clutches at his stomach, doubles over, and vomits the chips from earlier.

"Dude, what the hell is wrong with you?"

"She's dead. Holly Landon. She's dead." He starts crying again and then rubs at his face in frustration. "Why didn't my mom tell me? Why doesn't anybody ever tell me anything important that happens in this fucking town?"

"Who's Holly Landon?" I ask dully, already knowing somehow this is connected to the girl that I know as Holly.

"She was this angel I dated in high school once. God, the whole reason I took up with Marla was to make Holly Landon jealous. You know how it goes—the one person you care about is the one you hurt the most."

I slump down on the hard ground and grasp my arms around my knees in an attempt to put it all together. *Lay the Landon girl because she fucking needs it.* The sick feeling resurfaces because somehow I *know* this story. Charlie joins me after a few minutes.

"I'm sorry. About Holly." I lie down on my back, clasp my hands around my head, and stare at the blue sky overhead, unseeing. The persistent sick feeling from earlier returns. Charlie lies on his back next to me, mimicking my movements. I look over at him when I hear him taking these deep shuddering breaths. I've never seen him like this.

"I loved her, man. I never told her."

"Holly."

"Yeah. Holly Landon."

"Ah, shit." I take my time in an attempt to formulate the story just right. I take an unsteady breath and start to talk. "Remember that freak car accident? I told you about it. I'd just finished baseball practice. I was driving back along the 101 in February. Valentine's Day. I rescued a girl from a burning car. That girl? She's the same girl I was with at your party last night. I wanted to know her name. I wanted to know her because I haven't stopped thinking about her since that day. She didn't even remember me—carrying her, running away with her—from that accident. Some weird twisted part of God's plan had us hooking up at your party last night. The night of that accident, I went to the hospital—three hospitals, *actually*—before I found the right one where they'd taken her after a black SUV collided with an old Mercedes on the 101 head-on. The car caught fire. It was raining. The girl's sister died at the scene." I stop and let it all sink in. He makes the connection in the next ten seconds.

"Holly." There's so much despair in his voice that it slams into me, and I jerk back in response.

I sigh deep. "So, you think the girl from your party is actually her sister, right?

"Right. Her twin."

"But do you know for sure?" I'm suddenly desperate for a different answer. "I mean *for sure*. That it's the same set of twins—"

Charlie turns and stares at me. His face is one of total devastation. "I thought I *saw* Holly Landon at my party last night. They're *twins. Identical.* It wasn't Holly. It was *Tally.*"

"Tally." I roll the name over my tongue, hoping it isn't true. "Twins change places all the time." My voice shakes.

this much is true

This can't be true, even though I already know it is.

"This isn't twins changing places, Prez. This is *her* lying to you, fucking with you. Don't you get it? Holly's dead. Holly Landon is dead. They used to pull that shit all the time in high school. They were identical. They could fool all of us, even Marla, pretending to be the other. They're as different as night and day. Holly…was the nice one. Tally? Not so much. Sorry." He winces at my sudden scowl. "Holly's dead," he says slowly and closes his eyes. "I can't believe it."

I wonder if he feels if he says it enough that some part of his mind will actually believe it. "I was at the accident where this girl—the one from the accident and the one I met at your party—laid in my arms. She had to listen to her sister's screams in that fiery crash until they weren't there anymore. It was…bad."

"Holly." Charlie's voice breaks. He starts to cry again.

"Yeah. I'm sorry."

After another fifteen minutes, the real world invades. His mom calls wondering where her pies are. We trudge back to the Jeep in silence. On our way back, Charlie shakes his head at me and then pretends to concentrate fully on the road. After a few minutes, he takes an unsteady breath and blows it out with a heavy sigh. "If Tally Landon is your mystery girl, I'm just telling you that you're screwed, and I thought I had it rough."

"Why would you say that?" I get even more anxious at the look of despair on Charlie's face.

He frowns. "Tally Landon is one of the up-and-coming ballet dancers in the world. She's got a shot at the big time with her ballet. She's always been a bit of a rebel, slept with half the guys at Paly, by the time she was a sophomore." I wince at his graphic portrayal of her. "Sorry." Charlie shakes his head side-to-side and takes another shuddering breath. "But she's not the kind of girl you could actually fuck around with. No pun intended."

Charlie looks worried and his obvious concern transfers to me like an infusion of some kind.

"She's incredibly beautiful, incredibly smart, and incredibly talented—but elusive. She's someone you'd never really get to know. I don't know how to explain it better than that. Her father is this brilliant surgeon. They live in Atherton."

"*This* coming from a guy whose dad and *my uncle* is a venture capitalist," I say dryly and then attempt to laugh when Charlie winces.

"The Landons do just fine, believe me. I knew Tally from school through Marla, but she didn't give any of us the time of day. She was solely focused on ballet and would hook up with guys willing to go into the ring with her.

It's not that she's bad news, *Prez*; just trust me when I say that Tally Landon is *way* out of your league."

Charlie doesn't say anymore. Instead, he picks up speed and moves across two lanes of traffic in a matter of seconds. It's only after he navigates past the oncoming traffic that he turns and gives me this full-on warning look that scares the hell out of me. "Look, I'm not trying to bring you down. It's just this girl is trouble. She'll fuck with your mind as much as your soul. *Trust me.* I've watched her do it to a few of my friends." Charlie shakes his head. "She can turn it on, and she can turn it off. She told you her name was *Holly*— her twin *sister's* name. *Her twin.* Who does that? Especially given what we've just learned happened to Holly. She lied to you. Holly's dead," he says with disquiet. "Tally lied to you about *everything.*"

"That's fucked up," I say slowly.

"Yeah."

"She lied to me about everything." I try hard not to let the despondence overtake me completely, but it does anyway.

"Yeah."

"So what do I do now?"

Charlie scrutinizes me closely. "Dude, you walk away. You fucking *run.* Tally Landon is not a girl to get your head wrapped around." I tune out his lecture. "Like I said, she's a year away from hitting the big time with her ballet. That's all she cares about. Didn't she tell you any of *this*?"

"Kind of. She danced for me. She said she was the next Polina something or other."

"*She is.* Seriously, dude. She's a rising star in the ballet world. Trust me when I tell you that world is fucked up. They barely eat. They barely shit because they starve themselves so much of the time. Hell, they limit themselves to two drinks at a party if they go to one because, if they do drink and allow themselves the calories, they get fucked up on two drinks alone. Don't you get it? Ballet is everything; nothing else matters to them."

His rant about Tally Landon goes on for another five minutes. I thought he was done, but then he launches off on another tangent and gets even more pissed.

"Marla has always talked about Tally with this kind of reverence. She *worships* her and the way the girl operates. Damn. It's one of the many reasons we broke up. I didn't completely trust Marla since she was hanging out with Tally Landon so much. And I couldn't be around Holly, not after…because… I left for UCLA." Charlie sounds so forlorn that it catches my attention. "The three of them together were…too much. It was like flying too close to the sun. They fucked with guys, fucked with them in every way, and basically enjoyed doing it. Not Holly so much, but Tally and Marla to a greater extent, for sure." His shoulders begin to shake again. *Shit.* He's crying again.

Finally, he wipes his face and looks over at me.

"She *lied* to you, Prez. Think about why she did that. She doesn't like attachments. You can't *own* her. She's aloof and uninvolved. That's her deal. She'll screw with your mind and cruelly move on when you least expect it. You'll just serve as one of her boy toys, and then she'll leave you behind. That's what she does. Look, she already has." He shakes his head side-to-side. "I should have warned you. I didn't think she was there with Marla. I thought I saw *Holly.*" He frowns. "Holly's the angel. *Was,*" he shudders when he says it past tense. "I thought Thorn was there with her. I thought I saw him. Parties weren't always Tally's scene. She liked her privacy, and she remained focused on her ballet. That's all she cares about. I was hoping Marla wasn't still hanging out with her. I should have paid more attention to who you were talking to last night. Prez, are you even *listening* to me?"

"Yeah, I heard you." Dejected by the news of this girl Tally, I lower my baseball cap even further to hide my face from Charlie.

"Okay, what did I just say?"

"She lied to me about everything."

"Yes. Think about that. Why would she do something like that? It's fucked up, man, but it's what she does."

"She left me a thank-you note." I wince at the irony even as Charlie attempts to laugh.

"Well, you got more than most then. *She thanked you*, Prez, but you've got to stay away from her. She's trouble. I'm telling you this for your own good." Charlie sighs and looks more uncertain. "I guess that goes for me, too. I should just stay away from Marla. Look what she does to me by just seeing her again. I can't even think straight. And Holly's dead." Charlie slaps the steering wheel and looks irritably at the traffic up ahead and groans. "I missed the turn. *See?* That's what Marla does to me."

I sit up straighter and barely glance up at the cars passing us. Charlie slows down and makes a U-turn in the middle of the street and begins to race back the other way. I have to remind him to slow down because he still seems distraught with the news about Holly Landon.

Holly. Shit. Tally? Why would she lie to me like that?

"Well, at least we found out the truth before either one of us got in too deep," I say with forced bravado.

"Yeah. There's that."

We trudge into the kitchen, holding the pies in weak triumph to Aunt Gina. "What's wrong with you two?" she asks as soon as she sees us.

"Women. You can't trust them, and the good ones don't last." Charlie looks at his mom and relays the tragic story of Holly Landon's demise. I can't bear to hear him tell it again. I'm already reliving the horrible images of that accident. I can still hear the girl's screams. There was nothing I could have done, but that doesn't make it any easier in recalling it now. Imagine being the dead girl's sister. Her twin, no less. *Tally.*

After a few minutes, Aunt Gina eyes me warily. I haven't said a word since we got back.

"Everything all right with you? And this girl?"

"Not exactly. She's Holly Landon's sister. *Tally.*" I can't quite keep the misery out of my voice.

"Life must be so hard for her right now," my aunt says with a heavy sigh. "It'll take some time for her to work it all out."

Spoken like a true psychologist, which Gina Masterson is. All I can do is nod. It's hard to breathe, to think. *Everything's screwed up. I'm tired. I have a game. I'm a train wreck; all because of this girl Tally.*

"Mom, I just told him to forget all about that girl," Charlie says irritably. He glares at both of us.

He seems to be fighting for control. I'm sure he doesn't want to break down in front of his mother.

Aunt Gina looks over at Charlie. "Both of you need time and distance from these two girls. Time. Distance. It'll be hard. It'll seem impossible—but if it's real, it'll survive."

"Not true," we both say at the same time.

I head back across the lawn toward the guest house, intent on getting ready for my game against Oregon State. I have four hours to get it together. I attempt to concentrate on my father's three favorite words for me these days. *Focus. Baseball. Winning.* Yet I keep thinking about this girl. *Tally.* Her image runs through my mind over and over. *Tally. Tally Landon.* Why does her name roll so easily off my lips even as I shower and dress and get ready to throw a baseball? *Why?*

She seems to have taken my soul. I'm going to have to figure out a way to get it back.

CHAPTER ELEVEN

Tally · For the love of baseball

I SIT BETWEEN MY TWO BEST GUYS—MY dad and Tommy—and take solace in the fact that I can be a spectator and have free reign to watch the pitcher on the mound without anyone questioning how closely I do, including the guy himself. According to my little brother, the Stanford is up nine to seven in the top of the eighth over Oregon State. All I know is that Lincoln Presley is winning in more ways than one. *With me.*

I still like him. I still want him. Intrigued by the unexpected possession that Lincoln Presley has over my mind, body, and soul, I have trouble breathing most of the afternoon.

"Awesomely good at baseball," Tommy says more than once over the course of three hours.

For his part, Lincoln Presley remains focused on the game. He commands the entire field of play with his indelible presence. He doesn't even glance up my way.

The field dust permeates the air and my psyche, obviously, but I still manage to love the way the sun lights up his dark hair whenever I get a glimpse of it sticking out from under his red and white baseball cap. I ran my fingers through his gorgeous, wavy head of hair just last night. *I'm possessed. I have to stop thinking about him. I have to stop staring at him. Stop it, Tally. Stop now.*

Yet I find myself intently watching the way his leg muscles move and stretch as he winds up for another pitch or the way his fingers curve around the ball each time, just before he throws. *What the hell is wrong with me?*

My heart speeds up the longer I watch him. My face gets hot, too. It's time for a break from the spontaneous combustion that seems to be taking place inside of me. I steal a glance at my dad. He looks over at the same time and smiles wide.

"Thanks for coming today. You made Tommy's day and mine."

"Sure. We won't get to do this all summer." I frown. "I wish Mom would have come."

"She wanted to. She's tired today."

"She's tired every day." Bitterness seeps into my voice. I look over at him with a silent apology. "Dad, is she going to be okay?"

"She's trying. We all are. It's hard on her—between losing your grandmother last year and Holly; it's all been a bit much for your mom. Don't worry. I'm keeping a close eye on her."

"Are you?"

My dad gets this guilty look but doesn't answer for a long while. "It's hard on all of us, Tally. What's happened."

"Yes. It is." I look unseeingly at the baseball game. My interest wanes. The catapulting emotions for this guy I just met and the upheaval in which I find myself and my life just about pulls me under.

"So," Dad says with a little hesitation, "You *know* him, kiddo?" He subtly gestures with his right hand toward the pitcher's mound.

Tommy.

I'm going to have to have a chat with my little brother about what we share with the parents. My dad gets one of those *worried-father-please-don't-do-this-to-me* looks. Dad suddenly seems unsure if he really wants to know how I'll actually answer. After all, what does *knowing him* imply? I sort of laugh when he presses his lips together and gets this vexed look. "Barely." I shake my head side-to-side. "We met last night at Charlie Masterson's party. He's nice," I add in an offhanded way and shrug a little for emphasis.

"All I care about is what *you* think," my dad says.

"I think he's nice." I glance away from my dad and back toward the pitcher's mound where Linc winds up for another perfect throw. "He's good; isn't he?"

"Very good. There are a ton of scouts here just to watch him pitch. He'll be drafted in the next couple of weeks."

"What does that mean?" I ask, still keeping my eyes on Linc as he winds up to throw again, and manage to avoid my father's probing glance. *Bonus.*

"His life's about to change. He'll probably play in the minor leagues for a few years, maybe less, depending upon how he does there. They'll sign him to a huge long-term contract, provide him with a hefty signing bonus, and bring him up through the ranks. He'll pitch at the major-league baseball level soon enough."

A guy in front of us turns around and gets this unapologetic look for eavesdropping and says, "That's the Giants' scouts over there." He points toward the North. "And that's the Oakland A's and even the Yankees' scouts on the other side."

I look around at all these avid fans that watch Lincoln Presley so intently and can almost pick out who the scouts are for myself. They hover together near the fences on either side of home plate, assessing Linc's abilities with their speed guns and applying quiet verbal critiques to those around them, and write stuff down on their prized clip boards.

Scouts. Baseball star. Wow.

"I read that he's going in the first round," the guy says while still looking up at us.

"What does that mean?" I ask him.

"It means he can write his own ticket, young lady. He'll play for the big leagues within the year. He's got quite an arm and quite a legacy with his dad. And you *know* him?" The guy looks impressed.

"We've met. We're friends." My face gets hot again as the guy looks me over. He nods, apparently satisfied with my honesty on that front, and eventually turns his attention back to the game.

Breathe. This is getting weird. The longer I sit here watching Linc, the weirder the whole thing gets. I sense additional scrutiny from my dad with one of his studied sidelong glances. I'm fully aware that my dad would still like to believe that I am still his innocent little girl, that I'm still ten and virtuous besides.

Yes, Dad, I know him. I slept with him just last night. I know him quite well. But really? Not at all. I wince and take a deep breath. *Shit. What was I thinking coming here? This is all wrong.*

I finally look over at him. "We're just *friends.*" My dad breathes this little sigh of relief while I consciously hold mine as I deliver this all but blatant lie. "I'm leaving for New York in a few weeks, remember? Nothing to worry about."

"But you'll be careful in New York. Allaire Tremblay will be there," he says, looking more uncertain.

"I'm always careful; and yes, she'll be there—and Marla, too. Rob Thorn is going to NYU. Plenty of people around that I know who will watch out for me." I'm not sure why I felt the need to add in the Rob Thorn trivia, but my dad looks relieved.

"Good," he finally says.

Tommy returns with his third hot dog and moves in to sit between us. He takes turns staring at my dad and then me, before shrugging and devoting his attention back to the game and his hero, Lincoln Presley. I'm surrounded now by all these rabid fans of Lincoln Presley, which proves both surprising and alarming. *They worship the guy. All of them.*

I feel bad that I have really no idea what they're talking about or can't fully appreciate the talent they obviously see. Fans of Linc's examine and pick apart every pitch from the way he holds the ball to the way he lets it go and as to whether the strike zone is high or low or the pitch was outside or dead-on. I'm overcome with confusion and utter amazement at the same time. I don't know any of this stuff. I don't have an appreciation for the game the way even my little brother does. They live and breathe this stuff. *Baseball. Stats. Runs. Walks. Errors. Wins.*

Winning.

Impossible. This situation with this guy is impossible. I shouldn't be here. This is all wrong. This is an impossible situation.

"Baseball is my focus," he'd said last night. He'd said it almost apologetically. Now I think I get why he said it that way, as well as what he was really trying to say to me. *I don't get involved. Baseball is my focus.* That was his warning.

My heart contracts. It seems to literally cave in on me as I splinter inside. *What the hell is wrong with me? Why did I come? Why am I still here?* I shudder with the recognition of that kind of pressure. *Lots of it. To be perfect. To be the best.*

My focus is baseball. He wasn't kidding.

The air leaves my lungs swiftly and doesn't seem to want to return. I'm aware enough to realize the beginnings of yet another one of these confounding panic attacks. I stand up. My dad looks at me funny.

"Gotta go. Can I have your car keys?" I ask, holding out my hand.

"Are you okay?" he asks, reaching into his coat pocket for his keys, and then drops them into my hand.

"I'm fine. I just need some…air. The dust is getting to me. I need to drink some water…soda. *Something.* I'll meet you at the car after the game."

Miraculously, I climb down the bleachers and through the throngs of people with relative ease. Baseball fans are an accommodating bunch—nice and thoughtful. Some guy helps me jump down from the last row of bleachers where the promised land of the hard ground shimmers just three feet away from me. His hand stays on my waist a moment too long. I pull away after thanking him without really registering his face because now I'm intent on an escape from all of this. The crowd suddenly roars with the umpire's call of "Strike!" I glance over and watch a stream of Stanford Cardinal baseball players run across the field. I'm just about home free when I spy Lincoln Presley running straight towards me. My breath hitches at the sight of him.

Then, some tall blond calls out his name and waves. He moves off in the other direction toward her. My nemesis is tall. An Amazon. I can't quite place her accent. Yet I stand here and crazily watch him go over to her while I semi-hide behind the bleachers and watch the two of them interact. He works his fingers through the holes in the fence that separate them and in the next moment, she's brushing her lips along his fingers.

What the hell is this? Who is this?

I close my eyes for a few seconds trying to get air while this unexpected jealousy wends its way through me like a flame that bursts to life at the flick of a match following an inevitable trail of gasoline. *Oh. My. God. I'm jealous. At an almost visceral level. I so want to scratch her eyes out. Right now.*

I take in air and open my eyes only to discover she's still kissing his fingers through the fence. And he doesn't seem to mind.

She's laughing. A sexy laugh. *Holy shit.*

"Nice pitching, Lincoln Presley," she says.

Russian accent. She's Russian. Tall. Blond. Sexy. I've never felt more inadequate in my life. I turn away because I can't watch anymore.

"Thanks for coming," I hear Linc say.

I can't help it; I'm turning back around and watching him study her face intently.

"Did you come by yourself?" he asks.

Did she come by herself? An interesting, all-telling question. My mind automatically wraps around the intimation he's going for in those few spoken words.

"Yes, of course." She laughs.

He laughs and kind of nods. "I'll see you after the game then."

Whore. Manwhore. Whoreman. I hate you.

I'm pathetic. Even my silent name calling is pathetic.

I blindly make my way toward the women's restroom. Five minutes later, I'm ensconced inside one of the stalls—locked and loaded and attempting to breathe. *Holy shit. I'm pissed. Disillusioned. Disappointed. Panicked. Unloved. Unwanted. Fucking jealous.*

"Fffffuuuuuuuuuuuuucccccccccckkkkkkkkkkkkkkk," I say aloud.

"Are you all right?"

It's the Russian bitch.

No way.

"I'm fine." I search for a lie. I want her to leave, and I manage to take a few shallow breaths as I hear the water running and then the subsequent rattling of the paper towel dispenser. "My period started," I lie. "Do you have a tampon by chance?"

"But of course," she says in her sexy Russian accent.

Her slender hand appears along the edge of the bathroom stall proffering a pink wrapped tampon within the next sixty seconds. *Girl power.* I don't feel particularly beholden to her thoughtfulness and unnecessary rescue. I can't even explain why I just said what I did. *You're Tally Landon; you don't have to.*

"Are you going to be okay now?" she asks.

"Yes. I'm fine. Thanks."

I throw the tampon into the trash, flush the toilet thirty seconds later, wait another two minutes; and have to hope that she's left. I open the door and step out.

She stands at the long mirror on the far wall, fixing her long, silky blond hair. She's redoing her ponytail. She's wearing all black. Jeans. Jacket. Blouse. Tight. Fitted. Designer. *How absolutely fucking fabulous is she?*

"Thanks," I say for what must the third pathetic time.

I wash my hands slowly using plenty of soap like I have time and youth on my side. *True. I do.*

And yet.

I combat this sudden urge that has me putting my hands firmly around her slender neck and squeezing out her very breath until there isn't any more. Until she is no more. *What the hell is wrong with me?*

Jealous much, Tally?

No.

I can't even breathe while I'm thinking these murderous thoughts. *What the hell is wrong with me?* My breath gets jagged. I look up in time to catch her studying me via the other mirror. She gets this almost expectant look as if I owe her my life for the gift of the tampon. I wonder how many times I'm going to have to thank her for it.

Don't, Tally. Don't.

Walk away.

But no.

"So how do you know Lincoln Presley?" I ask. Fish wife. Jealous much? Tally, what are you doing?

"We go to Stanford together. We're *friends.*" She lingers on the last word and licks her lips after saying it and knowingly smiles.

Friends with benefits. Fuck friends. How absolutely fucking fabulous is this? She gets this wider secret smile, even as she blithely lines her lips with an expensive lip liner. *It's forty bucks.* I know this because I have the same one. Holly ordered me one for my birthday last year.

Our birthday. Last year. Because we are twins. Were twins. Now I'm a party of one.

My hands shake as I valiantly dig through my purse in search of the elusive fucking lip pencil. She still watches me with this little supreme smile.

"So how do *you* know Lincoln Presley?" she asks.

I've got this.

I take my time drying my hands and formulating the exact words to use ever so carefully because they need to be delivered just right.

Don't mess with this bitch.

That warning goes unheeded. By me.

"We're friends, too. Good *friends*. I'm Tally Landon. And you are?" I hold out my hand. She stares at it for a long two minutes and then directly at me and still doesn't take it.

The battle lines have been drawn.

She gets this vindictive taint to her features. Her eyes go wide and then narrow, while her perfectly-lined lips form into a grim, straight line. *No smile now.*

I want to step back from her because she's stepped forward into my own personal space, but I hold my ground as she gets even closer. She's close enough now that I spy the faintest of lines around her eyes. She's beautiful now, but she must do some partying on the side, because the frequent use of those vices is beginning to show up there on her face.

"What are you—all of nineteen? He wouldn't date a slip of a girl like you," she says with a wide fake smile. "Linc likes his women older, sophisticated, and worldly."

She's describing herself, and I suppress a laugh. "Older? Really? I didn't get that impression from him."

She looks taken aback. I'm pretty sure this woman is used to things going her way without a fight every single flipping time. I slowly nod. She stares back at me—scrutinizing, assessing, evaluating. I avoid flinching under her laser-like scan but just barely.

"Nika. Nika Vostrikova. I'm a senior at Stanford. I do computer work on the side. For Linc. I capture his stats? And we're good friends. He has a special way of paying me for those." Her eyes practically shimmer as she says the last part.

We're back to that.

My bravado falters for a myriad of reasons—exhaustion from a virtually sleepless night and the greatest sex of my life and now seeing Lincoln Presley again and meeting his friend with benefits, Nika Vostri-*fucking*-kova. The truth is, in this pivotal moment, I need my sister. I'm pummeled inside by the constant worry over my dad and what's really going on with my mom. There's Tommy. Who's going to take care of Tommy after I leave for New York? I'm missing my family already, and I'm not even gone. Then there's this Lincoln Presley. Baseball. Ballet. Paly. Graduation. New York. Ballet again. And now? Nika Vostrikova.

Where's the focus, Tally? Where's the focus?

I swallow hard, steady my breathing, and stick out my hand. "Thanks for the tampon, Nika Vostrikova." She lightly shakes my hand while I glide towards the door and exit stage left.

"Nice to meet you, Tally Landon." There's isn't a hint of sincerity in what she's just said, but I laugh. And laughter releases me from the threat of tears and propels me toward the concession stand.

Ten minutes later, I work my way through the parking lot and toward my dad's gleaming silver Lexus. Grateful for the solitude, I slide into the backseat and roll down the passenger window and freely breathe in the inevitable dust and vaguely hear the announcer as he calls out the end of game.

Lincoln Presley gets the win.

Now we can all go home.

I console myself with the fact that he doesn't even know I was here at his game, watching him pitch, meeting his good friend with benefits—Nika Vostrikova. *No.* He doesn't know anything about that. Why would he? His one and only focus is baseball. He said so. He meant it. *Why? Because there is only baseball. We all know that.*

You stupid, stupid girl.

What were you thinking?

Get it together.

Now.

⁓⁓⊙⁓⊙⁓⁓

My dad drives home but continually steals looks at me via the car mirror. "Are you okay?" he asks for the sixth time.

Tommy is oblivious. He waited in a long line to have Linc sign his ball and glove with a black sharpie pen. This simple gesture essentially makes my little brother's life, while mine seems to have fallen apart in the same equally short amount of time because of the very same guy.

Hero to Tommy.

Manwhore to me.

I take solace in my anger.

I let it burn through all of me.

Anger is good.

"I don't feel that well," I finally say to my father's question when he asks for the seventh time.

This will buy me some much-needed alone time at home. My dad looks all concerned. I manage a weak smile back at him in the rearview mirror.

"Thanks for coming today, honey. It was fun," Dad says.

"It was fun. We'll do it again." *Not.*

Never again.

I will never watch baseball again. Ever. Never. *Ever.*

CHAPTER TWELVE

Totally Addicted

"Y OU KNOW WHAT YOUR PROBLEM IS, don't you?" I ask Marla and glance over at her anxious face.

She's been moping around since she got here. We lay side-by-side on my queen-sized bed amid all the packing boxes in preparation for our trip to New York in a few days. Yet, we're lost in our own private thoughts. It's been three weeks, twenty-two nights actually, if one wanted to get technical, since I first met the baseball player. It's been a week since Charlie and Marla's third official break-up since that initial Friday night. I predict if she ever utters the phrase, "we're done; we're over" again neither one of us will actually believe her. Marla's officially an emotional wreck. I'm barely holding it together myself because thoughts of Lincoln Presley continue to invade my psyche at all these inopportune moments. I trade between fantastic thoughts about our one night together and the seething anger at him over his *friend with benefits* Nika Vostrikova.

"My problem is Charlie Masterson," Marla says without shame. She covers her face with one arm, so I can't really see her agonized expression, but I hear it.

"Yes! I told you that party was a bad idea. And, look what he's done to you in a matter of three weeks. Make up; break up. Make up; break up. There's a pattern forming here. Why can't you *see* it?"

Marla sits up from the bed and looking chagrined. "At least, we're trying to work it out. We're not *ignoring* how we feel about each other. We're trying to find a way to make it work. Even so, you're the one that is all but impossible to be around. You're the one who needs to work things out with the guy you screwed three weeks ago because your mind is clearly still tightly wrapped around him. I know we're not supposed to talk about him, let alone mention his flipping name, but let's be honest for once because this bitchy *I-don't-give-a-shit-about-the-guy* attitude is wearing me out. You obviously *do*."

"He has a girlfriend. Her name is Nika. She's older, Russian, sexy. I saw them together. He was pitching for Stanford that *same* weekend, and she was there. I went to the game with my dad and Tommy, and I saw them. It was the day after he and I…" My voice breaks. It's my turn to hide my face because now I sound jealous and pathetic. *This will not do. Not at all.*

"Nika," Marla says with disquiet. "Are you sure?"

"I talked to her in the women's restroom at the field. She said they were *friends*. And I *saw* them and how he reached for her through the fence. She was kissing his fingers, and he didn't seem to mind."

I'm bitter. Disillusioned. Pissed.

I let Marla see it all. She's gazing at me with notable indignation and looks taken aback at the same time.

"Have you thought about calling him?" She frowns. "Confronting him? To work things out?"

"There's nothing to work out." I glare at her. "This situation is *way* different than yours. You *know* Charlie. He knows you. You have something together to work out, whereas Lincoln Presley and I are nothing more than a one-night stand." I shrug but my shoulders tremble negating the nonchalant attitude I'm going for and Marla sees it. "We had a little fun. We're a premise— nothing more—that is clearly *over*."

"If it's so *over*, why are you still moping around here like somebody…?" We're instantly caught in the riptide of Holly again. Marla looks contrite at what she's almost said. "I'm sorry. You just seem so devastated on a lot of levels. You're not yourself and even Tremblay's noticed. You *know* that. And I think, maybe, if you can just talk to him one time, there will be some form of inevitable closure with him. He's just getting back from the baseball draft and he's flying out to wherever the L.A. Angels have him play on one of their minor league teams. Charlie says he'll be on the road all summer through the fall."

How does she know all of this stuff about the baseball player who I will not name?

"Well, maybe Nika can follow him all around the country and take down all those baseball stats for him."

Fish wife.

Really, Tally?

What is wrong with you?

Why do you care?

My mind swirls with the image of Lincoln Presley's face right above mine.

"And how do you know all of that anyway? I thought you weren't speaking to Charlie," I say attempting to breathe.

Something feels *off* with Marla. Yet, somehow, she distracts me when she squeezes my hand and smiles and manages to convey sympathy all at the same time.

"Well, I *have* talked to Charlie, and that's what he told me. I asked him about Linc for *you* because I care about you. I thought you might want to know so maybe you would stop acting so crazy."

"I'm not crazy," I say sadly. "I just want to get to New York and concentrate on ballet. Besides, he thinks my name is Holly." I wince at admitting this particular lie.

"You are one sick puppy," Marla says softly. "Geez, Tally. Why do you always have to give guys such a hard time, both figuratively and literally?"

We both start to laugh. It eases the tension in the room. She lies back down beside me on the bed. I close my eyes because fresh tears sting them because she sounds just like Holly, and it's sad and funny at the same time.

We've been over this whole scenario of what transpired at Charlie's party a dozen times already, but I never confessed to the part about going to see Linc at his baseball game the next day. I've never talked about Nika Vostrikova before because this insane jealousy spins me out of control. A foreign feeling—this jealousy. I don't like it. I've never experienced it before. I've never *cared* before.

The five-mile runs I do every day since then have done little to erase the lucid memories of that night with Lincoln Presley. Even my attempt for normalcy by serving my grieving parents a few true home-cooked dinners these past few weeks—where I was clearly influenced by the memorable culinary efforts by one Lincoln Presley—has done little to erase the memories of the night with Elvis. No. None of these good deeds have damped down the memories of that incredible Friday night escapade with him three weeks ago.

Marla and I have been basically wallowing in misery over these two guys, like all girls do, most girls anyway, but not generally us, usually not me, in particular. Yet, something is definitely going on with the two of us over these two.

We've lost our focus. Not good.

We've graduated; but nothing's changed. Still? At other times, it seems everything has changed. We came to that conclusion earlier today when Marla called and said she was coming over to work it all out. We leave for New York this Sunday. I'm not sure what we need to discuss or work out.

"It's okay to like him," Marla says now, turning to closely scrutinize my face. "It's okay, Tally." She traces the lone tear that carelessly trails down my face while I swipe her hand away.

"No. No, it's not. It's not *okay* for me. The last thing I need right now is a distraction—*a guy* distracting me this way. And I lied to him. I'm a terrible person. The worst. And I miss Holly, and it hurts to miss her like this. My parents are still so out of it. I don't think it's even registered with them that I'm leaving in two days. I'm worried about who's going to take care of Tommy and my mom when I'm gone. My dad does what he can, but…they barely made it through the graduation ceremony earlier this week. It's just too damn hard—missing Holly and doing all this extraneous thinking about Lincoln Presley. It's insane. I'm insane."

"He knows your name is Tally."

"What?" I practically choke on the word.

"Charlie told him who you were. I guess they ran into Stacy that first weekend, and she told them what happened to Holly." Marla takes a deep breath. "Anyway, Charlie figured out that the girl *Holly* that Linc was going on about was *you*. He was pretty upset. They both were." She gets this uncertain look. "But I guess Linc liked your note."

"Oh…" My face gets red at her mention of the note. *Why did I leave a note? Who does that?* "Linc told Charlie about my note? And, Charlie told you? When exactly did you *talk* to Charlie? I thought you were on another break."

Marla gets this vexed look. I slide off the bed in the next instant while Marla studies me and appears to be waiting for something. *A clue. A signal. A phone call. What?*

"So how bad is it?" she asks, avoiding my question.

I gaze at her more closely. I'm more tuned into her now because something is definitely going on with her. She's acting stranger than I am. I cross my arms and stand across from her shaking my head to clear of all the wayward thoughts of one Lincoln Presley.

"It was one night. It means *nothing.*" I stumble on the last word. "*Nothing,*" I say again for both of us. Then, I sigh because the truth wills out. "There have been a dozen other guys, as you well know, but for some reason…this one stays with me. It's pretty bad." I get this wry smile. "I need to exorcise him out or something."

"You *like* him. You *more* than like him."

"No. Not possible."

"Tally, it's there all over your face and I've never seen you act like this before. I'm not sure what's going on. Sometimes, you have this look of absolute joy and then at other times I've never seen you look this devastated. Even with Holly," she says gently. "Either way? I think you need to work it out with him…whatever it is." She flips her right hand through the air. "We leave in two days," she says, sounding more forlorn.

I look at her more closely again but she looks the other way taking a sudden interest in the open doorway of my half-empty closet. I'm half-packed for New York. She takes a shuddering breath and blows it out.

"And I just think *this* may follow you there, unless you confront it *and him,* once and for all." She frowns. "What you need is closure, my friend."

"Closure," I scoff. "Because what you and Charlie have been able to attain is *closure?*"

Marla laughs nervously and gets this angelic serene look as if she's figured out all of life's answers and just needs to tell them to me.

"Not exactly," she finally says. "But at least we're moving forward instead of just left wondering about it all. If I hadn't seen Charlie, I wouldn't know that I still have all these amazing feelings for him." She displays this blazing smile. It's like a light has burst forth from inside of her. "I would have gone to New York and gotten engaged to Devon and probably ended up in the Hamptons. I never would have known that Charlie Masterson still holds my heart…and my hand."

Now she holds out her left hand with this dramatic wave, and I spy the diamond that sparkles there that I failed to notice earlier. Her green eyes glitter with tears. Happy ones. She's getting married. *To Charlie. Holy shit.*

"Marla." I stare helplessly at her left hand. *Breathe.* "Wow. When did this happen?"

"Last night. He came over around eight, talked with my parents, and then asked me on bended knee and everything." She gets this dazed look. "He's just so amazing and wonderful. Charlie really wants us to be together. He's going to be busy with school for the next couple of years finishing up his undergraduate degree at UCLA. I'll be in New York for the summer and maybe the fall. I've applied at UCLA because my dad really wanted me to, but I can just see how the summer goes first. See, Tally? It all works out."

"How does it work out? He's in L.A. and you're in New York. How does that work out? When are the two of you *together* exactly?"

"Well, we haven't gotten that far. Like I said, I want to see how the summer goes. See how things work out with Tremblay and ballet. We've given ourselves the summer. We'll do the long-distance thing and just focus on being engaged."

I nod slowly while my mind calculates all these various scenarios—none of which seem to work out in their favor. I shake my head.

"Aren't you happy for me?"

"Yes. Yes. Of course. I'm happy." I move in to hug her and manage to push all the anxiety I already feel for her—and for me—way down.

New York and the NYC Ballet the dream all three of us shared crumbles a little more with this news. All I can see is that Marla is breaking rank, just like Holly has inadvertently done, but it's there all the same. The dream is being destroyed by every change we encounter—devastating or joyous. It's changing everything for us. Marla won't last without Charlie for more than six months. I already know this.

Selfish, selfish Tally. Be happy for her. Smile for her. Do it.

"So." She looks uncertain. "We're celebrating. My parents. His. Charlie. Me. You. Linc," she adds with a nervous smile. "There's a party at the Mastersons tonight with all of them to celebrate our engagement and Linc's draft news. He's flying in some time tonight from New York."

"Wow. Double billing and sharing the celebratory news with the baseball player," I say with little enthusiasm.

"You'll be my maid of honor so you're going. You have to. And, Linc will be his best man. So, there you are. It's all worked out. You have to do this for me."

"Damn it, Marla. You've put me in an impossible situation here."

"I know. But you'll do it; right? Because Charlie's parents are a little intimidating, and I want things to be perfect and the only way I see that happening is if you're there with me. Please say you'll come. *Please?*"

I'm too weak from endless weeks of angst and her clearly emotional plea to say no. I don't even try.

She picks out a dress for me to wear, pushes me off to the shower, and re-does my makeup when I return. She unabashedly changes into an amazing white designer dress she's brought just for the occasion and instantly looks like a true bride-to-be. The dress hugs her in all the right places. She's tanned and beautiful and seems to sparkle like the unique, pear-shaped diamond on her left hand. I hug her close and tell her all of these things by borrowing heavily from every chick flick film I can think of, in the space of ten minutes. In less than an hour, we've transformed into bride-to-be and maid-of-honor. I wear black because Marla designates it so. She tells me that she wants me to be comfortable and relaxed and be myself. The color black suits me just fine. And as far as being comfortable and relaxed? These are two states that I would never describe myself as being in, but I go along with the charade for Marla.

Truthfully? I look like a dressed-up, dark-haired Barbie. The dress is made of too much taffeta and chiffon and flounces at the mid-thigh. I pirouette in the mirror, and the bride-to-be gets this satisfied smile while I force my lips to form one.

My goal tonight is singular in scope: to make Marla happy. It's an achievable goal. At least, that's what I keep telling myself.

We leave in two more days for New York. I keep consoling myself with this fact while I'm getting ready under Marla's doting tutelage. I convince myself that nothing has changed, even though I know all of it just has. I don't have time to examine any of these competing thoughts too closely. No. I just wave at my parents, tell them I'll be late, and follow Marla out to her car and try not to think of anything or anyone, for that matter.

Marla's engaged. To Charlie.

Can the night get anymore surreal?

Yes. Yes, it can.

I go along with the charade in exhibiting pure but unexpected surprise and happiness at Charlie and Marla's engagement. The Mastersons and the Stones are gracious but seemed to be as equally stunned with the news that Marla and Charlie are getting married as I am. Lincoln Presley isn't here yet. I can breathe. I stay busy by helping Charlie's mother in the kitchen. There are drinks and appetizers to be served, and Gina Masterson seems grateful for the additional help. She watches me with a secret smile that makes me a bit uncomfortable, but I manage to return one and make a concerted effort to join in the fun and be cheerful. Fun. Cheerful. *Me?*

We toast. We celebrate. We drink. I stay with seltzer and so does Marla. The whole underage issue lingers beneath the surface of every adult conversation. Dismay that Marla is only eighteen silently floats all around both sets of parents, but no one voices their actual concern aloud. Instead, the parental units trade these dazed looks with only hints at the anxiety that lurks beneath. Both sets looked absolutely shocked that things have spun out of control in this way with their kids.

I move between the outdoor patio and French doors leading into the kitchen in a regular devised pattern carrying out appetizer trays and drinks while Gina Masterson bewilderingly hovers. I get the feeling she wants to stay busy to avoid the silent rumblings taking place with just about everyone else. I console myself with the undeniable fact that we're headed to New York in less than forty-eight hours, and this night will end soon enough, and Lincoln Presley is still not here.

"Come on, Tally," Gina Masterson says to me. "It's taking longer than they thought. Let's take them some of this food and some drinks. They won't miss us for a few minutes out here." I look at her blankly not understanding who or what she's talking about. "The draft," she says softly. "They're holed up in the study going over PR stuff and logistics with the Los Angeles Angels."

"He's already here?"

"Yes. I thought you knew that."

"No." I try to smile. "I didn't know his schedule and I'm not a baseball buff. I'm not all that familiar with the…game."

"Oh. I thought you were. Interesting," she says with a little laugh.

Gina Masterson is pretty. She has dark blond hair that she keeps in a stylish bob. I think Marla mentioned to me once that she is a psychologist or something. I covertly watch her as she puts together a tray of sandwiches for the *draft set* as she puts it. Then, she proceeds to tell me who makes up the draft set—Linc's agent, Linc's dad, their publicist Kimberley Powers, and Linc himself—all apparently on a conference call with the Los Angles Angels and their coaching staff.

"Juggling a lot of celebratory stuff tonight, Mrs. Masterson," I say with a forced smile.

"Call me Gina." She smiles. I nod. "He knows you're here," she says softly. "He asked me about a half-hour ago if you were here yet."

"He did?" I can't hide the tremor in my voice fast enough.

Gina's lovely brown eyes narrow in on my face. "He really likes you. Which is going to be a problem for Davis and Kimberley." She frowns slightly.

"I don't know who any of those people are. I don't want to know who they are. I just want to go…home or to New York or be anywhere but here." I've said this all aloud and Gina looks at me with this recognizable maternal sympathy. She puts her around me and hugs me close.

"It's okay, Tally. *Really.* You two will have time to work it out. I don't see any reason to rush things the way my son has with Marla." Her forehead creases with worry. "Don't get me wrong. I'm thrilled with Marla. I just wish they would wait."

"You couldn't ask for a better daughter-in-law than Marla," I say into the waning silence between us. "Marla's amazing. She's talented and steady and loyal and always happy. I wish I could be just one of those things."

"I think you already are," Gina says, but then her smile fades. "His mom would have loved you. You're perfect for Linc. He…he hasn't had an easy time of it in growing up without his mom." She sighs. "And my brother Davis expects a lot of Linc." She shakes her head side-to-side. "There are a lot of expectations of him with baseball. Maybe, you understand some of those pressures. Those must come with your ballet, too. Marla's told us you are extremely talented."

"I've studied ballet since I was four. There's a lot of pressure. A lot of expectations. You have to really want it." I frown giving in a little to one of my fears of not making it—*failing.* "We have this once-in-a-lifetime opportunity in New York with SAB. The School of American Ballet? And after that, a possible internship with New York City Ballet. That's the big plan." I catch my lower lip and glance at Marla and Charlie. "I guess plans change."

"That's amazing. You've worked really hard to get there from what Marla has said."

"All three of us have. Yes."

Gina Masterson gets this confused look at my mention of three of us; and I'm filling in blanks to her unspoken question before I have a chance to think it through.

"My twin sister Holly? We were all supposed to go to New York together. Holly and I...were in a bad car accident...a head-on collision on the 101 on Valentine's Day. She died at the scene." *Breathe.* "Like I said, plans change." I again glance over at Marla and Charlie, who both stand before her parent's and Charlie's dad with their arms wrapped around each other.

"You're the one Linc saved that day. He just told me the whole story recently," she says. "He was so upset by it, so distraught over the girl he saved from that car fire. That was you. He went to three different hospitals to find you." She touches my hand and I involuntarily flinch while all avenues for air desert me. "That was you," she says again.

I manage to look up in time to see Linc standing in the doorway.

"The Los Angeles Angels want me there in the line-up with the Salt Lake Bees on Tuesday." He's smiling, but it fades when he looks over at me.

I can't hide the pain...for all of it. Him. Holly. Me. Life doesn't make sense. None of this makes any sense.

My thoughts are all jumbled. Now, his eyes look so familiar because I suddenly remember them from that day.

"It was you that day? Elvis?" I whisper.

He nods slowly and looks uneasy.

Marla comes through the other door from the dining room. "Tally, what's wrong?"

"I have to go. Thank you, Mrs. Masterson...Gina."

Somehow, I manage to set the tray of drinks back down on the counter even as this feeling of spinning out of control takes over. I start to lose my balance as I push through the French doors and race out onto the terrace. My mind takes me somewhere else. *All I can see is Holly's face. She's smiling. Running.* I follow her past the Masterson's hedge, down the drive, onto the street. Marla's car beckons. I've got to get out of here. I welcome the way the darkness envelops me. I want to hide. I want to get away.

CHAPTER THIRTEEN

Tally Friends and benefits and lies

I RACE TOWARDS MARLA'S CAR AND THIS unknowable peace that I am sure I now so richly deserve.

Keys. No keys. Shit.

"Holly!" Linc calls out. I keep running, putting my head down to make my body go even faster toward the sanctuary of Marla's car and away from him. "Tally, I mean."

"Save it. I've heard and seen enough." I reach the car and lean against the passenger door willing it to miraculously be unlocked. It's not. I try the door handle twice. "Shit."

Then, Linc's there.

"I know it sounds bad," he says in a low voice. "I wanted to tell you, but I was worried about how you would react since I know you're still struggling with the aftereffects of the accident, and everything associated with it. I just wanted to know your name the night of that party."

His body somehow enfolds into mine from behind. My body involuntarily reacts by leaning into his. "Well, now you do, but I'm not Holly."

"You're not Holly," he says with knowable sadness.

I turn, trapped between his arms, and face him. "I'm Tally." I lift my head in defiance.

"I know."

His fingers entangle in mine. His hands are warm while mine are cold. He leans in closer to me.

"Let me go. Please."

"No. Not until you hear me out. You owe me that much for the lies you've told, *Tally Landon*. Please listen to me. I care about you. I have since that first day, since Valentine's Day. Aunt Gina's right. I recently told her about the accident and you—*this girl*—I couldn't get out of my mind. And then, at the party, I couldn't believe my luck in finding you again."

"Luck," I say dully. I'm sure he can feel my racing pulse through his fingertips where his hands rest along each of my wrists. Gravity already feels off center in just being this close to him again. His fingers brush along my waistline and in the next few seconds, he sweeps my hair to one side and lightly strokes my neck with his magical fingers. I can't help but react to it. This half-mournful, soul-destroying moan escapes my lips. "Don't do this to me, Linc."

He still manages to imprison me against the door Marla's car with his whole body. I can't really move. Tears threaten. *What is with this crying when I get around him?*

"I'm not your flipping wild horse."

I hang my head, embarrassed that I've turned on him within the first few minutes of seeing him again. I sigh and catch my lower lip between my teeth. Then, I remember Nika.

"And I'm not your friend with benefits either."

I struggle within his forceful arms that imprison me, even while his attraction for me becomes more apparent. His hardness travels up against my thigh, and my breath gets jagged for a whole new set of reasons.

"I never said that you were." I turn in his arms and note his confusion in the shadow of the street light that shines across Marla's car and the two of us. "But you've done pretty childish things now; haven't you? *Tally.*" He closes his eyes for a brief moment as if summoning patience from some hidden place and leans into me further. "The question is *why*? Why do you *lie*?"

"Because." I force my hands to stop shaking in his.

"Why do you lie?" he asks in a gentle, seductive tone.

"I lie because that's what I do." I steal an uneven breath between clenched teeth. I can't even look at him. Instead, I glance over his shoulder looking for gravity's center. Guilt and remorse for lying to him from the very start overtake me. "Because it's easier." I wince but can't really find the courage to say anything more. "I'm sorry?" It comes out as a question instead of an apology.

"Are you? It doesn't sound like it." He laughs low.

It's sexy, and it's infuriating at the same time.

We don't say anything for what seems like an eternity. We just stare at each other. Our breaths seem to match up after a few minutes.

"What is it with girls in high school and older guys?"

"Would you like most girls' version or mine?"

"Yours."

I exhale slowly. "It's easier. I don't like…complications. Commitment. Relationships. Older guys seem to get that."

"You mean older guys are willing to put up with your shit," he says softly.

I look up at him a little taken aback by his sudden change in attitude. Now he sounds pissed.

"It's not like that." My voice shakes. I cringe because I sound needy and uncertain.

"Look, baby," he says with an edge to his voice. "I—"

"Don't. Call. Me. *Baby*. Ever."

"You didn't seem to mind three weeks ago."

"What? I don't remember *you* using that particular term of endearment with me. Maybe it was with someone *else*." I glare up at him in the dark. "I don't like it. I never have," I pause while my swirls around with thoughts of Nika and the way she was behaving at his game. "Come to think of it; I don't remember much about what took place with you all of three weeks ago. *It's long forgotten*. Believe me; I'm just trying to be nice here."

"Well," he says, drawing in a long breath. "It's nice to know that Charlie was at least telling me the truth when he said you are a real piece of work."

"Charlie said that?" I ask, incredulous. "He…he broke Marla's heart. Then he proceeded to flaunt his relationships with every other girl at Paly that he had taken up with, including my sister Holly, before her or after her, I can't remember. Flaunting every relationship in her face until he finally left for UCLA. And now he's back again—messing with her mind all over again and getting engaged to her out of the blue like this and making promises he surely can't keep. Yet, he has the nerve to call me out for my less than stellar, perhaps some would say, unsavory behavior with guys? Wow. Just wow. I've heard enough. Go back to your party."

"From what I've been able to figure out," he says slowly. "It's Marla and Charlie's engagement party, not mine. I agree that they are rushing things but Marla's great and Charlie's great. We can all be friends. I have every right to be standing here just as much as you do. We're *friends*—you and me." He gets this victorious smile. It gleams at me in the dark.

"Friends?" I practically spit the word back at him. My chest heaves as I struggle to catch my breath again. This conversation has upset me on a number of levels that I haven't even begun to fully realize yet. I fight for breath and control. "Friends," I say again with more contempt. "Like you and Nika Vostrikova are friends?"

"What? How do you? When did you?"

He gives up on words and shakes his head and blows out his breath in exasperation.

I want this to end this thing with him but for some inexplicable reason, I have to know about Nika, how he feels about Nika. "I saw her with you at your game three weeks ago when you pitched. She was on one side of the fence, and you were on the other. She was *kissing* your fingers."

"The Oregon State game? You were there?" He looks taken aback.

"Yes. My dad had tickets, and my little brother Tommy begged him to go and so the three of us went. I saw you with her, Linc, up at the fence. It looked like you were *good friends*. And that's what she told me later on, when we happened to meet up in the women's restroom. She wanted to ensure that I knew that you were *good friends*."

He sighs deep. I've hit a nerve and the prickling sensation races up my spine again. *I'm still jealous. This is an impossible situation. We both know it. And I'm jealous. And it's pathetic.*

I hang my head, and my hair falls forward covering my face. I take shallow breaths in an attempt to control my breathing, to get a grip, and keep these confounding tears at bay. *What is wrong with me?* I need to get as far away from this guy as humanly and cosmically possible. We should not be in the same air space. *He drives me crazy.*

Then he reaches out and tucks my hair behind my ear and fingers my jaw line. For some reason, my head automatically lifts. He gets this apologetic face. "She was more than a friend for a while but that's *over*. She knows it. Nika is…complicated. We met when we took a statistics class together. She's just finishing up at Stanford and puts together my stats from my games. She's does freelance work. Computer research? She's smart as hell—"

"Tall. Beautiful. Russian. Sexy. Smart. Yeah, I got *that*."

"Nika doesn't lie about who she is. She puts it all out there."

"Well, good for you—for the two of you. It's so important to have friends like that so you can freely take advantage of all those benefits whenever you feel the need. How nice for both of you." I bite at my lip to keep myself from saying more. I sound like a jealous girlfriend; and I know he hears it because he gets this little smile. In that moment, I want to slap him and ensure it permanently disappears from his face. "I think we're done here."

"You know what your problem is, Tally? You won't let anybody in."

There's this quiet fury in his voice that has me looking at him more intently. His jaw flexes with tension, and he clenches his teeth together. His eyes narrow at me. He sighs deep.

"So, *please* answer my question: Why is that? Why do you lie like that? I'd really like to know. I mean, I know you don't give a shit that you could have a direct impact upon my life or my career; because how would it look to the world if anyone were to find out that this almost twenty-three-year-old, who is about to sign with the Los Angeles Angels, just recently slept with a minor? Yeah, he slept with some girl still in high school who may not even be eighteen yet. Jesus, Tally! Think about *that* the next time you set up shop in somebody's house and seduce the hell out of him and have the nerve to leave behind some damn thank-you note to further drive your point home that all it was to you was a complete and total mindfuck or fuck over. Take your pick, little girl, whichever term suits you best. Maybe it's both. Who the fuck knows? Am I right? Because you…you don't even care what you do to the people you run over that happen to be in your way."

He's really mad.

And like an accelerant added to a fire, my fury has risen exponentially with every word he's uttered. All I can see are flames. My car. *Holly.* My mind goes somewhere else even as I quietly say, "I turn eighteen in a few weeks. You're safe. I won't tell anyone. Thank you, Linc. Thank you so much for the advice. But I have other places to be. Go find Nika for all I care. It looks like she is more than willing to entertain you." I gasp at the air now, struggling for breath.

All I remember is opening the car door and falling to the ground. I hear Holly say, "Run!" But, nothing moves. I can't move.

It was this kind of emotional outburst that triggered the last panic attack with this guy, three weeks ago, but I press on, even though it's become a struggle just to get the words out and to breathe at the same time. "Maybe next time you can check for ID before you fuck somebody just to ensure they're really deserving of you and your particular brand of charm if you know what I mean. Ensure they're a good friend. The best kind. A good friend with benefits. Like Nika!"

My vision gets wacky. There is less light and more darkness streaking across my vision.

The darkness closes in on me even faster.

"I. Can't. Breathe."

"Hold on." I think I hear him say.

<hr />

I come to on top of Lincoln Presley's bed under very different circumstances from three weeks before when the same thing happened to me while I was with him. Marla's face is about eight inches from mine on one side while Linc comes at me from the other. Even Charlie Masterson gets in on the act offering up a glass of orange juice as soon as I try to sit up.

"Here, try this," Charlie says, shoving his way past Linc and handing me the full glass of juice.

"Back off," Marla says like the true mother hen she is. "Tally, are you okay? God, I was freaking out when I saw Linc carrying you in here. What the hell happened?" She shoots Linc a daggered look. "Did he hurt you?"

Yes.

"No." I shake my head side-to-side for added emphasis but then the confounded dizziness returns. I take a few swigs of the orange juice and abruptly turn off the calorie counter that automatically starts up in my mind. "No, we're fine. We've agreed. It's just best to be…friends. Right, Elvis?"

Lincoln Presley looks like he just got hit in the chest by a wayward baseball. He takes a jagged breath. "Right. That's what we decided. We're friends. Just friends." He frowns at me, drops my hand, gets up from the bed, and leaves his bedroom without another word.

"What did you *do* to him?" Charlie asks in an accusatory tone. "He really likes you, Tally." Charlie runs his hands through his blond hair and looks extremely unhappy.

"Now, that would be a real mistake; wouldn't it?" I say with derision. "He's got his whole life ahead of him. Why would he want to get involved with someone like me? You warned him about me; right, Charlie?"

I've forgotten Marla is privy to this conversation. In my still seething rage, I forgot this little detail.

"What?" she asks, incredulous all at once. "Charlie? You warned Linc about Tally? Why would you do that? It's so…cruel. She's my best friend. She's been through so much." Tears trail down her face. "You jerk! Damn it, Charlie. I thought you'd changed, but you're the exact same prick you were over two years ago. And, you're lying to me. Even now. About everything."

I slide off the bed in one less than graceful swoop. "Enough. Don't you two break up over someone as unimportant as me."

"Tally, never say that!" Marla's fuming mad now. I can see it in her face. She grabs my hand and pulls me along Linc's hallway. "Come on. Let's go. We shouldn't have come."

No truer words have ever been spoken.

We reach the great room. He's standing there looking completely devastated. It's disconcerting. It's not supposed to go like this.

Things have spun out of control in a matter of thirty minutes and wielded emotional damage in so many directions in all four of us that it's almost unbelievable. I can't quite bring myself to reconcile it now, because deep down there's this part of me that anticipated this kind of ending. I *need* this kind of ending in fact.

"I love you, Marla," Charlie says from behind us. "I want to marry you. Build a life with you. I know you're going off to New York to pursue your dream. Just know that I'll wait for you. I'll wait for you always." His voice breaks.

I turn and spy the tears in Charlie's eyes. It's hard to watch. I cringe while Marla makes this guttural sound next to me. In the next moment, she wipes at her face with her free hand. I extricate myself from her firm grip and gently push her in Charlie's direction and start for the front door, alone.

"Tally, I'm sorry," Linc says.

His sincerity stops me. I turn back and look at him feeling both helpless and completely lost at the same time for a few precious seconds.

"I wouldn't lie to you, Tally."

I recoil backward at his words and concentrate solely on the steady pulsating movement at his throat without looking directly at his face. "I'm sorry I lied to you," I finally say. "I shouldn't have done that. Lied to you like that. That first night. Holly, my twin sister, we…"

I take a minute to better compose myself. *Best to get this over with. Clean break. All that jazz.* I look past his right shoulder in a valiant attempt to keep it together.

"We used to play this game when we were feeling out of sorts in a strange situation or circumstance. It wasn't intentional…until it was." I look straight at him and start to get this rueful smile regretting my behavior and all the lies. "The point was to be Holly that night, to be charming and fun and nice, like she always was." I shake my head back and forth. "That's not really who I am. I'm not…any of those things." I glance over at Charlie and Marla. "Charlie knows. He's right, too. I'm not any of those things."

"I think you are," Linc says.

He starts to cross the room, but I hold up my hands out in front of me and gesture for him to stop. I nod slowly as if I'm taking a practiced cue for my next solo performance.

"My name is Tally. Tally Landon. That much is true." I catch my lower lip between my teeth and look at him more closely.

He waits. He has this little smile as if he's certain how things will work out.

He's not afraid of the joy, but he should be.

He's not afraid of me, but he should be.

"Don't be so afraid," he says from across the room as if reading my thoughts. He gets this vexed look. "Trust me. We can work this out. Somehow." He sounds a little uncertain.

I need to finish this thing. Heartless Tally finally shows up. *Where have you been, girl?* "Linc, I can't do this. It's not a good idea. It's not what I want." Apprehension rolls in on me as my voice begins to shake as much as my body conveying the exact opposite to what I'm saying to him.

"Endings are inevitable." I shrug my shoulders in an attempt to appear nonchalant, casual, and cool. *Or is it cruel?* "Am I the only one that believes this here?" I force myself to laugh. My lips quiver with the effort. I swipe at a wayward tear and stare at my wet hand suddenly unsure as to where it came from. "I. Cant. Lose. Anyone. Else. Wonderland doesn't last, Elvis," I say with such sadness that I think all three of them might start to cry now. "This isn't supposed to be so hard. This is the easy part. But you…you make it hard and complicated. Two things I don't need…or want."

I start toward the front door and Marla and Charlie, who are in each other's arms now. It's almost unbearable to watch. I've got to take back some semblance of control. However, I can find it. I turn back from the door.

"You're a great guy, Linc. It's been fun. Take care of yourself. Congratulations on your deal with the Angels." I sound dismissive, sincere, and completely in control. I turn towards Marla. "I'll catch you later. Go celebrate with the parents." I give her the wave-off signal that means text me later when you're on your own.

And, I leave.

This burst of adrenaline carries me down the front steps and directly across the Masterson's massive backyard. My mind races to catch up with my fast-moving legs. There was a different gate entrance on the other side of this property that I suddenly recall seeing the first time Linc and walked back here. It's more hidden than the normal one everyone else uses. I find it, unlatch it, and scale the neighbor's adjoining fence within the next twenty seconds. All the running I've been inadvertently doing in the past three weeks to forget about the first and last amazing encounter with Lincoln Presley pays off. Linc calls my name from the far side of the property at the opposite end of it. *I've escaped. He isn't going to be able to find me in time.* Relief courses through me because this is what I want. This is what I need.

I take off the strappy sandals which free me up to fun faster along the darkened path. I easily sprint away from the turmoil and the heartbreak. I'm numb to it all. I feel somewhat unscathed. I'm home in a matter of ten minutes after having taken the back streets through the upscale neighborhoods at double-time, until I reach the familiar streets of mine. I sigh with relief when I finally see my darkened house where my parents predictably wallow around inside. It's the most welcome sight I can think of for once.

Yes. Endings are inevitable. And I've made sure of this one with Lincoln Presley. Yes. Yes, I have.

CHAPTER FOURTEEN

Linc ~Day into night

WE PUT IN A FEW MORE hours of celebration with the parents. Marla encourages me to give Tally some time. She stays to ensure that I do. The party revived enough to celebrate my draft news. My publicist and family friend Kimberley Powers seemed satisfied enough with what she heard about the contract offer and left shortly after promising we'd get an early start in the morning. She warned me that there would be more interviews and photo ops with the local press and to be prepared for it all. My agent breathed a continuous sigh of relief and promised to go over the entire contract in detail tomorrow mid-morning before I sign. I heard it all, responded to most of it, although my own thoughts remained strictly centered upon Tally Landon. She knew about Nika. I'd glossed over Nika. I wasn't exactly forthcoming about Nika. I still can't believe I didn't see Tally at my game a few weeks ago. The fight we had tonight leaves me unsettled. *I owe her an explanation. An apology. Something.*

Conflict. Avoidance. All I want to do is go hit a few baseballs and work out the uncertainty and rejection that Tally has just unceremoniously shoved upon my psyche, but Charlie and Marla convince me to hang out with them, when later we back walk over to the guest house when the Stones finally go home, and my dad and aunt and uncle go to bed. It's painful to watch the two of them be around each other even more than I thought it would be. They hold hands and watch a movie while I slink around and drink a little too much Jack Daniel's for all three of us.

It's during a break in the action of the second film they've started, after Charlie goes out to get Marla some ice cream, she insists she need, that she finally comes over and sits down directly across from me at the kitchen counter. She's checked her iPhone a number of times during the movie, so I know she's communicating with Tally.

"How is she?" I finally ask and then wince at how pathetic I sound.

"She's fine. She's packing because keeping busy is what Tally does when things get too emotionally hard for her. She's complicated." Marla sighs and stretches her long legs, pointing each toe like she's working out the kinks all the way from her feet up to her lovely thighs. She grins at me when she spies me watching her movements so intently. "Look, I'm only going to tell you this because I do think you're a nice guy, and I think you'd be good for Tally. She'd kill me for saying this but somebody needs to say it." She takes a deep breath and holds it for a long moment. "She's not as strong as she comes off. She's been through a lot. Her dancing and the pressures she lives with to perform at that level are immense. And now? With what happened to Holly? They were close." She holds up two fingers and twists them together. "They were as different as night and day, but you know how the night needs the day and vice versa?"

She gets this wistful tone, and I think she's going to cry right then and there. I swallow hard because this was way out of my comfort zone.

What is keeping Charlie anyway? This girl makes me nervous. She's incredibly beautiful with her long blond hair and these amazing eyes and a body that doesn't stop. No wonder Charlie is so into her. And on top of that she seems like a downright angel. She smiles and gets this pink tinge to her lovely face. It travels up her neck to her cheeks when she catches me staring at her again.

"Tally is the night, Linc. She's not normally afraid of anything, except maybe now *you*. Do you understand how talented she is? She's going to go places with her ballet. She's incredible—even Allaire Tremblay believes this. She's better in many respects than even Tremblay was; because Tally stays singularly focused upon her artistic talent. Do you know what I'm trying to say here?"

"I think you're trying to tell me nicely that I need to back off."

"Not exactly." She gets this vexed look. "I don't know about you." She shakes her head side-to-side and then grins. "You have your own stuff; right? Trying to be perfect? Pitch the perfect game? Do you focus on doing that every time you're out there on the mound?" I slowly nod. "Well, Tally does, too. There's a fine balance to it all. It's a unique talent. For both of you. And Charlie and me? We're just privileged to be in the same stratosphere as the two of you and have fun along the way and enjoy the amazing ride to stardom with you both." She laughs. "Anyway, I love Charlie and he loves me. It seems getting engaged seems crazy to everyone else but the two of us. But for us? It's something to build toward, to hold on to. If it's real, it will pass the test of time and distance. I like to believe that's how it works." She gets this faraway look. "Tomorrow is our last night in town. Tally and I are supposed to go to a few summer parties, but I want to spend some time with Charlie. You should spend it with Tally and her family. It's been rough on all of them. You're exactly what she needs, even if she can't see that yet." Marla gets this thoughtful look and eventually nods. "Yes, go see her tomorrow and meet up with her family. It'll be good for both of you."

"Meaning?"

"She's acting very strange these days. Distracted. Moody. She's happy one minute, unhappy the next. If I didn't know better I'd say she's in love for the first time in her life." Marla smiles and then gets this serious look. "Don't break her heart, Linc. Please don't do that."

"I won't."

"Okay," she says. "Here's the Landon's address. They live about a mile from here. I'm beat. It's been quite a day—quite an exhilarating and heady twenty-four hours since Charlie proposed. Just tell my fiancé that I'll see him tomorrow. Congratulations on the baseball contract. The Los Angeles Angels. Wow."

"It'll be a few years before the big leagues. I'll spend most of my time in Salt Lake with their minor league and up and down the West Coast."

"Ah, well, when I'm not so tired you can explain all of that to me again." She yawns. "Long distance relationships," she says. "Nothing like testing love this way; right?"

"Right." Uncertainty must show in my face.

Marla gets this serious look and sighs deep. "So. It was you." All I can do is nod. "She got a bouquet of flowers from some guy who signed his name Elvis. She didn't remember what he looked like other than to say he had dark hair, wore a baseball cap, and had saved her life when he picked her up and took her away from the car before it exploded. That was you."

"Yes."

"The mystery guy who left the flowers and the note card…Elvis?" I nod again. "She pretty much tries to block all of that out because it's too painful for her." Marla gets this thoughtful look. "She focuses upon her ballet in total. I think it keeps her from falling apart altogether. Look, she broke three ribs and her wrist in that car accident, sustained a concussion, and they didn't know if she would walk again. They couldn't explain much of that. She would have died without being able to dance. That's how she's wired. Ballet is her life. Her entire focus. She walked out of that hospital and wrapped her broken ribs tight enough to dance as soon as she physically could. For Holly. For herself." Marla takes a deep breath. "Her parents have fallen apart, and

Tally has had to soldier on for their sake, for her little brother Tommy's, for me—all of us. Ballet is about all she believes in and I'm all she's got. Well, you too, I guess." She shakes her head side-to-side. "She doesn't drive anymore because it freaks her out too much because—as you must know—she was driving that day.

Marla pauses and takes an unsteady breath while I hold mine. "Holly's funeral was attended by the entire high school. Hundreds of Paly high schoolers attended that day all of us questioning how life can go on without Holly." Marla sighs. "But it does go on, doesn't it? It's hard to believe, but it does. And some of us spend each day just ensuring we don't drown in the sadness. *Tally.*" She looks at me hard. "The panic attacks…she hides them well, but how many have you seen?"

"Two."

"Shit. I'll try to keep a closer watch on her. She can't be upset like this. It's too scary. I'm afraid something bad is going to happen to her when she has one, and what happens if none of us are there with her?"

I don't say anything because I don't have an answer for that and the thought of Tally suffering alone with one scares me, too.

Marla looks sad for a moment and shakes her head. "Holly was the epitome of everything good. So, if Tally was busy personifying her that night, don't ever forget why that was." She hesitates. "It gave her a little break from the pain she still carries. Tally's just trying to find herself in a world that she doesn't really feel she should exist in anymore. Occasionally, she'll say something like that because what is the night without the day?" She swipes a hand at her face to clear away the tears and tries to smile.

I grab her free hand and squeeze it between my thumb and finger. "Thank you for telling me. What can I do?"

Marla slips off the bar chair and heads for the front door. "Give her some of your time, Elvis. Go see her tomorrow. She'll say she doesn't like it—*you,* but she does." She gets this secret smile. "Wait up for Charlie. He's bringing back ice cream. See you around. Good luck with the baseball stuff. You're going to do great."

"Are you always such a cheerleader?"

"Have to be," she says with a little laugh.

And then she's gone.

⁂

Charlie sails into the guest house holding up the container of ice cream up in triumph. Then he looks around the great room in a barely veiled panic.

"Where's Marla?"

"She left?" I shake my head at him. "She said she will see you tomorrow."

"She's great, isn't she?" Charlie's smiling like he's won in Vegas. The guy is seriously gone over this girl, even if he thought he could only love Holly Landon. "Marla is the one for you," I say slowly. "But, dude, are you really ready to get married?" I frown not completely on board with the whole commitment thing.

"We'll work it out," he says with a laugh. "We will. I'll be in med school after next year. She'll do the ballet thing for a while, and then she'll miss me so much that she'll come to L.A. and be with me. We'll get married in a couple of years. Marla's cool with that plan."

"Does Marla *know* about that plan?"

"Not all of it. Some of it." He looks uneasy all at once and then frowns.

"I'm just not sure what I'm supposed to do now about Tally," I admit with a hesitant laugh and tell him about Marla's suggestion.

"So, you're going to go see her tomorrow. She'll come around *eventually*. At least I think she will." Charlie goes behind the kitchen counter and retrieves two huge soup spoons from the drawer. "But first, we're going to finish this ice cream, and soon we'll head back to L.A., and you'll sign your major-league contract with the Angels, and I'm going to finish at UCLA and go to med school and eventually marry Marla." He grins. "Besides, just think, a year from now? The world will look and be a lot different. We'll be older. *They'll* be older. *Thank God.* And I'm going to seriously get my act together and so are you."

"My act *is* together," I say irritably.

"Dude, you're more messed up than I am." He laughs. "I mean Tally Landon is seriously out of your league. At least Marla loves me back."

"You don't mean to crush all of my hopes and dreams; do you?" I ask only half in jest.

Charlie has a serious point. He has a relationship with Marla—a future. I am pretty much holding on to nothing, but a connection that I may have all but imagined with a girl who doesn't want commitment, encumbrances of any kind, and who tends to suffer from panic attacks every time we spend any length of time together. I have nothing to go on here really, except my belief in this girl, myself, and baseball. It isn't exactly a stable start for any kind of future relationship, as a friend or otherwise. *I can barely breathe.*

"I didn't mean it quite like that."

"Stop talking."

The night and day analogy stays with me. I just need time to figure out what all Marla meant by it. Could I be the daylight in Tally's life? That's what I decide the blond angel must have meant by that reference.

Day into night. It can serve as my new mantra.

Idealistic now, I decide I just need to dedicate my time and attention to this gifted dancer of a girl and show her in some way that there doesn't have to be an ending of us at all.

CHAPTER FIFTEEN

Tally ~ Promises made, kept, then broken

*I*T'S OUR LAST NIGHT HOME AND Marla and I have already decided that the best way to say good-bye all at once to all of our friends that we're leaving behind is to attend one last party together.

I'm in my room putting on my usual attire—black jeans and a T-shirt when my mom shows up in the doorway. She gives me the once-over, incredulous, *you're-wearing-that?-why-can't-you-put-a-dress-on?* look that only a mom can.

"You and Marla are headed out?"

There's so much angst and disappointment in that simple question.

Just for a while," I say soothingly although I remain pissed at her. I've been pissed off at her for months. Instead of looking at her, I concentrate on the mirror and put the finishing touches of mascara on my lashes.

"Your dad will be home soon. I thought we could spend your last night all together. With you. I mean you'll be with Marla all summer. Maybe into the fall with the internship..."

A whining complaint from my mother about missing me? Say it isn't so.

"Tremblay told you about that, huh," I say in flat voice. My mom has been so out of it that I'm surprised she even knows I'm leaving for New York tomorrow, let alone that the summer session could morph into being invited to the winter term at SAB or the coveted internship with NYC Ballet. She nods and looks anxious.

"It's just for the summer," I add quickly. "We might not get into the winter term. I probably won't get the internship."

"You will," she says emphatically.

"Mom, what's going on?" The woman has barely said ten words to me all these months. We pass each other in the hallway with contrived waves and forced smiles. I arranged for the housecleaning service and meals to be delivered because my mother has been sorely lacking in the ability to function in any capacity whatsoever—beyond a brokenhearted one—for months. I frown. *Anger. Remorse. Bitterness. Rage.* All these emotions assail me. Dear Mom hasn't been here for any of the shit going down around here. I *have.* But I really do worry how it's going to be around here when I'm gone. Yet I'd go bat shit crazy if I had to stay.

"I'm just going to miss you so much." Her eyes get watery.

She is the exact replica of me. Well, *me* of *her.* I take solace in the fact that I resemble her so much and that when I'm older, I'll still look more than halfway decent. Maybe, even as good as her when I can eat properly again and gain a few pounds without anyone noticing. Her dark long hair has the same kind of wave and texture to it as mine. Her eyes are this amazing green. 'Jaded and green' she used to say and would always laugh. She doesn't laugh anymore. I never really did. That was Holly's thing. Holly and my mother Tessa's thing. *Me?* I was this strange little replica that mirrored their physical traits but none of their amazing vitality. I've been too concentrated on ballet to care about anything or anyone else. Remorse swells up inside of me. *I'm not the good daughter.*

"Mom, it's going to be okay." I look at her closely. "Someday. You have Dad. I'll be a phone call away. I'll be with Marla so you don't have to worry about me. I'll be fine. This is something…this is something I have to do. Believe me, it would be a whole lot easier to stay…easier than you think, actually. I'm going to miss you guys like crazy, too. It's just…this is something I have to do. I have to see if I can make it."

"I know. And, *you will.* I know that. It's just, well, Tally, please take care of yourself and don't be so hard on yourself. And *eat something* and *have fun* and make mistakes because as we all know now…life is short and it can be taken away so suddenly. Just tell me that you'll try to be happy."

I'm speechless by what she's just said. *Happy? This* prophetic ideology comes from a woman who has effectively shut herself off from the world. I'm sure the irony of her words must show on my face. She gets this twisted smile and frowns slightly. "I realize that I have no right to expect you to be happy since I've been such a colossal failure at it."

I let the words hang there for a moment between us. "I'll try to be happy… if you try to slow down on the drinking," I finally say.

"Deal," she says with a slight nod. "Yes, I can agree to that." She bites at her lower lip. "Your dad will be happy about that promise, too."

"Good."

The doorbell rings.

Marla.

My mother breezes out of the room which seems so unlike her. She's surprisingly intent on answering the door for me when I tell her it'll be Marla. I stare across at the space she's just vacated, stunned by her almost bordering-on-cheerful exit, because it is so unlike her—answering the door, breezing to do so—after all these months and after what she's just promised me. I actually need a minute or two to recover from it all. I'm taken aback that she knows that I know she has a drinking problem. I'm relieved she wants to admit to it and possibly deal with it. My dad and I have had a few conversations. I showed him the black Sharpie marks I made on the Grey Goose vodka bottle weeks before. I told him again a few weekends ago that someone needed to be watching over Mom. He'd gotten this weird almost guilty look and promised he'd take better care of her especially now that I was leaving.

I strain to hear the stranger's voice coming from downstairs. *It's not Marla's. It's a guy's voice.* And it's only a good ten seconds before my mother and this unknown person stomp up the stairs and make their knowable presence down the hallway just outside my room.

"Tally, you have a visitor," Mom says in this singsong voice from the open doorway.

I don't even have time to pick up the castoff clothes from the half-dozen blouses I tried on earlier after finally settling on the standard uniform of T-shirt and jeans in my customary black. I'm already half-prepared to have the usual fashion argument with Marla about my clothing choice. I turn around with my hands on my hips in a battle-like stance and open my mouth to start it. But, of course, it isn't Marla standing behind my beautiful mother; it's Lincoln Presley. He hangs his head a little and gives me this sheepish *I-know-I-shouldn't-be-here-but-just-go-with-it* look.

My normal penchant for fury deserts me and for a second or two, I'm at a complete loss for words.

I finally say, "Mom, this is—"

"I *know* who it is, sweetie. Lincoln Presley. We just met. Downstairs." She gives Linc this wide welcoming smile. "Tally's talked so much about you."

And you wonder where the ability to finesse a lie comes from?

My mother gives me one of these implicit looks that implies *we-will-so-be-talking-about-this-later.*

Linc has said all of two words since he walked into my bedroom. "Hi, Tally."

A loaded salutation if there ever was one.

"I didn't know you two were friends," my mother says sounding mildly accusing.

I wince. How do I explain Lincoln Presley to my mother?

He's this guy I hooked up with three weeks ago. Yeah. That's him. That is all it was, Mom.

That explanation really isn't going to fly. It doesn't even sound right to me for once.

"We are. Just *friends*, Mom." I look over at Linc with a raised eyebrow. "He's on his way back to L.A.; I thought you were gone—on your way by now, Prez." I seem to remember Charlie calling him *Prez,* and it seems like a guy thing—*a platonic friend thing*—to call him.

Meanwhile, my mom gets this secret smile and proceeds to carry on this innocuous little conversation with Linc. It catches me off guard. I'm just staring at her for a few brief seconds because I don't even recognize this woman who is talking and smiling and nodding as if she doesn't have a care in the world. It's been months. *Months.*

Then I realize she's giving me a golden opportunity to get the room and myself in order so I do my best to hide my anxiety level and grab my castoff clothes from the floor and hastily toss them into one corner of the room. My mom turns on the Tessa Landon charm, which has been long absent and effectively captivates Linc's undivided attention, while I scramble around my bedroom like a mad woman and attempt to figure this whole thing out starting with: *What the hell is he doing here?*

After another indeterminable five minutes, my mom excuses herself to rustle up cookies and refreshments for all of us. Two terms she hasn't used ever and two things she's very unlikely to find in our kitchen right now, unless Linc thinks she's referring to stale bread and vodka. I tell him this as soon as she closes my bedroom door when I think she's far enough down the hall. Bad, heartless Tally talking like this about her mother. Linc gets this confused look while I retreat a few steps back from him. I'm intent on distance and forgiveness—from God, Holly, and my mother—for being such a bitch and revealing this particular family secret in the last ten seconds to him. I shouldn't be telling this guy any of these things. *Why am I?* I take a deep breath and settle upon a different tactic.

"How do you know where I live? What are you doing here? Why are you here?" All three questions leave my mouth in quick succession.

"Marla told me," he says patiently. "Because I had to see you. Because we need to talk." He gets this beguiling almost defiant look. "Where would you like to start?"

"What the hell is Marla doing telling you where I live?" I ask intent on ignoring that look of his. He sighs a little. I feel a little guilty for starting the conversation off at such an inquisition level. "Sorry." I take a deep breath. "Hi, Elvis." I force a sweet smile. "What. Are. You. Doing. *Here?*"

Now he laughs a little. *That's more like it.* I smile for real this time.

"I leave for L.A. tomorrow. I changed my flight. Talked to Charlie, got Marla's number. Found out her plans and changed them up a little. I thought that maybe we could be friends. You said we could. Last time."

"What?" I hold my breath and let it out slowly. *Think, Tally.* "I leave for New York. Tomorrow. Afternoon."

"Great. We'll be at the airport at the same time. That's what I worked out with Marla."

"What's with you and Marla?"

"We're friends."

"What?" I ask, incredulous. "Like you and I are friends?" I blush, recalling our very first encounter. "Because that's going to get mighty crowded. All of us being friends like this. It seems like you have enough *friends*."

Nika invariably comes to mind, and I'm instantly pissed at myself because I'm thinking of her and the inevitable jealousy that follows. *Again.* I sweep my arm across the room, and he follows my arm movements and slowly smiles.

"Don't make it complicated."

He brazenly looks around my bedroom. I cringe a little when he spies my green cap and gown from two days ago hanging up on my closet door. He reaches into his pocket and brings out a little gift box. A small little gift box. It's ring size. I look at him suspiciously—prepared to launch into all kinds of questions and accusations. *Something.*

"Don't freak out quite yet. It's nothing really. Just a little something for your graduation. I didn't know about it, and so I thought I should take care of that now. Since, you know, we're friends and all."

"Do you know you get this little southern accent sometimes? Where does that come from?" I ask while attempting to disarm all these uneasy feelings spinning through me even as I unwrap the red ribbon from his little white gift box.

"My mom was from Georgia. We used to visit my grandparents there for years every summer. I picked up a little of an accent from those summers at least some of the time. *Why? Does it bother you?*"

"No." I stare at the charm inside the box. It's this little golden sun. "No."

"I know you can't wear it much of the time because of your dancing. The *no-jewelry-you'll-impale-yourself* kind of thing. I'm sure Allaire Tremblay has all kinds of rules about that."

I nod and look over at him still wary. Enough for both of us.

"Yes, she does." I swallow hard. *How does he remember Tremblay's name? How does he know so much about me?* All the remaining lies I've told him have unraveled right in front of us at the point. He gets this little smile like he already knows that, too. Then I scrutinize his gift—this little golden sun charm.

"I guess it's kind of impractical from that standpoint," he says, getting this weird, hopeful look. "But I thought of you when I saw it. So, I thought—"

"I remind you of the *sun?*" He looks a little surprised by the scorn so obvious in my tone. My face gets hot. I'm sure there's some kind of hidden meaning with the gift that I'm just failing to get.

"No," he says gently. "It's supposed to remind you of *me*. Wait. There's more."

He looks thoughtful for a moment and then reaches into his other pocket and pulls out a silver bracelet with more charms attached. He does the clasp around my left wrist before I can protest.

I carefully examine the various charms there while he's clasps the sun one into place and commands me to stay still. There's a baseball and bat in platinum. There's a silver moon with a little smiley face and a gold star. There's a gold heart separated into two halves that fit together when you hold them a certain way, which he promptly demonstrates. I'm busy trying to register what it all means and fighting off all these incredulous feelings of gratitude because it's basically one of the best gifts I've ever gotten when my mom reappears.

"Oh my," she says with a little laugh. "What is this?"

"A graduation gift," I say, suddenly feeling uneasy. "Elvis, you shouldn't have." I glare at him.

"You call him *Elvis?*" My mother asks with a little laugh. "I love that. That's so sweet, so…" This little hint of sorrow travels across my mom's features. I know it reminds her of Holly because it's something my twin would have said. "Tally," she says gently. "What a wonderful gift."

"I thought I would take her out to dinner on her last night in town but I don't want to take her away from you and Mr. Landon. We could all go."

I'm looking at him and then at my mom in complete bewilderment. I helplessly watch as the two of them exchange these strange, knowing glances, like they've known each other for a decade, and openly share the burden of being personally acquainted with all of my most unlovable qualities.

"I have plans with Marla," I say. "Lest, there be any doubt about what I'm doing tonight."

"Tally." My mother adopts the gentle, scolding tone in just saying my name.

"No. Those got canceled. Lest, there be any doubt, you're with me," Linc says with such amazing confidence that I could slap him, but then he gets this amazing smile, and I'm momentarily bewitched by it.

My mom studies him intently as if he is the last man on earth and some kind of god besides. I've got my hands full with just these two in the same room when I hear my dad call us from downstairs. *Great.*

We sail down the stairs. Well, Lincoln Presley and my mother sail down the stairs, arm-in-arm.

I haven't seen my mom act this happy in a long time. There's a part of me that is seriously reluctant to disrupt the strange dynamics taking place between the two of them on any level. Savoring the moment, I trail behind them a good five feet and attempt to contemplate my next move; because, clearly, this is going to get out of hand, and I need to be ready.

Linc is shaking hands with my dad, who is still completely enamored with Lincoln Presley already, and proceeds to tell him he's met him briefly once before at the Stanford versus Oregon State game during his long stint in the autograph-signing line waiting for the baseball star to sign Tommy's glove. Before I can even steer the conversation back in the right direction and remind them all that I have plans with Marla and Linc really needs to go, the guy is telling my mom and dad that he brought steaks for the grill, and he's prepared to make dinner for all of us. That he wants to. *Here.*

My mom openly sighs because *I know* she was just being polite earlier about even considering the possibility of going out dinner with Linc and me. Because as we all know, except for the baseball player, she hasn't exactly left the house in months. My dad is busy offering Linc a beer which he judiciously declines. We all settle in on the offer of sodas within two minutes at the lovely Tessa Landon's suggestion. My dad and I exchange glances but even Linc seems okay with the idea of drinking diet soda to keep my mom on track for the evening.

I take a breath because I've been holding it again. *For obvious reasons.*

Ten minutes later, Linc is out on our back deck grilling steaks while my mom and dad are rushing around clearing the patio table since we haven't used it since last year; because, *oh yeah, my sister died and the world literally stopped at the Landon house. It's impossible to explain. It really is.*

"What are you doing?" I ask guardedly as soon as my parents go back inside to get the rest of the stuff.

He's standing over the grill, tending to the steaks like he's taking care of a newborn child. I'm taking advantage of the opportunity—now that we're alone—to chastise him properly for this ambush of me and subsequently, my parents. Thank God, Tommy is spending the night at his best friend's house. My little brother would be beside himself at the thought of the Lincoln Presley in our house because now he is a huge lifetime fan of said star pitcher.

"I'm grilling steaks."

"What are you doing *here* grilling steaks for me and my parents?" This is so not okay—what he's doing.

My parents *like* him. They're practically in love with him already. *This is not good at all.*

"I thought we were friends. I guess, since you said we could be friends; I thought we could start that up before you left for New York. I wanted to give you your charm bracelet. And frankly, Tally, I like your parents. You really should spend your last night with them and me. You'll see Marla all summer, whereas you won't see your parents or me that entire time." He smiles wide, pleased with himself that he's got it all figured out. He rewards me with this *determined-to-win* look while I shake my head at him.

"I believe I said we could be friends before the fight at the guest house front door where I essentially told you—*warned you* might be a better description— that I don't do relationships. And you have a lot of *friends* already."

He looks disenchanted with what I've said. "How many?" he finally asks. "How many *friends* have you had?"

"Oh." I'm stalled out. This could get messy but my mind already starts to do the tabulations. My face gets hot and the heat spreads downward to my neck. He's looking at me intently now. I shrug. "How many innings are there in a baseball game?"

"Nine. *Why?*" Then he lets out a deep sigh as he begins to understand what I'm getting at. "*Nine* friends?" He looks incredulous.

Now I decide to mess with him. "How many games have you pitched?"

"Don't mess with me, Tally." He looks decidedly unhappy.

It appears the whole Nika thing has run its course with me. I don't feel as threatened by her anymore. I laugh nervously. "How many for you?"

"Before you?" he asks.

Stalling.

I roll my eyes.

"Easy. Four. I've been pretty focused on baseball," he says.

"Longest relationship ever?" I ask.

"Two years in high school. She dumped me for my best friend. We weren't friends after that."

"All right. My actual number is seven. Not as high as you imagined, right?"

"You're younger than me," he says miserably and then looks at me intently. "How long was your longest relationship?"

Oh. He's backed me into a corner now. I take my time in answering and watch as he turns the steaks and then still waits patiently for my answer. I'm reminded of Marla. "I've never had one—a relationship," I finally say. "Honestly. That's the truth," I say hastily at his questioning look.

"I told you, I don't *do* relationships. I've never really trusted anyone that way before."

We stare at each other, clearly assessing and weighing one another for just about everything.

"Don't you have a game or something? Isn't it baseball season somewhere?" I ask softly.

"I signed some stuff today. Uniforms and a workout for the press are in store for tomorrow. I've got some press conference and a photo-op with the local hometown press with Kimberley. Then it's back to L.A. with Kimberley. She's a friend of the family. My dad's publicist and now mine. We're friends. Real friends. She used to go out with my brother Elliott years ago." His voice breaks after he says this. I'm caught off-guard by his unexpected emotion.

"Elliott. Your brother?"

"He died. In a car accident along with my mom. Eight years ago. I don't usually—"

"Talk about it," I say, finishing the sentence for him. I study his face. Sadness reverberates from him. "I'm sorry about your mom and your brother."

"Yeah. It's tough."

He glances over at my mom and dad who both traipse through the back door carrying supplies. When I hear my mom actually laugh, I turn to savor this sweet sound and get a glimpse of her serene face. It's an unexpected gift. Lincoln Presley is full of surprises. He's like this living glimpse of Wonderland eliciting all these small miracles all around us.

My dad comes over to check on the steaks and us. "So, Linc, don't you have a game tomorrow? Regionals?" he asks.

Exactly, Dad. I flash my dad a grateful smile.

"I gave up my scholarship with the Cardinal a few months ago before the season started so there wouldn't be a conflict of interest. It's not been made public everywhere yet, sir; but I've signed with the Los Angeles Angels. They flew in with the contract this morning, and I leave for L.A. tomorrow afternoon and then on to report to their minor-league team in Salt Lake City. According to the coaches, they'd like to see me in the line-up by the end of next week. I'm ready to go."

"Wow. Congratulations. I'm glad about the Angels, but I was really hoping the Giants would come through."

"Me, too. The Giants showed a lot of interest, but I went early, the seventh pick."

"Wow. Congratulations, Linc." My dad shakes Linc's hand and goes in for a guy hug. I'm kind of surprised by the level of enthusiasm. My dad seems to sense my confusion. "Tally, it's a big deal. Your friend here is going to be a superstar—actually already is a superstar. It's incredible. An incredible opportunity. Wow. The Angels. The big leagues. That's amazing, Linc."

"I know, Dad," I say with a little petulance. "He's a great pitcher. I've seen him play."

"The seventh pick is a big deal, Tal," my dad says giving me this stern look.

"Oh, congratulations," I say, turning to Linc. "But I thought you wanted to play for the Giants?"

"I really wanted to play for San Francisco. My dad played for them. The Giants were his preference, too; but, like I said, it goes by team rank and where you go in the draft."

"That's right. You went to Paly. A few years back." My dad runs his hands through his blond hair and gets this contemplative look.

I think he's beginning to go through the age difference between Linc and me that I'm not sure even the baseball player has calculated exactly. I wince at watching my dad make those calculations in age difference. Adam Landon is a handsome guy. And it's so great to see my dad smiling again and watch the stress of the past several months leave his face for a little while. I quickly tabulate that he and Linc are about that same height. *Why am I thinking of that? Why does it matter?*

I get uneasy. What am I doing? I can't like Linc. I can't be involved with anybody. *Stop it, Tally. Stop it, right now.*

"Five years ago. I graduated five years ago from Paly," Linc says, sounding completely apologetic.

Now I can definitely see my dad doing the math.

"Wow. So Tally would have been an eighth-grader when you were a senior."

The statement hangs in the air between all of three of us for a few minutes. I glance down at the ground in embarrassment at all the lies I've told this guy. Linc probably would have talked to me all of five minutes and clearly moved on if he knew I was still seventeen to his twenty-two. He could have picked up some college girl that night instead of me. Or called Nika. Jealousy resurges at that wayward thought.

I glance up and over at Linc and discover that he's watching me closely. He kind of smiles and inclines his head at me. I return it and then scold myself for doing it. *What am I doing? We're just friends.*

My dad watches the exchange between us and slowly nods. "I guess that's the same age as your mother and I." My dad gives me this twisted yet extraordinary look of approval.

"Dad," I say, touching his arm. "We're just friends."

"*Please.* Give your old man a little credit. Okay? Even your mother isn't going to buy *that* story."

My dad inclines his head towards my mom, who is busy setting the table with our better China. Yes, the Landons have three kinds of China: good, better, and best. Holly always liked the better China. It's this intricate sage-green Lilly pattern on white with a silver lining. I'm glad my mom chose it, and I give her a grateful smile as I walk over to help her set it out.

"Truly, Dad. We're just friends. Right, Elvis?" I turn and give Linc a quizzical look, daring him to disagree with me.

Linc gets this defiant look before he turns to look directly at my dad and says, "Sir, I think you should know that I think your daughter is amazing and if being her friend is all I can be then I'll take that. Although I want to be completely honest with you, I want to be more than just friends with your daughter in due time."

In due time? What is he? A lawyer negotiating a deal for me with my father?

"Well, I appreciate your honesty. I really do." My dad sighs, "Tally has a mind of her own. She does things her own way but I can already tell that you understand that about her." My dad laughs and shakes his head side-to-side and leans over towards Linc and says, "Probably more than a lot of the guys that follow her around do."

"Hey, Dad? I'm right over here. I can hear every word you're saying about me."

"Good," he says to me and winks before turning back to Linc again." Tally's one of a kind."

"I know that, sir."

I can't listen anymore. The soul-bearing statement from my father just about does me in. But then my mother picks that moment to drop one of our prized dishes. It crashes to the cement patio and splinters into hundreds of pieces in a single instant and serves as a stark reminder of how fragile life can be. How one moment you're whole; and then in the next, you're shattered. It almost feels like Holly is here and just forcefully pushed the plate from my mother's hands in some cosmic way. My mother—in our newest sphere of normalcy—should have burst into tears, but instead she starts to laugh.

Eventually, we all do. In that powerful few seconds, I know we actually take a step forward in life for the first time since Holly died. *Together.* We effectively breathe as a trio. Although it's a silent communiqué between the Landons, it's the first time in months that we actually have done this together—breathed. It's a miracle that we all quietly acknowledge when we finally manage to look at one another.

All because Lincoln Presley dropped by. Eventually, all four of us smile.

It's a little after ten when my parents finally go upstairs to bed. My heart rate speeds up as soon as I hear their retreating footsteps along the upstairs hallway because I am now essentially alone with Lincoln Presley. He's completely won over my parents and I'm beginning to wonder if that wasn't the entire purpose of his impromptu visit upon us.

For the last ten minutes, he's been strangely quiet and there's this little crevice between his brows as he frowns slightly and then looks over at me with such a palpable intensity. I sit across from him in one of the opposing chairs by the fireplace in the living room. We came in here after my mom served him a second piece of chocolate cake. Up until that point, I'd done a pretty good job of eating everything that was put in put in front of me but I had to draw the line at the chocolate cake. Now I can tell he has a problem with it.

"What?" I finally ask.

You need to eat, Tally."

"I do."

"You need to eat *more*."

"I will."

"Starting when?"

"Tomorrow."

"Funny. You leave for New York, where it's bound to be twice as competitive for you from a dance perspective, and yet you're going to sit there and tell me you'll try when you won't."

"I'm not going to fade away, Elvis. I'll be good."

"How good?" He gets this thoughtful, determined expression.

It becomes clear that we're not talking about chocolate cake or my diet regimen anymore.

"You want to ask me something? Then ask."

I stand up because I'm in dire need of control and power. He's fast because he stands up, too, and grabs my wrists from either side pulling them into his chest. I can feel his heart race.

"I want you to wait for me."

I let his request sink in on me for a few minutes. And for a long while, that's all there is—the two of us breathing. We seem to be taking it all in. Most likely, we're both beginning to wonder where we can actually go from here.

"What does that involve, exactly?" I finally ask, swallowing hard. He's so close I can feel his breath as it stirs my hair. His cologne begins to drive me crazy, and it does all kinds of things to my body from a heat perspective.

"Thank God, my parents are home," I say with a nervous laugh.

"Yeah. Thank God for that."

He dips his head and trails his lips along my jaw line. I think he knows that turns me on. He pulls me into his body, and we are right back to the same kind of moment that started this whole thing between us. It's all the same, except there is no music and what was once a mystery about physical attraction has been explored and duly noted. Sex with Lincoln Presley is definitely a known factor and one I know I will always remember. That thought alone has my heart beating faster. My body starts to move further into his. I'm excited at the memory, even though my mind starts to reject the idea that he affects me at this astonishing level in any way at all. *I want him. He wants me. And my parents are right upstairs.* I take in these jagged deep breaths, gasping for air. It becomes clear that I haven't been…breathing.

"I want you to wait for me," he says against my temple. Then he slowly kisses my forehead and each side of my face as if he's branding me. "I want you to be good. Wait for me. And stay far away from every other guy."

"You want me to be exclusive to you while I'm in New York; and you are God knows where? That's what you're asking of me?" I can barely get the words out. My pulse races out of control now. I've truly forgotten how to breathe.

"Yeah." He takes an unsteady breath because apparently he's been holding his, too. "I know it's a lot to ask but I'm asking anyway. Tally, will you be good? I'm going to be exclusive to you, and I want to ask you to be the same for me."

"Why would I do that?"

I pull away just enough and warily look up at him, trying to discern from his face what he's thinking. He looks uncertain. I assume it's an unfamiliar feeling for this amazing guy. *Vulnerable. Undone. Worried.* This whole parade of emotions crosses his face.

"Because I want you to. *Please,*" he says with hesitation.

"For how long? What does that involve, exactly?"

"Through the summer? Until baseball season is over? Christmas. New Year's. Your birthday. Which is?"

"This August. The second of August. I'll be eighteen." I smile sweetly at him but can feel my face getting hot.

"Geez, you really *are* seventeen." He groans. "You're too young to ask anything of."

"Ask me again," I finally say, stepping closer to him. He waits so long before forming the words, I begin to get uneasy. His lips part but nothing comes out. His features twist with uncertainty and doubt. He seems to wrestle with the whole idea now and there's this nagging disappointment that's about to rain down on me. This long silence just drags on between us.

"Will you wait for me?" Linc finally asks and then he lets his breath out slowly. He awaits my answer. I remain completely still for a long while because this is serious and what he's asking of me could change everything from here on out. Eventually, I reach up and trace his jaw line with my fingers. The charm bracelet he gave me earlier brushes against the side of his face, and he leans into my hand. He closes his eyes and slowly inhales the scent at my wrist. It's the sweetest gesture I've ever witnessed from a guy. This outright bliss surges through me. It's as if I've been lit from inside.

"Okay," I finally say. "I'll wait for you." It's such an intriguing promise for something more. *How can I say no to such an honest request? The truth is I don't want to say no.* I like the idea of him being mine, and me being his. It's a foreign concept—something I've never wished for or contemplated or thought I would want. It's so sweet and corny and good that I want to try. "You make me want to be a better person, Elvis."

"There is no comeback to a line like that."

"It's not a line."

He kisses me then. It's a long and passionate kiss as if he wants to imprint on me all the way to my soul. He lifts his head when he's done and stares at me. "Thank God, your parents are home."

I laugh, and it's like I just turned on all the stars at once in the night sky for him—or something along those lines—because suddenly it feels like I wield that kind of power over him. "Do you hate it when I call you, Elvis?" I ask shyly.

"Nah," he says. "I'd hate it, if you stopped."

"This is going to be complicated," I say for both of us.

"Only if we let it."

I walk him to the front door. We kiss one more time but it's sad this time and so we end it quickly because we both admit that good-byes aren't really our thing. He picks up my cell phone from the foyer table and programs in his number under...what else? *Elvis.*

I grin at him. I feel like a school girl with her first boyfriend. *Let's not examine that thought too closely.*

"So," he says with uncertainty returning to his face.

"I'll see you at the airport then," I say with a wide benevolent smile.

Promises made. Promises kept. Promises broken.

We start out with such good intentions, and then life does the unexpected, and we're instantly reminded once again how things can change in an instant.

CHAPTER SIXTEEN

Linc - Lightning strikes

I'VE THROWN FORTY PITCHES FOR THE cameras, so they can get me from every angle. Normally, I wouldn't mind but as the time slips by and annihilates my plans for making it to the airport with enough time to spare to see Tally, I get uptight.

Don't get me wrong. I love baseball. I want to pitch baseballs professionally or otherwise. I love the game. I want my new employers to be pleased. I don't mind doing the publicity to help the team, to sell more tickets down the road so that everyone who loves baseball as much as I do will come out and watch me play. However, I want to see Tally Landon one last time before she gets on a plane bound for New York and, most likely, a new life that is clearly far away from me. With the promises we've made to each other—in being exclusive for the summer and the possibilities of eternity—I want to be there to see her off and essentially pass some kind of monumental test, which I'm sure she's definitely made up in that pretty little head of hers, because she's invariably waiting for me to screw it all up.

Trust issues? *Most definitely. We both have some of those.*

Hers? *We can plainly see.*

Mine? *Nobody really knows about those.*

Yes. It's true: I'm beholden to this amazing girl and the newly-found pledge and commitment we've made. *I can't explain it. Her. Me.* My reaction to her and the why as how I've fallen so hard for this girl. Okay, let's call it what it is: *I'm in love with this girl. I am in love with this girl. It's all wrong. The timing sucks. Her age sucks.* Even so, I choose to ignore all of that because I am in love with Tally Landon, and that's all that matters.

Wayward pitch.

It sails past the catcher's glove and hits the backstop at ninety-five. The various pitching coaches are busy calling out the speed that registers on their guns and debating its accuracy under their breaths as if there is any. *Fucking baseball.* Stats are everything. I'm blowing mine because I'm worried about getting to the airport on time to meet up with Tally Landon, a newly graduated senior from Palo Alto High School that I happen to be in love with, who is five years younger than me and all of seventeen. The press would have a field day with that information. Kimberley Powers would have a heart attack if she knew. Instead, Kimberley quizzically watches me from behind the fence and pretends to be no more than a mildly interested spectator. Yet I can feel her eyes blaze right through me. They narrow suspiciously in my general direction after I throw another wayward pitch to match the last one.

She gives me the look—the one that silently screams: 'What the fuck is your problem, Presley? Throw the fucking baseball, so we can catch the damn flight back to L.A. and civilization'. Kimberley is not enamored with my home town. In addition to my agent, she is the most relieved that I signed with the Angels earlier today.

Another bad pitch. The photographer looks up from his camera lens.

I need to focus. I need to end this on a high note. At least five sports reporters are here as well as a few of the Angels' staff that delivered me the contract. A few hold their speed guns to capture each of my throws. I manage to get a strike by the umpire called in quick succession but struggle with the next two throws.

Suddenly, I hear Kimberley say from close by, "Let me talk to him."

Her stilettos sink into the compacted dirt along the outer fence with every step she takes but Kimberley doesn't seem to notice because she stalks toward the pitcher's mound so fast she seems to fly.

"What the *fuck* are you doing, Prez?" she whispers as soon as she's near enough. "God damn it. There are reporters here as well as some of the Angels' staffers. It's not a Kindergarten tryout. They want a demonstration of what they just signed your huge contract for. I know you don't see the money right away; and God knows I could personally spend that six-million-dollar signing bonus inside of a week, but get your head on straight. Throw the pitches at ninety-seven, hit the guy's glove, and let's get out of here as soon as Jimmy gets the money shot. *Jesus!*"

"I need to get to the airport on time," I say through clenched teeth.

"Why? There are *hundreds* of flights to L.A.; we can get one *tonight* for all I care."

"I have to be there *on time. Today.* This afternoon."

"Why?"

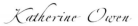

The entire group of spectators, including the main photographer, look up and over at us. They're clearly more interested in what she's saying to me than watching me pitch or taking down any more of my stats.

"I'm meeting someone at the airport. I need to be there on time. It's important."

"Fine," Kimberley says and gives me a withering glance. "Concentrate for the next half-hour on *baseball* and then *we'll go*. Get it together, *Prez*. Now!" She yells the last word so loud all fifteen heads go up again at the exact same moment. "You're buying me a new pair of shoes at the Duty-free," she says for all of us to hear as she settles herself back in her designated spot behind the chain-link fence. Then she stands there with the expectant stance of a general manager for the next five minutes and proceeds to watch me pitch nine strikes in a row including the money shot where the ball zips from my hand at ninety-seven miles an hour.

I manage to put Tally out of my mind for the next twenty minutes and finish up with a nice slate of stats: ten fast balls, five sliders, six curveballs, and even a few changeups and enough called-strikes to make just about everyone happy, including the entire Angels' pitching staff and their minor league coach Bud Schuyler, who sauntered in a half-hour ago, to meet his newest player.

The photo session ends only five minutes over. I did all the interviews earlier in the afternoon, and after I have a quick chat with Coach Schuyler and promise to meet with him first thing on Tuesday—in two days time—the world of baseball is relatively happy. And true to her word, we leave in thirty. Kimberley doesn't even protest when I ask the driver to step on it to make it to SFI in twenty-five minutes if that is at all humanly possible.

"Okay," Kimberley says as we settle down in the town car for the challenging drive to the airport at a break-neck speed. "Who is she? And what is she to you? Because that was not your best moment back there and I want to know why and effectively *who* just destroyed your concentration like that."

I'm reluctant to answer, although I'm fascinated by her innate ability to so quickly comprehend the situation and figure out how it affects me, even though we do go back a number of years since she was once engaged to Elliott. We still share in the grief at his loss all these years later. She's like a sister to me, but as my publicist, I'm still amazed at how Kimberley quickly picks up on things. People, places, and things. She pulls out her laptop and rewards me with this stern look compelling me to answer.

"Who is she?"

My mind races and essentially debates, whether to formulate a few plausible lies or tell her the truth. In some ways, Kimberley reminds me of Tally. Granted, Kimberley's older, but both women exhibit similar characteristics and wield incredible almost hypnotic power through their minds, bodies, and souls in the same exact way. Kimberley is more aware of hers. I think Tally is just catching on. For this reason, telling the truth wins out. I take a deep breath and gaze over at Kimberley and steel myself for her reaction.

"You may have seen her briefly last night at my aunt and uncle's house. Her name is Tally Landon. She's Marla Stone's best friend. She's a dancer. *Not that kind*," I say hastily when dread starts to spread across Kimberley's face. "She studies *ballet*. She's headed to New York for the summer to study ballet with some prestigious dance school. I can't remember the name of it. We met a while ago. She's—"

"*Seventeen*." Kimberley holds up her laptop that accusingly displays Tally's photograph. "I remember her. She didn't stay long. All of you disappeared soon after the call with the Angels ended. She is gorgeous. Just stunning."

She tabs through various pictures of Tally Landon that she's already pulled up on the Internet. There's even a photograph of the car accident where her twin sister Holly was killed. It's hard to even recognize the burned wreckage of what was once a car. My stomach twists when I see it while Kimberley gets this almost fatalistic look. I inhale sharply.

"Lost her twin in a fatal car accident earlier this year. Wow. Okay," Kimberley says. "She just graduated from Paly High with honors. She's lovely." Kimberley sighs and then immediately takes a deep breath while I just hold mine.

Here it comes.

She looks at me intently then. "You. Can't. See. Her. Anymore." Kimberley enunciates each word so slowly they become individual salutations all by themselves. "She's seventeen. You're twenty-two—almost twenty-three. You've got that star-crossed lovers look all over your face, Romeo; but you can't see her anymore. Not today. Not tomorrow. Not next week. Not a month from now. Not a *year* from now. Maybe two years from now. Yeah, maybe then." She gets this stern, unhappy look. "You're a *brand*, Prez," she says softly so the driver doesn't hear her. "You don't get to *do* seventeen-year-old girls when you're a famous baseball player and newly signed by major league baseball. Your dad would have a heart attack if he knew you were even thinking about playing around with one." She takes a deep breath and looks at me intently. "So *please* tell me you just *thought* about it, nothing more."

"I can't tell you that." This sinking feeling invades me. I know Kimberley is right on every level. My dad would freak. *She's seventeen. I'm almost twenty-three. No math required. What was I thinking?*

Kimberley looks incredulous for a few seconds, and then it morphs into this obstinate *there-will-be-no-arguing-with-me-on-this-one* look. "Holy shit."

She whistles long and low and catches the interest of our taxi driver with her sexy sound. She performs this dismissive wave prompting him to concentrate on the road and get us there on time. "Okay," she says, exhaling deep and finishing with a slight sigh. "Let me think this one through."

And so she does. Kimberley types away on her laptop and doesn't say another word to me for a long ten minutes.

With nothing left to do or say because there is no defending this impossible *situation*, I stare out the window at the grey nothingness of it all. The onset of inclement weather matches my mood. *This is bad. I screwed up.* Tally lied about her age, but I eventually went with it. I subconsciously convinced myself she was old enough; I didn't spend time analyzing why she would lie to me in the first place, and I didn't walk away after I knew. I screwed up. I know better. I know what it means. I told her once—*accused* her once—of potentially screwing up my career because of our age difference, but I never stopped long enough to think through the implications of what I was doing when I started pursuing her again. The consequences for me and for her are immense. No. I wanted to be with her at any cost. And just last night, I forced her to make an exclusive promise. To me. That wasn't fair.

The truth is simple. There is…only baseball. I attempt to take solace in that lone fact, and that I did tell her that upfront the first night we met. *But who am I fooling exactly?* Neither one of us took the time to analyze the alacrity of that statement at the time. *Baseball is my focus.*

Kimberley makes a few cryptic phone calls and finishes them up just as the town car pulls up to the passenger drop-off area in record time. She hands the driver six twenties and alights from the car before anyone can even get her door open for her.

"Follow me, Prez," she says. "We've got a special pass for SFI."

I'm still reeling from my own self-recriminations in the car. I'm not certain as to exactly where we left things on the subject of Tally after the car ride. *Where do we go from here?* Kimberley doesn't keep me guessing for too long.

"I've got a conference room reserved on the second floor. You have fifteen minutes. You will say good-bye to her in your own sweet Lincoln Presley way. You will tell her *you're sorry*. You *will not* give her false hope of any kind. You *will not* let her down easy. You will tell her how it is." She takes a deep breath and forcefully blows it out. "And let me tell you how it is—lest you not understand the gravity of this fucking situation. If this were to ever get out, your career would most likely be over. It's pedophile material, Prez. That's how the public would see it. You're the older guy, who took advantage of the innocent young girl. She's *seventeen,* and all the papers would report it that way if the story broke *today*. No matter that she turns eighteen in a few months. No paper would print that little detail. The facts are these: she's seventeen *today*. Her twin died a horrific death earlier this year. And, it looks like you—"

"I was there." I hang my head suddenly unable to look her in the eye. "Remember?" I told Kimberley this story. Part of it. She'll put it together.

"What?" Kimberley gets this dazed look and starts shaking her head.

"I was there. At the accident on Valentine's Day."

"The accident. On Valentine's Day. The girl you rescued? This is unbelievable. Now, you *look* like you've been stalking her…Oh Christ, *Prez*. It doesn't look good. You *can't* pursue this girl. It's stalker material no matter how innocent your hook-up." I flush at her harsh words. "She's too young. She's got her whole future ahead of her, and you have yours. She's going to be a star ballerina. You've just been signed by a major-league baseball team. You can't do this."

"But Kimberley, I—"

"Don't say *it*! Don't. Even. Say It. Your baseball career is *on the line*. You cannot get involved with this girl. Your contract is done. The money is on its way. You're a *brand*, baby. You have a *reputation* and a *baseball career* and a *future* with *Major League Baseball*. All of it is going just the way we thought it would. You're going to be on the road six months or more out of the year for the next five; and she's too young for you right now. Frankly, you need to stay away from Palo Alto and this girl for a long time. Thank God, you'll be in Salt Lake and then L.A., and she'll be in New York." She gives me the *do-not-fuck-with-my-plans* unyielding look. "Listen to me. You're going to be a star pitcher in the major leagues inside of a year or two or *sooner,* but *this story* would have legs because the good-looking baseball player screwed up or rather *screwed* the ballerina. You might get a pass. You might not. Public opinion could exalt you or crucify you, but it's a huge risk either way. It's your career we're talking about here. It's what you've worked for all these years. It's what your dad worked for and wanted *for you*. It's what you've wanted. You can't throw it all away for this girl, Linc. You can't."

She takes a much-needed breath.

We both do.

"Go end it," she says gently while she checks her watch. "I'm sorry. Her flight leaves in thirty-five minutes. You've got twelve."

At that exact moment, Kimberley stops at a side door on the second floor off of SFI's main terminal where an older, wizened security guard stands. She quickly flashes him her ID as well as her best, red-lipsticked smile and the guy lets her pass through within seconds. "Ms. Powers. Mr. Presley," he says with a wide grin. "This way. She's waiting."

Tally stands at the far window gazing out at the runway. She turns when we enter the room. *God, she is so beautiful.* She has this expectant look on her face as soon as she sees me. She looks so happy and she smiles wide, but it quickly fades when she spies Kimberley, who judiciously goes over to her as if they're old friends and re-introduces herself from last night's engagement party celebration. Kimberley even hugs her tight for a moment or two before letting go.

I'm reeling by now. My mind races with the possibilities of what I should say and how I should say it. *This is fucked up. This whole thing.* I'm not sure I could even say what needs to said but then my dad's disappointed face flashes through my mind and spurs me on in the next few precious seconds.

As Kimberley promised, she leaves the room within thirty seconds of re-introducing herself to Tally, but not before she says to me with true meaning, "Ten and half minutes, Prez. That's it."

Tally waits until the door clicks shut before she says anything else. "Who *was* that again?"

"That's Kimberley Powers. She's a good friend of mine." I wince at the look on Tally's face at the friend reference. "She was Elliott's fiancée…She's my publicist. She's my dad's publicist. And now she's mine, too. She was my brother's fiancée. Remember? I told you? She was Elliott's…fiancée."

"Elliott. Your brother. His fiancée."

Tally seems to struggle with making the connection. I haven't really told her very much about Elliott or my mom, but I can't say anymore about it because the hazy threat of my own of panic attack—that used to happen years ago—starts to surface. I focus on breathing even as my throat goes dry. I can't even swallow as all these competing emotions still try to take over. This feels all wrong on so many levels.

I sigh deep and run my hands through my hair and then shove my hands into the pockets of my pants as if that will somehow make this breakup thing with her any easier. This is impossibly hard and time ticks by at an alarming rate. I keep thinking about the utter feeling of loss in not being able to see her anymore or touch her or kiss her. Those are the only things I want to do now. Yet even now, I can't do it. I shouldn't do it. I shouldn't *want* to do it, but I still do.

I take a deep breath and start again. "She's my dad's publicist. She's mine, too, now. And, she's right about—"

"Linc, what's going on? They called my name over the loudspeaker, and that security guard escorted me *here.* Marla's probably freaking out just about now because our flight leaves in less than a half hour. My parents and hers and even Charlie already left. And, you're late."

"Hey. I'm sorry. The photo session took forever and there were a few of the Angels' coaches there to watch me pitch..."

"Oh," Tally says and gets this sheepish look. "How'd that go?"

"Not as good as it should have. I didn't throw my best pitches. I was worried about getting here on time. To see you off. To say...good-bye. "

"You were worrying about me during your interviews and photo session? Huh." She gets this vexed look. "And Kimberley *knows* about us."

I nod. I'm stalled out and take another deep breath and pray for courage or bravado or something that would provide me a little backbone to say what needs to be said and just cut her loose. *Six minutes.* I try in vain to recall Kimberley's exact words because they are the only ones that seem to make any sense to me. "Tally."

Her head whips up at my serious tone. Her beautiful green eyes zero in on my face.

We are five feet apart, but it can be measured in miles in that instant because I feel the separation from her so severely. I'm pretty sure she's feeling it, too.

"No." That single word sounds like it whooshed from the deepest part of her soul.

"Kimberley thinks." I stop. "It would look..." I take another breath. "We can't be together. You're seventeen. I'm twenty-two—almost twenty-three. It's not good. I could lose everything if anyone were to find out about us." I hang my head. "Besides your parents, me, Charlie, Marla, and now, Kimberley that we...were together." I look over at her. "That we've been together. That we *were* together at all."

She looks utterly stunned. Her throat moves slowly as if she's attempting to swallow. It sounds like she's having trouble getting air into her lungs. I am half-prepared for another panic attack. It has become our thing after all, but she gets this resigned look instead. She nods slowly as if the world has suddenly begun to make sense to her again. Her eyes glint with tears, but her voice is strangely steady and unemotional when she says, "Baseball's your focus."

It sounds rehearsed—almost rote—the way she says it. The moment is surreal as if it's all happening in slow motion and not really taking place right in front of us at all.

"Yes. It always has been. Until now."

She seems to weigh my answer after a moment. She cocks her head to one side and studies me for a few seconds. I almost thought she might laugh, but then she gets this steely look of resolve. "Sounds like it still is. Wow." Her words sound hollow. Her hands tremble as she brings them up to her face and absently runs it through her long hair all the way to the ends of it. She's worn it down because, at one point, I told her I liked it that way.

"Tally—"

"This. Is. Wow. Unexpected. Well, not really." She tries to smiles, and her throat convulses a little. "I gave it a month." Her smile disappears and then this incredible sadness traverses across her beautiful face.

This is what heartbreak looks like. I feel it. She epitomizes it. Right there.

She seems to wither away right in front of me and then she shrugs with unexpected nonchalance, clearly summoning up bravado from some place deep inside. "I gave it a month."

She stops and takes a step back from me and smiles even wider. I miss the warning then of her true intent for absolute fury. *She isn't done, far from it.*

"You," she says quietly. "*You?* You couldn't even give it twenty-four hours. Yet *you* extorted a promise from me. And now? You've...stomped all over it with all this hand-wringing angst about your precious career and your fucking loyalty to *baseball.*"

I reach out to her then, intent on trying to save what we have by holding on to her in some vital way because in the next moment, I know she's intent on destroying it, but she steps back from me.

We're wasting precious time with anger and fury and hate. All three. A part of me knows it's the end of what we have. Yet I want to try to save it in any way I know how. Preserve the memory of us. I glance at my watch. We have four minutes left.

"I love you," I say into the vast emptiness that threatens to engulf both of us, even as I grab for her hand. My words sound trivial, meaningless, and definitely arrive too late for these final moments. *This is what desperation feels like.*

She shakes my hand off and laughs bitterly even as tears begin to stream down her face, and she steps farther back from me. Then she latches onto the hatred for me and essentially saves herself, even as it swiftly envelops and pierces my soul with her next words. "Go fuck yourself, Elvis. *Please.* Save it for someone older and wiser than *me.* Save it for *Nika.*"

She walks out the door before I have a chance to say anything else.

She's gone. Gone forever, it seems.

I did this. I made the choice for baseball instead of her. And somehow, I'll have to live with that truth if that's at all possible.

"Well," Kimberley says as soon as she sees me. "It appears that didn't go any better than what went down on the baseball field today."

Words desert me. I can't think of a great comeback because she is absolutely right about everything. And, I did this. I made this choice. "You were—"

"Save it, Romeo. I just saved your career. Someday? You'll thank me."

"I was going to say you were right," I say with a grimace. "I *should* thank you but I can't, not today."

"Cheer up, Linc. You'll have a press conference with the Angels a few hours after we land in L.A., where you'll announce your newly signed long-term deal, and your life will begin. Such as it is." She searches my face.

Remorse. Regret. Guilt. It's all here.

She gets this weird, little smile. "Get over it, Romeo."

No sympathy from Kimberley Powers.

"You're about to ascend to the big time," she says. "Enjoy the ride. Our flight is in thirty minutes. Let's get on board and get back to L.A. because soon enough you'll be pitching a baseball and spending all that signing-bonus money on an apartment and a new life even if it is on the road. Oh." She pauses for a long moment and stops in the middle of the stairwell that leads back to the main terminal and grins mischievously. "I *like* her. She's awesome. *Sorry,*" Kimberley says upon spying the heartbreak that inadvertently travels across my face at what she's said. "Like I said in a couple of years, *maybe.*"

"She hates me now."

"Well, that'll fade." She looks me up and down. "I'd say you're pretty much impossible for her to hate. You guys have quite the chemistry going. My God, I felt it between the two of you as soon as I walked into the room."

One part of me wants to dislike Kimberley intensely for her cruel thoughtlessness in saying that aloud, but another part is weirdly cheered up at her candid assessment of my relationship with Tally---my *now non-existent* relationship with Tally.

"We are good together. Tally and I."

"Hey, Prez. You *can't* even say her name or even *breathe it* for *two years.* I thought I made myself clear on that point."

"We're clear," I say with a little smile. "We're clear."

I will have to take these small little moments of happiness where I can find them. Somehow, I already know they will be few and far between because all I have left is baseball, while the only thing I truly care about just walked out of my life. I'll be the first one to admit that I have no right to say or even think this after what just transpired with Tally; but I love her, as in always, even if I can't be with her. I love her all the same.

PART 2 — FAILING

"So, I LOVE YOU BECAUSE THE entire universe conspired to help me find you."~ Paulo Coelho - *The Alchemist*

CHAPTER SEVENTEEN

Tally ~ The war is over

I MANAGED TO KEEP IT TOGETHER ON the plane all the way to La-
Guardia and even hours later after we unloaded all our stuff in the
rented apartment loft that Marla was able to land for the next six months
through the still devoted Devon St. Claire. I managed to keep it together
while we chose bedrooms and purchased groceries for our new place and
shared a pizza. I managed to keep it together as we anointed our new life on
our first late night in Manhattan by opening the bottle of expensive champagne that Devon sent over even as Marla shrugged and told me she'd talk to
Devon later about her engagement to Charlie. I managed to keep it together
the first time she called and talked to Charlie, letting him know that we
had arrived safely, which directly wreaked havoc upon my psyche in reminding me all over again of his first cousin Lincoln Presley. I managed to keep
it together long past midnight as the most horrendous day—since Holly's
death—finally ended and became another.

And another.

Our summer in Manhattan flies by with the swiftness of a Kaleidoscope--
constantly shifting with each of life's subtle turns. Time essentially blurs. My
day-to-day existence and the vivid memory of one Lincoln Presley start to
fade. I do everything I do all I can not to think of him. *Ever.*

Our daily routines consist of dance classes and the follow-on rehearsals.
We spend the majority of our waking hours trying to please (*or is it appease?*)
SAB's newly appointed director and our mentor, Allaire Tremblay. We do our
best to anticipate her every whimsical need and perform our best in every

class, at every rehearsal, and with every performance. We take turns fetching her coffee and getting her lunch from the deli nearby SAB, while, at night, Marla and I openly commiserate about Allaire Tremblay's discernible disdain and indifference that she's lavished upon the two of us in front of everyone since we got here.

Even after those first days when we first walked into the school of American Ballet with fresh enthusiasm and naiveté, Marla and I still focus upon setting up our new life together in Manhattan with almost concerted effort. We determine the best places to eat and be and somewhat eagerly drink in the sights and sounds of New York City (both literally as well as figuratively). We want a life here. We do. So we do our best to make it work and put the guys on the West Coast out of our minds.

By mid-August, we manage to find our way around to just about every place that two eighteen-year-old girls on their own need to go and develop a somewhat unforgettable love affair with all things related to New York City— the greatest city in the world.

In all these discernible ways, I manage to stay numb about Lincoln Presley and manage to keep it together mostly. I don't think of him at all if I can help it. In this way, I manage to stay sane, mostly.

I don't speak his name. *That helps.*

I don't cry. *That helps.*

I focus on breathing. *That helps.*

I focus solely on ballet. *That proves to be everything.*

Tremblay moves slowly towards me inspecting and assessing like she always does these days. I cringe inward but try not to move at all while I continue to hold the arabesque the exacting way she expects me to. My leg muscles strain with the effort. I hold my breath trying to inspire my body to hang on to the difficult ballet pose, while Tremblay takes her time observing my form from every angle. "What's going on with you, Tally?"

I strain to hear her because she asks this so quietly. "Not sure," I say still holding my breath. I hold the form, even after she tells me to relax. A full minute goes by before I acquiesce and step out of the pose and away from her.

"We have our last summer performance in less than three days, Tally. Three days! We should be working on refinement, and instead we're rehearsing basic steps because *you* come to class exhausted and unprepared. Don't argue! I can see it for myself. What's going on with you?"

I turn away from her, catch my lower lip between my teeth. I bite down so hard that I soon taste blood. I'm afraid I'll burst into tears or go into fiery rage in response to her open criticism in front of the entire class. Everyone looks at me with veiled sympathy, including Marla. There's been too much pressure to be perfect and for the past couple of weeks, I've been far from perfect. *No.* I teeter upon the breaking point more than half the time now. It's not like I didn't know that working with Allaire Tremblay wouldn't be so demanding; but what I didn't expect is for my sister to die or that my unexpected break-up with Linc would continue to haunt me all these months later or that all the lies would eventually catch up to me and ultimately reveal a singular truth that I'm still unable to face even on this day.

In defeat, I gather up my things and start toward the door. "I'm sorry. I can't *do* this today."

"Talia," Tremblay calls out to me. "It's not time to go, yet. Class isn't over."

"It is for me."

The heavy entry door clicks closed and cuts off her angry response and the surprised looks of all the dancers who watch me leave.

———

It's two hours later when I hear Marla judiciously undo the four locks to our apartment located some ten blocks away from the dance school. Within a record three minutes, she slides in next to me on the sofa we fondly call '*red velvet*' that we carted home from the second-hand store around the corner on one of those first days we spent here in New York.

Marla gives me the once-over. "Hey, what happened to you today? Tremblay was pretty pissed." She gets this vexed look while a little crevice forms in the middle of her forehead.

"I don't know. I just couldn't do it today. Tremblay's right. I'm exhausted. I came home and took a long nap." Marla looks surprised, probably because I don't take naps, and I don't get tired because I never stop. "I feel a hundred percent better."

"Good." She nods, looking a little unconvinced. She puts her arm around me. "You push yourself too much. Sometimes, just backing off a bit actually improves everything."

I nod at her simple assessment of my overly complicated life. "True," I murmur striving for consolation of some sort for both of us.

We glance sideways at each other and eventually smile. It seems we're both relieved by the shared camaraderie. Things have been tense between us for the past few weeks. Summer Term is about over. Tremblay has yet to post the coveted list for those students who will be invited back for Winter Term. For me, SAB's Winter Term is the fall-back plan but Tremblay has become cagey about that, too. The coveted awarding of the NYC Ballet apprenticeships is expected to be announced soon, too. *Tense.* Things have been tense because all of it is highly competitive. I've begun to doubt myself. I think Marla has begun to doubt herself, too. There are only two open slots with NYC Ballet and limited ones for SAB's Winter Term.

She and I want the same things—the apprenticeship with New York City Ballet—or, at the very least, Winter Term with the School of American Ballet.

It's put a strain on our friendship and the two of us. For the first time, it appears neither one of us will get in. The dream feels too far away and out of reach for both of us.

Tense. Things have been tense.

I still refuse to talk about Linc and what happened. Marla has given up asking me about it. I've made a conscientious effort to display a modicum of happiness by doing less moping around the apartment.

I smile to myself; maybe I'm moping less because I'm never here. I've pushed myself even more in the past few weeks by staying late and working on lifts and routines beyond SAB's standard repertoire. I've been dancing with some of NYC Ballet's Corps and principal dancers—the ones who sneak into the dance school's building late at night—clamoring for more space, more solitude, and the never-ending quest for perfection.

Marla doesn't know about these late-night rendezvouses. She's been off doing her own thing—whatever that is. Rumors about the upcoming award of the two apprenticeships with New York City Ballet dominate all the dancers' conversations. Everyone's talking about it, except Marla. *No.* Instead, my roommate slash best friend does the bare minimum. She attends dance classes at SAB and shows up for rehearsals for our upcoming last performance where she'll be dancing in the Corps like so many others. Yet it's clear that her interest in what's going on at SAB or even with the NYC Ballet's apprenticeships wanes. I assume her attention centers on what Charlie Masterson has going on at UCLA, but now I wonder if it isn't something else entirely.

"Sasha Belmont was there late last night…at SAB," I say in an attempt to fill in the growing silence.

I have a mini crush on Sasha Belmont. She's NYC Ballet's artistic director and a former principal ballerina. She's a star. She's grounded. She's encouraging. She's so different from Tremblay. It would be a dream come true to work with her.

"She follows you around everywhere," Marla says with a hint of a smile, while she absently picks at the loose thread on her fashionable denim skirt that she scored at some basement sale she went to last week.

"I think it's just what she does this time of year," I say diplomatically. "They'll award the apprenticeships, and things will get back to normal soon enough. I think Tremblay has the Winter Term schedule just about lined up for SAB. I'm sure she'll post it by the end of the week."

Marla sighs. I look over in time to catch her rolling her eyes. Her lips part like she has more to say, but she seems to hesitate.

"What's the matter?"

"I'm not going to make it," she says simply. "No Winter Term. No apprenticeship." She glances at me sideways with this surprising, completely *at-peace-with-herself* expression and gauges my reaction.

"What are you talking about? That's not true. You've had a couple of off days, but it's nothing to worry about. Look at *me* today." I groan at the memory of not doing it right and walking out of Tremblay's last class in frustration "I didn't have it together at all today, not even in pointe class early this morning. I was a mess. Everyone has an off day. It happens."

I reach for something encouraging to say, while Marla looks even more determined. "We'll be doing *Midsummer Night's Dream* this fall, and you love that one—"

"Tally," she says softly. "I'm not going to make it. Tremblay told me that four days ago."

"What? Why would she tell you that?"

"I asked her what she thought my chances were for the apprenticeship and even Winter Term at SAB. Tuition is due by the first of September. I needed to know so I asked." She shrugs like this doesn't matter to her in the least.

"Why wouldn't she ask you back for Winter Term? That's the plan. She knows that. She invited us here. She promised."

Nothing is going as planned. How can this be?

"Tuition is almost six grand. I have better ways to spend the money. I gave it my best shot, but I can't keep throwing it at more ballet classes," Marla says. "Truthfully? I appreciated Tremblay's honesty. It's made my life and the decisions I've started to make a whole lot easier. Of course, she said she'd still try to work something out for Winter Term if a slot opened up. You know how things go. No slot is going to open up." She sighs. "I've spent enough money on ballet and after being here and realizing all the sacrifices I would have to make, I can't do it. I won't do it. I don't want to. I'm not like you, Tally. I'm not as gifted nor as incredibly talented as you are when it comes to ballet. I have to work ten times as hard as you do just to be in the Corps."

She gets this resigned look and cocks her head to one side and studies my face. "Look, I ran into Rob Thorn a few weeks ago. He's here in Manhattan. He's tending bar at Dahlia's on 5th at night. He told me the tips there are great for cocktail waitresses and…drum roll please…I got the job! I start this weekend." She laughs like she's just told me she's won the lottery.

"Why would Tremblay tell you that you're not going to make it? Why would you give up on ballet after all this time? And when did you become so chummy with Rob Thorn?"

"The apprenticeship is yours. It's just a formality." She waves her hand through the air dismissively. "They'll be sending you a letter in the next couple of days or Sasha will hand deliver it herself. Everyone knows that. As for Rob? We're just *friends*." She gets this defiant look.

"What does Charlie think about all this?"

She shrugs and turns away. "We broke up four days ago. Let's just say that he wasn't too keen about the idea of me working with Rob or going to NYU. He thought I would go to UCLA and be with him. We'd been fighting. *Again*." She frowns. "Because, let's face it, trying to conduct a long-distance relationship over the phone is such a hopeless endeavor." She tries to laugh. "Who would have known Lincoln Presley would be so right about that? Sorry," she says when I glare at her.

We have a pact. We don't talk about Linc. Ever.

"He said he needed an answer right then and there as to where he fit into my life and with everything going to shit for me with ballet, I didn't have one." Tears form on her lashes. She's not completely pulling off the *it's-all-for-the-best* act. "Well, it pissed him off enough that he hung up on me, and I haven't heard from him since." She slowly nods when she sees me frown. "Yeah." She sighs. "So right before pointe class this morning, I get a text from Cynthia Paulsen. She's at UCLA now. She asked me if I'd broken up with Charlie because he asked her out for this weekend."

"Oh, God. What did you tell her?" I ask, grabbing her hand. It trembles in mine even though her voice remains steady.

"I sent her a text back and told her she could have him." Marla shakes her head and actually tries to laugh, but it sounds forced. "If he can throw away our relationship so easily, it must not mean that much to him."

"You know he's just doing this to get a rise out of you. He knows seeing another girl, who was at Paly with us, will get back to you somehow. He *knows* that. Like I said, he's just trying to get a reaction from you."

"Maybe." She gets this wicked glint. "I sent his ring back to his mother this afternoon via FedEx." Her smile fades a little and her eyes glint with tears again. "It just makes me more determined to pursue my dreams while I still can. Because marrying Charlie Masterson doesn't hold as much appeal to me right now as going for what I really want. I'm going to be nineteen in a few months. I have my whole life ahead of me. I want to *live* it." She moves her head side-to-side. "I don't know what I was thinking getting engaged and thinking I'd marry Charlie next year. Crazy talk."

"Crazy," I say in an attempt to console her.

Where have I been? How could Charlie do this to her? Discard her just like that? I'm instantly reminded of his cousin. *Why am I so surprised?*

I start feeling light-headed while all these thoughts race through my head. This conversation has taken me completely by surprise, and I feel bad for not being there for my best friend while she was going through all of this with Charlie. It makes me wonder who has been there for her with all of this. Still, she manages to smile. *It's so Marla.* "And what do you want to do if it isn't ballet?" I ask.

"Well, I didn't want to say anything to you just yet. It's in the early stages… but there's this fashion photographer—Kandace Daniels? She's been working with me for the past month, off and on. She's started putting together a portfolio for me, and she's gotten some interest." Marla's face lights up. "She's heard of my mom, and she has connections here in New York as well as Paris and Milan. Kandace says being a dancer gives me an advantage as a fashion model because I'm tall enough, thin enough, and I know how to keep the pose. Clothes, fashion, and good fortune all rolled into one. You should see the photos she's taken. Somehow, she made me look amazing."

"You *are* amazing. Wow. You're serious." I slide off '*red velvet*' and intently study Marla's face. "This is what you want?"

"I've always had the dream of being a fashion model," she says slowly.

"You never told me."

"Holly knew." She gives me an apologetic look and hurries on. "I just didn't think it would ever happen. I met Kandace in Starbucks one day about a month ago. She was just staring at me and finally came over and introduced herself. She's pretty well known. She discovered Helga Swenson three years ago. She thinks I have *the look*."

My penchant for a black T-shirt and jeans for all occasions doesn't afford me to know who Helga Swenson is or what *the look* entails. I'm sure Marla will teach me soon enough. Right now, her blond ponytail swings through the air as she pirouettes around our living room. Her outright enthusiasm manages to deflate and effectively burst my bubble of an only-ballet world and the two of us in it. I'm bewildered by it all. She glances over at me.

"What will your parents say about all of this?" I'm confident all at once. Surely, her parents will talk some sense into her about this crazy fashion model idea. It's so not a part of our plan.

"Well, unlike *you*, I actually do stay in touch with my parents." She laughs.

Her utter joy is contagious, and I start to smile. "They're *thrilled*."

"You told them already?" It's obvious that I am way behind on the news around here.

this much is true

She's so giddy that I actually step back from her just in case it's contagious. Giddy is not a feeling that I normally ever allow myself to feel—with one exception—with Linc that night, when we'd promised to be exclusive to each other. *Giddy.* I'd felt giddy right up until the moment at the airport when he said, "Tally," like it had become a personal swear word to him and then shattered my heart in the next for all time. *Giddy. I hate giddy.*

Even so, I force myself to smile. I even make an effort to flit around the living room with Marla a couple of times and start rearranging picture frames to drum up some elusive cheer for all of this. Marla doesn't seem to notice my general lack of enthusiasm for all of her news.

"They're thrilled. They might even be willing to fund my trip to Milan this spring. So, I need a job that *pays,* until I can afford to pay Kandace for her stellar photography work on my portfolio. I also have a plan B and even a plan C, which includes working at the Dahlia on 5th, taking classes at NYU per Rob's smart suggestion, and working with Kandace on building up my fashion portfolio until I get my first gig. Rob thinks it's a good plan. All of it."

Rob again.

"Rob? NYU? Slinging drinks at the Dahlia? Where have I been?"

I feel more and more left out of all these plans.

"Rob's been supportive that way...as a *friend.* I've already registered for the fall quarter at NYU because I'll have time for classes during the day now," she says. "My parents are thrilled with that, too. And the Dahlia is fine. The tips will be fabulous, and there are a lot of fun people that work there and hang out. The money's going to be great."

"And the fact that you're not yet nineteen, let alone twenty-one?" I ask suddenly intent on following all the rules.

Marla just laughs. "That's what fake IDs are for. Rob has a friend, who knows someone, who fixed me right up. According to my ID, I'm twenty-one."

"You're killing me."

"Rob can hook you up, too."

I shake my head suddenly bent upon being a rule follower to the death.

"I just never took him for being one to break the rules like that," I say in confusion.

"I never took you for one to follow any of them."

Point taken.

"Rob's actually a lot of fun. *Truly.* He's funny and capable and good."

"Rob Thorn," I say. "Funny. Capable. Good?" I look at her closely feeling this twinge of jealousy for some unknown reason. Maybe, I'm just defending Holly at this juncture. "Huh."

She looks out the window at the lit-up Manhattan sky and then looks back at me with this sad face. "As for Charlie? Well, he'll just have to figure it all out on his own. The truth is he needs to grow up. I can't help him do that. In the meantime, I have an opportunity to do something I've always wanted to do, and I want to try to make it as a fashion model more than anything. Kandace thinks I've got what it takes, and I want to go for it. In the meantime, I want to have some fun, go to college, and live life on my own terms. If Charlie Masterson ever figures it out, he'll have to work hard to win me back because I'm moving on." She sweeps her hand through the air. "Just like you have."

She looks over at me in triumph. The heady bliss of promised fame just reverberates off of her. Who am I to *argue* with her? I've chased that feeling since I was ten for ballet.

"I haven't been the best example of moving on." I shake my head side-to-side and get this rueful smile.

"Yes, you have. You've put your *all* into ballet. Look at you. You're a day or two away from getting the apprenticeship offer from NYC Ballet and the chance of a lifetime. *Everyone* wants to be you."

"I don't think so. Everyone is going to want to be you. Marla Stone—fashion model extraordinaire."

"Can you believe it? Just think, one day you may be walking by a newsstand and casually glance at one of the magazine covers and see *me* on the front cover."

Her happiness fills up the whole room for a few moments and attempts to work its way inside of me but there's another part of me that still hesitates. She'll be in Milan by spring. And what will I do without Marla? Because I surely won't be in Milan this spring.

Where will I be? Nowhere whispers this little voice inside my head. I hug her tight. "I'm sorry about Charlie."

"Me, too," she says pulling back to look at me. "The thing is…love shouldn't be this hard. Maybe, Cynthia would be the best thing for him right now." She stands a little taller and straighter. "What I do know is that Charlie isn't ready to get married. As much as it hurts me to end it with him, I'd rather do it now—then find out down the road when I'm *married* to the guy—only to then discover that he isn't really committed for the long term. I mean if the biggest test of our relationship is making it work when we're apart—and yet we can't make *that* work—what are we really trying to save here?"

She shakes her head side-to-side in disbelief. "It's over."

"I'm still so…sorry about you and Charlie."

"I know. Me, too." Her voice catches and she gazes out the window for a few moments before looking back at me. "I thought we had something special, but it turns out we didn't. He hasn't called me for almost five days. We usually talk every three hours. And now he's asking Cynthia out. I guess, in the end, he just doesn't care about me."

"He cares about you. He's just being stubborn and mixed-up about his priorities. That's all. Guys do that. All the time." We share this knowing look. "Thanks for being there for me. God, I wasted the whole summer on Lincoln Presley. Remind me never to do that again."

"As long as you keep reminding me never to do a long-distance relationship again," Marla says softly. "You know? On some level, it feels good to be free. *Really.* Now, I can just concentrate on living here—building a life here. Working, going to school, and maybe I'll even call Devon. Someday," she says. "Not now. Later. New Year's or something."

"Better. Let's not rush into another relationship when we're still trying to get over the last one."

"Are you lecturing me or yourself? Because the one remedy I have in mind for you is mindless sex with a stranger."

"Is that a drink call you're memorizing?"

"No. It's a solution to all this moping around. Not for me. For you. You need to relax and stop being so committed to ballet. It's not the end of all things as we know it, you know."

"I feel, like if I let up even once, I'll fall or fail or both."

"I know. I get it. But if you don't let up and have a little fun, you're going to lose the best part of you—that feisty, fuck-it-all Tally that we all know and love so much. Even Lincoln Presley loves that girl."

"I thought we agreed some time ago not to talk about *him.*"

"We did, but you're in a weird place," she says. "You're stuck between joy and sorrow. You're in no man's land. *Literally.* You're so caught up in trying to forget about him that you can't move on. Instead, it just keeps you here—in this awful, dark place. It's not pretty."

"Heavy-duty stuff coming from the girl who just sent her engagement ring back."

"Well, I'm in an introspective mood. I'm just trying to figure it all out, too. What I want. What I don't want."

"Hard questions to ask, let alone answer."

"Funny. That," she says with a little laugh. "You've always known what you wanted. Maybe that's what's going on with you. Maybe you've changed your mind about what you want."

"Impossible. I'm not allowed to do that. My dad just sent me the tuition for SAB's Winter Term." I start to smile, but it quickly fades when I catch this look of disappointment flit across her features. "Sorry."

"Don't be," she says, starting towards her room. "It's been a long day. Crazy. I just need some sleep, so I can try to focus upon moving on. I'm sleeping in by the way."

"What about class? Rehearsal?"

She turns back and actually smiles. "That's what so great about making decisions about my life. I don't have to go to class or a rehearsal. There's a wait staff meeting at three at the Dahlia tomorrow. Rob's meeting me here and we're going together so he can introduce me around beforehand." She shrugs. "Why should I be in the last performance? What? So I can put it on my resume?" She rolls her eyes. "I already told Tremblay about my decision and declined her offer for being on the Winter Term wait list. Like I want to be on a wait list in case someone drops out," she says. "I told Allaire I wouldn't be there anymore. She's cool with that."

"She's *cool* with that?" I ask, incredulous. Tremblay is never cool about anything. Cool is never a way to describe the woman.

"She's fine with it," Marla consoles. "Truth? I just want to go to bed and have a good cry over Charlie. Then, tomorrow? I'm going to wake up and start a new day and a new life. I've been in limbo for far too long. It's time to move on."

I don't know what to say to that because her words ricochet through me like a stray bullet. My heart hurts as much as my head in just thinking about what all Marla's revealed tonight about her relationship with Charlie that inadvertently reveals even more about mine with Linc. She's handling the disappointment over her broken engagement with Charlie amazing well, whereas I have been all but falling apart over a guy whom I spent less than twenty-four hours with in total.

I need to move on.

I need to move past this thing with Linc and forget all about him.

That needs to happen. It does.

And, I need to start thinking of a back-up plan for my future just in case ballet doesn't work out.

The fears rise again after being buried for some time in my psyche. Failing. Falling. Losing. I shake my head, wondering if I'll ever really outrun them and if Lincoln Presley finally has.

CHAPTER EIGHTEEN

Tally – I have arrived

LIFE CAN CHANGE IN AS LITTLE of fifteen seconds. *I know this.*
Fifteen seconds.
An SUV clips my car, kills my sister, and changes me and my life forever.

Thirty seconds.
The time it takes for a stranger to lift me up and carry me away and save me from the burning wreckage.
Thirty seconds.
Thank you, Elvis.

One night.
The time it takes to fall in love with Lincoln Presley and forge promises that neither one of us can keep.
One night.

Thirty seconds.
The time it takes for him to tell me he loves me in one breath and then in the next says that he can't be with me in just the way he says my name.
Thirty seconds.
In thirty seconds, a heart can break.
Right, Elvis?

Sixty seconds. The time it takes to read the offer letter for the apprenticeship at one of the most prestigious ballet companies in the world—New York City Ballet. Only mirrored by the same amount of time it takes me to sign the offer of a lifetime.

Four weeks.

I'm allowed four weeks of almost pure bliss at NYC Ballet, where I finally feel that everything is actually right with the world.

Four weeks.

Miraculously, I seem to be in a better place. I've overcome the grief of losing Holly and the heartbreak over losing Lincoln Presley.

I am here. I have arrived.

I embark on my new life at New York City Ballet with new zeal. *Zeal.* This inexplicable almost energized happiness combines with equal parts gratitude and surreality. I pay homage to luck and timing. I smile more. When my parents call, I tell them that I'm fine and actually mean it because life suddenly feels amazingly grand for the first time in a long time. It's still surreal, since Holly, since Linc, but I'm better. So much better.

This is me. This is me moving on.

I am put back together; I'm not the same—but I'm stronger, more determined, and freer.

Almost…dare I say?

Happy?

Four weeks.

In four weeks, I feel almost worthy and certainly beholden to both the unbelievable good fortune that got me here. Yet, at the same time, I acknowledge the entire truth—all the hard work that brought me here to this triumphant moment in my life.

I've made it.

I am here.

I have arrived.

This much is true.

Still.

I can't quite fight off the effects of this seemingly endless flu. It feels chronic these days just like the heartbreak I finally admit to Marla to experiencing all summer long over Linc.

And, still?

I think it's temporary so I push through this unknown malaise because I believe it's just a nuisance and nothing whatsoever to worry about.

After all?

After all, the dance world awaits.

Yet this much is true: It waits for no one.
I push through this sick feeling to the third week of September.
Still, it doesn't make any sense.
Until it does.

Four months to the day.
I'm free. *Free.*
I'm on my way. Almost a star. A dancer. An apprentice. At eighteen.
This much is true:
The world awaits.
But really? It waits for no one.

I blow eighty bucks on my father's credit card—the emergencies only Visa—, but it doesn't matter how much money I spend at the pharmacy.
It doesn't matter.
It doesn't matter because the results are in.
They're the same with every test I take.
Three minutes.
Test and wait.
Five Tests.
Five times.
Test and wait.
The results are all the same.
Plus lines. Pink lines. Blue lines.
The results are the same.
The results will change my life.
Again.
Either way.

Silly me.
I kept thinking that thoughts of Lincoln Presley would eventually fade away.
But he's here to stay.
And how.
Now he haunts me…in such a surprising way.
Three minutes.
Just three minutes to turn my life upside down.
Again.

Marla sails through the door like she's on roller skates. Tips must have been good at the Dahlia. It's late. One in the morning. I've been pacing for four hours. Test time is long over. Reality settles in on me. I have to tell someone. That someone is Marla.

"Hey," she says pouring herself lemonade in a ready shot glass. She makes it fresh every day now. We got on a kick about two months ago for old-fashioned lemonade when the temperatures eerily soared here in Manhattan. I watch her drink it down. She wipes her lips on the back of her hand when she finishes. "Great night. These New Yorkers are good tippers when they want to be. And Kandace booked me for a shoot next week with *Fashion Sense*. Can you believe it?"

"That's great. She's amazing." I try to sound upbeat, but I'm not sure it's working.

"How was your day? How's the Corps?"

"Sasha tagged me for the Lilac Fairy in *Sleeping Beauty*."

Marla looks amazed. "Oh, my God. That's fantastic. I knew you'd get it." She starts dancing around the living room. "God, that's so amazing. You're in! Sasha Belmont wants you to dance the lead part in Sleeping Beauty. That *never* happens this fast. It's incredible. I'm so proud of you."

"I know it's really great. It'll run through the first week of November." I sound like I'm giving a speech at my sister's funeral. I cringe in thinking of that because now I do feel awful for not speaking at Holly's funeral.

Marla stops twirling and looks over at me. "So, if it's so great, why do you look like you're about ready to cry?"

I take a deep breath because telling Marla will make it *real*. *Too real*. But telling Marla will make it possible for me to figure out what I'm supposed to do here. "It's not that simple anymore."

"What's not that simple?"

"*This*. All of this. It's just not that simple anymore." I sweep my arm across the room like she did a few minutes before. I'm barely holding it together for an entirely different set of reasons that begin and end with Lincoln Presley. The irony of it all almost makes me want to laugh or cry. It would be funny if it wasn't so damn serious. *I'm going to cry.* My ability to survive from one moment to the next has been largely centered on a true concentrated effort that has been solely focused on breathing for the past several hours. I'm surprised Marla hasn't noticed this about me sooner, but she does now.

"What the *fuck* is your problem, Tally?"

We made a recent pact to use the f-word sparingly to give it more impact and meaning when we actually say it. Holly had always insisted upon this rule, and we honor her with it now.

I gaze at Marla in an attempt to form the necessary words, so she will begin to understand the gravity of my situation. "I'm late," I finally whisper. The heat rises to my face in delivering this truth. The hormones rage right on schedule like flipping clockwork. My body knows it, even if my mind refuses to admit it, despite this somewhat insistent fluttering in my midsection and five positive pregnancy tests.

"Late?" Marla looks momentarily confused but then gasps. "How *late?*"

"Possibly four…*months*…late," I say slowly trying to find air. I hang my head. "More like four. Late. I don't know." I raise my arms feeling helpless and give her this pleading look. "I'm not sure."

"Holy shit! When were you going to *tell* me?"

"After I tell myself," I say softly.

Marla begins to laugh but then she stops. She's caught between joy and sadness just like me; because, yes, being given the part of the Lilac Fairy in *Sleeping Beauty* with the NYC Ballet is a dancer's dream, although finding out you're pregnant the same day…not so much. *Welcome to my world.*

We stare at one another and share in this utter bewilderment and silently acknowledge this cruel twist of fate. I'm unable to hang on to the funny yet still refuse to openly capitulate to the sadness—the tragedy of it all. There is just no right answer for this one. We both seem to know it when we look at one another. I know because I've searched for it again and again in the past couple of hours.

"Are you sure?" I don't answer. Instead, I make my way to the bathroom while Marla follows closely behind me. She gasps when she sees the pregnancy sticks and sort of groans as she compares the test results with each package's set of instructions. "Holy shit," Marla says in disbelief.

"Yeah. I aced my tryout for the solo part for the Lilac Fairy in *Sleeping Beauty.* Sasha was pleased. She made a special point of coming up to me afterwards and telling me what a great job I did and she didn't waste a lot of time in announcing to the group that I had the part. I wasn't the only one surprised." I try to breathe. "Things were looking up. Right then. Until Benson made a casual remark about our last couple of lifts. I wasn't twisting in his hands as well as I usually do. He said, "What you'd do, Tally, gain three pounds?" I leveled him with a bitchy stare, but his teasing caused me to race back to the dressing room when we had a break and step on a scale. I've gained three pounds. I kept asking myself how can that be. I mean I've been eating better but not enough to gain weight…"

"This can't be happening," Marla says in complete sympathy.

"Oh, but it is. Now that I think about it…it explains so much about this summer. How I just felt sick and tired all the time. I blamed it on Lincoln

Presley." I sigh. "I guess I still can…just not for the reasons I thought. He didn't just break my heart; he knocked me up." I start to laugh softly, but then I'm gripping the counter as I feel a panic attack coming on. I close my eyes and concentrate on taking deep, steady breaths.

"Okay, let's not panic," Marla says from behind me.

"Too late for that."

"You're handling it quite well. I think I would have screamed or something."

"That might be next."

This sick feeling overwhelms all of me. I race to the toilet and vomit the last remnants of dinner from earlier. At least, I can breathe again. Marla disappears giving me a few precious moments of privacy. I brush my teeth and pull my hair back in a ponytail and try for some kind of order both physically and mentally in my otherwise wrecked life.

"Come on. Let's go." Marla dutifully hands me my favorite black T-shirt and her black leather bomber jacket. She grabs my hand, pulls me out the door, and then down the fifteen flights of stairs and through the apartment building's heavy steel doors into the rush and bustle of lower Manhattan. I actually begin to feel better. There's nothing quite like a crowded sidewalk of people rushing every which way who don't give a shit about you and whether you're five months pregnant or not. These strangers as well as Marla provide enough solace and comfort in an otherwise cold, cruel, twist-of-fate world.

There's nothing quite like having your best friend hold your hand and navigate the uneven sidewalk for both of us. Her actions alone implicitly tell me that everything is going to be okay somehow. In true heroic fashion, she leads me to our favorite place—the all-night diner we discovered our first week we were here—where she quickly orders two cups of black coffee from the waitress, who wears this crisp white uniform dress and purses her spunky red lips while sporting the wildest black punk haircut I've ever seen. I can't help but admire the woman for her daring to wear it that way. She blatantly displays her personal fashion statement and doesn't need an endorsement of any kind nor does she implicitly require a sense of belonging to an otherwise staid world from anyone else. No, it can all be damned. The waitress smiles over at me while Marla proceeds to order the juiciest well-cooked hamburger possible, an extra side of fries and a heaping pool of ketchup, and the biggest slice of coconut crème pie that the waitress can find along with two forks and two knives. *Why?* Because the situation as Marla puts it *"demands it."*

My best friend holds up two fingers to the waitress to further demonstrate all the things she wants in twos in double-time.

In this moment, the person I love the most, without question, is Marla Stone.

We don't say anything for the first half-hour. Ironic, because there is plenty to say, and we've been talking incessantly to mostly each other since we arrived in New York. We've clung to each other in all these unexpected ways, in search of courage, as we braved this new world. We nimbly navigated our way into the most preeminent ballet academy in the United States as many aspirants tend to describe SAB. While Tremblay may have considered us her favorites back home, however implicit, she didn't show it at all here. She'd been a taskmaster—demanding more, expecting more from both of us, and we'd given it back to her a hundred-fold. We were the best in all the classes that we'd taken at SAB; but it didn't make us popular with anyone. We'd been somewhat ostracized by the intermediate and advanced students who had been at the SAB for much longer and who fully expected the newbies to pay their dues via this quiet torment that had been exuded with such force and cruel intent that most dancers would have quit. Yet, we shouldered this heavy burden of being Tremblay's protégés and silently accepted our fate, even when Marla didn't make it, and I miraculously did.

Yes. My best friend has hung in there with me through all of it. She's here for me now.

"It's going to be okay," I finally say on a manic quest of some sort.

My words go unheard. She gets this pensive look instead. "Charlie called. He left a voice mail *again.* Do you think I should call him?"

"Do you *want* to call him?"

"I don't know. It's complicated."

"Complicated." I frown. "That doesn't even begin to cover it, does it?" I try to smile but fail as my new reality washes over me. *I'm pregnant. What am I going to do?*

For a much-needed distraction, I pick up the knife and cut into my half of the hamburger and then proceed to judiciously cut the half into fourths. I pop the first one into my mouth and slowly savor the flavors of Swiss cheese and juicy, well-cooked ground sirloin and sweet onion and pickles. "I have had a craving for this burger for a couple of weeks now," I admit to Marla. She stares at me open-mouthed.

"You never crave anything. Your willpower is amazing, bar none."

"Not lately." I laugh softly and steal another part of the burger from my plate. "You don't have to stay."

"Yes, I do. I want to. I need to. We both do."

"You should try to work things out with Charlie."

"If Charlie wants things to work out with us, he can come to New York and work them out. In the meantime, it's me and you." She gets this defiant look.

For a distraction, we split the rest of Marla's half of the burger and ask for a second serving of fries. It's an unheard of request from both of us. The pie remains untouched. We consume more calories in these first forty-five minutes than we've ever expended in a ballet class. I enjoy every single bite. The flavors of the burger and French fries and the ketchup are utterly fantastic. Marla teases me about my religious experience with food, and I just nod with my mouth still full, savoring every amazing morsel in the congenial silence. I'm reminded of Linc when he cooked for me. I stop chewing, swallow hard, and attempt to keep it together. My eyes water and I try to smile while Marla just stares at me from across the booth again.

"What are you going to do?" she finally asks.

"I don't know, yet."

I shrug my shoulders and sort of laugh and hand her one of the forks. We start from opposite ends of the coconut crème pie working our way to the center. Marla remains quiet, waiting me out. Usually she jabbers but today she seems to sense my inherent need for complete and utter silences—intervals where she seemingly recognizes my desire to be fully engulfed in enormity of it all for a good long while.

There is constant chaos all around us. New Yorkers come and go. Regulars clink their coffee cups, and waitresses crack jokes with the cooks, and the diner seems to take on a life all its own with the hustle and bustle of eating and drinking and just being. It soothes the two of us. We just sit there taking in the ambiance of the place. It's a joint if ever there was one. Tourists and regulars coexist with a staff that probably serves as a quasi family for many of them. Eventually, I anoint the diner's sounds for what they are: continuous motion. *Life.* It makes me smile. I glance over at Marla and acknowledge her insistent tap tap on the blue speckled Formica with her bright-red fingernails, which have become more prominent in last few months. Tremblay always had a problem with red nail polish and insisted we use demure colors on our nails, unless a performance calls for something more "colorful," as she once put it.

Marla's moved on. Why can't I? Life. Continuous motion. *Life. Here it is.*

I give Marla the *I'm-okay-just-don't-ask-me-anything-hard* smile. She shakes her head side-to-side in quiet disbelief. My best friend groans in sympathy as she leans back on her elbows, while her long blond hair graces the back of the booth behind her. "Talk to me," she says. "You never do anymore, not in a while anyway."

I play with a cold French fry and silently count the number of times the bell dings at the restaurant's front door as people come in and go out. *Eight.* Eight dings signal the diner's customers going in or out.

"I didn't pay much attention," I say slowly. "I haven't had a period in a long while before the accident. What with the Boxer's Diet and stuff. I didn't think anything of it. Then, with Benson teasing me that I'm heavier than usual, which is weird because…you know that I tend to track that stuff. Only I haven't been. Not since Holly died. I mean I get on the scale on a regular basis, but it's weird because when I do I've gained three pounds all of a sudden. And I'm thinking, why is that?" I exhale. "I haven't been eating all that much, so I kept thinking why is that? I can't quite believe it. I mean, you know I'm such a stickler about birth control but when Holly died, I took antibiotics for a while to ward off an infection from the gash in my leg, and I'm popping birth control pills more sporadically at times. My life was a mess, and I wasn't paying attention." I take a breath.

"Then I met Linc." I try to smile, but the heartbreak over him remains with me, and it's never far enough away. "He had it covered that night—with the best of Trojan—but there was this one extra time, and I thought it was okay. I told him it would be, but I did some research earlier tonight. Antibiotics can interfere with contraceptives, and I guess they did."

"Holy shit."

I move my head up and down so slowly as if it will make it untrue, but I already know it's true. I just did five pregnancy tests five hours ago. And now that I know what it is, I can feel it. *I feel different. Fluttery. Weepy. Outside of myself.*

"All those lectures about having it covered. Geez, the paper you wrote for Hennessey's class about contraceptives leading to the ultimate freedom of women."

"*Please.* Let's not rehash my academic accomplishments, especially when the irony of it all is so, let's face it, flipping ironic."

Marla starts to laugh.

And truly? Levity is what I need at a time like this. I slowly smile.

"What do you want to do?" Marla leans in closer from across the table so our conversation isn't overheard.

"I don't know. I don't want my parents to find out. It would kill them—their only daughter left—screwing things up this way. I don't think they could handle it right now. My dad is still burying himself in work at hospital, but my mom seems to be doing so much better, at least that's what they tell me when I call. I don't want to upset them right now, until I know what I'm going to do." I trace the pattern in the Formica table.

"You don't have to decide anything right now," Marla soothes.

I glance up and find her busy downloading something on her iPhone. "What?"

"Pregnancy calculator," she answers.

"They have an app for that?"

"May 22nd, right?"

"Let me think." My mind is not cooperating the way it normally does. I can't think or do simple math. Marla passes me the phone, and we look at the month of May together. "May 22nd, then." I groan.

She keys in the date and gets this dazed look. "February 14th," she says slowly.

"Valentine's Day." The irony isn't lost on either one of us.

CHAPTER NINETEEN

Linc ~Off-season

"MORE MONEY THAN GOD," CHARLIE LIKES to say about my contract with the Angels. The promise of money is there. I have to deliver first.

Early December finds me settled back in at the guest house at Uncle Chad and Aunt Gina's after a long season in which the Angels placed second in the NL West. I played a small part in the short-lived victory of my third outing in Major League Baseball, pitching for the Angels. We finished with a just below five-hundred season, which still isn't good enough. "Well, done for a rookie," I was told by just about everyone. I should be happy. I should still be riding that high from late September when all my dreams and achievements for baseball essentially came true, but I harbor these uneasy feelings. Fears. Fear of failing, falling, and losing, just like Tally and I talked about once. And I still pine away for the girl I lost because of baseball. The fact that she is clear across the country doesn't help me in any discernible way. Granted, for the majority of the year, I was either in Salt Lake City or traveling up and down the West Coast with the Angels' triple A team, the Salt Lake Bees, until they brought me up to Major Leagues with the Angels in early September when one of their starting pitchers suffered a shoulder injury that put him out for the season. It felt good to ascend to the Major Leagues. I did well.

Now, I'm just glad to be back home in Palo Alto for a while. However, with all this free time on my hands; it inevitably leads to continual thoughts of Tally Landon.

I've begun to question Kimberley's edict that I have to stay away from her. Tally is over eighteen now. What's the big deal? Intent on resolving this, once and for all, I dial Kimberley's number. Her regular insertion into my life with these weekly *check-ins* as she fondly refers to them are a requirement for working with her, especially since she's in New York more often than L.A. these days.

"Powers," Kimberley says on the second ring. I can never understand how she picks up her phone so fast, but have decided it's because it is never more than two inches away from her face.

"It's your favorite baseball player," I say. "Checking in, as always and forever."

"Charmer," she says with a laugh. "What gives? I thought we weren't scheduled for another week? And, it's almost Christmas or haven't you heard?"

"Is it?" I pause, formulating a plan on the fly. "I'm at loose ends. I was thinking of taking a trip to New York and just wanted to—" She cuts me off before I have a chance to even launch into all the reasons I need to see Tally.

"That's a bad idea. Linc, you can't see her. I'm not kidding around. Where before you had potential for the big contract, you now have one. You can't allow anything or anyone to interfere with that right now. We have to be squeaky clean. Can't you like take up a cause or something? Go out and have some fun. Date someone else who is actually your age."

"I don't want anyone else."

"I know but it doesn't work that way. She's still too young for you. You're twenty-three; she's just turned eighteen."

"Her birthday was in August. Ages ago," I say.

"Like I've said at least a million times before, all the papers would speculate, and then the questions would start. How did you first meet? And then someone would remember seeing you two of you together early last summer. Some Starbucks barista that needs the cash and is willing to sell you out for ten grand or some damn idiotic reason like that. It wouldn't even have to be *true*. Listen to me. Trust me on this. I know what I'm talking about. Please hear me. Move on. Go date some older twenty-five-something-year-old that is preferably blond and way different than Tally Landon. Do it for me?" She sighs. "What about the Russian girl you've mentioned? The girl from your Stats class."

"Nika."

"Yes," she says with a laugh. "Nika would be perfect. You like her. She's your age, right? You told me she was smart, beautiful, and Russian. She's the complete opposite of your girlfriend. Go out with Nika. You'll have fun."

"I don't want to go out with Nika."

"Do it anyway. *Please*. For me. She'd be entertaining and occupy your mind, body, and soul, at least for a couple of days. What does she do anyway?"

"She's into computers. She freelances. The last time I talked to her; she was moving to Seattle."

"Seattle's not that far away. Same coast. She sounds like fun."

"She's a hacker," I say, hoping to put Kimberley off.

"So she's brilliant, besides. I'm sure she'd blow your mind. *Literally.* She's sounds perfect for you, just what you need right now, Mr. Presley."

Kimberley seems preoccupied. She's talking about her new job in Paris and meeting some new guy. Even though she's thousands of miles away from me in New York, I hang on to every last word she utters because of something she's just said, "I checked in on Tally a few months ago. She's doing great."

"How did you do that?" I ask in perceptible wonder.

"I have my ways." Kimberley laughs. "I'm here in New York over Christmas and I may see her or call her again," she says using the somewhat flippant tone I've come to expect from her. "I thought I'd catch one of the New York City Ballet performances. Sasha Belmont's a friend of mine. They're enthralled with their latest intern. Apparently, they're talking about a European tour this coming spring and Tally's being considered for it. She already had a solo part in Sleeping Beauty this past fall. She's doing exceptionally well. A star on the rise already according to Sasha and the press."

"Wow. She got the internship?" I sound pathetic. I clear my throat in a weak attempt to correct my over-enthusiasm just in case Kimberley starts to read too much into it. "How do you know all of this about Tally?" I suddenly feel a little uneasy over what her answer will be and invariably start to spin out of control in the next few seconds at just the idea of getting to see Tally perform. I hold my breath awaiting Kimberley's answer. *Why can't I just move on from this girl?*

"You pay me the big bucks to ensure that I know what I know. You care about her. I care about what's going on with you. It is part of my modus operandi to know what's going on with all of my clients and every aspect of their lives, as unseemly as that might seem." She laughs but then her voice catches. "Besides, we're friends."

"Right."

"I have to admit I've been a little remiss," she says with a little sigh. "I should have checked up on her again, but she's been a little harder to track down. Sasha mentioned the internship and the solo part in September or October, but I haven't heard anymore about that, or Tally, or who she might be she seeing, for example. It's always good to keep tabs on your competition."

I wince on my end of the line at the jealous thought that Tally is seeing anyone. I have no right to dictate who Tally might be seeing at this point.

"I just want to know what she's been doing," Kimberley says. "And I know *you* want to know how she's doing. From what I've heard, she's had a very quiet year. I realize you're relieved, but it's a little strange that our little Paly high school grad isn't making a bigger splash on the NYC social scene. I've put it down to her being busy with her ballet career just like you're busy with baseball, but I just want to ensure that everything is copacetic on Ms. Landon's end of things. I feel…somewhat responsible for how messy things got between you two, and I just want to ensure she's doing okay."

"Right," I say and openly sigh taking a much-needed breath. There's instant relief on my end that Tally Landon led a very quiet year. "I really want to go to New York and check in with Tally myself and ensure she's doing okay and not seeing anybody."

"I know," Kimberley consoles. "*You can't.* I'm here in New York for a while. I'll see what I can do. I'll be in touch. Now, go do something fun for yourself; *call Nika.*"

I groan openly at her maniacal laugh as she ends the call seconds later after wishing me a Merry Christmas. I barely hear her. I'm consumed with thoughts of Tally because all I want to do is go to New York and see her for myself.

⁓⸙⁓

As a distraction, ten minutes later, I'm dialing Nika's number because I've decided there may be a way she can help me. I want to find out more about Tally and her life and what she's really been doing for the past six months. What better way than asking someone who has awesome hacking skills to help me out.

Nika cell phone rings four times. I'm just about to hang up when I hear her sexy voice. "Lincoln Presley. It's been…a while."

"Has it?"

"So, how's the off-season?"

The way she's said *off-season* makes it sound dirty. I laugh despite my best efforts to resist her charm. We're just friends now, but the longer I talk to her, the more I realize how lonely I am. Nika is entertaining. She's giving me the rundown on life in Seattle. One thing holds true; Nika knows how to find fun wherever she lands, while my life consists of attending practice, throwing a baseball, and preparing for next spring even in the off-season. I haven't had any fun in a long time.

"How's the hacking business?" I ask after a few minutes when there's a lull in the conversation.

She laughs.

"I'm always looking for legitimate work."

"I have something for you to work on." I spend the next ten minutes giving her the lowdown on what all I know about Tally Landon.

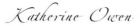

"So what am I looking for exactly?" Nika asks, sounding somewhat impatient after my long spiel about Tally.

I take a breath and try to focus because in just talking about Tally Landon again all this turmoil over her resurfaces. When I'm solely focused on baseball, as I should be, I rarely think about Tally. It's more about the next game. How fast is my fast ball? How good was my pitching in the seventh inning? When is the next game and will I be in the rotation? Nothing else. But here in the late December when my world has finally slowed down, all I do is think about is Tally. I sigh.

"She was important to me. I just want to know how she's spending her time. What's she's been up to in the last year and who she's been spending time with. I'll pay you triple your going rate."

Nika laughs again. "You don't even know what my rate is." She pauses for a few seconds and her breath catches. "I'm expensive."

"I'm sure you are."

"Okay," she says slowly breathing into the phone as part of her answer. "Okay. I'll see what I can find out about her. I'll be in touch. *Soon*…Lincoln Presley."

After hanging up with Nika, I sigh deep with relief because I'm doing something, at least, in hiring Nika to find out everything there is to know about Tally. That's what I tell myself, although another part of me starts thinking through the ramifications of having invited Nika back in my world. That part concludes it might not be a good thing, but I ignore the deep-seated fear beginning to surface in knowing Nika could invariably wreak more havoc on my life in all these unpredictable ways even more than Tally has. No. I ignore that wayward thought. I'm just focused on learning more about everything that Tally has been doing for the past several months. Yes. I'm less concerned about meeting up with Nika again than I should be, even though a small part of me knows that could prove to my undoing.

CHAPTER TWENTY

Tally ~ In more ways than just one

THE LIES TAKE HOLD. THEY GET bigger. My parents believe me when I call like clockwork to let them know how Marla and I are getting along in New York. Marla is busy working at the Dahlia with Rob and takes modeling and photo gigs wherever she can find them. Competition is fierce, worse than ballet, according to my best friend. I stayed in the background in the Corps after having come clean with the New York City Ballet creative director Sasha Belmont after my first lead performance in *Sleeping Beauty* end in the first part of November. I hid my pregnancy. Spanx helped. Layers helped. Not eating too much or often helped. I've been told as long as I stick to a healthy regimen and return ready to dance and perform in early March that Sasha was good with everything. She saw me dance. She appreciated my talent and eventually told me she admired my decision to raise a child even as she hinted that it's not an easy choice for a dancer to make. I didn't have the heart to tell her that I've since decided to give the baby up. No sense in bursting her little bubble of happiness about me and my choices.

Like I said, the lies just keep on building, one on top of the other. *Why stop now?* Nothing feels like it is in any kind of order. I try not to think of the money dwindling from my savings because I stopped attending NYC Ballet's rehearsals six weeks ago at Sasha's insistence. No dancing. No paycheck. I'm officially taking a paid position at NYC Ballet with the Corps in the spring, if only to start generating an income again. It wouldn't be fair to ask my parents for more money, since I'm holding back from them on so much of what is actually going on in my life.

The good news is that despite all the deception with everyone else back home, we have found suitable parents. At least, that's what Marla thinks.

I've only met them a couple of times. They seem nice enough, desperate enough. Their questions are few, and we've been able to mitigate most of their concerns about my age and why I'm giving this baby up in the first place as well as the permanent absence of the father—the usual red flags that would have most couples walking away at this juncture. Jamie and Elissa Mantel seem grateful for the opportunity to adopt this baby from me. I've been given the designation of surrogate mother since all I'm asking for is that my medical bills be covered, and that they call her Cara. I don't really tell Marla that this is a request I made of them. Cara. It means beloved. It's a cute little girl's name to me, and it is one implicit way that I can give her something that tells the story of who she is to me without ever really meeting her. *Beloved.* Cara Landon Presley Mantel. It makes me happy in some small way. *Cara. Cara Mantel.* I mean, who couldn't be famous with a name like that? If that's what she wants, of course.

The contract that the Mantells and I will have to sign is pretty straightforward. Marla hits up one of our neighbors, some attorney she met in the elevator one day and asked for his legal expertise. Bryan Davis was more than happy to help us out. He seems to have taken a vested interest in Marla, who remains oblivious to his interest in her. She just goes on telling him about her modeling sessions and helping me out and remains immune to the guy's advances. As far as the adoption contract, I have yet to scrawl my signature upon it. It rests on the coffee table where Marla set it when she first brought it home. Every time I think about signing it, I think about Lincoln Presley and his part in all of this.

I should tell him. I shouldn't tell him. I go back and forth. His knowing would jeopardize his baseball career. Yet, by not knowing, he can deny it, if ever asked.

And yet.

I constantly combat these wayward thoughts of him, knowing he's out there somewhere being famous and playing baseball. He's going to be father and never know it. *Linc.* His faraway presence still reaches for me. I have tried not to examine too closely why that is. He broke my heart. He ended it. And yet, I still think about him. And I wonder. Uncertainty. Guilt. Remorse. Hormones. These things make me feel conflicted. That's all it is.

I am a little over two weeks away from the big day when this baby arrives, and I give her away and start my life all over again. All I focus upon is my knowable future—ballet. This sideshow is almost over, and then I'll be able to breathe freely again. *I'll be able to breathe. And be free. Again.*

It's the end of January. Marla returns to the apartment looking worn out and not her usual bubbly self. She's withdrawn, unhappy. It's only a little more than two weeks before Valentine's Day, and we both seem to have begun a secret countdown. We need to get a cheaper place. We have determined that much. The rest of our plans remain uncertain. The resigned look on Marla's face makes me sad. I have to set her free. I can't take her down this abyss with me, not like this.

I watch her fill a tall glass with ice cubes. She pours a healthy dose of vodka, followed by a mere splash of pink lemonade. It's Thursday. It's four o'clock in the afternoon. We haven't really partied since we got here. I consumed a single glass of champagne on New Year's Eve. It was the one and only night, I allowed myself to feel reckless and free and not pregnant and not gangly, all these things I feel regularly now. I gaze at Marla from my designated position on the living room sofa. "What's up?"

Marla's hand trembles as she brings the glass to her lips and takes a long swallow. "Charlie's seeing Cynthia again. He's going out with her tomorrow tonight. I thought it was a one-time thing, but I guess not."

"How do you know?"

"She sent me another text, letting me know how excited she was to be going out with Charlie again. He's in Palo Alto for the weekend. And she came home, too. I don't like this!" Marla moves her head back and forth in disbelief. "She was sure I'd be okay with it since I never came to L.A. to be with him. And Charlie must have apparently told her I'd broken off the engagement, and we were done for good. He hasn't called in a while." Her hand slices through the air. "Damn it."

"Like I said before, you know he's doing this to get a rise out of you," I say. "He *knows* that just the idea of his seeing Cynthia *again* will drive you crazy. He's mad because you stayed with me in New York, and he doesn't understand why, not all of it, anyway. My part in all of this."

Marla slumps down next to me and rests her head on my shoulder. "I know."

"You should go back home and figure things out with him."

"What about you?" Marla asks. "You're just weeks out from delivering the baby. I can't leave you. And what are you going to do? After the baby comes? About the Mantels versus Tremblay's offer?" She makes a face.

Marla isn't exactly happy with me right now. Tremblay showed up two nights ago offering to adopt this baby. Marla is pulling for the Mantels, but I'm drawn to the idea of not giving this baby away to strangers. Tremblay's offer is intriguing. She hinted at helping me further my career. No details. They were just these subtle remarks of hers that she could help me in some way with NYC Ballet's next offer this spring beyond dancing in the Corps. Guilt surges with that particular admission; however silent, because I want to do more than dance in the Corps.

"What are you going to do about Tremblay's offer?" Marla asks as if reading my thoughts.

"I don't know yet. I'm thinking about it. I *know* Tremblay. That makes a difference to me."

"I know Tremblay, too, and that makes a difference to *me.*"

There's a bit of an edge to her tone, and it sets me off. "It's not your kid."

"No, but we've both made sacrifices to see this through."

She's pissed. She resents me. It was bound to happen.

We share a stormy five minutes of pure silence.

My anger turns to remorse. I can't keep her here. She's been the most loyal friend to me, but I can't keep her from Charlie just because she feels this overwhelming obligation to take care of me.

"Go see Charlie," I finally say. "Go. Catch a red-eye to San Fran and go work it out with him. And quit worrying about me. I've got this."

Now she looks conflicted. I feel guilty for having kept her here for so long.

"I thought it would all be so different. You know? Fun, freedom, parties, new things, love, guys," Marla says with a hint of disappointment. "We haven't been able to do any of that. We've both been working all the time. You're worrying all the time...about everything. It's all so messed up." She dabs at her eyelashes.

"I know. It's supposed to be the best time in our lives, but it feels like the worst," I say gently. "The truth is it's not supposed to be this way, not this hard, not like this."

"And the thing is I miss Charlie. I do love him, you know? The longer we're apart, the more I realize it."

"You two are meant to be together," I say gently. "So go work it out with Charlie. You love him. Go to him. I'm okay. *Really.* I can handle this. Go home. Work it out with him. I'll be okay. Promise. Now go catch a flight back to San Fran tonight and go see Charlie. You know he'd drop any plans with Cynthia with you in town. That's what he's been waiting for, for you to come back. So go."

"The whole Cynthia thing just pisses me off. It's not much of a show of commitment from him for me." Marla gets this wounded look.

"Don't let your ego get in the way. He's crazy about you. He has been for years. He's just doing what guys do; he's trying to get some kind of reaction from you. So? Show him how much you care because you *do* care. You love him. Anyone can see that. Go home. I can handle things here on my own.

You missed Christmas and New Year's with him. All because of me. Besides, if something happens, I can call Tremblay or the Mantels."

"Jamie and Elissa are out of town." She gets this vexed look. "They went to North Carolina to see his parents."

"Oh."

It's disconcerting to have to readily admit that Marla knows this couple better than I do. I should be more involved, but there is a distinct part of me that remains detached from all of this. *I love this couple; don't I?* They'll be good parents to this baby, but there is a larger part of me that secretly resents that about them, too. It's not something I can really share with my best friend who has sacrificed so much to make it right for me. No. It's hard to share these ungrateful parts of myself with another person, no matter how much I love them, not even with Marla because my ingratitude makes me feel shallow and unworthy. It's not something I'm proud of this resentment. I hate feeling this way, but I can't help it. They get to love this baby and have her be a part of their lives. *And I? What do I get? Nothing. Nothing. Nothing.* It stretches out before me into this hushed oblivion, this endless nothingness. And I resent it and them for being so perfect, so loving, so worthy.

"It's fine. *Really.* Like you said, I'm not due for another two weeks. I can handle things myself."

Marla looks torn for a few more seconds. I busy myself with looking resolute until I realize that Marla is talking to me. I've missed everything she's been going on about. It takes me a few seconds to catch up to her after this long reverie where I've done nothing but feel sorry for myself. Now I struggle with the guilt for feeling this way. It buries me a little. I'm not quite following what Marla is going on about.

"I'll only be gone the weekend," Marla is saying. "Maybe, five days max. It'll be fine. I'll call Rob and have him check on you."

"Nooooooooooooo," I say. "I'm fine on my own."

"Somebody needs to be watching over you. Rob can do it."

"Nooooooooooooo."

I've managed to avoid socializing with Rob Thorn for months. He works with Marla, and they take classes together at NYU. They've become the best of friends; it seems, but I stay out of it. Up until two months ago, I continued to dance with NYC Ballet, but they finally told me that for insurance purposes, I couldn't perform or rehearse anymore.

Dance. Rehearse. Perform. Suddenly, it was a no-go on all fronts. I've taken up the practice of ballet and yoga at home in the privacy of our living room and have become proficient with a wooden chair and the kitchen's highest countertop using it for barre work, even if I do look awkward doing it.

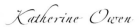

"I'm not going to go unless you cooperate. Tally, you're on doctor's orders to rest. The last thing we want to happen is for you to go into labor while I'm gone and when Jamie and Elissa are, too. Come on. Rob can do a run to the grocery store later in the week. He'll just pop in to check in on you. I'm sure he'll be fine with it."

"Does he *know* about me?" I look at her intently.

"No. You asked me not to tell anyone, and I haven't." She gets this vexed look. "I guess he can drop the groceries off at the front door. He doesn't have to come in unless you want him to."

"No. I don't want him to come in. This is my thing. I don't want the world knowing about it. I'm so close to being done with all of it." I don't hide my sudden agitation with all of it, as I stalk past her towards the kitchen and begin unloading the dish rack. Marla follows me into the confined space and watches me intently until I've put the last dish away.

"You're sure that you're fine." She looks unconvinced and crosses her arms and practically glares at me.

"I'm fine. Great. Fabo."

She laughs at the screwed-up face I make. It's been months since I've seen her quite this happy. The modeling gig hasn't been as easy as she thought it would be and the break-up with Charlie has been hard on her, regardless of how often she's told me she's *just fine* with it. And then, there's me. *My stuff.* Marla's been there for all of it. The late nights when I've all but panicked and openly shared my fears about failing, falling, and losing. Marla's the one who has stayed up with me and told me everything was going to be okay. I sort of gasp suddenly realizing what a burden being my friend has become over the last four months. I'm certainly not going to spoil it for her now when my unwarranted panic at the thought of being left alone in New York by myself starts to surge. Me. Alone. Me, solely dependent upon Rob Thorn and his grocery delivery. I can do this. I will.

"Go!" I say with a rare burst of giddiness when she gives me another questioning look. I don't need to say it twice. Marla races to the hallway closet and starts jamming stuff into her suitcase. And, all I can do is smile and mean it for once.

Within a half-hour, I've lined up her airline reservation while she's set a world record for packing. Now, she's ready to walk out. I damp down my ever growing reluctance at her leaving and follow her out to her car.

We break Dr. Shimmer's first rule when I slide into the driver's seat to take Marla to the airport. I'm not supposed to be driving. Marla doesn't say anything about it, and neither do I. I relish the simple fact that I am driving. It's been almost a year since I got behind the wheel of a car. *I can do this. It feels weird. A decidedly good weird. It's somewhat freeing. And God knows I need to feel free.* Marla stows her luggage into the trunk, and we're off.

After going a mere three blocks, she points out Rob's building. I covertly glance up at his apartment window and note that it looks all closed up. Nobody's home. I feel this twinge of panic. *I'm alone. Don't I know it?*

I shake off this unsettling feeling and contrive to smile for Marla, who studies me intently from the passenger seat. "You okay?" she asks.

"I'm fine. Just fine." I smile wider as we make our way toward the tunnel and JFK.

"He's probably working a double shift. It's Thursday. Sometimes, he does that."

"Sure. Truly, I don't want to know the whys and wherefores of Rob Thorn. "I'm going to do fine on my own. Look at me *driving*. I'm fine," I add for good measure and concentrate on the GPS.

On the first part of our JFK journey, Marla gets quieter. She studies the sights and lights of Manhattan, taking them all in as if this is the last she'll see of them. Then she spends quite a bit of time on the phone, trading favors, getting her shifts covered at the Dahlia through next Friday. So, it's now it's more than a full week in San Francisco, more than a weekend, but I don't say anything. No. I just navigate the traffic and manage to look cool, calm, and collected, as if I'm doing a Saturday afternoon performance. I suppose I am even though it's Thursday. Yes, I willingly partake in this innocuous adventure that will take Marla back to Charlie and away from me.

Marla gets this motherly gaze as soon as I judiciously park in a designated, no-parking zone at JFK. *Was it really only eight months ago that we marched down the aisle arm-in-arm with our high school diplomas?* I feel about thirty now. Yes, I'm going on thirty. *Linc would be pleased.* Ensconced in a white lace maternity top and a chic denim skirt that Marla procured for me from some discount fashion boutique she discovered last summer, I probably do look about thirty. I laugh to myself and glance over at Marla, who just beams back at me. *Bottle up this happiness and give it to me.*

"I'm going to surprise him," Marla says softly.

I nod. My throat gets tight, and my eyes start to sting. "Good idea." I miss her already, and she hasn't even left. I'm consoled by the fact that I'm driving her car. She has to come back to New York if only to retrieve it These thoughts buoy me up. I affect nonchalance, while Marla redoes her lipstick in the car mirror and checks her hair one last time.

"Tell Charlie hi for me," I say hugging her tight when she's finished.

"Anything else?" Marla flashes a megawatt smile, unable to contain her excitement. It practically shimmers off of her now.

"No." I wanly smile back. "If you happen to see my parents, although you probably won't, just tell them I'm doing great and that everything is fine. That I'm busy with NYC Ballet." My smile fades. "Yeah, just tell them that."

"Don't do *anything* while I'm gone. Just rest. Eat every day. Read a book. Relax."

"I won't do *anything* while you're gone. I'll eat. Promise." I hold my breath and let it out. "Remember, you can't say anything to Charlie about *this*." I point to my stomach.

"Paranoid much, Tally? I won't say anything. We've come this far and there's only a little more time to go."

"It's not a Juno flick," I say irritably. "Just don't talk about me. That way, nothing gets shared that shouldn't be."

It's easy looking at life from Marla's end of the spectrum. She isn't wafting around with a five-pound baby in her belly like I am. Paranoia sets in again. My ballet career may be in jeopardy. I can't quite believe Sasha's okay with everything, and I may get no more than a vacated spot in the Corps this spring. I'll take anything and count myself lucky, but the fear of failure surges through me anyway. *Anything. I'll take anything.* I've already told Sasha Belmont this, too.

Fears. I still have them. They still rule me. For a few minutes, I'm caught up in a memory vortex of Lincoln Presley and the intimate revelations about ourselves with that particular discussion with him. My sudden anguish must show because Marla's looking at me funny.

"You okay?" she asks again. I nod. "I left a message for Rob on his answering machine while you were changing. He said he should be able to check in on you this weekend. Don't give me that look. *Somebody* needs to be on call for you. Rob will be happy to do it."

"Okay. Great," I murmur and breathe out slowly. "Marla. I'm sorry I've had to ask so much of you, and that I've taken so much from you." I hang my head a little and then look up. "You've been the most awesome friend to me. The best. Thank you."

"Don't be silly. You haven't been any trouble. My God, Tally, you're having a baby. You're the one who's awesome." She squeezes my hand. "Don't forget we're in this together. You and me. The way Holly would have wanted it."

"Marla," I say trying not to cry. "Would Holly have given her up? Tell me the truth. What do you think she would have done?"

She looks uncomfortable with the question. "Tally," she finally says with a catch in her voice, "Holly was pregnant with Rob Thorn's baby."

"What?"

"They were going to get married." She groans and closes her eyes for a moment. "I thought you *knew*. I'm sorry. I shouldn't have said anything I just always thought you *knew* and just didn't want to talk about it." She looks heartsick. "But you didn't know and now you do."

"No. I didn't know but now I do. Wow. That explains so much—why she was so sure of Rob. She was so sure of him." *Breathe in and out. Just breathe.*

"Are you sure you're okay?"

"I'm okay. Better hurry, catch your flight." I force myself to smile. "You don't want to miss it."

"Are you sure you're okay?"

"Yes, yes. I'm fine. I'm just surprised; that's all. That she didn't tell me. That she didn't trust me."

"It wasn't like that. She didn't want to disappoint you or your parents by being less than perfect. She'd been debating about what to do. That's why she went and saw Rob that night. He wanted to get married from the very beginning, and she didn't. She'd finally decided that was best and went there to tell him and then planned to tell you on the way back. They were making plans, and everything was going to work itself out." Marla looks incredibly sad. "God, he was devastated about Holly, but he thought telling your parents that she was pregnant would just make things worse for them." She scans my face. "I'm sorry I told you. I really thought you knew and just didn't want to talk about it. *Her.* You *never* want to talk about her. And Rob thought you knew, too, and that you would eventually want to talk about it. But you didn't know," Marla whispers more to herself. "And I shouldn't have said anything. I'm so sorry."

I struggle to catch my breath and hide the ripples of despair that start to surface. "No. It's okay." *Breathe.* "Really. It's okay," I say slowly. "I don't think we should tell my parents now. They'd be devastated. It would be like losing Holly all over again. No. We shouldn't tell them. What's the point?"

"Are you sure *you're* okay?"

"I'm *fine*. Really. It's a shock, yes, but Holly loved Rob. She was so sure of him." I keep smiling, knowing Marla needs my reassurance in order to get out of the car. "I'm fine. Thanks for telling me. *It helps. Knowing.* And it doesn't change anything, does it? Now, go home and be with Charlie."

She sighs and takes a deep breath and turns to me. "I love you, Tally Landon."

"I love you, too, Marla Stone." She nods, squeezes my hand, and then gracefully slides out of the passenger seat. Within a few minutes, she's grabbed her luggage and is waving at me from the curb. I roll down the passenger window and lean over toward her. "Hey, do what you have to do when you get there. Just…be honest with Charlie about how you feel and what you want. Not that I'm the best one to give advice about being honest, right?" I shake my head side-to-side and she tries to laugh. "Don't worry about me. Okay? I've got this. I'm fine. Look at me." I force myself to smile even though it feels like I'm breaking up inside.

"Everything's going to be fine. It *is*," Marla says with enough certainty for both of us.

She gives me the thumbs-up as she leaves. All I can do is helplessly watch as the only lifeline I have gets swallowed up by the dark buzzing abyss that is JFK. I have to consciously fight the overwhelming devastation that washes over me as soon as Marla disappears inside.

I'm alone.

I do my best to ignore the underlying sensation that the very foundation of my life has just given way. *Again.*

CHAPTER TWENTY-ONE

Tally Seeking normal

IS CELL PHONE RINGS THREE TIMES before he picks up. It's six in the morning. I've been awake all night, waiting for what felt like enough time to pass, before I made this inevitable call. I'm holding my breath when he finally answers.

"Is it true?" I ask right away.

"Tally?" Rob sighs as he becomes fully awake with my early-morning phone call.

I ignore his greeting. "Sorry. It's early. Is it true? Was Holly pregnant?" Somehow I just need to hear him say it in order to believe it.

"Yes," he says with a heavy sigh. "Tally, I'm sorry. I thought she would have told you. She was scared but resolute about having the baby and us being together."

I wince at hearing his defensiveness. I've been cruel and bitchy to this guy for far too long. I close my eyes for a few seconds suddenly distraught when I hear the distress in Rob's voice. It wends its way towards me intent on colliding with all these mixed-up thoughts of my own about all of this. *This guy. Linc. Me. Pregnant. Holly. Geez. When did everything get this messed up?*

There's a muffled sound on Rob's end of the phone. He must have covered up the receiver. Somehow, I know he's breaking up on the other end of the line, and that he's going to cry soon.

Next topic. Is there another?

"How have you been?" I wince at the simple words and cajole myself to keep it together for both of us, even though I've been shaking nonstop for hours now. These weird sounds burble up in my throat, and my whole body aches from head to toe.

"Where are you?" Rob asks.

"At the apartment. Marla flew to San Francisco to see Charlie late last night." I pause and then sigh deep. "I just needed to know if it was true."

"Who told you? Marla?"

"Yes. She thought I knew. I didn't." I laugh bitterly. "I was just Holly's twin sister—the person who knew her best in the world; well, I thought so anyway. But *no*, Holly didn't tell me."

"She didn't want to upset you. She was worried about you about how you felt…about her and me. *Me*, mostly."

There's another heavy weighted silence. I can hear him breathing. It's a bit unsteady. "It's not your fault," I say grudgingly. "I blamed you but it was never your fault…what happened. Deep down, I knew that. I just went a little crazy, still am, I guess. I just want her back. I *need* her back." I sigh, debating what to tell him. "I need her now because…I'm in trouble."

"What kind of trouble?" Rob asks warily.

"A lot of trouble. Look, I can't do this right now. Thanks for telling me… the truth. I needed to hear it, I guess. I'm in a lot of trouble right now. I can't think straight."

"What kind of trouble are you in? Maybe I can help."

"No. No. No." I pause and close my eyes for a few seconds. "I'm in the same kind of trouble my sister was in," I say without thinking.

"You're pregnant? Jesus, Tally. Do your parents *know*? How are you getting along? Where are you right now?"

I can't answer all of his questions. I go for the last one. "In bed. But I can't sleep. I just…Marla's gone and my life's a mess. I only found out about you and Holly last night."

"Why don't I swing by and pick you up? I can be there in ten minutes. My car's in the garage. We should talk this through." I can hear Rob already going down the stairs. His feet pound along the steps at a fast pace. I feel this sense of relief. "I'm on my way. Keep talking."

"You don't have to do that." There isn't a lot of conviction in my tone. My breathing actually gets steadier in realizing that Rob is on his way to me. "Thank you," I finally say.

"It's not a problem. I've been meaning to call you. I wanted to say congratulations on the apprenticeship with NYC Ballet. It just never felt like enough time had gone by where you wouldn't hate my guts quite so much."

"I don't. It's not like that. It's just my life is very complicated. It has been for the past…year." I take a breath and slowly let it out. "Things just seem to be going so great with the internship after Holly and then there's this—me, pregnant."

"It'll turn out. There are options. Lots of them."

"Really? Because not that many are coming to mind. Believe me, right now? I'm just seeking to be normal again. Lead a normal life."

"Normal is good."

"My parents don't know, and I don't want them to find out. I can't disappoint them like this."

"Tally, I'm here," he says gently. "I'm parked on the street in front of your building. Come on down. Grab a coat and come on down."

"You don't have to do this. I'll figure something out."

"Get your ass downstairs, Landon," he says with a little laugh. "I'm here."

"You don't have to do this. I'll be okay. I'm fine *really*."

"You don't have to lie," Rob says. "We all do enough of that; don't we? I keep telling everyone I'm fine, but I'm not. I miss her so much." His voice breaks down. He sounds like he's about to cry again.

I'm not sure I can take hearing it because I feel like crying, too. "It's going to be okay, you know." I say, wiping at my wet face with the back of my hand as I struggle into my long coat. "Someday."

All I know for sure is that I have a little over two weeks before I have this baby. Surely, I can make it that far and figure out what to do next. Maybe, Rob can help me figure it all out. Maybe, Rob has all the answers.

Still looking for those, I spy a pearl-white Porsche, curbside, with its engine purring, as I exit the building. Rob Thorn leans against the car looking very unlike the guy I remember seeing more than eight months ago at Paly. I guess it starts with the sports car and his stylish clothes and the trendy haircut. He still wears it long, but it's more styled now. I guess attending NYU and tending bar at the Dahlia on 5th and living in Manhattan has changed him by multiple degrees.

Okay. Exponential ones. He looks good.

He stands tall and sure of himself as he hangs up his cell phone call with me. He pushes away from the car and half-smiles as he comes towards me. I almost roll my eyes, remembering his unassuming demeanor from before well enough. It is still hard to understand what all my twin saw in this guy. He always seemed all wrong for her. He has an uncanny likeness to the character Sawyer in *Lost*. The comparison has me smiling. I always liked Sawyer so did Holly. We thought he was sexy—combined with equal parts of honesty and dishonesty that made him that way. Holly used to say, "Sawyer lied for all the right reasons." Her analysis always made me laugh. Of course, I liked that idea because it gave me permission to be me. I catch my lip between my teeth as I move toward Rob.

Rather abruptly I'm brought back to the present, and a sobering early dawn where Holly is no longer here. I'm still pregnant in this reality and now mildly disturbed by Rob's very presence as we meet up, here in Manhattan. All these competing thoughts have me awkwardly shaking his outstretched hand. Together, we go in for a loosely-based hug. He hastily steps back and smiles down at me in that smirky way of his. His long golden hair hangs in his face, and he flips it back with one hand. I stare at him hard as if he is a complex math problem that must be solved.

"God, you look just like her," Rob says in the waning silence between us. "But then again, you're different in every way." He looks somber and apologetic at the same time.

I nod slowly. "She was amazing, beautiful, light, and airy. The opposite of me." My breath swarms the air with every breath I take, and he watches me closely now. "We all loved her."

A quick covert glance of his face reveals tears in Rob Thorn's mesmerizing grey eyes, and I scrutinize him more closely. *What is it that my sister really saw in him? Will I figure it someday?*

Up close, he still appears somewhat lost and out of sorts. He's a wayward line that is non-linear in formation. I've resorted to geometry within five minutes of meeting up with him. The thoughts won't stop. They continue to race through me at warp speed. He's a knight in shining armor just missing the shine, the armor, and the horse. Or, he was. Now I wonder. Now he seems to be golden and lit up with light, he seems bigger than life, and he drives a Porsche in Manhattan, not a Volvo. These incongruent thoughts make me smile ever so slightly, and he returns it as if I've provided him with much-needed air. In those first few seconds, he somehow makes me feel malevolent and powerful and not in a good way. It's as if I could wield it upon him, and he wouldn't care, he wouldn't fight me. *I can see that. I can feel it.*

And, let's face it, in the past half-hour; I haven't exactly thought through this whole scenario. I glance down at my rather pregnant form and inwardly groan.

What was I thinking?

He holds the passenger door open for me. At first, I'm too surprised at his chivalry to actually respond and move forward. No. I just stand there looking at him uncertain and attempt to quell all these senseless calculations that my mind is busy making about him. My assumptions about him may be all wrong. *I don't really know Rob Thorn. Do I?* I allow myself to accept that he's chivalrous and appears to be a benevolent knight without a cause. Yet here he is my rescuer. Rob Thorn got in his car at six in the morning and drove over here in record time to help me out.

"Thank you for coming," I say belatedly.

"I'm glad you called."

And there it is again—that smirky smile—complete with a row of perfect white teeth that would work fine for a Hollywood toothpaste commercial. I note that he has this inexplicable way of pushing his hair back from his face at inopportune moments and that this gesture inadvertently captures my attention and causes me to stop and stare at him.

"How do you like New York?" I ask and half-laugh when he gets this *deer-in-the-headlights* look. I'm not the only one who hasn't thought things through.

"Fine," he says slowly and gets this apologetic look. "NYU. The Yankees," he says with a shrug. "It's not all bad."

"Please don't tell me you're a baseball fan," I say feeling a little deflated by his answers.

"Are you kidding? I'm all about baseball…as a fan. I don't play or anything. I'm not Lincoln Presley if that's what you mean." He gives me a meaningful look.

He knows. How does he know?

"No, you're not." I catch my lower lip between my teeth and eventually nod. "And I'm okay with that."

"I saw you at that party with him. When you left with him."

All but accusing. No lies here.

"Oh. Yes," I say dully as the ability to lie deserts me.

It's strangely comforting to be honest with someone. How ironic that it would be with Rob Thorn—the guy I've blamed for Holly's death for almost a year.

"I'm sorry it didn't work out for you with him."

I gaze over at Rob and finally manage to shrug with faked nonchalance. "Not meant to be, I guess." I study the sidewalk for a few seconds and then look up at him. "He said I was too young."

"Asshole."

I nod slowly and eventually laugh. He stares at me for a long while and then finally grins back. Still smirky. It's fascinating just to get him to smile. I want to study it longer and figure it all out. I want to better understand just what all my sister saw in this guy. *Really* understand it, understand him. Somehow, I know if I can figure this thing out with Rob Thorn, then everything else will fall into place.

I've missed his question. He's going on about something. His features have transformed, and he's become more animated as he talks. He's actually even more handsome and endearing.

"You don't have to tell me if you don't want to," he's saying.

"I'm sorry." I pause. "What did you ask me?"

"I asked when you were due." Rob gets this little red flush it races up his neck and face.

"Soon. February 14th?" I glance down at my iPhone and avoid his quizzical gaze. I race through my calendar for the next two weeks and point the date Marla has highlighted on my phone. "February 14th. See? Valentine's Day." I swallow down the sadness. "But rehearsals will have already started at NYC Ballet by then. I hope to catch up by mid-March."

"Valentine's Day. Less than a month of recovery time, Tally? For ballet." There's judgment in his tone.

"Yes."

He looks apologetic. "You're really good. Holly always said you were amazing."

"She said that?"

"She did."

"I don't know. Not so amazing anymore," I say.

"You look fantastic. You really do. You hardly show even now. Your face glows. Holly's did that, too. She wasn't as far along as you but..." Rob looks sad for a moment and stares out at the passing cars without looking at me directly. His face is strangely illuminated but still shadowed by the overhead lights on the Parkway. New tears appear on his dark lashes.

"When was your baby with Holly due?"

"September 22nd. We were going to elope the first of May. We were working it all out that day." He winces and then lets out a long breath. His voice gets weaker. "Come back and graduate. We had it all worked out. We were really excited about the baby and getting married."

"In the spring. May Day," I echo his words as more of a distraction than actually registering what he's said.

"Holly thought that would be fun to get married when all the flowers were out. She wouldn't be showing that much. She had it all worked out. I mean, who wouldn't want to get married on the first day in May, right?"

"Of course. That would be fun."

He gets this weird expectant look. It makes me feel uncomfortable—the penetrating way he looks at me as if I can be Holly if only he looks at me long enough.

"Holly would think that would be fun." He looks taken aback at what I've said and shakes his head side-to-side as if to clear it. I reach out and touch his hand for a second, and then I lower myself into the passenger seat of his car.

He reaches in, slipping one arm behind my back to help me while his other arm grazes across the front of my chest. "Sorry. I didn't mean anything by that." He gets this sheepish look and bites at his lower lip.

He's fascinating in this weird way. I stare at him some more. He's not all that impossible to figure out. He's nice. Giving. Loyal. He's a Golden Retriever in the human form. He smiles again—the Sawyer smirk—I dub it for good this time.

I find myself easily returning it, so unlike me, because he has this uncanny ability of making me feel light, airy, and even normal, completely outside of my usual dark, edgy self. *He makes me want to be Holly.*

He still confounds me so I make an attempt to focus upon our surroundings—the Manhattan skyline at dawn. Lights still sparkle and dazzle from all directions. I feel weird, even light-headed. I try to remember the last time I ate something. Yesterday morning's breakfast? Yogurt? A piece of toast? Was that yesterday or the day before? My stomach growls in protest, and I'm just noticing this for the first time. With undetectable indecision, I watch him as he easily slides in on the driver's side, puts the car in drive, and pulls away from the curb.

"Rob?" I say after a few more minutes of contemplation. "I'm absolutely starving. There's this diner a few blocks from here. Want to go?"

He laughs. "I was hoping you'd say that. Yeah, I love diners. Let's go."

"Thanks for the rescue. Driving, I mean." I wave my arm about the small confines of his car. "Thanks for telling me the truth about Holly and being so understanding about all of this." I encircle my stomach and feel the baby move at that exact moment.

"It's a lot to take on. Having a baby. In Manhattan. By Yourself. I get it."

"Not all of it," I say quietly. I settle into the passenger seat and look away from him as he glances sideways at me with a curious look. "Later. I'll tell you more later. Right now? I just want to go to that diner and eat something. It's been a while."

"How long has it been since you've eaten?" Rob asks pointedly.

"A while. Breakfast? Yesterday, I think," I whisper.

"Tally." He shakes his head and gets this disapproving look. "You have to eat. We'll go to this diner, and then you can tell me everything."

He's hard to disagree with.

He's hard to dislike this time around.

"Okay," I finally say.

We order six different items off the breakfast menu. Rob wants to try their waffles and their pancakes. He tells me eggs and bacon is standard fare for him. "I eat a lot. All the time," he says after the waitress rushes away with our order.

Twenty minutes later, I am fascinated by the amount of food that arrives at our table, and I watch him tuck it all away and become completely enthralled and entertained. This guy can eat, and I enjoy watching him do it. There's no *only-two-York-Patty-candy-treat-limits-a-week* for this guy. There's recognizable consolation in knowing he's not like Elvis in any way. He nudges my hand where it lies on the table between us. In the next moment, he hands me a fork and pushes a waffle toward me.

"Eat, Tally," he says this so gently that it doesn't quite sound like a command.

The way he's said this reminds me of Linc and of course, it just about makes me cry but then Rob is looking at me and taking it all in and there's that smirky smile of his again. For a few precious minutes, I don't think about Lincoln Presley. Rob is amused at the New Yorkers' activity taking place in the diner—the way the bell dings every time someone goes in or out. He points out how the smell of bacon clings to the air and deems it as a sign of wholesome, good food. I get this wide smile because I recognize that he's been captivated by the place, just like Marla and I have been. I tell him we've come to love this place and think it's the best thing about New York, we've discovered so far. I listen to him intently as he goes on about the place. He's growing on me. I trust him. He's sweet. He gives me a little joy when there shouldn't be any. I smile again for what seems like the twentieth time already today.

"So what now?" I ask slowly.

I'm amazed at the amount of food he's just consumed, including half of my eggs and most of my hash browns and toast and all the pancakes and waffles the waitress with the black spiky hair delivered to our table just a half-hour before.

"Are you eating enough?" Rob asks now.

His eyes roam over my body in this brazen way that doesn't exactly make me feel uncomfortable. He reaches across the table and lightly fingers my stomach and then traces the hollowness of my cheekbone.

"You're too thin, Tally."

I lean into his hand with an unexpected need for his understanding and acceptance. "I try to eat," I say in a low voice. He nods. Apparently, he was informed of my eating disorder by Holly. "I'm better."

He looks at me hard, and I blush under his scrutiny.

"You have to *eat*. For the baby. For yourself. I know ballet is important to you, but you can't destroy yourself over it." For a second, he sounds almost like Holly had months before. I'm reminded of our argument just before she died about Rob, ballet, and New York—so many things.

"I'll try harder," I say. "Not much longer anyway."

He takes my hand and entwines his fingers with mine. "I know you will."

Being up most of the night begins to wreak dizzying havoc on my senses. He gets the intriguing Sawyer smirk once again as he helps me up from the diner's booth, pays our tab, and talks me into walking back to his apartment by way of Central Park. He promises me that it is a sight to behold this early in the morning before everyone is up. He is some kind of rescuer. I can see that now.

"Friends," he says at one point as if he's giving a blessing.

"Friends," I say back to him. I weave my arm through his, and he pulls me tighter to him. Being with Rob feels different. Safe, I guess is how I would describe. I can breathe freely again—something—I realize that I haven't been doing for a long time. Rob reminds me of home. And, I miss home. He's kind and worthy, and I know implicitly he won't set out to hurt me. Somehow that seems like enough for now. It's what I need right now.

"Want to stay at my place for a while? I mean, if you want to, until Marla gets back?" Rob asks.

"Yes," I say with only a little hesitation.

Rob displays that Sawyer smirk for me once again.

We walk arm-in-arm back to his apartment.

It's true that he fascinates me in this inexplicable way. He'll require further study before I can determine my final answer about what my darling, perfect sister really saw in this guy.

Yes, this will require more than sharing a meal at Jo's Diner, walking through Central Park or even exchanging '*we're-just-friends*' affirmations. I am sure of it.

This will require time and study and focus. I have all of these things right now.

And surprisingly, I notice once again that I can breathe freely. It appears I've been holding my breath all fall and into winter for all these reasons. *Further study of Rob Thorn is required. Yes.*

"Rob," I say as we ascend in the elevator to his apartment. "Thank you for coming to get me."

"Sure thing."

He hesitates for a few seconds and looks down at me.

I wait.

"You can always count on me, Tally."

And I believe him.

I wake up to the late-afternoon sun slanting through the window in an unfamiliar room. The clock says 1:07 PM, and I wonder how I got here. The last thing I remember is talking to Rob Thorn in the spacious living room of his apartment. We'd been sitting in opposing chairs and experiencing more of these jarring moments of awkwardness as the early morning dragged on between us. He was Holly's *friend*, not mine. In the quest to fill up the ever-growing silences, I told him more about the summer at SAB and the internship with NYC Ballet. He'd been interested and asked all kinds of questions. That's all I remember and now I'm in a bed waking up slowly and attempting to take it all in. I'm still dressed in what I threw on early this morning when he first picked me up. I sigh with untold relief as I conclude that nothing happened. *Why would it? I'm nine months pregnant.*

I'm sure Rob has other more viable options than a girl, who is pregnant and resembles a small refrigerator; even if she happens to look identical to the girl he once loved and lost. I'm sure as soon as I opened my mouth and spoke to him that he was disappointed in so many ways by what I said and didn't say; because it had to be painfully obvious, even to Rob, how unlike Holly, I really am. *Was.*

It's quiet. Too quiet. Curiosity has me going past the bathroom, stopping briefly in the middle of the living room and making a full three-hundred-and-sixty-degree turn and looking around with growing dismay for my host. *He isn't here.* This crushing disappointment swells deep inside.

Alone again. Naturally. The thought makes me almost cry. I stumble my way back down his hallway. I turn on the faucet and splash water on my face and let the tears flow. This crying thing has got to stop. I spend a few minutes making myself somewhat presentable. There's not a lot I can do with the wrinkled, white man's shirt and a pair of crumpled black maternity jeans, but I retrieve make-up from my over-sized bag and make the best of it. I console myself that in a few more weeks, I'll have answers. I'll make it through this pregnancy and figure out what's next for me. Life will return to normal again in whatever way that it's supposed to be. I'll have answers. I'll find them. I'll make them.

I look at my face in the mirror and feel somewhat satisfied. I feel better. I can handle this. I *will* handle this.

Somehow.

Ten minutes later, I emerge from his bathroom, instantly confronted by the smell of cooking bacon. I proceed warily, running my fingers through ends of my hair and somewhat holding my breath as I come around the corner. Rob is busy at the stove cooking breakfast. He turns at my approach. "I thought I'd make you something to eat."

"We just ate."

"That was *hours* ago. I told you I like to eat all the time."

"I can't."

He manages to hold up a book with his right hand that he's apparently been reading while cooking with his left. He allows me a glimpse of the title: *What To Expect When You're Expecting.* I'd started it half a dozen times and finally concluded that I didn't want to know what to expect when I was expecting.

"I haven't read it," I say with a careless shrug.

"*Obviously,*" he deadpans. "You're supposed to eat every five or six hours. Keep your strength up and stay healthy."

"I don't...I do what I can." Nervous, I push past him and reach up for a coffee cup I spy in the open door of his cupboard.

"Here I made you some tea. It's good for you. Herbal."

I turn to him holding the empty coffee cup and attempt to control my temper. "Rob," I say slowly. "I can handle all of this myself." I sweep my arm around the kitchen and then rest it along my stomach for emphasis.

"You don't have to."

"I *want* to."

"No, you don't." He hesitates but then he gets this obstinate look. "You called *me,* Tally."

"I don't know why I did that." I pause in search of a convincing answer. "Oh yes. Only to ask if what Marla had told me about Holly was true."

"You already knew it was."

I don't have an answer for that. I feel helpless and out of sorts. *He* makes me feel this way. *I don't like it.* This fury for him—for so many things—starts to wend its way to the surface. I carefully set the cup down on the counter and curl my hands into fists—preparing for a fight or flight. I'm not really sure which one.

But then?

He smiles.

It's that damn smirky smile again. Oh my God, it's going to be my undoing. I want to hate him so much, but I can't. I don't.

"I want to help you. I *can* help you. I *will* help you, Tally."

"I don't...want...your help. I can't..."

"I know." He gets this empathetic look. "We'll be friends then."

I have nothing to say to that.

The pan is smoking away behind him. I've obviously become a distraction. I shake my head and finally say, "Your...bacon's burning." He spins around and rescues the pan by removing it from the flame.

Remarkably, he manages to salvage just about everything in it. Inside of five minutes flat, we're eating his breakfast—scrambled eggs, crisp hash browns and bacon, and buttered toast—in this wondrous, companionable silence.

He encourages me to eat one bite of everything. I do two. Strangely, we're both happier for it.

⁓∘⁓∘⁓

He convinces me that another walk through Central Park is in order. I haven't run for last week, so I follow him out the door toward the infamous park. I covertly watch as he shoves his hands into his pockets, and we set upon the same pace toward the park's entrance. He's wearing one of those knit caps that have become all the rage with guys. Personally, I absolutely hate that look, but I find myself smiling at him and catch him gazing back at me. His eyes loom large in his face. They're this stunning blue—a different color than Linc's lighter, greyer than blue ones. Rob's eyes are clear and true. I silently cajole myself to stop comparing him to Elvis at every turn. *Just stop.*

We manage to walk the first mile in this acceptable silence, but then he nudges my arm with his. We've stopped near the top of a rudimentary stone bridge that overlooks a bubbling creek below. I've been staring over the edge at the gurgling water stream for some time while he's apparently been staring at me.

"Tell me about more of it," he says.

"*It.*" I glance over at him suddenly wary.

"Your life. SAB. Tremblay. Marla. The baby. NYC Ballet. Starring as the Lilac Fairy in *Sleeping Beauty*. What an accomplishment. *Him.* Start somewhere."

There's a long silence and he just waits. He's patient, accepting. I guess those are the two standout traits that seem to vibrate from him now. *Patient. Accepting.* Two things I could really use right now. From him. For me.

"SAB was hard. Harder than we thought it would be." I grimace and start to smile. "Tremblay took the directorship," I add belatedly. He nods. Somehow, it's disconcerting to learn that he already knows this, but I decide to ignore this fact and go on. "She's been a task-master, more than usual. All summer. Then Marla doesn't get invited to Winter Term. She and Charlie break up. I get the apprenticeship at NYC Ballet. Things are going along okay. Marla gets the job at the Dahlia. NYC Ballet is a dream come true. And, Sasha Belmont, the director? She's been amazing. I land the part of the Lilac Fairy in *Sleeping Beauty*. It's an amazing offer. A privilege. Nobody gets a part like that just starting out. But this whole time, I'd been feeling off. Awful.

Tired. Exhausted. I didn't eat much all summer because I'd been doing the boxer's diet, and I missed all the signs—"

"Because you weren't eating enough."

"Maybe." I sigh. "Anyway, this guy does a lift with me for another rehearsal and he's teasing me that I've gained weight. His remark gets me to thinking. Five pregnancy tests later, it's all but confirmed. I'm not panicked, not quite. I console myself with the idea of an abortion because I have up to twenty-four weeks to decide. But when it comes down to a decision like that? I can't do it. I kept thinking of Holly. Life is precious. I couldn't just take it away. *I know.* Who knew Tally Landon could ever have a conscience about anything?" I laugh a little. "So, the weeks just pass on by, and here I am…nine months pregnant."

"You're amazing," Rob says. His hand rests near mine.

"Not so amazing." I hang my head and swallow hard.

"Marla's been a great friend, but I'm holding her back from everything she really wants. She struggles with the modeling thing. She thinks I don't notice." Rob nods, confirming for me that Marla's confided in him, too. "She stays in New York for me. I owe her so much for doing that, but she belongs with Charlie. She went home to work things out with him. I'm just trying to keep it together, have this baby, and get on with my life." I take an unsteady breath. I should probably be out with all of it. "We had a disagreement about Tremblay a few days ago. Allaire came by the apartment with an offer to adopt this baby."

"Allaire Tremblay wants to adopt your baby?" He's taken aback. "That's pretty audacious."

"I thought that, too, at first. How do you know so much about Tremblay?" I look at him uncertain, and then it comes to me. "Oh. Holly."

He nods. "She used to fill me in on the stories about Tremblay," he says dryly. "The woman is…detrimental. Yeah, she's detrimental in all senses of the word—a *detriment* and *mental*." He laughs at his own joke. I can't quite bring myself to disagree with him because I've wondered as much about Allaire Tremblay myself.

"I'm not sure I can do it."

"Do what?"

"Give this baby up to complete strangers. Not after learning what Holly was going to do…I am thinking of letting Tremblay adopt her. That's a win… for almost everyone."

This conversation has become too personal. He looks surprised and then disappointed again.

In me? Of course.

I walk away from him because suddenly the idea of being suspended on this bridge above the water below and talking about this baby *with him* is too much for me to handle.

"I can help you," he says from behind me. "Let me help you."

"What do you mean?"

I whirl back around and stop him in his tracks with my sudden rage. He looks surprised by it. I'm sure Holly never lost her temper with him. Holly never got mad at anyone for long, including me.

"This isn't like buying a house or purchasing a car or deciding which college you're going to attend. This is *big*. It's life. It's a child. A commitment for a lifetime—a commitment that I'm not willing to take on. I'm not ready. I'm not good at this kind of thing." I grimace and turn on him further. "Please don't stand there and judge me because I've come up with a solution that works for me. Please don't do that. It's not like I haven't judged myself enough as it is already. I really don't need you doing it, too."

He looks disillusioned. He seems to search my face looking for a different answer. Finally, he says, "What does Marla say?"

"Like I said, Marla's not happy with the idea of Tremblay adopting this baby or *me* for considering it. There's this couple she found that want to adopt a child. We've worked out an adoption contract with them. Tremblay just showed up a few nights ago with this solution, and Marla didn't like it. Her life has been turned upside down by all of this, by being away from home and hiding my secrets from everyone we know, especially from Charlie. New York. *Me.*" I look up at him directly. "It's all a bit much for all of us."

Rob nods slowly and looks at me more intently. "I can help you."

I ignore what he's said. "Let's face it…I'm a drain on everybody I care about."

"That's not true."

"Yes. It *is*. It is true." I force myself to smile and then shake my head at him. "You've been warned."

"Your sister warned me about you a long time ago."

He gets this determined look that I've come to recognize in the past few hours. He's not going to take no for an answer—*any* of my answers. I'm bothered on a few different levels that he and Holly used to talk about me.

"What did she say? About me?"

"She said you were the most beautiful girl in the world—inside and out." He gets this little smile. "Talented? Oh yes. Amazing. Stubborn. Wicked. A rebel in every sense of the word but that underneath the edgy exterior, you show the world is this amazing wonderful girl, who just wants to love and be loved."

"She told you all of that? When?" I ask, incredulous and skeptical at the same time.

"That day. You were out there waiting in your car. I saw you from the window and asked what you were doing there with her. I was angry with you, especially when she told me how you had *concerns* about me and New York and NYU. About me '*tagging along*', as she said you put it. Holly insisted we all had to get along, or I couldn't come." He frowns. "I wanted to be with her, so I promised her I'd try to get along with you. We'd work out our differences."

"That's quite a promise."

Now he looks really unhappy. I'm a little put out and confused by the direction this conversation is going. I think it must show in my face. He sighs deep and so do I.

"Tally, I haven't been completely honest with you. I saw you a few months back. I saw that you were pregnant, and I should have—"

"You knew I was pregnant?" I step back from him while this weird vertigo sensation comes over me. "How?"

"Like I said...I saw you a few months ago. You were out running, and I saw that you were pregnant. I...I thought you still hated me, and I wanted to wait for the right time to talk to you. My parents were visiting that weekend. I had to sign some stuff for my dad. He took a hit in the stock market and had to move some funding around, and he bought a few places, here in New York, just after the market tanked last fall. We've just finalized a deal on an apartment by NYU, by SAB, by you and Marla. And I thought I could help. I want to help because I figured out you hadn't told your parents when you didn't go home at Christmas, and I thought...I could help. And then, you called. I know it looks bad, but I was going to call you this week anyway—"

"I don't believe you."

He isn't making any sense, and he sounds too much like a stalker at this point even for him.

"I know it looks bad, strange. She said I needed to understand you better. Holly wanted us to all get along and be friends. She'd told Marla she was pregnant, and she was going to tell you. That day. She wanted us all to be happy and live in New York together. And so I came to New York last fall— like we'd planned—and tried to put my life back together and keep an eye on you and Marla. I thought maybe we could eventually be—"

"What? Be friends? Live happily ever after? What, Rob? Jesus, you lay all this on me in a public place." I angrily sweep my arm across the general area. There is green grass and trees and sidewalks everywhere but not a soul in sight. Strange, given the time of day. It's after one in the afternoon after all when New Yorkers seem to be everywhere. "You can't just ride in on a white horse and rescue me, Rob Thorn. I don't even know if I *like* you."

He winces and so do I because I sound harsh and bitchy and ungrateful. I hesitate and take a breath while my mind races and my body contacts and my anger soars. "I have a life." I look at him hard, ensuring he understands. "I'm going to be a star ballerina. You're not a part of that. I don't even know if I *like* you. I'm not Holly. You can't just *buy* your way into my life."

I race down the sidewalk, gripping my protruding front and try for a dead run. Within three minutes, my right side begins to ache with the fast pace and this alarming pain starts up between my legs. I won't be able to keep this up too much longer, and it frustrates me that I can't physically do what I need to do. It's been this way the last month, and I hate admitting it to myself, let alone to anyone else. Tears of frustration blind me. I wipe at them with my right hand and keep a tight grip on my stomach with my left. I feel off balance. I almost trip. The stupidity of the situation wins out.

Why am I running?

What am I so afraid of? Rob Thorn? Surely not.

I am Tally Landon. I am doing it my way. I will be myself. I will do this thing. *Alone. Naturally.*

I will do this thing alone.

I stop running. The sidewalk materializes with people—regular people who mill their way through their lives and Central Park with little regard for me. There are only a few who offer no more than a cursory glance in my direction. I'm sure the out-of-breath, pregnant girl gripping her sides and staggering around on the sidewalk is only distracting for some of them and a non-event for all the others. *I am alone. Naturally.*

A hand touches my lower back. I look up into the dark-blue eyes of one Rob Thorn, not Lincoln Presley's dizzying light grey-blue ones. *No. Not Elvis's eyes at all.* There's this fleeting disappointment that comes along with that single crushing thought. Heartbreak crosses my features before I'm able to completely hide it.

But then?

He smiles. That smirky smile. Oh, God, the smile. It's distracting enough and endearing enough that it shores me up a little. It's crazy. I think I've all but drowned, and his smirky smile rescues me from the depths of myself and the despair of losing Holly, of losing Linc, of possibly losing Marla, and of giving up this baby. None of these losses quite touch me when he smiles like that. *At me.* I could stare at him forever when he smiles like that. I could possibly forget the loss of everyone else. It comes to me then. *That's what Holly must have loved best about him.*

"Well," Rob says, and then he pauses and gulps at the air. It almost makes me want to laugh. "She always said you were hard to keep up with. I guess Holly was right about everything, especially you."

"What do you want from me?" I ask somewhat gingerly while this unidentifiable emotion slowly makes its way through me.

This feeling is like a rush of warm air over bare skin, and this soothing calm soon follows. I gasp at the unexpectedness of it all. He makes me feel something new, however foreign.

And then it comes to me. It's this undeniable feeling of hope. *He gives me hope.* It's overwhelming…this feeling.

All my life, I've known how to remain indifferent. Since I was fifteen, I've known how to kiss a guy, have sex with him but keep him distant. Since I was ten, I've known how to command a stage, get the lead, and perform perfectly. I've known how to take and receive and take again. My whole life up to now, I've known how to love or not to. I've known how to be me, and I've known how to be Holly.

What I haven't recognized or understood or felt until this singular moment as I gaze up at Rob Thorn is the amazing capacity that hope brings. *Hope.* He gives it to me so easily. It's there in that smirky smile of his, in the way he gazes down at me, and then again, as he gently kisses my forehead. I frown with the gesture, close my eyes, and hide my face in his shirt.

My mind succumbs to the weight of uncertainty even as this unfamiliar feeling of hope races through me and proves to be a much bigger force to deal with. I can actually feel it extinguish the uncertainty. It's like a rush of air that inevitably snuffs out a candle flame.

Hope?

I feel hopeful?

He makes me feel hopeful?

It would seem he gives it freely without a requirement for anything of me in return. *No.* He just holds onto me in this loose embrace with his arms reaching ever so lightly across my shoulders. My head meets up with his chest in this perfect stance, and I can hear and feel his beating heart.

We're standing so close together that when the baby decides to interrupt the moment and kick, he feels it, too. I hear his soft laugh and his simple happiness travels straight through to me.

"What do you *want*…from me?" I mumble the harsh words against his chest and then quickly step back and scan his features in a desperate search for honesty, truth, and some indication as to what kind of price I will have to pay for all of this.

"I want to help you."

"What else?" I ask cautiously. "What else do you want from me?"

"I want to be your friend."

The words are sincere enough to make a girl cry, or laugh, or both equally in my case.

CHAPTER TWENTY-TWO

Tally Power shifts

NO ONE HAS TO EXPLAIN TO me how life can turn on a dime—how it can change in a single day or the next explosive second. My water broke just as Rob and I arrived back at the apartment. I blame it on the endless flights of stairs we judiciously climbed back up to the apartment. Both of us shared wisps of terror at what lay ahead of us (me), as we piled into a taxi and raced to the nearest hospital where drugs were quickly administered to me for pain, while the explanation was so easily given that it was too late for an epidural. That seemed flimsy to me. Yet, there was little time for debate because I was *going too fast* according to the rather cute ER doctor who first took care of me. A cute ER doctor was about the only good thing I could come up with in those first precious hours. Yes, in between those first few seconds when the reality of my situation made itself known and finally enveloped all of me—and in addition to the seven hours that have passed since then—I've managed to become a mother to one perfect baby girl because life can change on a dime. And it does. *Again.*

The baby stares at me from the bassinet that the on-duty nurse has placed right next to my hospital bed. Rob has taken a much-needed break for food and coffee. I am left alone with this infant because our frantic change of plans led to Lenox Hill Hospital in lieu of New York Hospital where my original birth plan is on file. *True.* No one here knew about my plan to give this baby girl up for adoption. I was the one that urged Rob to step away and take a break. I needed one, too. From him. From *this.* All of it. I require this alone time with this baby I'm not supposed to keep or want or love. Yet I recognize this unexpected gift, and I want at least thirty minutes with her all by myself in order to take it all in. *Her.* Alone.

My mind races with all these incongruent euphoric thoughts. I could raise her. I could find a nanny. I could get a job, at least one that *pays*. Hire a nanny. Get a job. Dance during the day. Work at night. Pay a nanny. I could become the cliché working mom in every love story ever filmed. And when would I see this baby exactly? I could go home. Give up ballet. Come clean with my parents. I can do any or all of these things. Any of these things. None of them. Options. Choices. *I can do this. Can't I? How would I do this? I can't.*

I stare at this baby, who stares back at me awaiting answers—*needing them,* in fact. She is so perfect. She is this angel, who seems to smile at me, although Rob read somewhere that this is impossible. Babies don't smile until they're almost three-months-old, he assured me of this earlier.

My hand languishes in mid-air, a mere six inches from hers. I'm afraid to even touch her, afraid of falling further in love with her—this miracle. I turn my aching body more fully onto my left side and just continue to stare at her. Eventually, she sighs deep and closes her eyes. I mimic her sleeping sounds from my ever-watchful position.

Allaire Tremblay's face comes to mind. Earnest. Determined. Serious. Ever calm. All these good qualities—a mother has—that seem to evade me. I can still recall Tremblay's understated joy from a few days ago when she offered to take this baby after explaining how the idea had just come to her the night before. She'd been thinking about my situation. It dawned on her that she was in a perfect position to raise a child, unlike me. *True.*

I shake my head. She probably won't name her Cara. Tremblay's favorite ballet is *Swan Lake.* I'd probably have to learn to live with the name Odette, or worse, Odile, because hands-down Tremblay's favorite ballet production is still *Tchaikovsky's Swan Lake.* Maybe I could talk her into Juliet. Probably not. Tremblay would most likely come up with a name that conveyed something sentimental or tragic or both, even if it wasn't after a character in a production. She'd hire a nanny, move back to San Francisco, and would ensure that I have the chance of a lifetime to pursue my dance career with NYC Ballet. She's hinted at that much.

Life would go on. Life would move on.

I would…move on.

Logical. All of it.

I could live with that. Couldn't I?

I reach out and trace the baby's little fingers with mine. She stirs in her sleep and emits this angelic sigh. *She's going to be okay.* I smile at this vacant thought, even as my body vaguely throbs with this fresh shimmer of heartbreak. Then I reach for my cell phone and dial Tremblay's number. The searing pain that came with delivering this little child dissipates with every passing moment she's here, but there's this other pain—this tangible heartbreak—that I recognize and honestly accept. It is so much worse. I'm already convinced of its permanence.

Allaire Tremblay doesn't waste time. Ever. Not even now. She bursts into my hospital room with this barely-veiled euphoria. She is a woman with a purpose and in awe of her unexpected gift—from me. I watch her struggle to hide her outright joy now. Her dancer's strut across the room to grab my hand does little to diminish the sudden anxiety Rob and the newly-arrived Marla display at her whirlwind entrance. Tremblay seems momentarily taken aback at their very presence. The duo takes an unconscious protective stance against the prima ballerina's unwelcome entrance, while I am restored, somewhat bolstered up, by her obvious happiness. I revel in it. In my decision. *This is good. This is right for all of us.*

"Oh," Tremblay says with a touch of dismay. "I didn't realize you were here, Marla." There's an unmistakable frozen quality in her tone and words. Her eyes narrow in the all-familiar, critical way that we know only too well, although these circumstances are far from the usual inspection of Tremblay's dance criteria, even for the woman herself.

"I flew back in early this morning after Rob called me." Marla rewards both Tremblay and me with a warning look. She's not happy with either one of us. Me—for not calling—and Tremblay because of her very presence here.

I sit up a little straighter in bed, profoundly aware of my intended power. I can change my mind at any moment in the next forty-five days and there's not a damn thing that Allaire Tremblay could do about it. No matter that I've pondered this consoling thought for the past half hour even as Rob and Marla have taken turns raging at me about my decision to give up the baby to Allaire Tremblay. With admitted reluctance, I had to confess to them that I already called her and told them my decision was final. I've tried not to let Rob's earlier derisive assessment of Allaire Tremblay about being *detrimental* influence me again, but it's hard. *All of this is hard.*

The room overflows with tension from all four of us while the little baby right next to me sleeps on. The crying infant stage has yet to materialize. Once I announced that I would be bottle-feeding this baby, the nursing staff (after one last carefully coordinated effort of convincing me otherwise) reluctantly produced a bottle of formula, and the baby was fed without mishap by Rob. I'm sure there have been private discussions at the nurses' station about my lack of mothering interest, but, so far, no one has said anything openly about it to me.

I've successfully checked off most of the things on their little chart that I must show I can do before being released from the hospital. *Eat. Go to the bathroom on my own. Eat. Drink. Be Merry. I'm a Christmas card.*

Dr. Shimmer swung by, apologized profusely for missing the baby's birth and adroitly made the hospital staff aware of my adoptive wishes. She assured all those concerned that I am properly informed and have consented and willfully give up my child in an open adoption arranged with the private-practice lawyer of Allaire Tremblay's choosing. This has diminished the questioning but not completely erased it. After Dr. Shimmer left, a few good souls ventured in inquiring, "If I was sure?" My assurance didn't exactly placate them.

There were more than few who looked beseechingly at Rob, hoping he could talk some sense into me. Until finally, at one point, I ungraciously said in exasperation, "He's *not* the father." This turned them around.

Now, with Allaire Tremblay on scene, things will finally move forward instead of backwards in deference to the general open concern for my well being. *Was I sure? Is anyone really sure?*

I'm adrift from it all. I fight lapses of overwhelming sorrow that combines nicely with this newfound mommy guilt. I can barely combat these two feelings that seem to be competing for my very soul, let alone spend more than few cursory seconds thinking through the ramifications of my decision. I experience all these unexpected thoughts of Lincoln Presley. These assail me in all these persistent ways and ignite this rising doubt that I'm doing anything right in giving up our baby for adoption to Allaire Tremblay.

It's true that the mind can handle only so much, and mine is maxed out.

"Do you have a name for her?" Tremblay clears her throat and gets this nervous smile. She's anxious, and I'm caught off-guard because I've never seen her like this before. It makes me feel closer to her somehow.

"Cara. I was thinking Cara. It's simple. It means—"

"*Beloved.* I love it."

"Cara Landon Presley Tremblay," I say in rote. All those names have been on my mind, and they tumble out of my mouth before I can take them back. I look up anxiously at Tremblay for an entirely different reason—to gauge if she heard what I just said. "Too much?"

She gleams at me but all she says is, "No."

Her hand trembles in mine. I glance down and watch her fingers collapse and convulse with nerves. The power has just shifted, and we both know. I just gave away Linc's last name. I know she'll trade upon that tidbit of good fortune. I don't have a choice now. I swallow slowly and try to follow what she is saying.

"Cara is a fabulous name. Cara. A little girl named Cara could have the world at her feet; n'est pas? But no need to decide right now." She practically purrs with her newfound power.

I lean back against the pillows defeated by my slip-up somehow already knowing that this mistake will cost me everything if I'm not careful. "Cara's good. I love it," I say into the stillness of the room. Marla is looking at me funny as if she just doesn't quite get what's going on here. I'm half hopeful that maybe Tremblay has missed what I said like Marla obviously has; but then, I look at the older woman's face. She hasn't missed a thing.

"It's perfect. Cara it is," she says with a clap of her hands.

Marla steps toward me, catching my eye. "What are you doing, Tal?"

"Everything's fine. It's good. We're good." I flash Marla a wide smile. We can't afford to upset Tremblay right now on any level. My eyes tell her this and signal with my left hand our familiar *we'll talk about this later*. Marla's eyes go wide. I think she's beginning to figure it all out—what I just revealed—and how it affects all of us.

"We can keep this as open as you like," Tremblay is saying. "However, you want to do it."

"Right. I don't know." I glance up at her. She withdraws her hand completely from mine. "Can we talk about it later? I just want to…I just want to get back to normal. Start dancing again. You know?"

"Of course." Tremblay licks her lips and gets this tight smile as if this is all a bit much for her as well. It makes her seem endearing somehow although these little warning bells go off in my head at the same exact moment. *She's playing me, and I'm falling for it.* "Anyway, no decisions right now. I have things in motion, but you can do what you want. A nanny for when I'm working. A pediatrician—unless you have one in mind. My place is big enough. All the baby's things are being delivered as we speak."

She looks a little uncertain now. I'm taken aback and then slowly realize how badly she must want this. The power between us shifts again. My mind races with this insight and these somewhat accusing thoughts that I've done *nothing* to prepare for a baby. *Nothing.* Allaire wants this. Maybe I never did. At least, I never thought about it—about being a mom and taking care of this baby.

"No. That's fine. That's good."

"Looks like you got it all worked out," Rob says from across the room.

We all glance over his way, temporarily stunned into silence by his surprising, insolent tone. He leans against the East wall with his arms crossed. His anger seems to reach for all of us. I can't tell if he talking to me or Allaire or Marla. Tremblay turns and acknowledges his presence for the second time since she entered the room and gives him a withering look.

"Rob," I say quietly in an attempt to diffuse the situation. *"Please."*

"Tally knows what she's doing. We've talked about this. She'll be as involved as she wants to be. We have an agreement. Cara will be told she's adopted as soon as she's old enough and Tally can be involved as much as she likes. She'll know who her birth mother is…always. I think that's fair for everyone involved."

"Fair." Rob lets the word hang in the air among us. Even Marla shifts uncomfortably at the harsh implication that underlies his derisive tone. "She's *eighteen*. She's making zero income; you've made damn sure of that. You wait until the last *days* of her pregnancy before stepping in and offering her this *perfect* solution. You've all but ensured that she's hopeless and desperate. Yet you have the audacity to stand there and stipulate you're being fair. *Fair.* Well, fuck the fairness of it all, Tremblay. I'm not buying it."

I'm speechless. Although I don't really know him all that well, I'm pretty sure that I've never heard Rob swear like this or look so angry. He pushes off from the wall and comes directly over to me and holds my stunned gaze with his the entire time.

"If you want to hand over your kid to this witch, that's your prerogative, Tally Landon, but I won't be a part of it. I told you. I can help you. The offer still stands." Rob gives me one last imploring look.

It's a look so insistent that it conjures up this profound new sense of heartbreak and takes my breath away. I jump out of the bed forgetting for a moment my scantily covered backside with the hospital-provisioned gown and step toward him. I'm determined to convince him of my decision, entreating him for approval, and needing his support for all of this for some inexplicable reason. My body rails with the sudden movement and all I manage to do is collapse into his outstretched arms.

"No," I manage to say. "No. Don't do this. Don't say that about her. She'll be good with her. She's helping me."

He grips my forearms to steady me and gently kisses the top of my head. *"You'd* be good with her, Tally." He sighs deep and just looks at me. If disappointment were a physical object, I can feel its direct transference from him to me. Disillusion forms in his eyes. It seems permanent and takes my breath away for a second time. There's a long silence throughout the room. Marla stares at the two of us and so does Tremblay. "Marry me, Tally. I'll take care of you and Cara."

"Rob, don't do this. Not here."

"Then when? I'm asking you to marry me. We can make this work. We can be a family."

I stare at him for a long moment. "I'm not Holly," I whisper.

He closes his eyes at my harsh words, and then opens them, and effectively pushes me away. He looks wounded as if I've slapped him. "True," he says quietly. "You don't have to be." Rob leads me back to the bed and tucks me into the covers again. "Okay then. I've got class," he says, getting this hardened look. "I've got to go."

I'm not the only one who lies.

Then he leans over the bassinet, strokes the baby's left hand with his own, and bends down and kisses her forehead. I'm reminded of the picture he'd shown me the day before of how to handle a newborn. "Kiss their forehead. Brush it with your lips. It shows great affection and doesn't spread unnecessary germs," he'd read aloud to me. Now, he looks over at me. The smirky smile is noticeably absent. I feel its loss at a gut-check level. "I've got to go. I can't stick around and watch this circus show unfold." He looks back once more at the baby and whispers goodbye only to her.

Then he's gone.

Marla gives me a similar beseeching look. "You want me to go after him?" She sounds as conflicted as I feel. I don't even stop for a moment to examine that thought too closely. *No.* Instead, I force myself to smile as a conscious way to eliminate this despondent feeling that seems determined to take a firm hold on me now.

"No." My new word for the afternoon comes out as a guttural, painful cry. "Doesn't change anything, does it?"

"Well, he's probably projecting his expectation of Holly on to you," Tremblay says callously. "I know who he is—*was*—to her. Forgive me. It's just he and Holly had quite thing going. Half the time she skipped class to be with him as if I didn't know *that* was going on."

I want to hate her in that moment for bringing my sister into this—for so effectively destroying the poignant yet earnest proposal and inexplicably painful good-bye with Rob that just transpired. For just being Allaire Tremblay and ruining it—smashing the dream as well as the romanticism and chivalry of it all. I actually shiver for a moment at the realization that I've just turned down Rob Thorn's proposal and agreed to hand my baby over to this person.

In the next minute or two, Tremblay seems to recover. Her smile gets wider and almost genuine. She laughs softly. "I am a witch—a bitch, actually. Do what you want, Tally." Her smile fades. "But I can tell you this much; you will be choosing between your ballet career and a child. That's the way it works."

There's the double-entendre in her words. A clear threat. I know it, so does she.

I lean back against the pillows and take a necessary breath. It's all a bit much, and now I just want it to be over. I don't want to think anymore. I want it to be done. Marla slides in on the edge of the bed next to me and grabs my right hand.

"Allaire, can you give us a few minutes please? I need to talk to Tally. *Alone.*"

Tremblay doesn't even bother to correct Marla for using her first name. Instead, the woman sighs deep as an implication of her frustration, probably with both of us, but acquiesces with a slight indication to the Kaleidoscope power that shifts with each progressing moment and backs out of the room as if she's doing Odile's last scene in *Swan Lake*. I bite my lip so I won't laugh out loud when I see this. The levity breaks up the dead seriousness of the moment for me.

"You don't have to do this, you know. You don't. It's a big decision. It's big deal. You can wait. That baby is rightfully yours until you sign the paperwork and forty-five days have passed. I want you to think about it, Tal. *Hard.* Like you've never thought about it before." Marla gets this anguished look. Her green eyes look turbulent, and this crevice forms between her eyebrows and gets deeper by the second. "I just want you to be okay with it all. You're going to have to live with it. I just want to know that you can."

"I know."

I glance over at the bassinet. The baby stirs. Her little fingers twitch, and she opens her eyes and begins to fuss about. I'm strangely calm as if I know what she needs. Maybe it's instinct. Maybe it's just part of the whole process of giving birth to a child who actually makes you feel like you can do and be anything for one magnanimous moment. Maybe that's what comes with bringing life into this world—it defines the meaning for you at last. No matter, how many other times so much gets taken away from you in life; it's this—this one defining moment—that essentially matters. I already know that I'll remember it forever, regardless of how everything else turns out. *This one moment.*

"Tremblay will destroy me," I finally say in defeat.

"Yes."

I try to smile as if we've just discussed the possibility of rain versus sunshine. "How'd it go with Charlie anyway?"

"He wants me to move to L.A." She looks away and then glances back at me. "I told him I would."

I nod and keep my tone upbeat and smile wide. "That's good."

"You should take Rob up on his offer and move in with him. It's cheap rent. You'll be gone most of the time."

"We'll see. He seems a little pissed off right now."

"Well, you're not Holly. He *does* need to realize that." She gets this wan smile. "He'd be good for you. I think he's a nice guy."

"He is. He just helped me deliver this baby. You'd think he'd taken Lamaze class with us. He was…amazing." I swallow hard as memories from eight hours earlier rush in on me. "He's a good guy. I don't want to destroy him, too. You know my capacity for being nice is limited."

"Not true." Marla walks over to the window and stares out. "It really didn't go the way we planned, did it?"

"No." I take an interest in bedspread pattern knowing Marla's gearing up for one of her more profound lectures.

"I just have to say this to you before you give her up. Make sure it's what you want. Don't do it as a way to get back at Linc because if that's what you think you're doing it's all wrong. Wrong on all levels—"

"That's not it. It's not. If I keep her, I put his career at risk. Dating somebody a lot younger is one thing, but an illegitimate child with some girl from Paly…would ruin everything for him."

"God, you're so altruistic. Does anybody else know this about you?" She tries to smile.

"No. Don't tell them either."

She looks uncertain. "I saw him. He just asked me all about you and wanted to know how you were doing less than twenty-four hours ago."

"You saw him?" I don't quite hide the agony in my voice. I cover my face with my hands, so she can't see it. *I can't get caught up in thinking about Linc.* It's hard enough as it is.

"He's doing all right. Consumed with baseball. Trying to keep his head above water and keep the fame at bay. He's fine, Tally. Yet he wanted to know how you were. You're the first one he asked me about when I saw him."

I lift my head up and look over at Marla. She still doesn't get what's just transpired. "Tremblay *knows* Linc is the father. I slipped up and said his last name. She *knows*, Marla."

"Maybe she didn't hear you."

"Maybe not. Regardless, I still need to protect him—an illegitimate child wouldn't exactly help his baseball career. His not knowing is the best thing for him; he can deny it, if it ever comes out."

"That doesn't make any sense. Linc would never deny his own child. You really need to think this through. Don't decide right now. Let's take her home. Take a few days to decide what you really want to do. You don't have to return to NYC Ballet for three weeks and by then everything will look and feel different."

"You've forgotten about Tremblay."

"Tell her you want to take some time with your—"

"If that's what you want," Tremblay says, strutting into the room in her usual definitive style but now with newfound purpose. If she didn't hear Linc's name earlier, it's obvious that she has now. "That's fine, Tally. Take a few days. I just wanted to give you a viable solution so you could continue to pursue your dance career."

And there it is—the subtle threat again.

Marla seems to suddenly understand; she actually flinches at what the woman's just said. Tremblay remains firmly in control while I too practically wilt under her sympathetic, all-knowing gaze.

The power between us shifts again.

"Come. Let's get out of here," Tremblay says, taking full control. "I have a car. I can drop you and the baby off. I've brought some things for her: an outfit, a baby carrier, formula, and a fully-stocked diaper bag. Surely, between the three of us, we can figure things out with one little baby. Go shower and get dressed, Tally. We'll get the baby fed and dressed as well."

A perfect plan.

I glance over at as Tremblay picks the baby up and holds her close and coos at her. Marla arches a questioning eyebrow in my direction. Neither one of us has seen this maternal side of Allaire Tremblay, not in all the years we've known her. I give my best friend the signal that we'll talk later and head to the shower after gathering up the fresh clothes that Marla's brought for me. I smile at the black T-shirt and jeans. I'm thankful that she's allowed her fashion sense to wane for the occasion. I just want to go home. Yes, the perfect plan is to go back to the apartment and think things through. Allaire Tremblay seems amenable to that idea, too. I breathe a sigh of relief, somewhat hopeful for the second time in two days that maybe everything will work out for all of us.

<hr/>

I re-enter my hospital room to find only Allaire Tremblay. She stands at the window. *No Marla.* Tremblay holds an expensive baby carrier containing a recently dressed-up baby Cara. *She's prepared. I am not.* I have got to give her that. Allaire Tremblay has thought of everything. She smiles at me. Her joy is obvious from the situation, and it even reaches her golden eyes today.

The shower's respite from the turmoil of my situation dissipates. I begin to envision my future if I were to keep this baby in my life. I give up ballet and get a job slinging drinks in a bar because I didn't go to college like my father wanted. Or, I marry Rob. For what? Friendship? And Rob pays for everything while I dance my little heart out and possibly make it without Tremblay's support. Yet everyone pays at some level to get me there, including this baby. Probably Cara, most of all. I close my eyes. *No.* I shake my head side-to-side. *No.* When I open them, I discover Tremblay carefully studying me.

Her body trembles ever so slightly. She seems to be holding her breath. *She wants this so badly. Cara. She wants Cara so badly.*

The power between us again.

I swallow hard and subtly try to breathe.

"So," she says taking the initiative. "Lincoln Presley is Cara's father. Does he *know*? Did you tell him? This could get complicated down the road if he wanted custody."

And the power shifts again in her favor.

I, of course, haven't really thought about this aspect. I was too intent on protecting Linc in some naive but altruistic way. By giving up the baby, he would never have to know, and I could move on and pretend it never happened. *Shit. How stupid have I been?*

Tremblay gets her recognizable critical teacher stance and looks at me intently now.

"He doesn't know." My words come out breathy like I'm being strangled.

"So you didn't tell him. Tally," she chides. "Were you just going to give her up to this other couple and go on your merry way?"

I nod and even though she's mocking me, I accept it. "That was the plan."

"Hmmm…not a very good one. So, he doesn't know." She gets this thoughtful look. I shake my head. "An illegitimate child wouldn't bode well for his baseball career. It wouldn't look good that a twenty-three-year-old baseball star has knocked-up a seventeen-year-old girl. My God, your parents only let you come to New York because I promised them I'd watch over you."

"He was twenty-two at the time. I was almost eighteen."

Tremblay waves her hand through the air with her usual dismissive flounce as if to say, '*that doesn't matter*'. She's probably right about that. I'm reminded of Kimberley Powers.

"My parents don't know about any of this, and I don't want them to. Right now, they're just trying to get over the loss of Holly. I can't disappoint them like this. With *this*." I glance over at the sleeping Cara. "With *her*," I whisper.

I swipe at my face when tears threaten. *Geez, I'm going to cry? In front of her?*

Get it together. This is Tremblay. Tremblay.

I look around the empty hospital room in desperation. *What's keeping Marla? Where's Rob when I need him the most?* I need somebody to help me fend off Tremblay's attack. This isn't going at all like I thought it would.

"So why didn't you tell him? Why isn't he involved?"

Silence. All the power has shifted to Tremblay, and I fear if I say anything more—anything at all—it will be irreversible.

"You're protecting him?" she asks, incredulous. I still don't answer. "How noble." She starts to laugh. "Does he *know* what you're sacrificing for him?"

"I don't think he would see what I'm doing as a sacrifice. We're not on the best of terms." I wince in recalling the last time I saw him at the airport. How I left him standing there because he'd just dumped me just like that. I've never gotten over what Linc did even after all this time. Why *am I* protecting him? This slow burn of anger surfaces and starts to wend its way through me all over again at his rejection and how easily he made the choice to protect his career. *And now, I'm doing the same thing.*

Tremblay shifts in her dancer's stance and starts to laugh a little. "I heard Marla's been working at the Dahlia and Rob did offer support—marriage," she says with notable disdain. "You *could* keep her. You might make it on your own with Sasha Belmont at NYC Ballet...*without* my help." She seems to pause for effect while her underlying threat about my career begins to resonate. "Regardless of whether the news gets out about who Cara's father is, however famous." She actually smiles at me as she delivers this last part.

Her threats land like acid she's purposely splashed upon me. I hold my breath for a long ten seconds and attempt to gain back some semblance of control. She's put it all out there. *She will tell.* And it will most likely ruin Linc's career as well as mine. *She wants Cara.* I almost admire her for owning up to this singular contemptible detail that is so intricately tied to her ultimate power over me, but some part of me wants to hear her actually say it.

"What do you want?"

She snorts in exasperation. "I want to adopt Cara. I've been very clear on what I want." She sighs deep. "The question is what do *you* want? You have the talent to take your ballet career incredibly far. Without my help...and if you're taking care of a baby, it will just take longer, if it happens for you at all." Her face hardens. She's just laid down the gauntlet. She'll tell all if she doesn't get Cara.

The one thing I can't abide is taking everyone else down with me. Eventually, Marla would resent the sacrifices she'd be making for me. Rob, too. The lies and keeping secrets would catch up to all of us. Linc's reputation would be destroyed because I was selfish in keeping Cara and in effect, admitting to the world, she was mine. His. *Ours. A baby I can't even provide for. What kind of life is that for Cara?* I take in air and attempt to breathe.

"You'd figured it out...eventually," Tremblay says grudgingly. She sounds like a mother for a few seconds. I'm remembering mine and stare at my mentor intently. I've never loved or hated Allaire Tremblay more in these few precious seconds.

"Cara is a perfect name for her," I say after a few minutes.

Tremblay slowly nods and gets this introspective look, while she stares at me intently. Her golden eyes actually soften. Her sympathy reaches for me from across the room.

I'm ten feet away from Cara—this miracle. Yet it seems like a part of another lifetime already. I brush at my face to ward off tears. *Don't cry. Just get it over with.*

"Where would you go?" I ask because it's suddenly important to be able to envision Cara's life with Tremblay. I need the picture painted for me. I want the exact scenario of what Cara's happily-ever-after life looks like.

"Back to San Francisco," Tremblay says softly. "I have a house there—in Alamo Square. A nursery. A nanny. *A life.* I've decided to cut back my hours at the dance studio when I return because I want to spend as much time with her as I can. God knows I've spent enough time dancing, teaching, and performing. Now, I want the chance to do something else—something worthwhile and life-changing."

Her lips part. Her eyes get watery. *Tremblay is going to cry. I've never seen this before.* I'm moved beyond words. She cares about Cara. Less so about me. But she already loves Cara and somehow knowing that makes it easier.

"Okay. Take her. Take good care of her. Make her happy. Make yourself... happy. All I ask is that you name her Cara and tell her about me and Linc some day when she's old enough." I nod slowly and impatiently wipe at the tears streaming down my face.

"You can stay at my place until the lease is up, longer, if you wish. We could work some things out. I had my lawyer work up an agreement. Standard adoption papers. You give up all rights as the known parent; we've kept the father's name out of it. You'll have forty-five days to change your mind. Standard stuff. He also added that you can see her any time you like. It's an open adoption. Cara will know who you are to her, and I'll personally tell her when she's old enough. I don't have any other living relatives. If something should happen to me before she's eighteen, I've put you down as her legal guardian." She hesitates, assessing my reaction. I can't even breathe. "I took the liberty to get in touch with the ballet master at NYC Ballet." She reaches in her bag and pulls out a sheaf of papers. "Three years. Three lead performances a year, more if you want them. Nice salary. They want you to headline the European tour. They've wanted to expand for a while over there. It's a good gig. Just be careful in a foreign country. You're young, beautiful, and soon will be a star, so just be careful, Talia. *Always."*

"That's…fine." I swallow hard. This is a chance in a lifetime. Am I the most awful person for wanting it? For wanting to take this chance?

"I'm doing all of this because adopting Cara makes my life complete, and I want to ensure you get what you want. You're a star, Tally. *Know that.* I'm proud to have taken you this far. You're ready for the big time. The question on the table is this: Are you willing to take it?"

She hands me a pen. My hands tremble as I take it from her.

I feel sick inside. I can't even look over at the sleeping baby still bundled up in a cotton pink blanket that Tremblay invariably reaches for. *Guilt. Remorse. Grief.* I recognize them all as they battle over the rights to my conscience.

In three minutes time, I've signed up for my future in three places, while Allaire Tremblay continues to stare at me intently. She affords me the single courtesy of not smiling in triumph for once when I hand her the signed documents.

"Cara Landon Presley Tremblay is going to have a great life. I promise you." Tremblay says softly. "I don't want you to take this wrong way but *thank you*, Tally."

Tears fall unchecked. "I just want her to know that she's loved…because I do…I love her. I want her to always know that." I steel myself to look at Tremblay directly and grab her hand. "If anyone were to find out she is Lincoln Presley's daughter it would destroy his reputation; maybe, even his career. They can't find out. No one can." I swipe at my face. "Please," I finally say.

Silence.

"Done." Her single spoken word undoes some of the tension in the room.

I watch Tremblay quietly kiss the sleeping Cara's forehead. In the next moment, she gets this look of pure elation and doesn't even try to hide it from me. It's no surprise to either one of us that I just made her life. I physically shudder at her undeniable joy and my insatiable quest for fame. *At any price, apparently.*

"You know you can hate me a little for getting everything I've ever wanted, but you tipped the scales in my favor when you said his name."

I take a shallow breath and slowly nod. "I know."

"So someday, Tally." She looks at me hard. "You're going to have to ask yourself why you did that. Because you held all the power." She gets this little smile and slowly shakes her head in apparent wonder at my stupidity. I cringe inward in learning what I so thoughtlessly gambled away. "I didn't know. I didn't *care*. Just know we share the same goals—to protect Cara and ensure your amazing rise to fame."

I just look at her. I can't speak.

Self-hatred runs at all-time high through me now. I swallow hard and strive for some semblance of control even through the tears that course down my face.

"You love her. You just showed her how much regardless of what your mind is busy telling you now. Don't forget that. I see it. Maybe, someday, even Marla and this Rob Thorn will figure out what you've just done for them, for Cara. Maybe, even Lincoln Presley." She pauses for a full minute. "Someday," she says with a touch of sadness.

I watch Allaire Tremblay leave with the bundled-up Cara and search for any oxygen she may have left in the room. *I can't breathe.* Part of me doesn't even want to.

I don't have a soul left, do I?

I just traded my daughter for Lincoln Presley's reputable baseball career and Allaire Tremblay delivered everything else to me in order to get Cara. *It's twisted—this mother's love.* I'm caught up in the throes of this all but debilitating sorrow. It feels like an undertow I can't escape. *What have I done?* Because now? It's the love of one little girl and her happiness—that's all I truly care about. I just wish that I was the one who could give it to her. And for that, I'm sad on a whole new level deep inside.

CHAPTER TWENTY-THREE

Tally · Denial is good

ALMOST TWO WEEKS HAVE GONE BY since I gave up Cara. My body aches in new and mysterious ways that I didn't know were humanly possible. As a dancer, I've suffered short-term injuries, the peculiar aches and pain that come with jumps and lifts and twisting the wrong way at the exact wrong time, but this pain brings about a whole different set of sensations. My body reacts in mysterious ways to raging hormones and a physical recovery that ebbs and flows (literally). All these factions serve a singular purpose—to get back into balance and return to the old Tally pre-pregnancy. But some days I feel a little hopeless. I'm assailed by constant guilt and punish myself with daily five-mile runs and again follow the strict regimen of the Boxer's Diet. Today's commemoration of Valentine's Day also marked a year since Holly died. It was a day I attempted not to recognize in any way, but my parents called and those horrible memories managed to engulf all of us, even now, a whole year later. And, of course, I think about Elvis. Of course, I do.

Nothing lasts, Elvis, nothing.

Then there's this new unrecognizable part of me that yearns to hold Cara and see her just one more time. Tremblay has already sent a few pictures, but it's too painful to look at them. Instead, I stash them in my dresser drawer beneath my best lingerie, just in case I ever decide to attempt sex with a hot guy again and need reminding as to why that would be a very bad idea.

Not really. Kind of. I don't know.

Sex is the farthest thing from my mind a little over two weeks postpartum, believe me. Right now, I eat every other day and drink water by the gallon, utterly beholden to getting my life and all of me back to normal. Although I'm somewhat back in dancer form in a matter of a few weeks because of this strict regimen I've put myself through, there's this general malaise that threatens to consume what's left of me from the inside out.

Tremblay left for San Francisco with Cara within a day of our secret deal being struck. Allaire's lawyer, Everett Madsen, managed to hand-deliver an updated dual-signed adoption contract to me, and Tremblay delivered on everything else involving New York City Ballet. The dance company expected me at rehearsals in another three weeks. I just wanted it to be all over with because this insistent remorse and an utter sense of failure have begun to take over. I thought the sooner we got things settled with Tremblay returning to San Francisco with Cara; the sooner things would return to normal. I underestimated what guilt, fatigue, and remorse would do to me. All I can hold on to now is that it was the right thing to do. If I keep telling myself that, then eventually I'll believe it, right?

Marla hands me a cup of tea and cozies in next to me.

"You okay?"

"Hmmm…" I glance at her sideways and give her the I'm-not-in-the-mood glare, while she conveys the I-told-you-so face along with this visible empathy. Neither sentiment provides comfort or absolution. I feel it all—remorse, guilt, physical nausea. What have I done? When will I ever stop thinking about Cara? Marla's conflicted look matches mine.

"Are you really okay?"

"I don't know," I say. "My body hurts. My breasts are killing me. Shimmer said the sports bra would help, but it doesn't seem to. Maybe, I should try the hot packs like she said…" My voice trails off. "Besides that?" I take a sip of the hot tea, so I can avoid looking at her and hope she doesn't begin asking me any tough questions. I didn't tell Marla everything. I don't want to tell her everything now. I don't actually tell myself everything.

"Other than that…you're good." She laughs a little and so do I because it's ironic, twisted, and almost funny all at the same time.

"Right." I catch my lip between my teeth and shake my head side-to-side. "I keep thinking of her. Cara. Holly. I wish I would stop doing that."

"I know. Me, too. Both of them." After a couple of minutes, she slides off the sofa and starts down the hall. "I'll run you a hot bath. That'll work. I read about it somewhere."

"Okay." I contemplate the silence versus actually saying something worthwhile, but all I can come up with is, "Hey, thanks for being here on Valentine's Day." I look over at her. She hesitates, obviously weighing her words as closely as I do mine. I know Marla is on her own little guilt trip about Cara. She played her part in this whole thing, too. She supported my decision to give her up but never actually volunteered what she would have done. Yet her nonverbal communication these past few weeks conveys these contradictory messages about me and what I did about Cara. Marla is pissed on a whole separate level at me, but she never says anything to me about it. This much I do know; Marla would have kept Cara. I didn't. In the aftermath of all that went down, we're both a little disappointed in me for that.

She avoids looking at me while she twists her hair around her finger. "Valentine's Day is not my favorite holiday anymore. Charlie understands. I'll see him in a few days." She shrugs. "I wanted to help you move into Rob's place." She just looks at me for a long time and then finally says, "Tally, I know you're going to be okay. You are. You will be okay because you are Tally Landon, but you have to start believing that too." She gets this determined look. "Thank God, Tremblay went back to San Fran so you don't have to see the two of them every day."

"Thank God." I force myself to smile.

My decision to give up Cara elevates my career almost immediately because Tremblay made it all happen. Tremblay delivered the updated countersigned contracts with NYC Ballet, the adoption paper documents, and everything else by eight o'clock that night. Marla hasn't quite figured out the price I paid yet. She looks troubled half the time as she starts to see things unfold with the NYC Ballet for me, but she doesn't say anything about it.

Rob called me the day after I came home from the hospital. He apologized for what he'd said to Tremblay and in general for how horribly he reacted to the whole situation and said he supported me in whatever I decided to do and that his offer still stood. Moving in. "All of it," he'd said in his roundabout way in proposing marriage.

I told him I'd take him up on the offer as a roommate and that Marla would help me move in before she left for L.A. if that was okay.

"Great." Then he'd asked, "Tally, what did you *do?*"

I didn't answer for a few minutes and then finally said, "I did what I had to do. For everyone. Tremblay has her."

His disappointment came at me through the phone after that. "You should have listened to me," he said.

"I didn't."

At least, I was honest for once. Did it count?

Soon after, we'd said good-bye. I felt sick inside enough already. I didn't need Rob reminding of what I had done. I figured he'd call again after a few days, but he hasn't called again. He'd just sent a text with his exact address, so I could start forwarding my mail to his place. *Cold. Distant. Punishing.* My roommate-to-be is unhappy with me. I put it on the to-do list. *Make nice with Rob. Soon.* I'm going to need a friend in New York. *Soon.*

I still think about Cara. All the time. I'm desperate to remember her sweet little upturned face, but twelve hours with her wasn't nearly enough time. I can't decide which I'm more afraid of: forgetting her or never actually moving on and getting over her. It doesn't feel like I win either way, unless self-hatred counts for something. I've begun to wonder just what kind of a trade I've really made and if anything I have left in my life can be considered a win in any way.

A deal was struck. I have to live with it. I have to learn to live with it.

"A bath it is then." Marla gazes at me with her infamous *I-have-a-million-and-one-questions-for-you* look but bites at her lower lip most likely to keep herself from asking me about anything at all. "Tally, I don't know…what to say," she whispers after a few minutes.

"There's nothing to say."

Nothing lasts. Nothing.

I swallow hard, push myself up from the confines of *red velvet*—the one piece of furniture we both agreed we needed to move from the old place to Rob's in the next couple of days. I turned down Tremblay's offer for her apartment. I just couldn't do it. And, I'll hardly be home, and I need to make things right with Rob.

We don't talk about it, none of it. All the lies, the secrets, even the wishes; we just don't talk about any of it anymore.

I move down the long hallway while my body silently protests the deliberate movements of walking the entire way. I'm stiff from running because I forgot to properly stretch afterward. I was too desperate to outrun all the guilt and sadness that still races through my head about Cara and Holly and Valentine's Day and Marla and Lincoln Presley and even Rob Thorn.

Cara. Linc. I count the days I've been away from her and him, like a kid with an Advent calendar counting down the days until Christmas, even though my days away from both will be infinite. There will be no Christmas to look forward to. There will never be a happy ending or a reunion. *There will be nothing.*

Tremblay offered to set up some kind of schedule for me to see Cara, but I decided it would just be too hard. It's been a few weeks, but it feels like I'm serving a life sentence of forever already. Yes. A deal was made because of all the lies I told and the secrets I now hold. I can't take any of it back. Wishes? I can't even wish for it to be different. What good would that do me now?

"I got everything." My voice echoes back to me as I traverse the empty hallway. *But, what is everything anymore?*

Minutes later, I stand at the open doorway of the master bath and watch Marla as she estimates the water level with one hand and dumps in bath salts

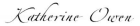

with the other. I'm assailed by the mixed fragrance of vanilla and lavender. She turns the faucet off, slips past me, and closes the door behind her without saying anything, which communicates volumes.

I need a break from all this unexpected pain and anguish. Marla needs a break from me already. She leaves for L.A. in two days. I already know she won't be coming back.

The water drips with methodical, judging sound. I take some kind of weird solace from that while I attempt to shut off my mind from all these relentless thoughts about Cara and even Linc and what I could have or should have done differently. A half hour goes by. The water turns ice cold. I still can't come up with anything different in terms of an outcome with either one of them. How could I sacrifice everyone else's time and happiness for a bit of my own? I couldn't take care of Cara; and if I'd kept her, Linc's baseball career and iconic reputation would have been in jeopardy. Mine, too.

So, why does doing the right thing hurt so much? I did the right thing—the only thing I could have done. I have to believe that or lose part of myself in all of this, as if I haven't already.

The tissue paper crackles beneath me with each movement as I slide across the edge of the examining table. I warily eye the stirrups and push back at the memory of delivering a baby twelve weeks ago. At eighteen years of age, I shouldn't know that experience, but I do. I'm not pregnant. That's not why I'm here at Dr. Shimmer's office. No. I'm all about preventing *that* from ever happening again, which is why I am here. My gynecologist wanted to meet with me in person anyway, a postpartum visit, and talk about contraception since she wouldn't even consider the idea of allowing me to get my tubes tied right after I had Cara. So today I'm here for an IUD—the compromise we've agreed to—but she's still not enthralled with this idea because she says I'm too young for one.

I've donned the cotton hospital gown that only a mother could love and don't count myself as one of those. Feelings of denial as part of the six stages of grief have finally taken hold. I *like* denial. This stage almost makes it seem like getting pregnant and giving birth happened to someone else. *I lie to others; why not lie to myself?* The modus operandi of the old Tally has finally shown up. I move through the world at almost full speed again. *Denial is good.* I practically swim in it.

Dr. Jane Shimmer sails into the exam room with a ready-made smile. She's a paradox with this long blond hair that she pulls back in a ponytail from her beautiful face; yet she wears clear lip gloss and hardly any makeup. She has the bluest eyes but overtly hides them behind a pair of black-rimmed glasses. My guess is that her constant quest is to be taken seriously—in lieu of being designated as Barbie. It appears she has to constantly fight these stereotypical, competing forces of beauty in combination with brains. Apparently, this is her way of completely dismantling that particular persona for anybody who spends time around her. *Take me seriously* is written all over Dr. Jane Shimmer's lovely face. I admire her for it. I get it.

"Still want the IUD, I take it?" She half-glances at her chart but manages to keep a vigilant eye on me. It makes me smile. I've met my match in Dr. Shimmer.

"Not unless you've changed your mind about tying my tubes."

"Tally, you're not yet nineteen. Your whole life is ahead of you. I'm not going to perform something as permanent as a tubal ligation. I seriously doubt you'll find any gynecologist around here that would. You're young. You may change your mind about children, and I want to give you the opportunity to do that. An IUD is relatively safe. It's good for five years. I wouldn't normally offer it up as an option to someone your age but yours is a special case. I know you don't want to talk about another pregnancy right now."

"Absolutely not." I wave my arm around the small room for emphasis.

"*Someday*, you might want another child." She grabs my outstretched arm and takes my pulse. "You did a great thing. You brought a beautiful baby into this world, and you gave her up to caring adoptive parents who love her. That is not a small thing. It is generous and worthy and wonderful. Like you."

My eyes start to sting. Her *Mary Poppins* speech is bringing me down. I'd rather take the constant torment that dominates all of my senses inside but instead Shimmer lavishes praise on me. It makes me feel slightly sick. Denial fuels me. Her praise and the look of sincere wonder leave me more than a little undone as guilt and remorse pay a silent visit to my psyche. I force myself to smile and swing my legs back and forth hoping to appear nonchalant. "Um…hmmm."

I'm still doing my damndest to bury the memories of last night's panic attack and the unfortunate circumstances with…what was his name? I draw a complete blank for a few seconds.

Jack.

Jack, who yelled: "What the fuck is your problem, Tally? Are you *crazy*? Are you really going to leave me like this with a fucking hard-on because you freaked out? What the fuck is your problem, baby?" Did I walk out of his apartment slamming the door as hard as I could because he called me *baby*? *Or,* was it because of the panic attack or because I couldn't breathe? All three equally, I decide. I won't be seeing Jack again, which is too bad because he was great, up to a certain point. Jack was the exact opposite of Linc in every way, a bonus, indeed. Jack was intimately in touch with the old Tally, until I lost it for both of us, for reasons, I refuse to explore.

Yeah, after that, it was dark and scary and when I came back to reality and discovered he was on top of me and taking things further than I actually found myself willing to go, in that frozen moment of panic, I didn't exactly recognize myself any longer. I managed to push myself out from underneath him and brought things to a decided halt. After that, things went from bad to worse. Thank God, I can avoid the bar he frequents. His choice words for me wouldn't be as pretty-sounding as they were when we almost hooked last night. Luckily, the Upper East Side contains plenty of bars and plenty of Jacks. *Lucky me.*

My reason for making the appointment with Dr. Shimmer became vital after what transpired last night. I'm now convinced that reliable contraception will make all my problems go away—well, *most* of my problems will go away. These will disappear as it relates to attacks of panic. I'm realistic, after all. I freaked out with Jack because I didn't trust a condom. An IUD will solve these unforeseen inhibitions about random sex. I'm sure of it. My panic attack had nothing to do with Linc. *Nothing.*

I break away from my reverie to find Dr. Shimmer regarding me closely. *Too close.* I manage a little smile again and hope I portray the easygoing *I-don't-have-a-care-in-the-world* Tally. I don't; right?

"So…Is everything okay? We can still try the birth control pills for a couple of months if you want."

"No." I shake my head emphatically. "Messing up with birth control pills is what got me into trouble in the first place. This is good. I read the pamphlet if that's what you're worried about. I want this."

"No. I know you did. We've talked about it enough. They've improved these devices a lot. There are risks. We've discussed them."

I nod.

I nod and smile.

Nod and smile.

"Are you okay?" She's still looking at me.

"I'm great."

"One more nod and smile and I won't believe you."

I stop kicking, smiling, and nodding.

"Better." She gives me a stern look and then sighs. "So. How are things?" She writes down some number on my chart and glances through the rest. Then she frowns. "You're eight pounds under your starting weight with us. How did you do that?"

She gets this quizzical look along with this easy expectant smile—like we're old friends just having a chat, as if I can tell her anything.

It makes me wary. I just want the IUD, so I can get out of here and move on with my life all on the same day. *Shit. What would Holly say?* I lick my lips, stalling for time and try to remember some innocuous charming thing my twin would have said in the situation. "I feel really good. I've been training quite a bit and running."

I run five miles a day every day and train three times as hard as everyone else at the dance company. *I feel great.* A lie I tell everyone I know—from my parents to Marla to Sasha Belmont. For the most part, Sasha Belmont, NYC Ballet's artistic director, has been great to work with, but she's a perfectionist and a former prima ballerina like Tremblay. She doesn't say too much to me. She seems to be in awe of the implied influence and power I seem to have wielded over Allaire Tremblay, who so effectively ushered me into NYC Ballet's competitive dance program to the head of the line. Sasha seems to still be trying to come to terms with the expediency with which my contract came together or, at least, attempting to better understand all that must have gone down in light of Tremblay's direct sponsorship of me with the head ballet master at NYC Ballet. Tremblay isn't here to explain it, and I'm unwilling to elaborate. I do my best not to disappoint Sasha Belmont and to ensure she's got the star that Tremblay both promised and delivered. I do everything at an above-and-beyond level of dedication. I'm intent on perfection. Yet Sasha Belmont utters the word *again* as often as Tremblay did. She wants a perfect performance. And I'll give her one or die trying.

Again. How I hate that word. Again. Do it again. Again as to imply it wasn't perfect, so start over. Again, because you messed up the one-two count for everyone. *Miss Landon, can you please try to keep up with your peers?* Again. Do it again. *Again.* How I hate that word and Tremblay in so many new ways now. I know I made the deal, but now I hate myself for it and her on this inexplicable level for manipulating me with her power. She always knew what she wanted and what I wanted, or rather, what I was willing to do for what I thought I wanted.

I do want it, don't I?

Allaire Tremblay had it all figured out long before I did. She was way ahead of me. It's only taken me a little over three months to catch on.

"Are you eating enough?" Dr. Shimmer asks.

"I could eat a little better."

"Give me a typical day's worth of meals. What do you eat?" She gets this unrelenting look while I get even more uncomfortable.

Can we just get on with this?

"A typical day?" I stall. "A yogurt in the morning. "With nuts, walnuts or something." Not true. I skip meals every other day. I never eat nuts. They're too high in fat to ever cross my lips. I can't afford that. "Salad at lunch. With some kind of protein." Dr. Shimmer winces a little. I think she knows I'm lying by this point. I'm caught in between not knowing if I should proceed with the telling of this lie or just stop talking. "An apple or a banana. Oatmeal for dinner. It's quick. It's faster. There's not a lot of time what with all the dance classes and rehearsals…" I stop talking somehow knowing I've already blown it.

She steps back and starts writing down something on my chart. After a long four minutes of self-inflicted silence while I continually remind myself not to open my mouth again to utter another word, Shimmer looks up. Her left brow furrows. "That's six hundred calories a day, and I'm being *generous*."

I stay with the silence. I embrace it. *I need that IUD.* Well, check that. *How bad do I need it?* It's not like I have time for sex anyway, and I don't need another repeat of a Jack from a bar and the promise of fun, which ends up being anything but a good time. I shift my legs from the uncomfortable *help-me-out* position and cleverly cross them at the ankles. I dig in for the long haul even though I'm obviously in the weaker position because I'm still naked under this completely unattractive patient gown. Shimmer is the doctor, and she holds all of this power over me as it relates to contraception. I fold my arms across my chest and give her the *try-me, defiant* look.

Still.

An IUD would be nice. I could do whatever I wanted, and ensure *that situation* never happens to me again. *Cara's become a situation.* I wince.

"What's going on with you, Tally?"

"It's highly competitive." I shrug my shoulders as if it's not a big deal. "It's a dancer's world. There's always somebody there who is just waiting to step into your coveted role. After you get to the principal level, you get two understudies whose sole goal in life is to see you fail or fall. That's the way it is. But you do it, if you love it enough. If you're willing to sacrifice anything and everything and everyone for it, you do it. That's the way it is. You have to maintain a certain weight to do the lifts and to jump higher than everyone else. You have to eat enough to maintain your stamina and your muscle but not enough to where anyone will complain about your weight when they lift you. You have to sacrifice just like everyone else, sometimes more. And when you screw it up, the way I almost did—by getting pregnant in the first place, going through with it, and then just trying to make it back and be more perfect—well, it is what it is. I have to pay twice as much for that decision, and I still count myself lucky. Allaire Tremblay helped me make it to New

York City Ballet. I can't blow it now." I take a shaky breath and wince at the truth I've just exposed in my little impassioned speech.

"Allaire Tremblay?" Dr. Shimmer asks in awe. "I went to one of her performances once. A long time ago. She was such an incredible dancer. I was sixteen when I saw her dance."

"She adopted Cara."

"Oh." Dr. Shimmer's brow creases. Her lips part as if she has something else to say.

"She's back in San Francisco. With Cara."

Silence.

Nervous by her lack of a response and hoping to get her to better understand, I go on to ensure she does. "She was temporary director at SAB, the School of American Ballet? And she's the one that ensured I got the internship and was invited to join New York City Ballet with Sasha Belmont. It's a lucrative contract. In this industry, three years is virtually unheard of, and it's all because of Tremblay's connections and *support*." I choke on the last word. *Easy, Tally.*

"And your *talent*," Shimmer says. "Sasha Belmont is amazing. She's a good friend of mine from school. Yes, she's amazing, exacting, driven, but she wouldn't do anything she didn't see as being for the good of the ballet company. I hear she's leaving for Europe soon."

"Yes, I'm going on the tour."

"Wow. *Tally.*"

"We leave in a month or so with performances in Milan, Rome, and Paris, over the summer and into the fall. It should be fun. It means…everything." My pulse races out of control in reaction to the surprising turn this conversation is taking. "It's all I've got." I try to smile but find myself struggling to breathe. I look away from Shimmer needing a break from her constant scrutiny and subtly swipe at my eyes with the back of my hand.

"You did the right thing, Tally. You need to believe that. Your baby is fine. She's cherished and loved. Allaire Tremblay will take good care of her; I'm sure of it. You're doing well, too. You did the right thing. *You did.* Believe that. Believe in yourself and your choices. I do."

There's this little shared silence between us. I incline my head as I look her way. She nods.

"You're doing great, Tally. I'll get the IUD packet. It's a relatively painless procedure and takes about five minutes. So, I'll be right back." Dr. Jane Shimmer gazes at me and smiles—it's a Barbie type of smile that almost takes my breath away. I'm automatically reminded of Holly, for some reason.

Why can't I be happy like Holly?

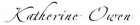

Why can't I be more generous with myself? Why can't I try?

I finally take a breath when she leaves the room. Then, relief overwhelms me—relief that I spoke the truth for once. Relief that somebody knows what I'm going through. Relief that Shimmer supports my decision, and she supports *me*, for that matter.

A modicum of unexpected joy follows because I've told her the truth. *Me.* Tally Landon said something that was true. It feels good. It feels right. Maybe I'll actually move on from here. Maybe I'll actually get my life back together just like I planned. Maybe I'll stop thinking of Cara and Linc every waking minute of every single day and actually move on from here. *Maybe.*

CHAPTER TWENTY-FOUR

Tally: This price for fame

"YOU CALLED THIS MEETING," I SAY with open defiance. "What do you want?" I eye Kimberley Powers with this unchecked disdain and inevitable wariness. It's probably unfair to blame her for Linc's obvious choice over a year and a half ago, if one we're going to get technical or maudlin or both equally, which I am. It's true, by the time I met up with Kimberley Powers at the small little café that has become our joint—our *hangout*—as Marla used to say, I'm in a foul mood. Rehearsal ran long. I'm burned out and in need of a well-deserved break. The lead for *The Nutcracker* hurt her ankle so just after a successful season in Europe, I was asked to step in, *expected* to step in. *I wanted to step in, didn't I?*

It's just that I am so tired after this long year that I really can't wait until it's over. After rehearsal, the ballet master asked me to stop by his office where he proceeded to carry on a one-sided conversation about a few of my missteps during rehearsal. It was a long twenty minutes about my obvious mistakes and his overreaching concern for a general lack of focus on my part and my sub-par performance.

Then one of his assistants interrupted with a *"Talia, you have a visitor"* reprieve—a reprieve that didn't last long once I saw who it was. Kimberley Powers, publicist extraordinaire, who, invariably, I could blame for wrecking my relationship with Lincoln Presley which, if one were being exact and honest, isn't really true. But I'm not one for honesty anyway. And right now? I don't give a shit about the truth or Kimberley or even Linc, for that matter, because it's been a long year.

Against my normal modus operandi, I order a hamburger and a salad and proceed to pick my way through this late-night meal while Kimberley sips at her coffee—black, no cream, no sugar—and scrutinizes me rather intently. She's most likely an older version of a future me in many ways. There's a large part of me enamored by her directness, so I can't help but like her. I need a soul sister. Marla's been preoccupied so our phone conversations have been short and infrequent. *Although…right now?* Kimberley Powers poses a threat to me in all kinds of ways that she doesn't even have a clue about, and I have to constantly remind myself of this fact during our conversation. *She's the enemy. She's the enemy with direct ties to Linc.* And I can't even think about Linc right now. There's too much at stake and too many secrets at this juncture.

"How are you?" Kimberley asks.

"I'm good." I force a smile at this lie, stall for composure by sipping iced water in front of me, and make a point of openly ignoring her penetrating jade-green gaze with a careless shrug. No, I just smile like Allaire Tremblay's taught me to do all those years ago. *"Smile through the pain."* It's what Tremblay always said. I do it now. *The pain is everywhere.*

Kimberley Powers is stunning. She's got this long, dark auburn hair. Her green eyes just pop with the designer turquoise and white outfit she's wearing. I'm a little self-conscious in my status quo of black T-shirt and jeans. Even my fur-lined winter black wool coat seems a weak attempt at being fashionable.

Within minutes, it's pretty obvious that Kimberley is the center of attention wherever she goes. This restaurant is no exception. Twice now, the waitress has come by with a proffered drink from some male patron sitting at the bar, intent on sending his admiration directly her way. Twice, Kimberley has leaned out of the booth and openly indicated her thanks with a little wave of her perfectly manicured hands to these earnest appreciative strangers.

She sips at one of the drinks like a queen would signal gratitude to her peasant people for their small kindnesses. I kind of laugh taking it all in, wishing I could take a sip from one of her gifted margaritas, too. Eventually, she slides one of the fluted glasses over to me in salutation and gets this secret smile—the *I-hope-you-have-fake-ID* smile.

I nod in acquiescence, confirming for both of us that wistfulness is an uncontrollable visible notion. I have it and somehow Ms. Kimberley Powers has picked up on it. And I have to be careful. I have to be very careful here. *She has direct ties to Elvis. Careful, Tally.*

"Your reviews are good. So how long did it take before New York City Ballet's finest offered you the position as the lead?" Kimberley asks with playful interest.

"Not long. You have to have recommendations…from the right people. Mine were…unexpected, but they helped tremendously this past year." I play with the edge of my water glass, twirling the contents back and forth. I'm a little unsettled. There aren't too many people who understand how the dance world works so I do my best to hide my surprise that Kimberley Powers seems to have a vague idea on how things work.

"I'm sure Allaire Tremblay pulled some of those strings." Kimberley waves her left hand around the restaurant as if by doing so it would somehow make this true.

"She did. I've been the lead through most of the European performances this year. It's a three-year contract virtually unheard of…" I frown because, despite my best efforts to remain detached and unaffected by what's been transpiring with this conversation; I'm combating this constant worry in keeping it all together in front of Kimberley. With Tremblay safely ensconced back in San Francisco with Cara, I naively thought things would end there. The deal was iron-clad on both sides for me and Tremblay. What I failed to anticipate were all the questions about my dance career and this contract and even the ties indirectly to Allaire Tremblay and Sasha Belmont. No. I didn't exactly think all of that through, and it's catching up to me now by the intrigued look on Kimberley Power's face. *Careful.*

"Three years. Impressive," Kimberley says. Her eyes gleam this jade green. "The NYC Ballet is one of my clients. Sasha's a good friend of mine. She likes you. She says you're very good. We go back a ways," Kimberley confides and gets this secret smile. "So really, Tally, who did you sleep with to rise to the top so quickly?"

She says this like we're old friends, and I should be willing to tell her. I take a shallow breath and cajole myself to tread carefully and play it cool. I need to end this conversation before it even gets started. I give her one of those meaningful winning smiles—the kind Marla and I used to exchange when we were out at a party. I think of Jack from seven months ago. I should go see Jack right after I'm through here and exorcise the last memories of Lincoln Presley right out of my system forever. "Other than the baseball player?" I sigh and then laugh at her surprised face. "It's been a long time since I've slept with anyone, but I plan to remedy that soon enough. His name is Jack. "

I look at her intently to ensure she knows where I'm going with this. *Where am I going with this?* "I've been focused on my career and dancing my little heart out. But enough with being the good girl. Look," I say with a sobering look. "I'm just trying to move on here."

"Aren't we all?" Kimberley sort of laughs then. I eye her carefully as she takes a sip of one of the margaritas and gets this sympathetic look. "He wanted to come. He had these naive plans about coming to New York and seeing one of your performances this year and last." She frowns a little.

"And you talked him out of it."

She nods. "Time. Has. To. Pass. This is a serious situation and the two of you *independently* just don't seem to understand that."

Her eyes glint. *She's serious.* "I get it. Take your lecture up with Elvis. It was a one-time thing. I've moved on."

"Have you? Have you, Tally? I mean, if that's true, why aren't you seeing anyone?"

Is she checking up on me? I sip the margarita to buy time and decide how to answer. "I've been dancing my ass off this whole year and last. It doesn't really leave time for anything or anyone else. Ask Sasha if you don't believe me."

"Oh, I believe you," she says slowly. "I just don't quite…get it. I mean you are a star in your own right. Sasha has ensured me of that. She wants me to work with you in fact. She wants to ensure I give you that extra star quality treatment that I give to all my special clients."

"I don't want to be one of your special clients. Besides, isn't that a conflict of interest with *him*?"

She raises an index finger to her lips after I almost say his name. "Separate problem. Separate client. It's probably better that I manage the two of you, so I have an idea of what's going on--separately, of course."

"Of course." I give her a somewhat resentful look for her insinuated interference in my life and my career. She isn't going to go away. She's made that clear. I sigh.

"So. A client. And friends." She smiles wide and then it fades. "We're good, right?"

"Do I have a choice?" I glare at her not enjoying the manipulation that both this conversation and our relationship seem to be taking.

"No. Not really." She laughs. "As I said, the NYC Ballet is a client of *mine*. You're part of the package. That's how it works out." She studies my face intently. "So, what did you give up to get here, huh?"

"Everything," I whisper.

"That's what I thought." She gets this thoughtful look. "That's what I thought," she says again.

We share this long protracted silence between us. I allow myself to smile a little and think of Linc. I envision his earnest face when he cooked me dinner that one night and how sexy he was when I watched him sleep and how much I still miss him. I hold my breath and finally swallow and incline my head toward her. "So." I take a deep breath and let it out slowly. "How is *Elvis*?"

"Good one. Catchy. No one will know who we're talking about. I'll call you Priscilla." Kimberley laughs outright.

It's so perfect and disarming that I eventually laugh, too; but then I'm nervous. To cover it up, I take another swig of the margarita and enjoy the alcohol as it burns my throat all the way down. "So. Not over him after all." She says after a few seconds of observing me. "He misses you, too."

She seems intent on gauging my reaction at every turn, and her blatant honesty catches me off-guard. This time I choke on the sweet-n-sour taste of the margarita because I gulp it a little too fast. In the next few seconds, I swipe at my eyes having forgotten all about the salted glass rim. It definitely stings when it makes contact. Soon, I'm dabbing at my watery eyes with the wet corner of a napkin in a vain attempt to hold back the tears that now mysteriously threaten. I laugh at my blunder while Kimberley takes it all in—assessing and evaluating my every move, my every reaction. My hands shake even as I strive for the control of a twenty-five-year-old but still struggle against the reality of having just turned nineteen a few months ago but going on thirty. I wish Holly were here because my sister would know what to say. Holly could handle Kimberley Powers. Holly would have charmed her into submission. Normally, I could do these things on my own. But tonight? It all proves to be too much.

The truth is that I miss Linc, and I find myself telling her this even though in the back of my mind, there is this small part of me constantly chanting: *you can't trust anyone and nothing lasts. Nothing.*

"I miss him. It's silly. *Really.* We probably spent less than twenty-four hours together in total, but he was great. You know? I liked him. And I don't normally like anybody for long."

"It's just a little while longer. Your birthday's in another eight months. I suppose at twenty if you guys met up; it wouldn't be so bad," she muses.

"It's not that simple. He broke up with me and—"

"He broke up with you because I told him to. Because you were seventeen at the time, and he was twenty-two. Seventeen-year-olds and twenty-two-year-old guys with their star on the rise do not mix. Capiche?"

For some reason, I decide to mess with her. "Does he always do *exactly* what you say?"

"All he has is baseball," she says with a heavy sigh. "Do you know anything about his life? His dad? Who he is? His mom? His older brother? What happened to them?" Her voice shakes.

I make a mental note to check out this part of Linc's story even though I promised myself long ago I wouldn't do this.

"His dad was a baseball player," I say slowly. "His mother died when he was younger. You were Elliott's fiancée. That's about all I know." Kimberley gets this tormented look and looks momentarily taken aback. "I've been busy. I have a lot going on. I really haven't had time to *Google* Lincoln Presley," I whisper his name and try not to sound too defensive, but I know I do.

Kimberley leans toward me and talks softly. "His dad is Davis Presley. Yes, *that* Davis Presley. The famous pitcher for the Giants from about fifteen years ago."

"Oh." There's this awkward silence. I'm intent on not being the one to fill it. I dig my nails into my palms to keep from saying anything more.

She takes a sip of her drink, sighs deep, and looks at me. "So, they were one big happy family. Davis married Cara Sanderson, the actress, before he hit the big time with the Giants and she with Hollywood. They were young and in love, and they had two sons, Elliott and Lincoln, and they all lived in L.A." Kimberley gets this faraway look, and her voice goes soft. I lean forward to catch her next words because, all at once, I can barely hear her and another part of me is dying a little that Linc's mother's name was Cara.

"I was…your age. I'd just gotten this great PR internship my freshman year in college at UCLA. Davis was my first client." She tries to laugh, but it doesn't quite work. "Life was good. For everyone. I met Elliott in one of my first meetings with his dad. He was destined to be a star baseball player just like his dad. He was twenty. I was almost eighteen. We fell in love within the first five minutes of meeting each other." She shakes her head side-to-side. "I resigned the account and gave up my internship because the firm felt there was a conflict of interest." She shrugs her shoulders and gets this anguished look. "I didn't care. I was in love. Elliott meant everything to me, and I'd follow him anywhere." She stops talking for a few minutes and swallows hard. She seems to be having trouble catching her breath.

I'm still reeling from the fact that Lincoln Presley's mom was the famous Cara Sanderson and I've inadvertently named our daughter after her without knowing any of this. I feel like I'm going to be sick. Kimberley misinterprets my distressed look.

"I know I came down hard on your relationship. I feel bad about that. *I do*. Linc had always been the dreamer. He had different aspirations. He was a bit of a rebel. He looked up to his big brother Elliott, who everybody loved, including me obviously. We'd been dating for six months, making plans for our future even though Elliott was focused on baseball and had just done a tryout for the Red Sox." Her tone gets more wooden. "His dad couldn't make the trip; he was transitioning over to work for ESPN and getting inducted into the Hall of Fame. So, Cara went with Elliott to the tryout in Boston. On their way back to the Boston airport to catch the flight back home to L.A., they were both killed instantly in a head-on collision."

Kimberley frowns. I can tell she's lost in the memory of that horrible day. I know the feeling all too well. She sighs and takes an unsteady breath and looks over at me.

"Davis fell apart. And Linc? He had to stay focused and keep it together for both of them. He's done that since he was fifteen, when he lost his brother and his mother and, essentially, his dad. It's been hard for Linc trying to live up to his father's exacting expectations in replacing Elliott and getting over the loss of his mother and his brother. Davis isn't easy to please. There's a lot of pressure to be perfect and unintentionally Linc wants to make up for all the loss for his dad. And there are worse things that can happen; right? He probably sees that in you so clearly…with your sister," she says softly. "Even on an unconscious level, you two are perfect for each other. I'm a bit jealous."

"Don't be." I try to smile. "We can't…be together."

"Not now," she says easily. "But someday."

Not ever.

I dig my nails into the palm of my hands again to keep from uttering another word, to keep from confessing to all the lies and the secrets I hold. Kimberley's eyes glaze over with unshed tears. I'm taken aback at all these revelations. I don't even attempt to brush away the tear that begins to run down my face because Kimberley is suddenly more openly than I am. Somehow, I know it's a first—to cry in public—for both of us.

"I'm sorry about Elliott. That must be so hard."

"Yeah." She nods and then gets this sad smile. "Ironic, huh? God, I loved that guy. He was…everything."

She swipes at her running mascara with the back of her hand, doing more smudge damage than actually repairing it. I retrieve a compact mirror from my purse and hand it to her. Kimberley laughs a little at my thoughtful gesture and seemingly her unusual tears. She gazes in the small mirror and avoids direct eye contact with me. She sighs deep and seems to attempt to get it together.

"Look." She gets this serious intense look. "I know it looks impossible. It looks like things will never work out, but you've got to trust me when I say that things always have a way of working out…I mean, it's an age difference that soon won't matter. Things will work out for the two of you," she says slowly. "Eventually."

"I'm so sorry about Elliott."

"Yeah." She gets this rueful smile. "Sorry, I don't normally lose it like that. I don't talk about Elliott to *anyone* but Linc. And then, only sometimes, but you…*you are good people*, Tally Landon. I like you."

I don't know what to say to that. I'm not really *good people* as Kimberley puts it. "I am incredibly talented at just one thing, and I traded away everything else that really mattered to me for that." Apparently, I've expressed this indiscriminate thought aloud.

Kimberley gazes at me even more closely and openly scrutinizes my own mascara-smudged, upturned face. Self-conscious, I laugh it off and attempt to repair my face when she hands me my mirror back.

"I'm going to help you," she says and nods as if she's got it all figured out. "Yes, I'm going to help you get everything you want."

I actually laugh—so I won't burst into tears again—because Kimberley Powers, of all people, would actually understand the price I've had to pay for fame.

CHAPTER TWENTY-FIVE

Tally ~ Unlikely alliances

ROB'S APARTMENT, WHICH IS STILL HOW I refer to it almost a year later, is strangely quiet for a Thursday night. Rob should be home. It's his night off. New Year's Eve is a night away, and we have plans like millions of others to be in Times Square. I have a reprieve for the night after having performed the role of the *Sugar Plum Fairy* seven nights and days in a row. Christmas is over, and the NYC Ballet takes the next three weeks off. Classes and rehearsals don't start up until mid-January. The thought of another long tour in Europe kicking off in Paris by April doesn't hold as much appeal this time around. I have virtually lived out of a suitcase for the past year. I've been thinking about making a trip home to San Fran. Marla will be there for a few weeks staying with her parents before heading back to UCLA. I need to see mine. And I allow myself to briefly contemplate seeing Tremblay and Cara.

Everything worked out. Europe was amazing. My performances got better and better. Sasha is pleased. Living with Rob is a non-event because I'm rarely here. He complains a little about me being gone all the time, but we are just friends. The strange thing is that he has been more distant lately, always helpful on those rare occasions when we run into each other and claims to be busy with his classes at NYU as well as this start-up software business he's trying to get going. I've managed to take a few classes this past fall after the European tour ended and before the Christmas season at NYC Ballet went into full swing. Rob tends to lecture about having a back-up plan in case ballet doesn't work out for me. I've even contemplated waiting tables at the Dahlia on 5th where he still tends bar part-time just for fun. Of course that was before I had to fill in as the Sugar Plum Fairy. Now I just want to rest.

On a deeper level, I think Rob is still pissed off at me about the whole thing that went down with Tremblay. I've been avoiding him and any sort of deep discussion on this front because he's too smart, and I'm pretty sure he's put it all together—the selling of my soul, basically. I already know he doesn't approve of any of it. So why give him the opportunity to guess the actual details? Cara will turn one a month from now. We've all moved on. The debts and sins on me have been paid; maybe, by all of us at some deep existential level.

Rob would still probably contend that we could have worked out the living arrangements between the three of us and taken care of Cara ourselves, or I could have married him. I shake my head at that selfless thought and smile. His altruism would seem to know no bounds. And it's true; there's a part of me that concedes that point that I could have married him and kept Cara, and it tears me up inside a little more each day because, as I get older, I see the world as more manageable then I did even a year ago. I see how Tremblay took advantage of the situation and of me. Nevertheless, I can't go there for long either. I can't think that way. Her postcards and photographs of Cara have become less frequent. I breathe a sigh of relief while at the same time I've begun to wonder why that is.

Most days, Rob's friendship is enough for me, and he's all I have since Marla's at UCLA. I anticipate we'll have more time to spend together since the performance season is over until mid-March. There will just be classes and rehearsals. I think we're both exhausted in different ways: me—after spending much of the year apart with me in Europe, and Rob in tending bar and going to NYU and working alongside his father on special investment projects and this start-up company of his.

I've even begun to wonder if he's seeing someone and doesn't want to tell me who it is yet.

I move quietly through the apartment to the kitchen and pour myself a generous splash of Dewar's. My dad likes a good Scotch. Tonight, I'm missing both my parents and Tommy. I want to see their faces; re-open Christmas presents since I've missed the event two years in a row now. I guess I want to turn back time. *To what? To before more than a year and a half ago?* So I could be more dutiful about taking my birth control pills or better know the side effects of antibiotics on birth control and undo everything that came after that? *Can I wish away Cara so easily? I can't do that.*

I spent Christmas here. It was a whirlwind day complete with two ballet performances. But now that Christmas is over, all I long for is to be home. Rob and I tried to make the best of it, spending Christmas morning together as friends, but there was still this underlying tension between us that seems to have started when I gave up Cara. It seems to have gotten even worse since my return from Europe. Our friendship—whatever this is—has never quite repaired itself after that.

I disappoint him. I get it. I'm not Holly. We all know that.

I'm sipping my self-appointed, *you-just-need-to-relax* drink at the counter when I hear muted laughter from the back bedroom. *Rob's room.* We don't normally invite people here. It's kind of an unstated rule that we established when I first moved in in late February. Curious, I walk down the hall and listen. I can't quite make out their words, although I hear my name come up. I instantly feel guilty for eavesdropping. I trot back to the kitchen, set down my glass, and contemplate my next move. I move to the living room and open and close the apartment door harder than usual—a clear signal to Rob and his mystery guest that I'm home.

"Hey, Rob. I'm home," I call out.

The muffled laughter stops completely. There's dead silence for the next few minutes. I feel stupid. I sigh, retrieve my coat from the sofa, and hang it up in the closet. Damn. Why would he do this? It's unlike him. We have a pact. We usually stay at the other one's place, although that only happened for me one time with Jack months ago. With Rob? How would I know? I'm never here. He probably didn't expect me tonight.

I move to the hall closet again, prepared to leave the premises as quickly as possible because somehow on a subconscious level I already know his mystery guest affects my life, too. *Shit.* My hands shake as I throw my arms into my long, wool coat. I lean down, snatch up my purse, and almost make it to the door when Rob calls out my name from directly behind me.

"Hey, Tal. Don't go. We just…well, we just got carried away." I turn back and stare at Rob like he's someone I've never seen before. I've never seen him quite like this—flushed and resolute. I've never seen him half-dressed either. His pressed white shirt is unbuttoned and only half-tucked in. His chest is nice. He does work out, and some weird part of my mind acknowledges this as an asset. Then I look past him and get a glimpse of a half-dressed Nika Vostrikova. *No.* All I can do is stare at the two of them with my mouth open. To say I'm floored is an understatement. It's probably more like the shock of the century for me, beyond Holly's death itself.

"I think Holly just turned over in her grave," I say. Rob hangs his head and won't even look at me. I don't regret saying this. Someone needs to defend and pay tribute to Holly. I guess that someone is me. "What the hell, Rob? How do you *know her?*"

"She's an investor in my new company," he whispers.

"Is she paying you in cash or just taking your fucking soul?" I ask.

Nika just gets this supremely satisfied smile at my clever remark. And, I suppose from her end of the slut spectrum it feels good to steal both of them from me.

"Rob and I are friends. *Good friends*," Nika says in the enveloping silence.

"I'm sure you are. You're just the best kind of *friend* that a guy can have," I say with true feeling.

Nika laughs, but Rob and I don't.

It's a multitude of things that make me cry. Me, Tally, who hardly *ever* cries anymore. It's the anguish over Linc and our daughter Cara, the manipulation by Allaire Tremblay and even the uncertainty of working with Sasha Belmont over the long-term, the mysterious meeting with Kimberley Powers that has left me more confused and disenchanted with her *I'll-help-you-out* promises that appear to be empty ones after all, the missing of my family, and now Rob, who looks ashamed of himself. As *he should be,* my mind whirs.

Where does all this self-righteousness come from? What part of me deserves to judge him in any role of the morality of his character? I can't judge him until I properly judge myself.

I say words to that effect, but I'm babbling now. The Dewar's made me do it. *Whatever.*

I move into my room in one fast long motion and face plant down onto my bed and start to sob like I've never cried before. I can hear Rob and Nika discussing the whys and wherefores on what to do from behind me. I don't care. *I have nothing left.*

The crying jag lasts a long ten minutes.

"Is there anything I can do?" Rob finally asks.

I can practically hear the wringing of his hands with the implied guilt and remorse for what he might have done or did with Nika Vostrikova. I answer as Holly would. I answer *for* Holly since she can't. I answer for myself and for Holly in equal parts. "Fuck off," I finally say. My voice is hoarse, but I get the words out.

With that sentiment, the door closes with a decided thud. I don't even wait for the click of the latch. I get up, pack my overnight bag, and grab my cell. My last parting shot is at Rob Thorn, where he stands alone—remorseful, undone, and clearly undecided—in the living room in the all-familiar, caught-lover's stance.

"I'm out," I shout at him and slam the door for good measure.

During the taxi ride, I charge my credit card with the nine hundred dollar one-way ticket to San Francisco and make my way to JFK. I'm going home. And everyone and I mean *everyone* can just fuck off.

My mom and dad are elated to see me. It was worth every penny I just blew on the plane ride to see their surprised faces, even though it quickly turns to looks of concern. I can't imagine what I look like. I'm still wearing dance clothes from yesterday morning. My hair is uncombed. I never even looked at my face in the bathroom mirror at the airport to repair my make-up before I boarded the plane bound for San Francisco.

"Are you okay, Tally?" Tommy asks, grabbing my hand and pulling me through the house.

"I'm fine," I murmur. I hug Tommy tight and follow him around. He shows me everything. His train set. His new bike. His gaming room. Things look festive. There's even a Christmas tree with lights and a few unwrapped gifts underneath. I'm a little surprised by how normal things look. I'm somewhat relieved and taken aback at the same time.

Holly would love this; wouldn't she? That they've moved on. Why can't I?

I trudge up the stairs an hour later after disentangling my arm from Tommy's clingy hands with a promise that I'll tell him about New York after I've had a chance to shower. I hear my mom noisily follow me.

"We packed up her room," she says in this false, airy voice. I hear it crack a little just before I train my full-on gaze to the open doorway that clearly conveys the utter emptiness of Holly's old room. "Dr. Anders said it was part of the grieving process, and that we needed to have a sense of moving on without her here. So we packed up her room a few months ago. I'm sure I told you about it."

"You didn't." My tone is flat—dead like Holly. I'm out of sorts. I thought by coming here after a year and half absence that I would find solace and peace. Instead, there appears to be as much upheaval at home as there is in New York. I shake my head side-to-side and moan the word *no* over and over. After a few minutes, I look over at my mother. She has this anguished look.

"I'm sorry. I thought we told you."

"You didn't." I look away from her. I can't take looking at the pure unchecked sorrow breaking out all over her face.

"Daddy thought it would be a good idea."

"I thought it was *Dr. Anders,* who said that." I do little to hide my mocking tone.

"You don't know what it's been like without you, without Holly. We just needed to move on and selling the house is a good idea."

"You're *selling* the house?" I practically scream at this news. I rush over to the window and spy the For-Sale sign that I failed to notice upon my grand entrance less than an hour ago. *No.* I alighted from the taxi and ran up to the house with all these naive expectations about coming home. *There is no home.*

"Oh. My. God." I turn and look at my mother *really* look at her. She looks thin. Too thin. Like me. Her dark hair is streaked with grey. She needs a haircut and color. There are fine lines on her face that weren't there a few years ago. She's aged a good five years, maybe ten. I have to wonder all over again when was the last time she left the house. I ask her this now.

"It's been a while." She gets this wan smile. "September?"

"So. We're not better," I say it for both of us.

"Not as good as we'd hoped."

I'd love to know who the *we* in that statement is. *Where the fuck has my father been?* Why have they been lying to me for the past eighteen months about how great they were doing? *And you wonder where I get it from.* I shake my head again, hoping to clear away all these incongruent racing thoughts, but I'm at a loss. I've got nothing. I can't even cry anymore. I'm all cried out. For myself. For Holly. For Cara. For my mom. There's no one left I haven't cried for. "Fucking Rob Thorn. Fucking Lincoln Presley. They broke my heart, Mom. I'm broken. There's nothing left of me," I say.

My mother is giving me this familiar once-over anxious look. "What about Rob? Linc?"

"They ruined everything. I can't trust anyone. They can't trust me. There's nothing. There's nothing. Nothing works out, Mom."

She laughs. My mother *laughs*. "Tally. Honey, that's not true. Some things work out." It sounds like it is something she has to believe. It's so sweet and innocent. I'm reminded of Cara, for some reason, while I'm just staring at my mother. *My mother.* She almost makes the situation bearable. I open my mouth to say something. I'm just about ready to spill out my entire story to her—all of it, but then pure terror stops me. I can't afford to lose the love of anyone else. My parents' disappointment in what I've done would just about kill me or them right now.

Then I'm distracted by the sound of the front door bell. It's this faint harp sounding ring from downstairs. I look over at my mom. "Who's here?" I don't even attempt to mask my accusatory tone.

She gets this guilty, worried look. *Yes. both, equally.* "Tally, you need to stay calm. It's not that big of a deal." She frowns. "It's probably…Linc. He's been taking Tommy to some of his batting sessions when he's in town. You know how your brother loves baseball. And, your dad." She gets this defiant look and then shrugs as if this is a normal occurrence—that of my ex-*almost-*boyfriend, the famous baseball player, coming by and taking my little brother to batting practice.

"No." I shake my head emphatically back and forth. "Tommy loves *hockey*. Hockey's his sport. And why would Linc get involved with my family? He…"

I stop talking when I hear the familiar timbre of Lincoln Presley's voice. "What the hell?" I stomp past my mom and fly down the stairs ready to do battle. "What are you doing here?" I rage at Linc as soon as I reach the landing.

Linc looks completely floored. It occurs to me that black mascara marks my face. I must look like a freak. All the energy drains out of me at seeing him and at what I must look like. I step back into the shadows of the foyer, while Linc steps forward and grabs my hand.

"When did you get in?" His voice holds all kinds of wonder.

Oh Elvis, I miss you.

"I took a red-eye. Home. Cheaper."

Not really. No. I flew into a rage at Rob, and I got the hell out of there and came here—home—because I need a break. From all of it.

"Does Kimberley *know* you come here?" I practically snarl when I ask him this. "She would have your head."

"No. I know." Linc hangs his head, but then looks back up at me with this pleading sexy smile. "You look like you've been up all night."

His voice is so gentle; it practically coaxes me to strip down for him right there. I can't move. I'm spellbound by his deliberate gaze. *Oh, God, please don't do this to me. Please.*

"All night," I manage to say.

"Hey, Linc. Are you ready to go?" Tommy asks from behind us.

Perfect timing as ever my little brother.

I start to laugh. "Yeah, you'd better get going." I slip my hand from his. Actually, I *pull* my hand from his ever-tightening grip.

He looks alarmed. "Can I see you?"

"You're seeing me," I say.

"I mean…*later.*"

"I'll call Kimberley and ask," I say sweetly, and then add, "Wait a minute, you *broke* up with me. So I guess it's up to me. *Me.*" I shake my head back and forth. "No. I can't see you later. I won't be here."

"Where are you going to be?" He looks uncertain and a little panicked.

"Anywhere but here."

Tommy is looking at both of us in typical, little-kid bewilderment.

Our faces are inches apart. I can clearly see the gold flecks that I remember so well in his amazing grey-blue eyes. I study him. He's tanner, thinner. He needs to shave. My mind goes to all these salacious places from the past, when his unshaven face rubbed up against mine, after he'd kissed me in the middle of that first night.

Only one night.

Just one, right?

I automatically lick my lips now, and he almost looks scared at what I might or might not do with those. He closes his eyes for a few seconds and opens them when Tommy pulls on his arm.

It's true. Little brothers don't understand the divisions that take place between love and hate. Fine lines—these boundary lines—that get blurred and undone with all the torment and passion. And then, there are all those lies that have been told. All the secrets. All those lies. Those lies that have been told and must be re-told, again and again, to keep the lines in place, to keep them from blurring, to keep the lovers from falling forward or falling apart, *equally*, in this case.

My parents enter the foyer.

Why not? Everyone else is here.

Tommy looks confused by the brazen way Lincoln Presley is looking at me. My mom looks hopeful for once, while my dad looks confident as if he has it all figured out. I take my cue from Daddy. "Well, you'd better get going," I say airily as I manage to move past Linc before he can react and move swiftly back toward the stairs, towards my dad, towards safety.

"I need to see you."

There's this obvious desperation in his voice. It causes me to turn and look at him more closely. I frown.

"You made your choice a long time ago, Elvis. Go play *baseball*." I break my gaze from his. "Tommy, have a good time. Just be careful and don't step out from behind the fence."

"I *know*, Tal," my little brother says. "Linc told me what to do."

"I'm sure he did."

I don't look at Linc again. I already know my hold on emotional power is about to run out. I can feel it slipping away. I'm minutes away from another crying jag. It's moving in on me like a thunderstorm you can see wending its ways toward you. These are dark skies I can't outrun.

My respite is a shower. Naked, locked in the bathroom, Linc can't get to me here, at least not physically. He wouldn't dare, not with my parents downstairs. I strip out of my clothes, sink down to the floor, and rest my weary head in my hands.

Eventually, I look up and the shower spray stings me with its untold power. It matches the rest of me in equal parts—mind, body, and soul—the heartbreak for pretty much everyone right now consumes all of me.

I let the tears fall for the second time in twelve hours when I'm absolutely sure that no one can hear me. I cry until I really can't cry anymore.

My breathing is rapid, so I pause in my soliloquy before starting again. "So that's the gist of it. I'm sorry. I can't believe he did that. It's so...so unlike him. Rob usually has it so together. Nika is a piece of work. Believe me, I know. He obviously wasn't thinking properly. I mean he's yours. We all know that. I'm sorry. I'm so sorry, Holly. It's not fair. And the whole other topic of Linc. Well, I can't even talk about that. Not even with you. Bad news. Trust me on that. Nothing good there."

I brush away the dead leaves and tidy up Holly's grave. It's the least I can do. I've neglected her for far too long. I don't think I've really spoken to her like this, since I found out I was pregnant, even before that. I just shut that part of myself off. I shut myself off from Holly, from the world.

And now? Here I am talking to a dead person buried six feet under. I'm seriously losing it on top of everything else.

Leaves crunch along the path. I keep myself from turning around by digging my fingernails into the palms of my hand—my normal modus operandi for such a moment. I remain perfectly still in my crouched position over Holly's grave.

Linc or Rob? Linc or Rob goes the mantra in my head. Who's it going to be?

"Tally?"

Rob.

I mete out the disappointment like a steady drumbeat that's tearing at my soul. *Of course.* Only Rob has a private plane and pilot who can fly him anywhere at a moment's notice. Only Rob would think to come to Holly's grave site because the only other person who visits more than I do is Rob Thorn. I've seen evidence of him, here and there, over the past few years on my infrequent visits. The love notes he leaves and the flowers he brings. Someone trims the grass and pulls the weeds from around her headstone or arranges to have it done. *Rob.* It's not like my parents are mentally together enough to perform these loving rituals. My parents wouldn't hang out here or swing by regularly with Tommy in tow. *No. It has to be Rob.*

"I loved her so much," he says.

I look up at him. He swallows hard in a vain attempt to control the sadness that inevitably crosses his handsome face. "I know."

"I'm just...I'm just trying to move on." He sighs deep, and I close my eyes for a second and feel his deep pain as if it is mine.

"I know."

"Do you?"

I open my eyes, jolted to the present by the hard look on his face and the unexpected anger clearly directed at me.

He shakes his head side-to-side. "I want to hate you so much. I want to get a rise out of you so bad. I want you to *see* me, Tally Landon. I want you to forget *him,* but you never do. You *waste* yourself on *him.*"

He clenches his hands at his sides. He looks like he wants to wrap them around my neck and press hard. A part of me wants him to do just that—choke the life out of me—press out all this pain and guilt and heartbreak.

"I just want it to stop. I don't want to feel this way anymore," I say.

He steps towards me and roughly pulls me up to him in one smooth motion. I fly into his arms, and he grabs my hair and keeps me there. There is no question about Rob Thorn this time. My mind registers that we're standing directly over Holly's grave and he is crushing me to him and trailing his lips along my neck, and I want him to. We fall to the ground, and he covers my body with his. We're desperate now—desperate to erase the memories of Holly and of Linc and, maybe, even of Nika. I willingly take up these betrayals and so does Rob. We take up where we left off almost a year ago when there was still this question about this forbidden longing for what might have been.

All these needs.

I need to forget. He needs to remember.

We forge an alliance right there in the cemetery, where Holly's ghost must surely watch. He undoes the front of my coat and blouse and then my jeans while I grab at his clothes. We're desperate to feel each other's skin and bodies on this inevitable collision course so we can discharge all these raging needs within us—of us—once and for all.

We forget the cold and the damp and the dead. We find warmth in each other. He's inside me within minutes, and I'm too ready for him to stop and consider any of this. He goes deep and fills me up in all these surprising ways. We both cry out at the unexpected pleasure even as we share in the indescribable pain between us. No one else knows but the two of us what it's like to go on without Holly. *Survive without Holly. Live without Holly.*

I feel this endless sorrow for all of them—Holly, Linc, Cara. People I love the most. I look into Rob's beautiful blue eyes, and he gazes back at me. He gives me solace that no one else has before; it's different from Linc. Rob's here. Perhaps, he always has been. *Rob's here. Linc isn't.*

I make a conscious choice, and my mind, body, and soul give way to Rob in this brief stolen moment. *I take him. I steal him.*

Our voices echo back to us among the trees and the granite and the dead. All judge but none speak. I've forgotten how much I need this. *I need sex. I need this.* And Rob's different from Linc in enough ways that I already know I'll survive this—all of this—because of Rob.

Peace, elusive peace finds me here. I feel like I might be able to breathe again, maybe even as long as tomorrow.

We finish slowly; look disheveled, and become shy but still revel in the awe of it all. We share this almost inconceivable wonder as we look at each other. Various pieces of our clothing have been cast aside in those first frenzied moments of need.

A few onlookers from the other side of the cemetery now glare in our general direction. I hang my head in shame but look over at Rob and eventually return his smirky smile with one of my own.

"I'm not sorry," he says.

"Me, neither."

It's true. It feels good to say it. It feels good to have someone there to hear it and believe me. There will be no judgment between us. It's all on us and no one else, not Holly, not Linc, not even Nika. My breath gets steady, and I stare at him as he holds my right hand and fixes my hair with his left. That's when he tells me, nothing happened with Nika, and I believe him. I breathe a shaky sigh of relief. It's short-lived because betrayal lurks inside my heart now—for Holly and even Nika and for what might have been with her and Rob. It divides and conquers me in that moment. *It. The distrust.* I push it all way down. Then guilt arrives and I take up the battle with that, too. I've betrayed Holly. I've betrayed Linc with all the lies. And now *this*, after all this time.

Seeking salvation, I gaze at Rob and it comes to me: *Our union, however imperfect, is perfect. It's that simple. We are lost when we're apart, but almost found when we're together. And, we can't go back. We can never go back. That's life's lesson for today.* Rob knows my secrets. Rob knows my lies. And he doesn't quite hate me because I remind him enough of Holly.

Within a few hours, we convince ourselves that being together is enough and that this is right. We hold hands when we finally leave the cemetery. I don't even turn around to say one last good-bye to Holly, even though I now hope to never return here.

On some level, I'm too ashamed of my betrayal of her. On another level, I'm too afraid of breaking the connection with Rob Thorn.

I'm too afraid to discover the truth behind our union and of seeing Lincoln Presley's disenchanted face when he learns of it; because this much I do know all lies eventually unravel and reveal themselves.

CHAPTER TWENTY-SIX

Linc ~ Game over

I DON'T WAIT FOR THEM TO FINISH. I've seen enough. Strange, I feel remorse, not anger. I suppose Nika Vostrikova figures into that sentiment somehow. I'm not a saint either; but then I didn't just brazenly fuck some random guy in a cemetery. The anger comes as I knew it would as I drive away from them. Tally never even knew I was there. She never even looked up when I called out her name before I saw she was with someone. No. She was flinging herself at some guy, like she'd been with him a decade already, and he was her long-lost soulmate.

My mind races. The vision of Tally fucking that guy won't go away.

I pour a glass of Jack Daniels as soon as I get to the guest house and drink it down like water. I have a personal trainer workout tomorrow. I have to fly back to L.A. in a few hours. I don't care.

If I hadn't gone into the Landons' place with the fervent hope of seeing Tally again, of talking to her, I never would have known about her and Thorn. But no. I had to play the benevolent ex-boyfriend, ensure Tommy was safely inside, hope to get a glimpse of Tally and beg for her forgiveness. Kimberley be damned. If Tally's mom hadn't mentioned the cemetery and speculated that is where Tally would have gone, I wouldn't have ended up there. If I hadn't gone, if I hadn't seen for myself how clearly Tally Landon has moved on, I wouldn't hate her so much now.

"What the hell are you doing?" Charlie asks when he walks in a half-hour later. The bottle is half gone. "Don't you have a flight back to L.A. soon?"

"Yeah. Can I get a ride to SFI?" I give him steely look. "She's fucking some guy who looks a lot like Kurt Cobain."

"Oooooohhhhh. Shit. Rob Thorn?"

"Yeah." I frown. "Rob Thorn? The guy from Paly that was dating her *sister*?" Charlie winces when I say this.

"How do you know for sure she was with the guy?"

"I *saw* them. Together. At the cemetery. Probably fornicating right over Holly Landon's grave because they certainly weren't planting roses." My words slur and my hands shake as I attempt to pour another.

"Ooooohhhhh. Shit. I…I'm sorry. I don't…Marla's mentioned Rob Thorn a few times. Yes, they all graduated from Paly in June. He's still in New York attending NYU. Tally stays there at his place, but she's like never there from what Marla said. I thought they were strictly friends. I mean seeing Rob Thorn would be kind of weird for Tally since he used to date her sister." He looks confused and sad at the same time. "I didn't realize they were *together* together. I think Marla would have told me."

"I don't…I don't want to talk about it. I don't really want his name mentioned again in my presence ever again. *Or hers.*" I pick up my cell phone and start dialing.

"What are you doing?"

"I'm calling Nika."

"Do you really think that's a good idea, given your state of mind?"

"All the good ideas are gone."

And they are. I'm done. I'm out. Game over with Tally.

They say there's a fine line between love and hate. They're right. I've found it.

CHAPTER TWENTY-SEVEN

Tally ~ He saw you

I NOTICE THE FLASHING RED LIGHT ON the answering machine as soon as Rob and I walk through the door, loaded down with suitcases and my mom's last-minute care package of stuff. We've decided to be straight with everyone. Apparently, Marla's decided to be straight with us; we just didn't know it right at the particular moment. I press the message button with this astonishing foreboding, almost like an electric shock before it actually happens. I take a look around Rob's place. There's not even a hint that I live here at all.

I look over at Rob, who looks amazing. Handsome. Secure. Rob basks in our love connection while I feel like a hologram about to disappear. I look up in the gilded mirror that Marla and I found at some second-hand store and push back my hair just as Marla's voice comes to life on the answering machine. And it dawns on me that *I'm barely here.*

"She *knows*," I say to Rob in this hollowed-out voice just before the message plays.

He looks over at me in surprise. *"How?"* His face transforms for an instant to this obvious remorse, but before I can ask him about it, I hear Marla's voice.

"Hey, Tal, it's Marla. Look, Charlie came home with a weird story about you and Rob?" She sighs. "Well, Linc...He *knows.* I guess...we all do." She lets out her breath slowly. "I don't know what to say. I'm shocked. It doesn't make any sense, and I tried to defend you. I went to talk to Linc myself, and that's when he told me he *saw* you—you and Rob at the cemetery, Tally. He...*saw* you and Rob." She takes a deep breath. I look over and attempt to gauge Rob's reaction, but he isn't even looking at me now. "I'm back in L.A. with Charlie.

I just don't completely understand it all, girlfriend. Anyway, give me a call when you get in. I'm sorry we didn't get to spend any time together. I do love you, Tal, but when are you going to start loving yourself?"

There's so much sadness and this underlying judgment in Marla's tone. It feels as if I've been stabbed. I clutch at my chest and hit the floor and gasp for air in an attempt to stem this inexplicable pain that burns through all of me from the inside. I reach over and press replay and listen intently to the message again. Only these words stay with me and inexplicably break my heart. *Linc knows. He saw you and Rob at the cemetery, Tally. He saw you.*

I should have known sooner. My mom asked me if Linc had caught up to me at the cemetery, but I was preoccupied with angst and guilt and remorse and regret, and all these thoughts of Rob were assailing me from all sides. I waited all the next day for Linc to drop by, unannounced like he always did, but he never came. I should have known. I couldn't even bring myself to go see Cara. I was too overcome with guilt about all of it. Everyone.

Then Rob called, offering me a ride—a flight back to New York—and suddenly I had a reason to return because Sasha had finally called and offered me the lead solo parts for both this spring and summer with the NYC Ballet's European tour. The chance of a lifetime. It's mine.

It's all so clear.

It's all there is.

He saw you.

Linc saw me. If he didn't hate me before, he hates me now. So I do what I've always done. I bury it as deep as it will go within minutes.

I saunter over to Rob and kiss him hard. I beg him to take me right there in the barrenness of that forgettable humongous apartment on the red velvet sofa.

"Make me forget. Take me away."

And he does. Rob does that for me. I have to convince myself that it's enough because surely this is all there is for me. Surely, this is all there is left for me to hold on to—this star-crossed lover of Holly's.

Rob.

Rob, who I now beg, borrow, and steal.

Rob can help me forget. Rob can take me away.

PART 3 — LOSING

*T*HE LURE OF THE DISTANT AND the difficult is deceptive. The great opportunity is where you are. ~ John Burroughs

CHAPTER TWENTY-EIGHT

Link ~ Always about the money

THE TALL, SEXY RUSSIAN DROPS A two-inch thick pile of papers on my glass coffee table with a decided smack. Her overt actions stir me from my normal malaise. Naturally, my eyes begin the long brazen sidle up her legs where they rest briefly. Then I become more intrigued when I take in the red fringe at edge of her pleated black-and-white miniskirt that generously offers a sneak peak at her delicate, black thong beneath. My gaze brazenly shifts to her midriff and finally settles upon her finely developed breasts, which look to be sheathed but just barely beneath her open-necked white men's dress shirt that she's casually tied at her fine waist. I could span it between my hands—her waist—and wished that I wanted to. How I wish I felt something for this girl and not the other one, but I don't. No. Not really. Not enough anyway. So I just vaguely stare at Nika Vostrikova because I'm unable or unwilling to feel anything more than this long-held disdain for eternal disillusionment that I am somewhat desperate to hide from her intense gaze. No. I'm not willing to share my private hell—this emotional empty vat of nothingness that appears to be without end that I constantly battle these days.

"She's still off the grid," Nika says.

"No kidding."

Nika gasps in frustration and shakes her head side-to-side. "I *told* you we had to move quickly."

"I had a *game*. You can't just *not* show up," I say with growing impatience.

"Okay. You had a game. *Several* games. An all-star appearance. Trouble in Toronto with your fastball. Seventeen walks in three starts following *that* debacle. Then eight consecutive strike-outs in another. And another. And a no-hitter in the last that effectively saves your season. But I'm telling you, darling Linc, she's off the grid. These are facts." She speaks a few choice words in Russian. It's sexy as hell.

"What does that mean—moy dah-rah-GOHY?" I ask.

She laughs at my garbling of her native language and gets this wicked little smile.

"Someday, I will tell you, not today." Nika *gleams* at me then. *It's possible. She does it.* She gleams at me and flaunts her incredible body in this not so subtle way with the slightest of dancer movements she's been making in just standing over me. She catches her lower lip between her lovely white, straight-edge teeth and I immediately think of Tally and how she used to do that, too. Misery swirls around me. *Again.*

"I'm just telling you how it is. And if you want me to keep looking for more info—keep tabs on her—"

"Let me guess," I say with a touch of sarcasm. "You need more money."

"Yes. Nothing comes for free." Nika smiles—this elegant bewitching smile at me.

I surprise myself by returning it. I haven't smiled in months, not since my spontaneous trip to San Fran and the unexpected encounter with Tally right before New Year's. It renders Nika Vostrikova momentarily speechless.

She stares back at me hard. *Weighs it. Assesses me.* I brazenly gaze back at her. A part of me is somehow a little mesmerized by this golden goddess that stands up to me and appears so willing, just like old times. She showed up in L.A. at my apartment doorstep just yesterday. We'd spoken by phone at least a hundred times over the past eighteen months since I first hired her to keep tabs on Tally. But she'd stayed in Seattle, did freelance work for Kimberley after I made phone introductions, while I just played baseball and tried to maintain some kind of focus. Nika. She was wicked, smart, and sexy. I remembered all of this about her from our brief encounters at Stanford. Nika Vostrikova. Trouble. Intrigue. Fun. Nika Vostrikova. The girl is beautiful in every way, but one; she isn't Tally. Would never be Tally.

For past eighteen months, I've lived for her somewhat infrequent communiqué about Tally—Nika's faxes and texts and phone calls—I waited and wished for them in every hotel from every town the team stayed in between the West Coast and the East Coast. I waited impatiently for Nika's updates about Tally only to be assailed by the stark truth of reaching yet another dead-end when I heard from her.

Nika knew my cell number. She even knew my stats. Yet I still knew next to nothing about her.

Until yesterday, I didn't even really recall her face. It'd been a while.

And after meeting Tally, I didn't see anyone else. All this time, I didn't care that I didn't really remember Nika.

Now, I do.

I have remained ever focused on two things: pitching a baseball at a high rate of speed and keeping tabs on Tally, or whatever the fuck she was calling herself these days, because it appeared that Tally Landon had made a conscious effort to drop out of sight. "Off the grid," Nika had said numerous times this season. One thing was going exceptionally well, and the Angels had awarded me the big contract I'd been hoping for at the end of last season, but at about the same time I gave up most of my soul for baseball, I had seen Tally with Rob Thorn. Fury coursed through me like a lit fuse that couldn't be extinguished. It spiraled ever downward toward its singular purpose, in exploding, no matter what I did to try and stop it. Anger at Tally flourished and grew. I had a plan. She just needed to wait for me but she didn't wait. *She chose to move on. From me.*

Eighteen months of celibacy for nothing. Even now. For what? What was I waiting for?

Anger. It fueled me, spurred me on to find her, and finally tell her what I thought of her immature, stupid move to drop out of my life so completely. I never stopped to examine the incongruence of this particular endeavor. *How could I actually be pissed off at a girl that I actually loved and effectively sent away in the first place? Did it matter?* I'd given her over a year and didn't try to reach and talk to her, but then I'd seen her with Rob Thorn, clearly having moved on.

Soon after, she'd vanished. *Off the grid. Nothing.*

Marla claims that she doesn't know where Tally was. Her best friend outright refuses to talk about Tally with me. She and Charlie live together in L.A. near my place, while I continue to try and stay focused on baseball and salvage what's left of my less-than-stellar season. I still struggle to understand and reconcile why I care so much about a girl who invariably broke my heart by being with Rob Thorn. Especially now, when this Russian goddess stands before me and appears so ready and willing for the taking.

Maybe I should do what even Charlie has begun to chant: "Forget the girl, Linc. Get your head in the game."

But which game? Baseball? Or life?

Even my shrink at three hundred dollars an hour—Hollywood's standard going rate—had encouraged me to move on with my life. "At the very least, get laid, Linc," Dr. Leitner had proclaimed at last Tuesday's session. "You seriously need to develop a focus on something else, besides your baseball career and this woman." It was the most Leitner had strung together in two consecutive and fully-coherent sentences in our seven sessions together. It's true. I'm going crazy because I'm too focused on Tally and not as focused as I should be on baseball.

Apparently, this little detail regarding my lack of focus did not go unnoticed even by one of my biggest fans in baseball, Nika Vostrikova.

I study the lovely Russian girl standing just above me some more. "Remind me again. Why are you here *in person*? You're a long way from Seattle and after all this time?"

Nika laughs as she retrieves a single sheet of paper from the stack she dispensed with earlier. "Do you know this guy?"

I glance down at the grainy black and white photograph. "Rob Thorn. How did you get *this*?" I ask, bewildered.

"Yes. It's Rob Thorn." She looks at me quizzically for a long moment. "It's a DOT shot just out of Manhattan. From over a year ago. I just found it."

"How did you *get* it?"

"You don't want to know," Nika says in a low voice.

I scrutinize the photograph and scan every detail of Tally's face. It's her. With Thorn. His dark blond hair is rocker length. He still has the Kurt Cobain look-alike thing going on, although he looks out of sorts, unsure of himself in the photograph. I search for applicable labels. A loser. A dork. All these stereotypes come to mind but fleet just as quickly because it doesn't do much to diminish the intimate look the two people in the photo share. I feel sick to my stomach all at once, somehow knowing that Nika has noticed their look, too. I run my hands through my hair and glance back up at the Russian girl again. She has this expectant look as if she's just waiting for me to figure it all out.

"What?" I finally ask and feel instantly afraid of her answer.

She makes this impatient sound and blows the air out between her teeth. "She's fucking him."

"I *know*." I struggle for air. My chest compresses and I try to hide it from Nika, who watches me even more closely now.

"When did you *know* that?" Nika looks unsettled. I didn't think anything could shock her but she displays all the signs.

"A while ago."

"*When?*" She seems to struggle with enunciating that single word.

"At the end of December. Right before New Year's. I was in San Francisco and I saw them together. What? Eight months ago."

A red tinge crawls up her neckline. She looks devastated by this piece of news. She spews a few choices words in Russian and starts pacing the room in sudden agitation.

"What of it? I pay you to keep tabs on her. I have my reasons as to why, you know."

"You went to see her," Nika says accusingly. More Russian words tumble from her mouth.

I'm confused by her unrestrained anger. "What is going on with you?"

"Nothing. It's just...*surprising* that he would be with her. *Then*. At that particular...time..." Her voice trails off. She seems to recover enough to rummage freely through my freezer. She finds the frozen Stoli and holds it up in triumph before pouring herself a generous amount in one of my favorite shot glasses. I watch her in this captive fascination. *Nika Vostrikova is pissed.* It's kind of a turn-on, when it's not directed at me. She fills one shot glass and then another and sashays over to me with them.

"She is with him," she says as if to convince herself. "There are others."

"Other *guys*?" I ask, sounding completely defeated, even as I down the cold vodka she's handed me.

"No," she says, looking surprisingly unhappy. "Other photographs of the two of them. *Together*."

Nika grabs a sheaf of photographs and drops them in my lap one by one. *Evidence.* Photograph after photograph shows the two of them together. Tally holding hands with this guy outside of some hotel. In another on a bridge. Another at Central Park. Still another at the Met. Smiling. Laughing. Happy? *Tally? This guy? What the hell?*

"He has a place in Manhattan," Nika says softly. "It took a while to figure it all out because his dad holds the deed. She's been there for a while. I checked it out for myself, and then came upon the Otis searches, as well." She's frowning as if trying to put it all together for herself.

"You check elevator security files, Nika?"

"Do you know how many security cameras there are in New York? And, the secrets they give up?" She gets this twisted smile. She's still pissed off about something. Her hands tremble as she grips the shot glass.

"I don't want to know."

She shrugs. It looks forced as she seems to strive for control. "They have a fondness for fast food. Well, he eats and she watches," she says.

I grimace at the memory of Tally and her weird love affair with food. She seems to have moved on to a guy who feeds into this particular obsession. No pun intended there. I practically wallow in the despair as it proceeds to roll in on me within a few minutes, while Nika seems to pause, assessing the effects of her news on me.

I knew this. No surprise here. I was just hoping it was a one-time thing but I knew better, didn't I?

Eventually, I look up at her in exasperation. She slightly sways, perhaps ensuring she has my full attention and I hate her more than Tally for a few brief seconds.

"What?"

"After these photos in Manhattan over a year ago, there's nothing. Months of nothing. No car. So no DOT photographs. Very strange." Nika shrugs ever so slightly and I get the distinct feeling that it's more for its effect on me than anything else.

Once again, I am automatically captivated by her very presence, caught like a voyeur. I stare at the sexy movement her beautiful shoulders make as she casually moves them up and down. The desired effect serves both of us on some level when her blouse slides off to one side. Nika secretly smiles while I'm instantly reminded of Tally. *Again.* I am caught in the memory of the first night we met when Tally's blouse did the same thing. I close my eyes, disturbed by the memory and the act of remembering when I'm clearly supposed to be concentrated on forgetting her, according to my shrink.

For a few minutes, I am only vaguely aware of the Russian who stands over me and way too close in proximity as it relates to client-to-hacker privileges or whatever we are to each other. It's a relationship I still refuse to define or pursue. She is a friend. I serve as the same. *Friends with benefits* Tally once accused me. She was right then. The crude thought has me opening my eyes again as Nika taps my knee with hers. This girl demands my full attention be upon her, whether I want to give it to her or not.

It's been a long while for me. Because of Tally. I'd been holding out for Tally. *Why? Why is that? It's not like she's been holding out for me.*

"So I went back and did some more digging in the school records. Palo Alto High School? Your high school? Hers? *His?* This guy. Rob Thorn." She leans down and stabs the photograph with a long red fingernail. "He dated her sister. Her twin." I start to nod while Nika seems to pause for full effect. "Holly Landon. That one was pregnant at the time of her death. Medical records indicate she was at least ten weeks along. They had a hotel reservation in Vegas for that spring, May first, I believe, and had filled out the online application for a marriage license in the state of Nevada. Robert Garrett Thorn. He's from new money. VC money. Venture capitalist funds? Daddy's a big time investor in San Francisco. The family lives in Sea Cliff. He's a trust fund baby and a prodigy. He was expected to go to Stanford, but ended up at NYU, studying business, much to his father's dismay. The Thorns have donated millions to the dad's alma mater Stanford. NYU seems to be a rebellious act for their one and only son. The family business is real estate in and around Silicon Valley as well as venture capital investments. He's worth millions. His dad is worth even more. No wonder they can afford to stay off the grid. And that is who your Tally Landon is spending her free time with now, I believe. Even when I input her real name, she's not showing up— *anywhere*. She hasn't for a while now. It's very strange." She gets this vexed look and cocks her head to one side, affecting deep thought. Her golden-blond hair falls along one side of her body, long and sleek, like the rest of her. "My guess is she doesn't want to be found and he's helping her," Nika says softly.

"How do you *know* all of this?" I shift uncomfortably as my body reacts to Nika while my mind scatters to someplace else entirely.

"Do you really want to *know*? Have you never done this before? The world is a very connected place, Lincoln Presley, unless people choose to not be connected. I see it all the time." Nika gets this serious expression. "This photograph was taken eighteen months ago. Weeks of photographs of the two of them that followed a pattern. She was *with* him then and she is most certainly with him again now. They started showing up again in late December up to now. She seems to have chosen. And so has he."

This hint of sadness crosses Nika's beautiful face and then it's gone and I begin to wonder if I just imagined it. There's a long, protracted silence between us. We both seemed troubled on some level by all these revelations.

"Why?" I finally ask, bewildered by Tally's alliance with Rob Thorn and stung by it on whole other level.

"My guess is she's hiding something or she needs his help or his money. People do strange things for a lot of reasons. They lie for a lot of different reasons. It's not like you promised her anything; right? You left. She moved on. Obviously, so did he."

Each word she says stings worse than the last. *I left her. She moved on.*

Nika's right. I did those things. What did I expect? Her to wait for me, until I…what? Got my shit together? Or, the world stopped judging our age difference because she was finally old enough for me? What was I thinking? *Was* I thinking? *Probably not. No, not at all, not on any level.*

"She's old enough, I suppose; she can do what she wants, except drink." Nika tries to smiles. It doesn't work. She seems to see and feel my pain as if it's her own.

After a while, she nods slowly as if having made a decision and begins to lightly sway above me again like she's performing some hypnotic dance and is just waiting for me to finally pay attention to it and her. I dazedly watch her swirling movements but am instantly reminded of Tally's spectacular dance moves. Nika's calculated assessment of Tally and Rob's relationship sinks in on me. This truth annihilates me all over again. *She's fucking him.* Nika's obscene expression runs through my mind like an unwelcome mantra but my mind holds onto the truth of the Russian girl's words. It's there in every photograph—the way Tally looks at this guy. She *trusts* him—Rob Thorn. I can see that for myself.

"She chooses to be with him," Nika says softly.

"I can see that."

"And I thought we should do this in person."

"Do what?" I ask with a faint smile and intently watch as her expression changes.

"Say good-bye or say hello. You choose. I know what she has meant to you—this girl. I just want to make sure you are…okay. *Fine*. Whatever it is you Americans say." She gets this secret smile.

"Really." I don't attempt to hide my sarcasm. I already know deep down that Nika could prove to be more dangerous. When I first met her at Stanford and acknowledged her beautiful face and the body to match and her lightning-fast mind, I knew she could be trouble. And then, yesterday, after all this time, she's just standing there at my L.A. apartment front door, looking resplendent and confident like she owned the world and a part of my soul already. Of course, she already knew my truths. And yet, somehow, a part of me already accepted that and another part of me wanted to better understand Nika's sense of control for the world. That part of me wanted her to take over because this much is still true: I just want to throw baseballs and concentrate on the one thing I'm good at for a while and let everything else fall away.

Instinctively, I know Nika will allow me to do this. Even now, in this moment when I look far into the depths of her crystal blue eyes and catch a glimpse of her soulless soul, I know she might be able to help me move on and away from all of this. Nika's dark in a way that Tally could never be. Nika can help me forget Tally.

Apparently, a part of me has already decided that maybe Nika Vostrikova is just what I need. In what swift estimation I still possessed in that first moment, even before I let her in, I knew full well that when I did that she would take all possession of me and would probably prove to be even more detrimental to my psyche than Tally has ever been. There's no doubt Nika Vostrikova lies better and more frequently for a myriad of reasons that I will probably never come to understand. I have no doubt that Nika's emotional wounds will attempt to cut me deeper and perhaps be no less painful than Tally's have been. Yes, getting involved with Nika again could lead to even more deep emotional cuts and wounds and eventual scarring, but I already know and accept this.

It's true. Nika will exact her pound of flesh from me in different ways; yet I allowed her entry yesterday and silently embrace her particular web of deceit—willingly, knowingly, and with true intent—now. I already sense I am her finest prey. I understand this, too. And yet, I willingly accept my fate in order to feel something with someone else. It's been too long. It's all been for nothing in the end. *Tally's found someone else. That someone isn't me.*

She casually shrugs again for the desired effect; while I just watch her fine bony shoulders move up and down as she seemingly tempts me in every way possible. Of course, my mid-section responds like clockwork this time. It's the only thing that isn't truly demolished by this latest news that confirms the permanence of Tally and Rob.

"Well, if you aren't *fine*," Nika says softly. "I'm going to ensure that when you I leave you that you are feeling *fine*. I thought I'd stay and watch you finish your season. I owe you that much after taking all this money from you." She waves her hand around my expansive living room.

And the seduction begins again.

"Ah, we're back to the money again." I sigh.

Resigned to her, I take a deep breath and hold it for few seconds. I know she is the Bering Sea, where the sea still freezes, and that she is just as deep and dangerous. This much is true. She'll take my heart and plunge it with an emotional knife that penetrates deep and beyond repair before we're through. I know this already, and yet most of me will go to her freely with the clear intention of playing this treacherous game because I have nothing left to lose. I face down my fear of losing. It's pretty bad—this losing. But I'll survive. With Nika.

"Is it always about the money, Nika?"

"I have found…that it always comes back to the money. At least, for me."

Nika retrieves the pile of photographs from my lap and tosses them aside. They splay across my Travertine floor like a collection of accusations.

I stare long and hard at the one photograph that's landed on top, Tally smiling at Rob Thorn. I wince while this incredible pain shoots through me from all directions. It feels like I've lost her all over again.

I look up as Nika. She still towers above me presenting herself as a golden opportunity. She is equal doses of permissible torment and pleasurable fun in the extreme. My hand of its own volition sidles up the length of her long, swanky leg. She moans and unwinds her goddess-like limbs down on top of me.

"Let me help you, Lincoln Presley. Let me make you feel better and not so lost; huh? Free of charge. I'll stay for the rest of your season. I'll be here for you," Nika says.

this much is true

I close my eyes and let Nika Vostrikova take all control. I shut off my mind and allow this woman to do whatever she wants because it's just game after all. A game I've been losing since I started playing. Maybe, if this girl wins, the memory of the other one will finally disappear once and for all.

CHAPTER TWENTY-NINE

Tally · Bereft of true emotion

EUROPE BRINGS MUCH-NEEDED DISTANCE FROM THE shredded mess my life has become. The time spent in Rome and then Paris brings unexpected solace and holds a distant promise for future inner peace. Someday. My mind doesn't race as much with all these uncontrollable thoughts of Lincoln Presley or the baby I gave away although I still subconsciously calculate the time since I last saw them. It's been more than four hundred days since I last saw Linc and more than two years since Cara was born. I dedicate a few minutes each day to this calling and determine her age at an almost a rote pace and allow myself to recall Linc's face the last time I saw him when he trusted me. Even so, it's true that the blameworthy noise inside my head is muted, almost absent, and I welcome that respite. It gets more tolerable, the longer I stay away. So I embrace the aloneness. I wallow in the solitude because all the turmoil goes away. It's as if a negative neutron has been forced by the physicality of nature into traversing in the opposite direction away from me. Nothing touches me. Nothing reaches for me. Ballet becomes my singular focus while the chaos that is my life effectively disappears.

Rob is busy with classes at NYU, living a separate life far away from me in Manhattan. He expresses his love for me in all these sweet, reachable ways through notes and flowers and little gifts that the hospitality staff leaves in my hotel room for me at each place we've stayed during the tour. I've already broken up with him at least a dozen times in my mind, at least six times on the phone, and three times in person. The topic of our being together is raised on every phone call. It begins like this: *"Rob, we can't do this anymore."*

His response is always the same. "Tally, give it some time. *We can do this. We are.*"

It's been more than a year, since the scene at the cemetery, more than six months since I've been home and that visit was brief—three days as a stopover on my way to Europe. I haven't even seen the new house my family has moved to. If I fly in to San Francisco again, I'll have to call and get directions to it. I'm still part of NYC Ballet's expansion dance troupe in Europe as the dance company fully establishes a reputation for itself internationally. This will be my second year on tour when we leave in a few months. *In exile.* I view it as an opportunity that nothing and no one can stand in my way. No one. Not even me.

I've changed my name and for the past eighteen months, I have taken on the professional persona of Talia Delacourt for my personal life as well. Tally Landon is long gone. I like it that way. "A rebranding of *you*." Sasha Belmont had called it when she first brought up the idea.

I was game. I was ready to forget who I was. I was ready to be someone else. I've told Rob and my parents about the stage name change; that's it. Marla's stopped calling. She never answered my infrequent texts. The roaming charges became so cost prohibitive that I finally turned off my phone and stopped trying to reach her all together. Since I so easily changed my name, I decided to change my look. My hair has gold highlights now, and the color catches the stage lights and all of me. I'm more golden blond than a brunette now. I feel and act differently as Talia Delacourt. And to the world, I shine and glow as the dance world's newest star. *Inside?* I'm dying little by little; yet, no one knows this but me and the critics.

The critics *know*. "Her dance is exquisite. Her form is perfect. Her performance is long on depth and beauty, but what it is bereft of—is true emotion."

"She performs. We applaud. But where's the feeling in this young lead dancer's exquisite performance?"

"Don't read the reviews," Rob had said more than a few times when he's called. "Stop reading them, Tally. They know not of what they speak." The way Rob said this makes me laugh. He always makes me feel better. *Mostly.* Rob always knows what to say, what not to say. That's probably why Holly must have loved him so much. I try not to dwell too often on why I can't feel the same way about Rob, or why I won't marry him, or why I still read the reviews, every last one of them.

<hr>

In early January, I land at JFK on a return flight from Paris after doing a bonus performance that Sasha Belmont insisted I be a part of after a brief return to NYC Ballet's holiday performances of *The Nutcracker* over Christmas. I automatically turn on my cell and hear the automated voice say, "You have eight voicemails." Strange. You would think the entire world would know that I've been traveling pretty much non-stop for the past two years. Seven messages are from Rob about: flight times, my passport, delays, he'll be there later, eat something, drink something, and see you soon. The eighth causes me to stand stock-still among the continual stream of deplaning passengers. "Tally, it's Marla. Hey, we're getting married. Charlie and me. On Valentine 's Day. I want you here in San Fran. You have to stand up for me. Call me when you get this. Your mom said you were coming home from Paris this week. Everyone will be there. You have to be there, too, *with me*. Bring Rob. Call me. Bye."

Marla sounds good. *Happy.* I resume my walk down the jet way and largely ignore the *lady-are-you-coming-or-going?* trash talk taking place all around me as New Yorkers hurry on their way to somewhere. She's getting married. She wants me there. We're going to be okay. I don't even want to think about who she's marrying, for the moment, or his cousin and most likely his best man. No. I refuse to dwell on that aspect of what she's asking me to do.

Two minutes later, I glance up and spy Rob holding a sign that reads: *Delacourt's Enterprise.*

Funny. Funny guy.

I fall into his arms and kiss him hard because, today, I need Rob Thorn and no one else. After we come up for air, he signals to our limo driver and tells him which bags to take; then he pulls me into his arms and kisses me everywhere all over again.

"I've missed you." He brushes his lips against my forehead and runs his fingers through my hair. I shiver at his touch. We haven't seen each other for a few months and the last time we did; we'd had a huge fight even though it was his last night in Paris. Pressing me for a commitment; I told him, in no uncertain terms, to quit asking for one. I look up at him now. He's dressed to the nines in a dark grey Italian suit and a silver and black silk tie. He took a financial position with one of the Wall Street investment firms. Something, he confided to me once, he would never do, but here he is, doing it.

"Is everything okay? You're acting weird, more than usual," I say stepping back and gazing at him intently.

"Yes. Just glad you're home." He sighs and looks away. He's nervous, and I become suspicious of this whole strange demeanor of his.

"I hope you didn't plan anything…you know, *big*…for my homecoming."

"No." He shakes his head but avoids looking at me directly.

"You're scaring me. What did you *do*?"

He winces. "I don't want you to freak out."

"Well, now I am. So, out with it, Thorn. Like you said once to me…a long time ago." I force myself to smile at him even while my pulse begins to race. "What did you *do*, Rob?"

"I got us something. A place. *To start over*. Ours. Not my father's. It's pretty nice with a view and everything and I just don't want you to freak out too much when you see it. I think you'll want to call it *home*."

"A place to call *home*? We *moved*?" There are too many implications in that little statement. We fought at Christmastime about where our relationship was going or not.

"Yeah."

"And you think I'll like it?"

"I do."

"Okay, show me," I say.

I can't really explain where the agreeable nature is coming from. We've had numerous discussions about our place, his place, my place, *a place*. *Us.* Because if we're getting technical, and that's what we're really talking about here, after the last year away from him most of the time, I'm actually ready to talk about all of that—meet up with all of that—with him. Marla's getting married. We've all moved on. Rob puts his arm around me tighter and leads me to the car. I climb into the limo and give him a hard stare as I look around because this is no ordinary car ride. There are white roses and champagne and two types of wine and a dozen chocolate truffles. It's not Valentine's Day quite yet. Neither one of us has found peace with that holiday yet.

"Red or white wine or champagne, Ms. Landon?" the driver asks.

"Champagne," I murmur and take the glass with unsteady hands from the helpful limo driver.

Rob's sliding in right beside me and looks even more nervous. He's shaking as he holds my hand in his and gives me one of his soulful looks. *Oh shit.* He's gone all out, and this isn't just a ride home to a place that he wants to be ours.

The limo moves out onto a more familiar-looking route towards Manhattan. Rob's drinks from a glass of sparkling wine and playfully kisses my fingers, one by one. *I want this; don't I?* I start to go through the list in my head as to all the reasons why I should want this because the aloneness of the last year all but engulfed me most of the time. *I missed him. I missed Rob. He's here. So am I.* I lean into his white-pressed dress shirt and breathe him in.

"What did you do?" I finally ask after a long shared silence.

"Like I said. I got us a place. To be together."

"That's not what you said." I shake my head. "Before. You said I got us a place to start over. Ours. Not my father's. It's pretty nice with a view and everything. *That's* what you said. So. Why does it feel like it's more than that?"

"Tally? Why do you have to complicate absolutely everything?" Rob asks sweetly.

I don't have to formulate an answer or a lie for that one because the limo pulls up in front of one of the taller buildings in downtown Manhattan. I choose silence.

I can't believe we sailed through forty minutes of traffic, and I didn't notice. The driver must be as magical as Rob right now. Rob jumps out and leans back in and takes my hand and pulls me from the car. It's like getting out at a film screening. I note the red-carpet treatment just as a few camera lights flash.

"What is going on?" I look over at him like he's lost his mind, and he's looking at me as if I'm the unicorn that he's just successfully captured for the very first time. Where are these fairy tales coming from?" I ask.

Now, it's his turn not to answer. He just gets a little smile while it begins to dawn on me that he is shrewdly forcing my hand.

There's a little round of applause as we make our way to the front doors of the building. There must be at least twenty people gathered there. I recognize a few faces from the dance company. Sasha. Kimberley. I'm really confused now. *A place. Ours. Together.* This doesn't look like a nice evening where we're sitting at home getting to know each other all over again and discussing our future now that I'm back.

We're rushed up a private elevator and I steady my nerves by counting the floors. We stop at the forty-ninth floor, not the penthouse level. That's one more above us, according to the lit-up panel. I breathe a sigh of relief; maybe, Rob didn't overspend on this idea.

There's twinkling white lights everywhere throughout the apartment, which is mostly white and sparkling glass and beautiful. The place is beyond anything I ever imagined living in. He's managed to replicate all the things that I mentioned that I did love when I once saw Tremblay's place into this one, including the Impressionist artwork displayed throughout. Although I have a feeling that some of the pieces displayed on the wall in the living room are actually original.

His parents are here. The older version of Rob walks toward me and grabs my hand and kisses the top of it. Rob's blond and beautiful mother is dressed in a long, black form-fitting dress. She comes over next and kisses each side of my face and whispers 'Tally' loud enough that everyone hears it. I'm being anointed here in some way. This is a party—a celebration—I'm the star attraction, whether I want to be or not. It seems we all need this. Rob is no further than six inches away from me. I hold on to him for all kinds of support—moral as well as physical.

After a half-hour of this, I'm in need of an explanation of some kind. I have to hope he's going to give me one, but I'm not sure that he will. He pulls me away from my parents and his. I mindlessly follow him down the long hallway. Black and white. Shiny and beautiful. Nouveau riche. This place must have cost a fortune. I'm enamored and terrified at the same time and left wondering how we're going to live here and afford all of this.

He stops in front of wide-open doorway and gives me the smirky smile. It's been a long time since I've seen it. I reach up and trace his lips.

"Here, I got you a dress to wear."

"What is all this?" I ask.

"I want to show you how it could be. How it could work. I want you to see me. To see what I see and show the world—our world—what I see with the two of us together. I want that for you and me. I want you…if you want me. Do you?"

"Rob," I hesitate, secretly begging for more time without saying another word. He winces. "You know…I do." I practically choke on the words. My heart rate speeds up because I already know where this is going, and I know what I want to say. *No. No way. No fucking way. Why are you doing this to me?*

"I do? Because the fight the first time you were in Paris left me…reeling. I didn't know what to think, and these fucking phone calls between us seemed more rote, as if we just recorded them in advance or something and just said the same things over and over again." He runs his hands through his hair in obvious frustration.

I close my eyes, intent on erasing the memory of someone else first. When I open them, Rob is staring at me. He's just a mere six inches away from my face, discerning every emotion that crosses it.

"I keep thinking you'll forget him. That time will erase all of him from your mind. It's hopeless, isn't it?" Rob gets this determined look as if he's hell-bent on finishing this tonight.

I take a little step back, uncertain where he's going with everything, uncertain I want him to go *anywhere* with all of this. "Don't."

"Don't what?" He sighs in frustration. "I wanted to give you this." He flips open a red velvet ring box and gets down on one knee in the next. "I wanted to ask you this…to be my wife in front of every single person out there." He frowns. "But I'm afraid to do that, Tally Landon, because I really don't know what you would ever say besides *no*."

He laughs a little and shakes his head side-to-side in disbelief.

My eyes fill with tears.

Why do I always disappoint him?

Why do I choose to do that?

"You've been gone a year. A *year*, Tally. Please don't stand there looking at me like that and then tell me you need more *time*. Please don't fucking do that to me."

I am over him—the other one, who neither one of us can name out loud anymore because in the past year by some unspoken agreement; we have stopped saying his name. And we can't say it even now.

And the other one. My secret—the one Rob knows—*Cara*. I haven't thought of her since yesterday, when I packed for home, until now. She is two. Talking. Walking. Tremblay's postcards have kept me somewhat informed.

I forget nothing and no one even when I want to, even when all I want and need to do is *forget*.

Easy. Easy mistakes. Easy lies. These are the easy ones we can tell ourselves.

Rob stares at me hard, willing me to say something.

I do the same.

"Okay," I finally utter. "Okkkkkaaaaay. Let's do this thing. I've got a few months before I go back. You can't hassle me about this next tour though. You get what you want. I get what I want. We make this place *ours*. Okay? Yes. Okay. Go ahead and ask me." I sigh and take a jagged breath because I'm surprisingly a little giddy at using all these unfamiliar words like *okay* and *yes* and *go ahead* and *ask me*. Yet, acquiescence and this inner peace of some kind come right along with them.

"Really?" He looks unsure.

I roll my eyes. "Damn it, Rob. Please don't ruin it for me anymore than I already have."

"Tally, will you marry me?"

I start to use the word okay, but he looks disappointed with that one. He drives a Volvo. He did. He used to. Now he has a Porsche but has a driver and gets driven everywhere. Safe. He is safe. He is nice and wonderful. *An easy mistake.* I cover my ears, so I can say the word without hearing myself say it. "Yes."

He looks surprised—an answer he wasn't expecting or rather is ill-prepared for. Then he smiles the smirky smile, and that's when I know for sure that's why Holly loved him. Holly still loves him. *And me? I'm a good stand-in for Holly.*

In this moment, I want to make him happy because one of us should be… happy. One of us should try to be happy.

I pull him to his feet. He folds me into his arms and kisses me as if I'm his sole source for oxygen. Thirty seconds later, he slips this brilliant diamond on my left ring finger. It feels weird and heavy and binding.

His smirky smile saves me again. I stare at him open-mouthed.

"I've always loved you, Tally Landon." He gets this extraordinary look as if he can't quite believe he's said this much aloud. "It was always *you*." He dips his head and kisses my ringed hand.

"A place. Us. Together. Okay."

He looks up at me. "Get dressed, baby. I want to tell the world we're getting married."

"Married," I grit the word out through clenched teeth and then force myself to smile. I even manage to avoid bitching at him about calling me *baby*. That particular discussion can wait for another day or two.

He kisses me again and leaves. "Before you change your mind," he calls out from the hallway. I listen to his fancy dress shoes tap away along the marble floor until I can't hear them anymore, and then I breathe.

Breathe. Breathe. Breathe. What the hell just happened?

Alone. I make a three-hundred and sixty degree turn around the sumptuous master bedroom and try to not to examine too closely to what just unfolded in the past forty-five minutes between his parents and mine and his proposal. I'm exhausted all at once. I stare out at the dark twinkling view that sweeps across one whole side of windows that face Central Park and the bay and include the best parts of Manhattan's skyline.

What's left of my soul has been taken, sold, and repurchased. And I've just consented to it all.

He's gone all out. There's a dress laid out on the king-size bed. It's a black velvet cocktail dress. It's expensive couture that I recognize having just spent the past few months in Paris.

Kimberley Powers chooses that particular moment to saunter in. "He picked it out. I told him it was too conservative, but he insisted you'd love it," she says with a tight smile.

"I do."

"He's great. Rob. Is. Great." She rewards me with the all-powerful Kimberley Powers stare that must include a Star Trek mind meld of sorts for free.

I nod, not trusting myself to speak. "How do you two know each other?" I finally ask.

"We met up a few times. I told you I like to keep tabs on all my special clients."

"So, you did."

"If he's what you want, I'm all for it." She gets this uncertain smile. Her bravado apparently falters as much as mine.

"What did he tell you, exactly?"

"He wants to make you *happy*. I believe him." She gets this defiant look.

This I can handle. Kimberley Powers defiant. It practically fuels me.

I grab the dress, strip out of my travel clothes—designer Parisian jeans and a silk blouse—and slip the black velvet dress over my head. A perfect fit.

Kimberley tosses me some strappy black sandals, and I put them on one at a time.

"Jesus, Tally what are you? A size zero?" Kimberley asks as she zips up the back of the dress for me.

"Don't start."

"Yeah, well, you need to eat a hamburger or something." She laughs and so do I.

"I've missed those. They just can't get it right in Europe no matter how you try to describe it when you order."

"I *know*. American food is so hard to come by there," Kimberley says. "So when do you go back?"

"May? A summer and fall tour. We'll be in Moscow through the holidays."

"God, it's worse than baseball."

I look over at her intently, take a deep breath but wait until my voice will sound steady and clear. "Hey, Kimberley, we don't ever talk about baseball; okay? I just want to be clear, since I'm one of your special clients. We don't talk about *him*. Not now. Not ever."

She gets this sympathetic look.

She knows something—something she probably wants to tell me, but I don't want to hear it, and I tell her that now.

"I don't want to know. I. Don't. Want. To. Know."

"Okay then," she says evenly.

Together, we walk arm-in-arm down the hall toward the party. Kimberley makes small talk with me about the great artwork and the great location and how great the place is.

I reward her with a dirty look.

"One more *great* and I won't believe you."

"Ditto," she says.

Then Rob introduces me as his future wife—the future Mrs. Robert Garrett Thorn—to all those suddenly gathered around us. Kimberley drifts off to one side, and Rob takes over.

Beholden to the task at hand, I spend the rest of the evening hugging people and smiling and nodding at them and showing them my left hand, until I feel as if I'll never actually be able to do any of these things again in this lifetime.

I smile and nod just the way Allaire Tremblay taught me years ago because you must do what you have to do to survive. You dance on. That's what you do.

CHAPTER THIRTY

Tally - Far far away from here

MY BEST FRIEND MARLA IS PROJECTING to be all kinds of things for this bridal audience, and my designated role is to sanctify it all. Marla says she's going straight to grad school after teaching for a while, after Charlie finishes medical school. I'm impressed he's still going and in the top twenty percent of his class. It's all coming together according to my best friend. *Oh, Marla.* I think it. I don't say, but I think it *a lot.* She's marrying him on Valentine's Day, three years to the day that Holly died. None of us are supposed to notice that, although it's hard not to. Clearly, Holly would have been her maid of honor and not me because Marla would have been fair that way. She would have included Holly in this huge honor, and my sister would have been great at this kind of thing; whereas, I am so *not. I am the fish out of water here. I cannot breathe. I need air and water and a place far far away from here.*

Rob decided to be a prick at the last minute and decided not to come with me. There was no real explanation for his last-minute change of plans. He just bailed on me when we got to the airport.

I boarded the plane alone, battled with myself a number of times on the five-hour flight about taking off this incendiary fucking rock on my left hand, but eventually decided I may need to be weaponized at this event. So, I left it on.

Marla announces she wants babies. Three babies in five years. She looks at me. I start to feel nauseous and must turn a little white. I look away from her and allow myself to think all these nasty thoughts. *Three babies in five years with Charlie? Are you fucking kidding me? That doesn't add up on any girl's wish list. Charlie Masterson. A father? Say it isn't so.*

Yet she lays out this family plan the way you'd say, "After yoga, I'll go to Lia's for the mani-special and then wax on about hairstyles and hemlines until dinner."

If I were gifted at making long-term plans, which by now we all know I'm not, and if I was at all hopeful, which we all know that I can never be, although it crosses my mind that it's entirely possible these are all just huge, fucking, temporary setbacks and nothing more, even though it's been going on for over three years now, since Holly died, and I met Lincoln Presley. Events that could be construed as somehow inevitably related. Yes, perhaps there's an expiration date on the said pursuit of unhappiness. Perhaps, things will eventually go my way after I actually discover what that way is supposed to be.

I don't get to finish this last thought completely because now everyone notices the rock on my left ring finger.

"Rob?" Marla asks, incredulous. She makes a weird shape with her mouth, not quite an O more of a Q. This streak of outright sorrow crosses her face like a flash of lightning, but then it's gone. She's hugging me and kissing both sides of my face. "Tally, you're getting married."

"When?" asks the bitch from Bel Air.

I don't like her. I don't bother to learn her name. In forty-eight hours, this thing will be done. She and I will never see each other again, and we are both already thanking God for that little reprieve in our otherwise extraordinary lives.

"No date."

That's all I say.

I look at them all imploring them with a single scary glare that it is best for all to just move on to another topic of conversation. Marla sighs and gets this secret smirky smile, which reminds me of Rob. Envious and sad, I just watch her through these rising misted layers of hair spray that linger on the air and co-mingle with the flotilla of dust particles and the pungent scent of Beyonce's *Heat* perfume. I'm not too sure of the bride-to-be's appropriateness with that particular scent, but I inhale deeply, while she sways to the lyrics of *Bad Romance* and taps Gaga's rhythm with her red stiletto-adorned feet in the cramped quarters of her one-bedroom, one-bath hotel suite.

She's got this dreamy look going—her *everything's-right-with-the-world-why-isn't-it-right-with-you-Tally?* face. It's such a carryover from high school that I almost laugh. Her golden locks wisp around her face every which way from her hair spray jag, minutes earlier. She manages to look absolutely stunning, and it comes together all so effortlessly. She's lean and tan and vibrant and so sure of herself. Marla really can do all the moves in her

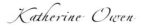

yoga class, including the Crane pose *Bakasana,* which she shows her L.A. roommates slash bridesmaids-to-be and me—her lowly maid-of-honor—in one smooth, sultry move.

I close my eyes, remembering how good she used to be at ballet. All of me is filled with instant regret and endless remorse at what went down with Tremblay and what she gave up for *this.*

I open my eyes and look around the sumptuous suite. The Oceana Hotel & Spa at Half Moon Bay Harbor is not a bad consolation prize for a wedded bliss, but she could have done so much more on stage with me.

"Yes," Marla confides to the vamps that surround her. "Yoga keeps me limber in all *situations."* It's the word she uses for all encounters of the sexual kind; now that she's so down with all things strictly associated with UCLA. I roll my eyes at this one. *If they'd only see her perform.* But she obviously doesn't talk to them about ballet. And, up until two years ago, she'd been incapable of a long-term relationship of more than six months at any given time; but then she'd re-connected with Charlie because of me, because of me and Linc, because her ballet dream disintegrated and her modeling one never materialized. *Because of love? Say it isn't so.*

I hang my head and twist the rock around so it doesn't sparkle so much in the blasted sunlight here.

"Just don't give up your dreams," I say only to her during a decided lull in the girlish shrieks of conversation happening all around us. I must be experiencing equal parts of inebriation and panic to talk like this out loud. *Here.*

Everyone politely laughs, except Tracey Rothfield, who judiciously files her nails and looks bored by it all and has informed the bachelorette party of five that she's been ready to go for an hour. I am definitely the odd one out with this whirlwind wedding nuptials' weekend. I'm designated the girl from New York, the bride's best friend from high school, the ballerina, whatever that means to these three—Tracey, Fay and what's-her-name—Marla's college friends, who get to see her practically every single fucking day.

Yet, after only knowing her for just over two years, they are asked to be in her wedding. It's true that it's been too long since I've seen her. *But still. These are her friends? This is UCLA's best offering for friends?*

And now, she's marrying Charlie. Why? Because it's what's expected? Because she's changed him? What do I know of Marla anymore? What do I know for sure of Marla anymore? What can she possibly know of me?

The bride-to-be takes a long swig of her margarita. She wipes the salt from her lips with the back of her hand and asks this Fay to get her a refill, who dutifully complies. I stifle a laugh in witnessing Marla's complete domination of this wisp of a girl. Marla smirks in my general direction. "I promise. I won't give up on my dreams. You can't either, Tally Landon, dancer extraordinaire."

Does she mean to ridicule? Is she making fun of my life? Does she disapprove of me? She knows all my secrets. Does she still judge me for giving up Cara? Even now? Does she still hate that she has to keep that secret for me? Or, is it Rob? Rob and me? And, this ring that I should have taken off, but a part of me wanted to show her, show *him* if he shows up, that I have definitely moved on.

The Xanax is not working. Mixing it with a margarita was probably not a wise choice.

Being worked up about these tag-alongs—these three Girl Scout cookie wanna-be's—is not worth it. I didn't come all the way back from New York to San Francisco's Half Moon Bay to hang out with Tracey, Fay, and what's-her-name. I came back home for Marla's wedding, to be with her, to meet up with my family, to stomp on the old stomping grounds of my past, and to reveal to the world as much as to myself that I have moved on with my life. Yes. I'm the girl from New York now. I'm Rob's fiancée. I'm a star. I've made it. This is me now. Of course, it's true that I also came back to San Francisco to finally sort myself out because who knew I'd still be thinking about that decision I made two years ago that only Marla knows? I intend to see Cara and Tremblay, at some point, before I go back. Just to know. To ensure that everything is fine. That things are as right as rain. That she's happy. Because if Cara's happy, then I can finally be happy. And, if Elvis shows, I want him to know that I'm happy with what I have—which is everything, just minus him and Cara and Marla and Charlie.

I'm happy, aren't I? I'm almost happy. Aren't I?

My eyes begin to sting. I blink hard. I swig the margarita and allow it to burn all the way down because I've gulped too much of it.

I have everything.

Rob. Career. Fame.

Don't I?

I do.

I'm almost happy. Almost.

Marla stares at me. Then, she grabs my hand and smiles.

We are the only two here. The other three just fade away and don't matter anymore. Her look tells me all of this.

I decide *no*. Marla's not being thoughtless. Marla isn't that way. She's a guardian angel. *Mine.* She's the lit candle lighting the way in my life, even when she isn't close by. During the darkest days of that angst-filled summer, fall, winter, Marla was there. She held my hand, told me everything was going to be okay. And it was okay, has been okay. But I just need to hear her say it—say it again to me now—everything is fine. Everything is okay. Things are as they should be. I just need to hear her say it. One more time.

⁓ ⚬ ⁓

It's late, and we drank too much. No amount of food, late at night, is going to soak up the amount of alcohol that we've consumed over the last eight hours. It's two in the morning, and the three bridesmaids went to their rooms over an hour ago. Marla and I sit out under the stars in comfy lounge chairs on the Oceana's expansive back patio.

Ten minutes ago, we dragged our bed comforters outside and wrapped ourselves up in them. It is forty degrees out, but it feels good to breathe in the salty San Francisco Bay air even out here in the dark of night with the stars glowing at us from overhead. We can see our breath. Every time we open our mouths and breathe, we puff out steamy air. For some reason, we both think this is funny.

We've waited hours to be alone like this. I don't waste it now.

"I hate them," I say without preamble and true vehemence. *Such honesty.* "All three." I hold up my hand and splay out three fingers.

"I know they're awful, aren't they?" Marla laughs. "I kind of panicked. I lived near them right by campus. We've hung out a bit. I guess I didn't know them all that well because I had no idea they were this catty and this slutty and this boring. Charlie's been busy. I've been working extra hours waiting tables so we would have enough money for all of this." She waves her arm around the hotel grounds like she's holding a magic wand. "I went to school with them, hung out with them for drinks and stuff and pool parties as part of the L.A. scene, but I didn't really know them. Not like you. You know? I've tried to stay busy. Charlie's got three more years of med school. Then, it's on to a residency. It all costs money and he won't ask his parents or Linc for anything."

I turn and look at her in the semi-dark. "He's really going to be a doctor."

"I know." She shakes her head and then stops. "I didn't even know until I got here. He fesses up about getting into med school right after I moved in with him." She sighs. "Charlie's in med school. He's going to be a doctor. Can you believe it?"

"No. That's just weird."

"You like that word a lot.

"I guess so."

She hands me the bottle of champagne because we are swigging directly from it at this point.

"So," she says. "Don't you want to know why he's not coming?"

"Does it matter? *Will* it matter?"

"He wanted you to be able to be here for me, and he didn't want you to be uncomfortable around him."

"That's stupid. That's ridiculous. That's weird. "

"I know."

I hand her the bottle back. We snuggle closer to each other in our blankets and rest for a little bit in the lounge chairs and don't talk for a while.

"I'm going to see her while I'm here," I finally say. "Tremblay sends these postcards and a few photographs; but I just want to check in for once. Make sure Cara's happy and all of that."

"I want to come."

"You do?"

"Tally, I need to see her, too. I'm sure she's great but I want to make sure she's okay, too. I think about Cara all the time. We should have kept her."

"It wasn't that simple."

"I know." Marla looks over at me in the dark. Her face exhibits this intensity I've never seen before. "Do you think he even realizes how much you sacrificed for him? I mean *really* sacrificed it all for him."

The mix of alcohol makes me tear up. *Too much alcohol. No food.* My throat gets tight, and I have trouble keeping my emotions under control. "I didn't think you saw it quite that way," I finally say.

"I *always* saw it that way. Always." She sighs. "He makes me so mad. He's being such a jerk these days. He's got more money than God. You'd think he'd be willing to help Charlie out. *But no.* My fiancé just follows him around like a puppy dog and Linc just doesn't even see that Charlie really needs his help."

"I'll talk to him. I'll call him tomorrow and tell him to come to the wedding. I'll tell him to quit being a jerk, too; and to help Charlie out."

"You will?" Marla asks with this undeniable wistfulness.

"I have his number."

"You do?"

"I've had his number for years."

"Nobody has his number. When they found out he was Charlie's first cousin, all three bridesmaids wanted his cell number, but even I don't have it. Elvis gave you his number," Marla says in awe and wonder.

"A long time ago."

"Maybe we should call him and Charlie now. Why wait? Let's call them now," Marla says.

I don't even stop to think through the implications of this. *No.* I just pull out my phone and dial.

He answers on the third ring. He sounds like he was sleeping, but he's wide awake within seconds.

"Tally?"

"Hi, Elvis."

"Have you been drinking?" Linc sounds somewhat alarmed, and it makes me laugh.

"A little. Marla's right here. We're starving though. What can you bring us to eat? The kitchen's closed, and the hotel restaurant is closed and the only other choice we have is the mini bar, which really doesn't have food." I pause and take a breath and then go on in a rush. "You can come to the wedding. You need to be here for Charlie. Marla wants you to come. I want you to come. You should come. You should come to the wedding, and you should come see me. *Now.* Bring food."

I hand the phone to Marla, who giggles the entire time, while she gives Linc better directions and reminds him to bring Charlie.

∗

They're here in record time. I clock it at thirty-five minutes.

I look up at Charlie. "You drive too fast."

"I know. I'm trying to slow down." Charlie gets this wide grin. "How are you, Tally?"

It's hard not to like him.

"I'm good."

I flash the groom-to-be a sly smile, fling off the hotel's comforter in the next, and stand up in my fine little black dress that Marla insisted I wear. I'm barefoot, hungry on a variety of levels, and suddenly very cold. I look over. Linc is staring right at me, gazing at me, and seems to be undressing me with his eyes. I extend my hand out to his. "Tally. Twenty. I dance for the New York City Ballet. And, you are?"

"In trouble," Linc says with an easy laugh as he takes my hand into his.

I've never seen him laugh quite this easily before. I incline my head and study him for a minute or two, while he gets this unexpected shy smile but doesn't let go of my hand.

Instead, he pulls me to him, and I quickly note he's different than Rob. Taller. Still so sure of himself. He's stronger, leaner, and tanner—a more fit version of himself than even a year ago. Time has been good to Lincoln Presley.

"I'm in trouble, too," I say back to him. "Did you bring food?"

"I did. You know how I like to see you eat something, in case we get to do the deed later."

"Right." *Breathe.*

This vague memory of him looking at me like that before stirs. *Was it that first night?* I kind of shudder—thinking about the consequences, thinking of Cara, who's not really a consequence anymore—but momentarily recognize that I'm older, wiser, and covered, tonight.

CHAPTER THIRTY-ONE

Linc~Some kind of record

*I*T'S FIVE IN THE MORNING, AND we've gotten forty-five minutes of sleep in total. I watch her sleep and try to think of five thousand different ways to keep her here. Yet I already know she will not stay. She's told me a little about the European tour coming up. She leaves in May. I'm two weeks away from spring training, and she pretends to hold interest in that but her face glazes over because the truth is she really has no interest in baseball any more than I do in ballet. She doesn't exactly understand what I do and what I sacrifice for it. I get it, even though a part of me is disappointed by her true lack of interest in what I love to do the most.

She looks so beautiful just sleeping next to me. She ate the hamburger I brought her as if she hadn't eaten real food for a week. Based on the size of her, I would hazard a guess that's true. She's taller; I think, although we've been horizontal since we got to her room. We lay right next to each other on the bed, while I fed her French fries one at a time, because she seemed to enjoy the undivided attention I gave her. She's seems…*lonely*, more than distant. I guess that's the best way to describe it. And, while she sleeps, she looks so sad. It's heartbreaking to watch her actually. The crevice along the bridge of her nose deepens. I wonder if she knows she does that. But how could she know she does that? I wonder what's made her so unhappy. I don't have to wonder for too long because she starts talking in her sleep about Holly and even Rob and someone named Cara, and sometimes she says Elvis or Linc. *No.* I don't have to wonder why or who makes her so unhappy anymore. It's all there. She says it all. Her face says it all.

How many disappointments can one girl have? And I have to count myself among them, too.

"Again," she murmurs now. "Do it again. It has to be perfect. Again."

It's another twenty minutes before she finally stirs awake. I ply her with a glass of water and three Advil and my best smile. I've already showered, and I prepare myself for the turn—the remorse and the regret about us being together—because, clearly, she has a whole other life in New York without me. I grab her left hand and study the brilliant diamond there on her finger. I slip it off and hold it up to the sunlight that begins to stream through the hotel window and splays across the bed and the two of us. She just stares at me without saying a word. Then, she slips out of bed, naked, blushes a little but makes no attempt to cover herself. She does that dancer's strut I remember so well toward the bathroom, while I listen to her as she runs the water and brushes her teeth. It makes me happy and sad at the same time just hearing her do these normal daily routines that we never get to do together.

The ending is coming. I can feel it. I don't know if I can take it this time. But then again, I say that every time and yet, every time I take it. And, I come back to her again for more. I will take whatever time I can get with her. I will do that for a lifetime. I will. I know that much about myself. She is my water. I can never get enough of her, and it appears that I will die trying to love her, to keep her, to hold her with me, even though our time together seems to evaporate so swiftly. It slips through our fingers so damn fast that we don't even have time to savor it when we're together.

She slips a white camisole over her head and pulls it down over her stomach. I watch every move she makes and hold my breath. I just wait for the signal of this ending. She brushes out her long dark hair just as my cell phone rings. She leans over and reads the name.

"Nika?" she says, looking uneasy. Her voice is husky from a lack of sleep and too much booze and something else.

"I don't want to talk about Nika. Not today." She glares at me.

This is new. I kind of like it and I pull her to me, and she falls back onto the bed. "I believe this is yours." I hold up the diamond ring just inches away from her face.

She stares at it for a few minutes. I sigh deep and slowly slip it on her finger. Then she kind of laughs and brushes at her eyes. *Is she crying?*

"It makes him happy," she finally says.

"Does it make *you* happy?"

"A ring doesn't solve everything, Elvis." She gets this solemn look. "I can never be Holly. We're both a little disappointed with that."

"Then why *stay* with him?"

"Because it's easier. Because he's been there for me. Because it's complicated." Her lips part like she has more to say, but she doesn't say anything more.

Anger burns through me slowly again. *Anger at her. Him. This. Us.*

After a few minutes of staring at each other, she fits herself into me closer and starts touching me in all the right places.

"Are we going to talk about all this other stuff all day? Or, are we going to make the most of our time together? I've got to be somewhere else this afternoon. Marla and I have to be somewhere, but I have this morning for *you*."

"The whole morning? That's like some kind of record for us, isn't it?" I try to sound casual and nonchalant, but it comes out pathetic and needy. She seems to take advantage of me at this point.

"Don't be such a baby, Elvis. *Really.* I'll be here for three days, and we'll work it out, okay? I might stay longer. I've got to see where my parents live."

"I can show you."

"Oh, my God, you're still working with Tommy on baseball?"

"He's really good."

"He's going to be a hockey player," she says with notable arrogance. Then she sits back on her legs, puts her hands on her hips, and glares at me.

"Tally," I say slowly, taken aback a little that she doesn't even know this about her little brother Tommy. "He's an all-star player. He made it last year. He's really, really good. I've got a few of the coaches and baseball scouts I know keeping an eye on him."

"He's only nine."

"Tally," I say gently, suddenly feeling like I have a rare glimpse into her psyche. "He's *eleven*."

She groans and lies back down on the bed with her arm over her face. "Oh, God."

"Whatever you want to call me," I say in an attempt to make her laugh. She eventually does. "Who's Cara?" I ask after a few minutes sliding right in next to her.

Her smile vanishes. "What?" She gasps for air as if I've just punched her. She lowers her arms and stares at me, open-mouthed.

"You said *Cara* a few times in your sleep last night. Well, in that forty-five minutes of sleep that we got. Were you dreaming of my mother?" I smile, but she doesn't return it. She gets this stricken look. Her eyes tear up. Now she really does look like she's going to cry.

I did this. I made her cry. What is wrong with me?

"What are you doing to me, Elvis? Why are you doing this?" she asks.

"I'm just asking because you said something about Cara."

"She's Tremblay's little girl." Her voice shakes. "She's two. Marla and I were going to swing by and see Tremblay this afternoon for old time's sake."

She gives me this steely look. Her beautiful eyes glisten with new tears, and she wipes at them with the back of her hand and looks away. I can tell she's fighting for control, and that I've upset her for some reason. I'm trying to figure out how to take it all back and to, in effect, reel back the last five minutes because our time together *is* like water evaporating. It's too fleeting, and we can't catch it or keep it because it runs past us both too fast. I'm rushing on trying to explain it to her, and she's nodding and listening and finally smiles.

"Stop talking then. Let's not waste it, Elvis."

So, we don't.

Just after one in the afternoon, Marla swings by looking like death warmed over with big sunglasses on that cover half her face. She barely says two words to us beyond informing us both that Charlie lit out for an early anatomy class a few hours ago. I watch the bride-to-be and maid-of-honor head off toward Tremblay's place wherever that might be. These two promise to be back around six tonight for the rehearsal dinner.

I've got things to do in order to make good on my promise to myself that I've suddenly committed to in saying what I need to say to her, showing her what I want. It's true: I have very little time in which to say or show it. I have to be ready because this time it's a full count, and losing is not an option.

CHAPTER THIRTY-TWO

Tally ~ Because it's easier

"So, how's it going?" Marla asks as soon as we pull away from the hotel's long-term parking lot. We are on a mission that is so far off the wedding track that Marla's mom will most likely be calling us within the hour, wondering where we are, because there is so much to do between these two events—the rehearsal dinner and this wedding. And yet? Marla is more insistent than even I am about meeting up with Tremblay, unannounced. For some obscure reason, we are intent on seeing this thing through together, too. It's like a girl pact. The kind we used to make in high school about every boy, every event, every dance, every recital, every plan we ever made. *We do it together* remains our standard modus operandi.

"It's going fine." I glance at her sideways. I've donned my own pair of big black sunglasses, so she can't see my face either. My head is pounding, and I'm hoping the additional Advil I took will simmer things down. I tell her this now, but I know that's not what she's really asking about. *Linc. Rob.* She's asking about those two, not my head, or how I feel physically. "Closure," I finally say with a tight smile. "That's all it is. Closure."

"With Rob or Linc?" she asks.

Oh this girl is smart, so smart. "You should work for Kimberley Powers. I'm dead serious. She would love you."

"I'm going to be a teacher," Marla says proudly.

"And waste your talent on *children*? When you could make more money working in PR with Kimberley?"

"It's never about the money."

I don't answer for a long time. "It never is, is it?" I finally say.

"How come Rob didn't come with you?"

"He bailed on me at the airport without a valid reason. He just said he wasn't doing it. Actually, he said he couldn't watch it."

"Oh." Marla gets this pink tinge to her cheeks. A few minutes go by, and she's wiping her face with the back of her hand. "Why are you with him?" she asks. There's an edge to her voice like it really matters how I answer this one.

"Him," I say slowly. "Linc or Rob?"

"Rob."

"Because it's easier. Because it's complicated. Because he's been there for me. Because…just because." I clench my jaw to avoid saying more, but I finally blurt out. "Why are you marrying Charlie?"

Two girls hung over with too many secrets between them shouldn't be answering these heavy-duty questions. But we are. And, she does.

"Because it's *easier*. Because it's complicated. Because he's been there for me. Because…just because. I'm pregnant. Almost four months. Due in August. So we do what we have to do."

Silence.

My mind races. Now I don't know what to say that will sound right. I have plenty to say, but I'm too afraid to say the wrong thing, and I don't want to lie for once. "All that drinking—"

"That was *you*. I'm battling morning sickness pretty much night and day. I was dumping the champagne onto the ground, and you were wasted enough not to even figure it out. Those were virgin margaritas earlier. Tracey made them for me."

"Why didn't you just *tell* me?" I half-turn towards her, while she continues to look straight ahead suddenly intent on navigating the curvy two-lane road and avoiding my intense gaze. She won't even look at me now, and I know it has nothing to do with the traffic. We're passing by all this beautiful countryside without either one of us even taking notice of it until now.

"Because you needed to get drunk and relax and figure things out with the baseball player and—"

"And cheat on Rob," I finish dully.

"Well, at least, I *love* Charlie."

I wince partly with guilt and at just hearing the truth from her. "We break up all the time," I whisper. Seeking solace of some kind, I stare out the passenger window, unseeing, and avoid her accusatory look. "All the God damn time."

"Well, one of these days, you're going to have to figure out why that is, Tally Landon *Delacourt* or whatever it is you're calling yourself these days."

"We do what we have to do. Surely, you know that by now," I say.

We don't say anything more after that. *What else could be said?*

Twenty minutes later, we're cruising Tremblay's upscale Victorian neighborhood of Alamo Square that most people actually equate to all of San Francisco. Allaire Tremblay bought in a long time ago with her hard-earned cash from NYC Ballet before the housing market surged. I remind myself to take a look at these kinds of investments at some point. Rob has been harping on me for the past year about that. If I won't take his money, I should at least be investing mine what little there is of it. I can practically hear his looping lecture about this very thing. Musing about Rob, I barely glance at the designer-dressed mom in a matching black and white striped jogging outfit running doggedly up the steep incline with the fancy red baby jogger with her dark long hair flying behind her. Then I take a second look and grab Marla's arm.

"It's Tremblay."

"Holy shit," Marla says. "She's bought into the whole mom package."

"Yeah."

We cautiously follow her via car as she runs the sidewalk. Five minutes later, she turns down a worn dirt path that leads to a city park and immediately starts unloading her precious cargo from the baby jogger. She's done this before. The only thing I've gotten a glimpse of so far is the little girl's pink and white walking shoes that continually bounced up and down while Tremblay ran. Then, in the next minute, she appears. Cara's bundled up in a snow-white jacket that's lined in pink fur. I can't help but think that even Tremblay has fallen for the blatant marketing ploy of Disney and dressed her up like a doll. I almost smile, but my heart is pounding so hard that I feel like I might hyperventilate right here in Marla's car.

Cara toddles over to the swing set and pushes at the swing and looks back at Tremblay, who is busy re-adjusting the jogger and grabbing a back pack from the side. She calls to her, and the baby turns and runs back to her. Her little face lights up at whatever Tremblay's said to her.

"She looks just like you."

Marla hasn't taken her eyes off either one of them since we parked. I haven't either.

"She does."

Cara's hair is long and dark like mine. I watch as she runs straight for Tremblay's outstretched arms. Mother and child embrace. Allaire kisses the little girl's forehead and brushes her hair back from her face and re-ties it in the next.

I watch them closely and mindlessly check off all these sentimental requirements that I need to see for myself. *Cara. She's happy. She's growing. She's not mine.* Tears trickle down my face, and I absently wipe at them. I can't look away from this mother and child scene that unfolds thirty feet and a whole other lifetime away from me.

"She looks good," Marla says through her own tears. "Don't mind me. I cry at everything these days." She removes her sunglasses to fix her face in the car mirror and glances at me sideways. "Let's go."

I nod, sigh a little, and lean back in the car's passenger seat thinking '*let's go*' means Marla's ready to drive away. Instead, she alights from the car and starts calling out to Tremblay. *Of course,* Allaire Tremblay hears her. Who else would be yelling, "Madame Tremblay," just the way we've been trained?

And so, I meet my child for the second time on the day before Valentine's Day.

———

Marla and I are both a little taken aback by this version of Allaire Tremblay. Her house is somewhat in order—clean, possibly immaculate; however, there are toys strewn about everywhere. Her focus is Cara. That much is obvious. Two hours into this astonishing visit, I'm still attempting to concentrate on being able to openly breathe. I can't take my eyes off of Cara for more than a few seconds at a time. I'm staring at Linc's grey-blue eyes reflected so clearly in Cara's. I can't stop staring at my daughter, our daughter—Linc's and mine—this miracle.

Allaire Tremblay seems to have noticed. Her smile has been surprisingly genuine, but she now seems more guarded then when we first arrived.

Marla holds onto my right hand and squeezes it occasionally. We are way late. We need to go. And, I don't want to. I just want to watch Cara forever.

Somehow, we've managed to have this exhaustive conversation about NYC Ballet and UCLA and Paris and Milan and Rome, mostly about me, but without me actually talking most of the time unless prompted. Distracted by this utter fascination with watching Cara, I only briefly tell them about the upcoming tour to Madrid and Paris again and then Moscow. Marla fills in the rest of the talk about NYC Ballet, Paris, Milan, L.A., her wedding, Charlie.

Now Tremblay looks as glazed as I feel. Yet, she catches my attention with an unnatural wave with her hand, and I openly stare at her when she just nods and rewards us with an unforgettable calm.

Tranquil. Serene. Composed. This is Tremblay.

I guess that's the biggest difference about her. When I tear my gaze away from watching Cara long enough and glance at Tremblay, I discover her smiling and even laughing sometimes. It proves almost impossible to reconcile this Allaire Tremblay with the one I know and have practically hated since I was ten.

Again. The memory of that word and the way she's always said it to me plays through my mind. This is a different Allaire Tremblay. She's patient, content, and *happy.* It's disconcerting. Yet, after more than two hours, I see the protective side of her towards Cara in deference to me and Marla so clearly.

She tells us that she's still running the studio, but that she's cut way back on the amount of hours she spends there. She has recently hired another dancer to help her out.

I nod at the appropriate intervals while Marla starts glancing at her watch more and more. Her own smile now fades. *We have to go.*

Cara plays on the floor near our feet. She has a fascination with my shoes and keeps touching them. They're the black Christian Louboutin pumps that I picked up in Paris. I think she likes the red sole. After only a moment's hesitation, I slip them off. Cara takes off her shoes, puts mine on and attempts to walk around in them holding onto the furniture as she goes. It's hilarious. Marla gets up and starts snapping pictures with her iPhone, while Tremblay and I share this weird, surreal moment as we look at each other. We start to laugh as we experience this enchanting scene with Cara all together.

It's weird. Surreal. Yes, surreal explains it all.

I finally stand up and prepare for this ending.

Allaire Tremblay hugs me long and hard and whispers, "Thank you, Tally. You made my life." She steps back and smiles wide. Her golden eyes glisten with tears. *Holy shit. She's crying.* Now, so am I. Marla started three minutes ago.

The moment ends with Cara hugging at my leg, asking me to pick her up, which I do; because you don't deny a two-year-old anything. She wraps her little arms around my neck and hugs me tight. A few seconds go by, and she leans back and then swoops in and kisses the side of my face.

"Tally, bye-bye."

"Yes. Tally's going bye-bye. Take care of yourself, Cara. Your mom is…so great."

"Great mom," she parrots as she claps her hands.

I hand Cara to Tremblay with a general ease that I didn't think I was quite capable of doing. This mysterious solace and the customary guilt swing in on me and start to do fierce battle inward. For once, solace wins out. I think it's the look of happiness I see on Cara's face as well as Tremblay's.

I can live with that. I, apparently, do.

"Surreal," Marla says after a much-needed twenty minutes of pure silence in the car after we leave Tremblay and Cara behind.

"No kidding."

We've navigated the challenging streets of San Francisco. I've wrestled with the idea of checking in with my family and pounded that idea into subconscious submission for another day or two. It seems we've both just begun to breathe freely again as we head toward the hotel and traverse all the winding curvy roads to get there all over again.

"Cara's happy, Tally. They both are. That's all that matters. You did the right thing. You can feel that and say that now, can't you?"

"Most of the time." *Breathe.* "Because someday she'll hate me. She'll be old enough to know what it takes to be a mother, and she won't understand why—all the reasons why—I gave her up. I think that's what kills me the most. And, keeping it all from Linc." I frown.

"Well, you can't judge the moment until you get to it." Marla looks at me hard for a few seconds, cajoling me to believe her by bestowing me with one of her all-knowing looks.

I roll my eyes and sigh. "What the hell does that even mean?"

"It means maybe someday you'll be able to tell him, and it will all work out. We both know that life has a way of changing on us before we can figure it out, and you can't predict what's going to happen in the next." She gets this wicked smile. "So let's get back to the groom and best man and see where they take us."

My iPhone goes off.

It's a text from Rob: *"I'm here at the Oceana. Where are you?"*

Where am I? What am I doing? What did I just do last night? I don't have acceptable answers for any of these questions. Do I?

I text back: *nowhere.*

CHAPTER THIRTY-THREE

Linc~Reacting badly

ALL THOSE PLANS FOR TELLING TALLY how I feel come to an abrupt halt the night of the rehearsal dinner when I'm introduced to Rob Thorn, by of all people, Nika Vostrikova, who informs me that they both have been kept waiting *for hours together* as she put it for my return as well as Tally's. I shook his hand and eyed him warily. It's confirmed; he still has the Kurt Cobain thing going on but, unlike the photographs I've seen of him before, this guy in the flesh is now one self-assured jerk. Rob Thorn *knows* he's already won. The only time I see his self-assuredness falter is when Nika walks in, right behind Tally, both of them arriving fashionably late to the rehearsal dinner. That's when it all comes together for me. The guy's in love with my girlfriend. Yet he's engaged to the only girl I've ever loved. It may be for nothing more than to harbor and enjoy the satisfaction that he beat me to the one and only prize I've ever wanted—Tally Landon. Rob Thorn does have more money than God, and his self-assurance tells me that he knows I know this already, too. Misery settles in on me, intent on a long stay.

On the other side of this complex equation is Nika. I specifically asked her to stay away from this wedding; once I told her I was going to go to it. We're on a break, one of several that we've had over this last particular off-season. Nobody supports me better than Nika when baseball season is in full swing. She comes to most of my games. It doesn't matter to her where they are. We've traveled the country together to all of these out of-the-way cities and towns for baseball. During the season, Nika serves as almost a lifeline to me—more than a friend, not quite a girlfriend—but we're both agreeable to all these unique benefits between us. We revel in them. We don't ask for more from each other. It is enough—us, somewhat together—during baseball season.

Our relationship didn't start out that way; it evolved.

Nika has no problem spending my money, guarding my time, ensuring I get my sleep and enough to eat during baseball season. She's like a veritable watch dog. It's not the kindest analogy, but that's what Nika's like. She constantly deals with the fan girls in this diplomatic sort of way of hers and deftly handles the press in Kimberley's stead. Nika ensures I get there on time and takes care of all the extraneous stuff in all these baseball towns after I arrive. She doesn't get hung up on our future any more than I do, which is probably why we keep coming back to each other.

Feeling guilty at times, I've tried to explain to her that there isn't a future for us and every time she just casually shrugs and tells me she understands. *We have an understanding.* She knows about Tally. Hell, she keeps tabs on Tally for me.

Nika doesn't even ask why I still need her to do this. Nika just understands. She's sexy and fun and carefree, and she spends all her free time with me. It's a turn-on in its own unique way. She tells me that she doesn't need anything from me, and she takes care of just about everything. For me.

Am I selfish that way? Yes. But she's willing and, at least during baseball season; I'm her singular focus and I like that. She makes me feel less alone. Nika keeps me focused on the game. She makes me feel like a winner in the way she effectively takes care of things and the things she says about me and the things she's willing to do for me.

It's during the off-season that we end up fighting. We always end up taking a break from each other during the off-season.

Charlie thinks Nika is some kind of an addiction to me—a drug that's probably bad for me, calling forth all kinds of hidden side-effects that I can't even fathom yet. He might be right.

It's still the off-season *barely*, but we're on a break. She knows this. And yet, she's here at Charlie and Marla's wedding. Part of me is pissed at her for showing up, unannounced; and the other part of me is fortified by her very presence.

Even tonight, Nika proves to be exactly what I need as I numbly watched Charlie and Marla exchange vows and say *'I do'* and proceed to get dragged into watching all these manufactured social performances going on here at their reception. I watch Rob Thorn look longingly over at our table while he nuzzles his fiancée Tally in the next breath. I drink my way through it on the other side of the room and just blatantly watch this sham unfold.

Now Nika whispers into my ear that I've had enough, and that we should go. I numbly turn to her and silently nod. *Nika gets me.* Right now, I need someone to understand the worst parts of me; in particular, my unrequited love for Tally Landon that still has a vice-like grip upon my fucking soul even though she's virtually ignored me the entire evening and last because Rob Thorn is here. *I don't exist. I don't like it.*

Nika sees it. She gets it. She's prepared to save me from myself and Tally Landon. Some distant part of me is grateful for this respite. Another part is longing to prove a point. That one wins out. I get up from the table where we've been nursing drinks all night and attempt to steady myself and find my balance as I start across the dance floor. Tally's dancing with Rob. Charlie's dancing with Marla. I surprise everyone when I cut in on Charlie. Rob gives me a stony look and squires Tally far away from me.

I grab on to Marla, slur a compliment about her dress and how beautiful she looks, while she gets this anxious look at my obvious hopeless state.

"Because let's face it; Lincoln Presley is spinning out of control right in front of everybody here, and it's all because of one girl," I say summing this up for Marla now.

"Prez, not here," she says gently. "Not now. Okay?"

"When then? When is it going to be okay to tell her how I feel?"

"You're *with* someone." Marla gestures wildly toward the far side of the dance floor where Nika closely watches the two of us dance while standing there in her lovely long gown. I shake my head. Only Nika would do her best to upstage the bride. She looks like a queen languishing there in this white slinky dress and glittery diamond earrings that probably set me back a cool twenty grand.

"I want to be with someone else. I want to be with Tally. It's always been Tally."

"You're drunk. You need to pull it together. It isn't going to happen like this, not in this way, Linc. She's in New York. You're in L.A. or every baseball town in between. How can you possibly be together? And frankly, where have you been for her?" Marla's voice goes up a few octaves and gets louder. "You *chose* this!

"I know," I say. "But I want something different. I want things to change."

"You want something different? You want things to change? With Tally?" Marla scans my face.

I nod while saying, "Yes."

She glares at me. "Then, do something about it or the outcome is going to be the same every single fucking time. *You did this.* I blamed her for so long, but *you* did this to her in the first place. You *broke* her when you chose baseball. You did that. *Own it.* You've got to start showing her that to even have a chance of winning her back. But right now? Go back to your girlfriend or whatever she is to you; or better yet, *go to bed* and sleep it off. This isn't going to resolve itself tonight. *Leave*, Prez. You're too drunk to do anything about it right now."

The music has stopped.

The entire wedding party stares at the two of us.

I look over and discover Tally standing a few feet away from us with her mouth open. Rob holds onto her like he owns her, while he openly stares at Nika with this inexplicable pain that's hard to even look at. Nika, who has walked up to this little party of five, and tells me, "We need to go." She doesn't even glance at Rob, and this seems to incite him even more.

I react badly.

"What the hell, dude?" I say to Rob. "You've *won* her. Tally's yours. And yet, you're staring at Nika, like she's the only one in the world that matters to you. Get your head on straight."

I don't even see his right hook coming until it connects with my face. No, I just stagger back at the unexpected force of his fist directly against my jaw line. In the next few seconds, I register incalculable pain, lose my balance, and then fall back hard to the floor.

The release feels good. After that, it's black.

CHAPTER THIRTY-FOUR

Tally - I have this

LINCOLN PRESLEY SLEEPS. IT'S A SIGHT to behold. I take these first few precious moments of solitude to gaze at him in unguarded wonder and trace my fingertips along his unconscious form. The ER doctor said he was going to be fine, but I have my doubts—my uncontrollable fears—and I just want a few minutes with him alone to be sure. I *demand* a few minutes alone with him from everyone—the doctors, the nurses, the family, his friends, his publicist Kimberley Powers, and his closest friend with benefits Nika Vostrikova.

Quick thinking by Charlie in performing CPR after quickly realizing his best man had stopped breathing saved Linc's life. The doctor informed all of us in the waiting room that Linc has a mild concussion; but added that the reason he stopped breathing remains a mystery.

Everyone breathed a sigh of relief that the star baseball player was okay. *Everyone, but me.*

I don't quite believe it. Equal doses of fear and wrath battle for my living soul. Seeing Linc not breathing brings it all back for me. It's like losing my sister all over again. Another loved one. Me. Loss. Love. I shudder remembering Linc's long prostrate form laid out on the dance floor. Charlie's frantic efforts to get him to breathe. Linc not breathing. The fears rise again with their all-too-familiar drumbeat—failing, falling, losing, Linc. They reverberate through me at an accelerated rate finding fresh life inside of me once more.

I haven't outrun any of them.

Not one.

Not him.

I can't do this.

I. Cant. Do. This.

I told the doctor I wanted to be with him. *Alone.* I demanded it. I sent that bitch Nika on her way. I sent Rob back to New York and told him I was moving out, and we were through. Tremendous relief comes with that truth, alone. I'm able to breathe now and being told Lincoln Presley was going to be fine allowed me my heart to beat once again. In a daze and with a remarkable sense of control, I encourage an anxious Marla and Charlie to go and catch their flight, because '*I have this.*'

I. Have. This.

This.

Whatever this is.

I have it.

I have to make this right because I've made it so damn wrong for far too long. I think seeing Cara yesterday gives me the strength—the fortitude—to move forward now, instead of looking back toward the past and remaining engulfed in all the lies. I think that's it.

I have this.

I can do this.

I can let him go.

I have to let him go.

The words fly through my head at an alarming rate. I clasp my hands tightly together in order to keep myself from falling apart. I focus on breathing. I close my eyes. I wait.

Eventually, I hear him stir. The sheets rustle and I look over at him, just as he opens his eyes.

A few minutes go by where we just stare at each other. His face creases with pain. I put a glass of water with a straw near his lips and help him sit up.

"Drink this." I sound pissed.

He groans. I spy pain and remorse in his handsome face. I decide that's okay.

"I'm a jerk," he says.

"Yes."

"Where's everyone at?" Linc asks as he weakly leans back against the pillow and sighs deep.

I put down the glass with a sharp rap. It startles him, and I check myself and my temper for a few minutes. I can't even breathe right away. After a few seconds, I sigh.

"I sent Marla and Charlie on their way. Their flight leaves SFI at midnight for the Caribbean. The doctors say you're going to be fine. It's just a mild concussion and one hell of a headache. Already, huh?"

I don't wait for his answer. "They want to keep you here overnight for observation, but you're going to be fine. The wedding reception ended about the time you hit the floor. Charlie did CPR. He saved your fucking life. You might want to thank him for that. Good thing they do CPR training early in med school; right? You. Almost. Died. You're weren't breathing. They can't explain why. You hit your head when you hit the floor."

"After Rob swung at me," he says, managing to look helpless and adorable at the same time.

I clench my fists at my side to keep myself from reaching out to him. *End it. End this.*

"We're done with Rob."

"I wasn't fucking him. I wasn't engaged to him," Linc says.

I cover my face with one arm and inadvertently wipe at my eyes. My breathing gets jagged. I feel like I'm going to have a panic attack right in front of him. I lower my arm and gasp for air only to find him looking properly chastised when he hears me.

"Tally."

"No. Don't say anything."

We stare at each other for a long time.

"You scared the hell out of me. This is me...*scared*." I hold up my hand in front of him, and it shakes uncontrollably. Tears come. "I can't do this anymore." I turn away, wipe at my face and attempt to summon the earlier anger for him again.

"Tally," he says bleakly. "Look at me."

"Rob Thorn has been dealt with *by me*. Nika went back to Seattle. Her purpose has been served. Right, Linc?" I whip my hand through the air for emphasis about that one. "I called Kimberley and she's handling the press as we speak." I pause with a sudden need for air and space from him. "Yes, you're a jerk."

I brush at my face again and step further back away from him.

The dress gets in the way. *The damn dress.* It swishes between my legs and I almost trip with my sudden need to get as far as away from him as his private hospital room will allow. I begin to pace. The dress is this red chiffon thing that Marla had us all spend a small fortune on. Mine is off the rack because I was so late to the party in even being a part of this event. It's a size too big and there wasn't time to take it in. So now, it's practically falling off of me— what with all the frantic antics from earlier—when I raced to Linc's side and managed to push Rob off of me at about the same time. It's torn on one side because Rob had been holding on to me so tight that when I dropped down to the floor to rescue Linc, it ripped at the seams at the right shoulder.

Now, I'm enraged at the improper functions of the fucking dress. I slip it off my left shoulder and tear it in two strips and re-tie it tighter so it will stay on. Linc watches this sudden dress-making ingenuity from me in utter amazement, but I think he's afraid to say anything more now.

As well, he should be.

I take a deep breath. "Of course, this isn't going as planned. The only time things come together like they're supposed to is when I'm on stage. But life isn't a stage; now, is it, Linc? Unless, of course, what you were discussing with Marla was meant for public consumption just for the drama alone."

He dips his head and looks away from me. "I just wanted…"

"To be with me?" I ask sharply.

"Yes."

"It cuts both ways, *baby*. You don't get to push me out of your life and then expect me to come back into it. *You chose baseball.* Live with that. And quit interfering in my life. I had a nice chat with Nika. Really, Linc? You've been spying on me. And you keep a list of who I fuck? Why? So you can reference it later?"

"Tally, I wanted this all to go so differently—"

"With this?" I slam down the black velvet ring box they found in the pocket of his tuxedo jacket onto the feeding tray next to his hospital bed. He turns a little white. "What? Were you going to ask me between the rehearsal dinner and the wedding? Thinking you had it all worked out? *Really?* You're not even *done* with Nika. She goes to all your games now. She knows all your stats. She works out for you during the season but not so much during the off-season. Is that it? She's a great fuck when she's recording your stats on your personal clip board and the way she follows you around to every damn town in America like a devoted fan girl. Yeah, she's great at keeping you warm at night and fucking your brains out when you need it on the road, but not so much when she's not doing all those things for you in the off-season. *Right, Linc?*"

I've hit a nerve. Some of it was stuff I was only guessing at, but now he won't even look at me.

"Tally, it's not like that."

"Don't *lie* to me."

"What are you most afraid of now?" he asks.

"The same things I've always been afraid of. They're still out there, Linc. Falling. Failing. Losing. And now, you. I'm afraid of you—maybe, *you*—most of all."

"You can't outrun the fears. You have to face them. You have to face *me*," he says.

"No. I don't."

There's a tipping point with rage. It's an all-consuming flame. It doesn't discern what's in its path nor determine what's worth saving. I'm blinded by fury, and I go too far in the next instant.

"I don't want this. You shouldn't want this. Marla's right. You did this. You chose baseball and the life you wanted for yourself a long time ago. You finished us...a long time ago. I want to be free of you, to make my own life. We're done, Linc. Don't call me. Don't think about me. Don't love me anymore. I don't love you anymore. You've killed it. There's nothing left of us. It's time to move on. We both need to...move on. We both knew that a long time ago."

Now, I can't even look at him. In the next fifteen seconds, I've made it through the door. Part of my mind registers that he hasn't said anything, which should really tell me all I need to know. It's possible that he doesn't love me. Maybe he never did. If he knew about Cara and what I did, he'd hate me for sure. There's no future for us. I guess we both made sure of that in our own selfish ways a long time ago.

I had this.

I did this.

I have to let him go.

I don't stop long enough to examine why it hurts so much to finally let him go.

The flight back to New York is uneventful. I watch Rob go off to work and class from the safety of the Starbucks across the street from our building. I move out in a matter of hours, leave his ring on the kitchen counter, and put everything of mine in storage. Sasha Belmont accommodates my urgent request to leave early for Milan and within seventy-two hours, I'm on a plane to Italy.

I text Marla with my new cell number and ask her not to share it with anyone, especially Lincoln Presley or Rob Thorn. The only other person, besides my family, that knows how to remain in touch with me is Allaire Tremblay. It's not that I expect to hear from her, but it feels like the right thing to do after seeing her doing so well with Cara.

I won't return to the States until after Moscow. I think by then I won't be as pissed as I am now.

The anger fuels me.

The critics love me.

And that's all that matters to me now.

After a long while, I realize that I've become more like Lincoln Presley because all I really do care about now is ballet. Nothing else matters to me anymore.

I let them go. I let them all go.

What I didn't expect to discover is how much it hurts when I do this.

CHAPTER THIRTY-FIVE

Tally ~ Need you now

ARLY NOVEMBER FINDS ME WALKING DOWN an unfamiliar street in Moscow having taken a wrong turn from the restaurant where many members of the dance company met up for lunch. I left early, not in the mood for banter and the ever-increasing questions about me and my personal life. *What do you do with your free time, Talia? Where do you go? Enjoy your two days off in a row whatever you do.*

I'm intent on keeping my eyes on the pavement, not daring to meet the probing eyes of every Russian I pass. I'm still a bit intimidated and fairly cautious here in Moscow. I've had a few close calls in this city—an almost mugging and a strange encounter with some avid fan at the theater last month, who tried to follow me home to The Savoy where most of the dancers stay. *Moscow.* Moscow scares me in all these distinctive ways, especially as a foreigner. I'm afraid all the time now and more than ready to return home—to New York, to Rob even, to wherever and whoever may be left for me back in the States. Rob and I remain wary after what happened at Marla's wedding nine months before. He still calls me though. And, after this tour ends, Rob wants me to move in with him again. We've spent a couple of long weekends in Europe together over the last several months since I've been away. It's been a half-hearted attempt to try to repair things between us.

There's nothing going on with Nika, so he tells me.

There's nothing going on with Linc, so I tell him.

He flies in when he can break away from classes at NYU or work; but even Rob is beginning to understand what I mean by *we can't do this anymore.* We haven't had sex since July while I was in Paris, and he'd flown in as part of his continual pursuit of reconciliation, but, even then, it was per functionary on my part. I couldn't wait for it to be over. I've tried to wrap my head around why I was feeling that way at the time. I told him we should see other people. I've demanded that we do this. I didn't want to tie him down. I didn't want to be tied down. I'd been with a few others since then in a vain attempt to figure it all out. It was a salvo—a blatant attempt—to return to the old Tally from almost four years before in what really was a whole other lifetime. There was Ian from the Corps, probably one of the few straight guys in our company. He tried to show me the way. He said it would help with the lifts if he knew me intimately. There was a time in Italy when I thought that was true but Ian had a temper and got jealous easily. In the end, I realized that I didn't need any more emotional baggage that what I was already carrying enough for myself. And, he was boring. All Ian wanted to do was talk about the other dancers and what he'd done with them—all these private, salacious things that he thought would turn me on but just as swiftly turned me off. He didn't take kindly to my decree that he was a bigger slut than I'd been. In the end, I told Rob about Ian, and he flew over to Milan from New York and convinced me to give us another try—begged me to give us another try. Rob insisted we didn't need a break and what we really needed was each other.

I remain unconvinced of this, but agree to give us another try when I get home.

I've been named the principal ballerina for our next performance opening night. It's all wrong. I'm still too young. I still lack experience and every understudy and former principal tell me this; but the choreographers and directors love me, especially Sasha Belmont. Now they all give me the best parts whenever they can. They want me because I give them my all every single day and night. There's nothing left for anyone else. There's nothing left of me. *I wonder why they can't see how tired I am.*

I lift my eyes from the snowy pavement and catch the intense gaze of a tall Russian in a long threadbare wool coat as he passes me. I hear the heels of his boots crunch the snow and just as suddenly instinctively sense his turning back toward me. I pull my coat around me tighter, pick up my pace, and wildly cast my eyes around the unfamiliar surroundings while my heart races.

No one is paying any attention to me. This is a desolate part of town—a shabbier section that resides just before the swanky cosmopolitan hotels actually come into view. I look up for a few seconds and thankfully spy the spires of the taller buildings of the hotel district just up ahead. They beckon to me. I breathe a sigh of relief that I'm close, so close, to being home free. I berate myself again for not taking a taxi back to the hotel and instead electing to take this ridiculous, stupid walk—these ten long blocks in this questionable neighborhood because of my stupidity.

I hear the deep sigh from behind me and then look up again into the dark eyes of the man who passed me just minutes before. He smiles slightly and then roughly grabs at my arm and pulls me into the side alley that suddenly appears to my right. Within seconds, he's dragged me into an offshoot of the alley into a shadowed doorway. I dully note the peeling blue paint and vaguely listen to the ever cloaking quiet, just as he wields a long knife and deftly holds it to my throat. The passing cars on the street are muted now and that no one can see us. *No one.*

Fear and adrenalin take over as he cruelly presses me up against the alcove's stone wall. I scrape the side of my cheek against the rough surface when I turn my head to avoid his searching mouth, while he attempts to devour my face with his lecherous tongue. I feel his hardness through his wool coat and mine.

I have seconds before this ends badly.

"You are a pretty little thing, Talia Delacourt," he says in broken English.

"Do I…*know* you?"

"Such a beautiful dancer," he says, breathing hard, and then mutters more words in Russian.

Tremblay's words of almost three years before come back to me. *Be careful in foreign country. You're beautiful, a star, just be careful, Talia. Always.* And here I am living the nightmare of all of that. The man's movements get more frantic. He seems to already know he has only so much time before we're discovered. His searing breath practically burns my skin as much as the cold Russian air does. Still, I try not to panic. I try to maintain a semblance of control looking for any chance of an escape from him. I take a jagged breath and try to breathe even as he covers my mouth with one of his gloved hands smothering my very first scream.

Why didn't I cry out sooner?

Suddenly, I fight the engulfment of all-out fear and the filmy edges of a panic attack, as I desperately try to pull away from his vice-like grip. He slaps my face so hard with his raised palm that my head crashes back against the rough stone for a second time, as he presses in on me further and roughly bites at my lip, drawing blood. Then he crushes my mouth with his while at the same time he pushes up my skirt. I hear the ominous sound of his zipper. My right hand feels his waistband come apart. I fight for my freedom and yank down on his erection causing him instant pain. My reward is a knifing pain at a gut level. For a brief moment, we're both surprised by it.

Blood pours profusely from my stab wound, and I go perfectly still. Now, I'm fully aware of how dangerous the situation has become. The knife glints down at his side now and streams with my fresh blood. *Seconds.* There are only seconds left before the last of my strength is gone, and he completely overpowers me. His right hand steadily grips the knife and in the next instant, he swiftly cuts the buttons off of my long, wool coat and expertly slices down the front of my skirt leaving deep slashes on my thighs. His fingers tear at my panties and push their way inside. I scream out in pain and shock as my clothing starts to fall away. He starts to work his way inside. The knife clatters to the ground when he lets go of it. He pushes me downward and I land hard on the ground. He roughly lands on top of me. I can't breathe. I dully watch as he picks up the knife again and holds it to my throat. *What I can live with? He's going to rape me or kill me or both.* I fight hard to get away from him, and that's when he plunges the knife into my side only deeper. *He's going to kill me.*

He withdraws the knife and violently shakes me against the pavement. My head hits the stone hard for a third time. My vision blurs. *I can't pass out. I can't pass out. I can't die. Not here. Like this.*

I turn my head to the right and see my blood pooling. Just the sight of it makes me gag. In that moment, he loosens his grip on the knife again, and I grab for it and plunge it deep into his chest. He goes limp for a few minutes, and it takes me what seems like forever to push out from underneath him. I try not to look at his dazed, agonized face. Then, I see him blink and the terror starts up inside of me again. I start to scream as he tries to pull me back to him by grabbing my left ankle and twisting it hard.

"Bitch!" he screams.

I'm focused on the ankle pain when he takes up the knife and stabs it directly into the top of my foot. Fury takes over. I kick at his arms and face with my good foot but that just makes him angrier. He growls in Russian and gets up and starts coming after me. When he reaches me, he pulls me hard by my hair, and I push back at his chest hard with all the strength I have left. He lands at an odd angle on the pavement and stops moving, and his eyes start to glaze over. Rebar sticks up from his chest. He's pinned to the ground by it. The horror of it all descends upon me. I move slowly, gripping the rough stone wall for balance and can only wonder where all this blood is coming from. Every few seconds, I look back to make sure he isn't coming after me again, but he just lies there now. I don't feel relief of any kind. There's only this soul-crushing terror. The fears come. Falling. Losing. Failing. I experience them all. I think of Holly's last moments, and I finally start to scream. *I can't breathe. I have to get away.*

Fast-moving cars speed by in both directions. In shock, I walk out into the middle of the street and raise one arm, like I'm flagging down a taxi, while maintaining a firm grip around my injured mid-section with the other. Finally, a taxi brakes hard and screeches to a stop and barely avoids hitting me.

Shaking uncontrollably, I grope my way along the car for balance to the passenger side. When the door opens, I helplessly cower in the arms of a stranger and seek protection inside the safety of his long grey wool coat. Strong arms close around me and steady me.

"Some guy," I say unevenly. "Attacked me. Don't know him. Do you speak English? Help me."

"Are you hurt?"

"He had a knife. There's blood everywhere." I point toward the alley and stare at the bright redness that coats my entire hand. I shove it into my coat in the next and grip my side tighter with my arm. I'm transported back to a different time and place and think of Holly. *Oh, Holly.* My breathing gets jagged, and my mind starts to splinter.

"Did he hurt you?"

"I don't know." I bury my face further into his chest as the sick reality of the situation overcomes me.

I need to get out of here. Take a bath. Assess the damage. Remember all that just happened. Stay awake and think.

Then my mind clicks with recognition because I *know* that voice. I shake more violently as a new kind of fear surfaces. I look up at him. I'd recognize those amazing grey-blue eyes anywhere.

No. Not a stranger. Lincoln Presley is in Moscow.

"Tally?" Linc looks astonished when he gets a glimpse of my upturned face. "Jesus, what are you doing here? Who are you running from?"

"I've got to get out of here." I begin to hyperventilate. "That guy. He's—" I can't finish the sentence. The reality is too horrible.

Linc guides me into the waiting taxi and shouts at the driver to stay with me and turns in the direction of the alley. In a few seconds, he returns and instructs the driver to get to the nearest hospital.

My entire body convulses with pain as he slides in next to me. His arm goes around me.

"Let's go," he says urgently to the driver. "It's going to be okay, Tally," he says to me.

I look away, unable to meet his questioning eyes quite yet, and whisper, "You think?" toward the taxi's dirty car window.

Thankfully, Linc doesn't say anything more. After a while, I steal a glimpse of him. He watches me closely and makes a Good Samaritan attempt to wipe the blood from my face and body with his wool scarf, but it makes more of a sickly mess, and it hurts like hell, which I finally admit to him with a shaky, inappropriate laugh. Dulled by shock and excruciating pain, I again look out the car window at the buildings we race past them.

"Where are you staying?"

Why is he asking such an innocuous question? I'm tired. I've been stabbed, apparently. Almost raped. Why does it matter where I'm staying? "I'm staying at The Savoy." I take a jagged breath.

"The Savoy?"

"We're on tour here. Close to the Bolshoi and the Moscow Theater. Fairly close," I answer tiredly.

"The Savoy. I guess things have been good for you, Ms. Landon."

I wince at his subtle sarcasm and glance up at him. "Things are okay, except for today," I say.

He gets this subdued look. It seems we both still harbor anger toward each other.

I suffer in silence with physical and mental pain. I try not to let him see I'm shaking or how badly I'm hurt. It seems to be a combination of what just happened and being this close to him again after all this time. *But we are worlds apart, he and I.* This much I can sense already.

I press against the back of my head and say "Ow," again. I stare absently at the palm of my hand that is now covered in even more blood. Linc gasps when he seems to realize that my injuries are more severe than I've let on. He makes a desperate effort to stem the blood flow on my right side by making a tourniquet out of his wool scarf.

He doesn't meet my gaze, and I avoid his, too. There is too much to say but neither one of us will say it. There's nothing left between us. I have to keep reminding myself of that.

"We're supposed to go to the ballet later this week and see that performance."

"We?" I ask dully.

"Nika and I." Linc gets this defiant look.

All the sins from the past separate us like an invisible wall. "Nika." I don't attempt to hide my disenchantment.

"Yes."

There's an apology in there somewhere. He gets this anguished look, and I know he has more to say about Nika. Why do I expect it to be any different? I had it right all those months ago when it came to Nika. "Oh," I manage to say.

His fingers brush across my lower lip. He gently caresses the side of my face with the palm of his hand. "I was scared back there. You're so brave, Tally."

"Bravery doesn't come to mind. Stupidity comes to mind."

"I wouldn't let anything happen to you. You have to know that."

"Do I? Promises, promises," I say in my best Russian accent. Mockery works. He looks a little pale under his fine tan. My harsh arrows against nostalgia hit their intended target quite nicely. "Don't test me though. I only know about twenty Russian words and half are swear words."

He tries to laugh. I attempt to at least try and smile, as if somehow being funny around him can undo the underlying horror of the current situation. But then, my upper lip throbs with fresh pain. "Ow," I touch it tenderly in a small attempt to keep him preoccupied from looking down at the blood that's beginning to pool in my lap. I draw the shredded edges of my coat tighter, so he won't see it.

A few minutes later, he's handing the driver enough rubles to have driven us across the entire city and back again. We alight from the car as one. I cry out when I step forward and my left foot buckles. Fear takes over. *What did that monster do to my foot?*

Linc sweeps me up in his arms, despite my visceral protest and constant pleas to put me down. He carries me past the waiting gurney that one of the hospital staff has procured and walks directly into the ER, demanding to talk with the doctor in charge, even though I try to protest loudly but my cries are somewhat smothered by his coat sleeve.

I weakly raise my head and attempt to give him my best derisive look.

"You're hurt," he says gently. "Don't start. What do you weigh all of a ninety pounds now?"

"Don't start."

Mollified somewhat and taking consolation in being in his arms, regardless of the eerie circumstances, I decide I'd better enjoy the damsel-in-distress routine for once—before Nika gets here or I pass out; both of which are becoming distinct possibilities. I look past his shoulder and see the long trail of blood that's flows behind us like dripping paint, retracing our erratic path through the ER. *Shit. Not good.* My head pounds. My dignity suffers both mentally and physically from all sides, while my entire body begins to convulse as if I'm being turned inside out. I'm not really sure how much longer I'll be able to keep up the *I've-got-this* brave front. My body already starts to betray me as I shake uncontrollably like I've just emerged from swimming naked in an Arctic lake. *If they have those.* I comfort myself with the fleeting thought that he's here. And right now? I'll take whatever part of him; he's offering because, in this peculiar space and moment in time; I need Lincoln Presley. It appears from all counts that he's saving my life *again*.

"Seems like old times."

"Don't do that." My voice is no more than a murmur. I'm losing the battle with consciousness.

"What? Force you to remember?"

"There's no forcing when it comes to remembering you. Just a wish to forget some of it, but I remember *everything*." I close my eyes.

"So do I," he says.

I open my eyes again and study his face. Lincoln Presley looks conflicted. I trace his furrowed brow with my free hand to try to smooth his sudden anguish away.

"We're getting...*married*."

He struggles in saying the last word.

And so do I.

I reach down deep inside of myself on a vain search for the right words to convey my true and honest feelings about this particular announcement from him and his thoughtless fucking timing. *Can't I just die in his arms and not know this?* In those first suspended moments of knowing, I hate Nika Vostrikova so much that all I want to do is destroy her in any way I can. I hate all of her with my entire being because she has taken what I have always held on to—this egotistical notion, *really*—that Lincoln Presley would be mine. *Someday.*

I finger his long dark lashes, trail my hand along his strong jaw line, and gauge the racing of his pulse at his throat. What I say next could undo all those marital plans. I could be honest and tell him the truth about us—him, me, *Cara.*

My throat constricts with all these pent-up emotions and truths as well as the agonized guilt and remorse that I constantly live with and the love I feel so strongly for Lincoln Presley right now. *Because I do...I do love him.*

I open my mouth to speak only to realize that he's been filling in my long, drawn-out silence with words of his own. Lincoln Presley is talking, and I haven't heard a single word he's said. But then, his words finally register with some part of my brain.

"She's due in May. We're pretty excited," he says. "I've always wanted a big family and Nika's game for one, too."

His face comes alive with such joy that it inadvertently sucks the last air out of my lungs with its unintended force. Remorse for what I said to him the last time, for not telling him about Cara, for all the lies returns full force and haunts me now.

You can't really hear heartbreak. It is remarkably silent but excruciating all the same.

You think you've already met up with the depths of sadness and despair. You've had your share. You think that there is no more that anyone can say or do to you that could make you feel worse, but you would be wrong even on this most terror-filled day.

I can't breathe. I'm staring into his face and noting the trace of happiness that lives there within him now; but I'm drifting away too far and too fast from him. *I'm evaporating right here, and I can't breathe.*

It comes to me swiftly how I never fully understood the ramifications of my decision with Cara until now. How this one decision has come back on me in all these visceral, unexpected ways. This one hurts the most. Linc has gone on with his life and is having a baby with someone else. I won't be a part of his life.

Some part of me believed in the fairytale. I skipped over the true ending of *Romeo & Juliet.* Yes, it's true that we do that play for an entire month during the season, so I *know* how it ends. *Still.* I egoistically and naively thought we would work it out. *Someday.*

Instead, there's *this. This heartbreak.*

It hurts like hell. It's as if I'm being burned alive.

"Thank you, Elvis," I manage to say just before my body reacts for me.

This feels good. Dying feels fine and I welcome the blackness with open arms.

Because today? I've truly lost everything.

CHAPTER THIRTY-SIX

Linc~Staying with the lies

*T*HINGS WILL WORK OUT; HOWEVER THEY'RE supposed to work out. My mother used to say something like that. It's a stupid saying. I never understood it. I don't understand it now. And yet, I stare at the unconscious body of Tally Landon and can only wonder at its truth. *Because she's here; and I'm here.* After everything that's gone down between us, that has to mean something for both of us.

I pray to God. I beg for salvation. I make a deal with Him. I ask for forgiveness for all the bad choices I've made and for all the transgressions I've induced and for the lies I continue to tell.

The hospital staff manages true discretion. They rushed Tally inside one of the first available rooms in the ER, after she passed out. "She's my wife. I'm Lincoln Presley," I said, having decided within those first few minutes that lying would be easier. And lying gives me this little window into Tally's psyche. *Yes, lying is so much easier.*

I fill out a few sheets of paperwork, pull out a Visa, balefully hand them a wad of American Express checks, and keep my vigilant gaze on Tally at all times, while they quickly assess her injuries. I provide the sketchiest of details to some police detective about Tally's assailant but keep my entire focus on Tally.

I all but freak out, when they finish cutting off her clothes in the ER. There are deep lacerations and bruises along both of her legs, especially her inner thighs, and my mind starts to go to the most horrific places. The medical staff automatically performs a rape test.

I have to leave the room after that. I throw up in the first restroom I can find and acknowledge how deeply I hate the man who did this to her and Moscow, equally.

After a half-hour, the first detective returns with an attentive look and informs me that they found a guy. He says, "Perpetrator," in perfect English but that seems to be one of the few English words he knows. He goes on to tell me in a mixture of Russian and broken English that the guy matches the description I gave earlier about who I saw in the alley. They want Tally's statement. I gesture towards the window of the exam room where, just beyond it, Tally still lies unconscious while they work on her. The detective tells me that the guy isn't dead. *Yet.* The perpetrator is in critical condition in this very hospital on a different floor and about to go into emergency surgery; I feel somewhat unhinged because I secretly wish he was dead, and that I could be the one to kill him when he tells me this. *What is happening to me?*

Sometime later, I call Nika with a relentless need for pretense. I need her to tell me that everything is okay and; for her part, it is. Hearing her say it helps. I continue to lie about where I've been all afternoon. "Practice—pitching, hitting, catching balls—*the usual,*" I tell her. I call my pitching coach. "There's been an emergency with a close friend of mine, and I may not make the practice. Don't count on it," I tell him. "I'll do my best to make practice, but I might not." Deep down, I know there's just no way I can throw a baseball right now, but I give him false hope. I cover my bases. *I lie. Again.*

I fill up the endless time in an almost unconscious daze and endlessly study the non-English-speaking medical and nursing staff as they work round-the-clock. Yes, I do my best to avoid the despair, but it's there all the same. My eyes glaze over at the gravity of the situation. Guilt assails me from all sides now because I'd been telling Tally about Nika and me and our baby; yet all the while she was bleeding out from multiple stab wounds, going into shock over a possible sexual assault, and suffering from a severe concussion. I was the jerk going on about the rare vein of happiness; I'd been able to find, in recently learning Nika was pregnant and making plans for our future, because I was determined on some sadistic level to make Tally pay for how she'd left me on Valentine's Day, after Charlie and Marla's wedding. Oblivious to the true horror of her situation and too intent on inflicting my own brand of emotional pain upon her, I didn't see what was fully going on with her, until she passed out in my arms; and I finally noticed all the blood that trailed behind us across the hospital's sparkling-clean floor, forming a curiously accusatory pattern that led straight to me.

I haven't exactly been forthcoming with the hospital staff about who Tally really is; because it was surprisingly easy to exploit my celebrity and just go with the telling of the first lie that I was her husband. I'd pretty much shouted this fact aloud to anyone that would listen, after we first got here, in quickly realizing how easy lying really was. It's true that I've taken advantage of the situation and my celebrity, and that I'm unstoppable now. The hospital staff is a little in awe of my baseball star status. They've heard of Lincoln Presley, the baseball player. The Los Angeles Angels. The Russians seem to love L.A. and I hear them murmur about this in broken English among themselves.

The deception quickly lends itself to my own personal fantasies about meaning more to Tally—about being more than just some guy she used to know but never should have known.

I stay with the lie. I revel in the lie. She's mine for now, at least. And, I'm most definitely hers.

Nika calls me back. She tells me she's decided to stay in the country with her family for another two days until the actual game and wonders if I'll be all right. I assure her that I'm fine, even though I can't stop shaking. I breathe a heavy sigh of relief that I have a brief reprieve when it comes to Nika. I can't even think about the implications of Tally and Nika right now, and how I'll ultimately deal with all of that.

I'm supposed to be getting ready for the Angels' exhibition game. Instead, I sit here holding Tally's hand because I'll take any part of her that's left. Meanwhile, my head swims with all these raging thoughts about marrying Nika and our baby, but then I'm equally assailed by all these memories of Tally. *I can't leave her. I won't leave her.* That tenet stays with me even as I only vaguely consider that it will destroy everything I have with Nika Vostrikova.

Choices.

I will have to make them. I already have, haven't I?

I'm bound to the magnitude of only one truth now. *I won't leave Tally. Ever. Never again.* My allegiance to it effectively blows me away. Yet another part of me wonders how that will be tested just like it always has been in the past.

At regular intervals, the hospital staff moves in and out of the room where they've put Tally without saying too much to me. The barrier for English and Russian appears infinite. I don't care. I have nothing more to say. As long as I'm willing to cover the medical bills, people don't ask me anything. I don't want them to ask me anything because I don't want to answer. I don't want to tell the truth, not on this day anyway. *I*

'll stay with the lies. I need them to be true.

She's mine. For now.

One of the nurses comes in and takes Tally's vital signs for the umpteenth time. Next, they roll in a portable ultrasound machine and gesture that I should leave the room, but I indicate in my own American way back that I'm staying and shake my head side-to-side to get that point across. I've come this far. I'm determined to go all the way.

The technician shrugs and then extends the wand over Tally's abdomen and lower extremities. We all watch the chaos unfold, as Tally's internal organs flash up on the 3-D screen. They seem to know what it means while I look on in a stupor of confusion, but with growing concern at all the turmoil that seems to race across the monitor. There's blood oozing everywhere inside of her. That can't be good. Their faces are somewhat grave, and it scares the hell out of me. The doctor strides in, visually takes in the screen shots, and then makes a few handwritten notes on Tally's chart. He says a few things in Russian and looks over directly to me as if I'm supposed to have an answer.

I shake my head. "English?"

So far, everyone here has babbled on in mostly Russian. I've given up hope of finding anyone who could really understand me beyond the Russian cop who knew enough English when I spoke to him a few hours ago to at least take down my side of the story.

"Ah, you're American," he says. "Me, too. I'm Dr. Michael Markov. My parents were Russian, but I was born in San Francisco. I moved here a little over two years ago when my father wanted to return to Moscow. So, we did, just before he died." He gets this despondent look. What he's just revealed explains just about everything. He's this blond, good-looking American guy whom I would gauge to be about thirty-five. I would have a beer with him under different circumstances. I decide I can handle him. Somehow, this makes me breathe easier.

"Lincoln Presley." I extend my hand.

He shakes it and smiles a little. "The baseball star. The whole ER is talking about you."

I nod. I stand up to my full height and face him. I'm taller. Tired. Put out. Adamant. I decide now might be the time to exert my influence because all that fucking fame and power surely grants me something. Surely, this guy can help me out. *Help me out here, man.* "Yes. Lincoln Presley. I pitch for the Los Angeles Angels." I glance over at Tally's still form. "We're here for an exhibition game. Day after tomorrow."

Complete recognition of who I am and an obvious penchant for baseball crosses his features at the same time. He knows me. He likes baseball. His stance and enthusiasm change right in front of me.

He glances over at the sleeping Tally, too, and nods at me slowly, effectively putting it all together in a single instant. "Her condition is critical. Two deep stab wounds to her abdomen have caused serious internal bleeding, and the IUD has perforated the uterine wall." He turns to the screen and points out a Y-shape on the screen that sits at a peculiar angle. "Stab wounds have caused the extensive bleeding. The IUD needs to be removed. The lacerations and bruising on her legs are mostly superficial. Her foot has multiple broken bones, and the ankle is badly sprained. We'll cast that." He sighs and glances back at his chart. "The ultrasound doesn't look good. The removal of the IUD and stopping the internal bleeding so we can determine the extent of her injuries are critical. We already confirmed there was an attempt at a sexual assault, semen along her inner thighs, and semi-detectable vaginal penetration but inconclusive."

"Semi-detectable. Inconclusive. What does that mean?" My tone is harsh, but I don't apologize.

"We don't know for sure. It looks like he tried to sexually assault her but may not have succeeded."

"Well, that's *great news.*" I don't attempt to hide my sarcasm, and he looks a little put out by it.

"It appears, she fought him hard, Mr. Presley. I know it doesn't seem like it, but she's actually very lucky." My face must show utter disbelief because he hurries on with his speech after that idiotic comment. "The internal bleeding has to be stopped. In addition to the knife wounds, there appears to have been blunt force trauma to her abdomen. It looks like the assailant kicked her." He frowns, probably because of the incredulous look on my face. "In any case, the IUD has perforated through the uterus, and we have to take her surgery to remove it. There's a risk." He pauses and looks at me hard. "We may have to perform a hysterectomy, but we won't know until we get her in surgery. Microsurgery has come a long way even for something as delicate as the uterine wall. Dr. Wallenski is the best, here in Moscow."

His qualification of *here in Moscow* worries me. "Can't we just wait and fly her back to the States?"

He studies me intently for a few seconds. "She won't make it to the States. She's lost a lot of blood, and she's bleeding out internally."

All the air rushes from my lungs, and I stagger back suddenly unable to breathe. It seems he was waiting for that kind of reaction from me. He slowly nods and then goes on without waiting for the words to make any more sense. "Depending upon how the surgery goes, she may not be able to have children. She'll need counseling about all of this. Eventually, she'll be fine, both physically and mentally, but an attack like this…well; she may not remember much of it, but it will take time and counseling and support from family and friends. She has all of that, right?"

I nod, not trusting myself to speak because I don't know anything about Tally's life anymore, as if I ever did. Marla won't tell me anything about Tally. Nobody's been able to find out anything of what's going on with her for months. *I let her down.* This single thought assails me now. I let her down when I let her walk out of my hospital room and didn't call her back. I'm sure she was waiting for me just beyond that door just waiting for me to say *something. Anything.* And I chose to let her walk out. I didn't say a word, blinded by anger at her for the things she'd said. Yet I was the one who had let her down in first place. *I couldn't afford to do it now. Not again.*

"Mr. Presley? We need your signature on the surgical form. You said you were her husband?" He looks unconvinced.

"She's my wife," I say, lying for the second or third time in less than four hours, although it feels very real when I say it this time. It seems like I should be the one who decides Tally's fate. Who's going to question a star baseball player for the Angels here to pitch a baseball game in Moscow? Hell, I'll give this guy tickets to the game for saving Tally's life.

In the next few minutes, I actually promise him a ticket to the game as I irrationally go on and on about baseball, while Dr. Michael Markov prepares the paperwork. He eventually slides the forms over in my direction and smiles with sympathy as if he knows I'm fighting the shock and pain of this day, both for Tally and myself.

I hold my breath and say a little prayer and have to hope he doesn't begin to question my authority over Tally's health directives. I scribble my signature across *Tally Presley's* patient form. I can't even look over at her now.

"I'm sorry," the doctor says. "It's a horrible thing that's happened. It's a risk—the surgery, but it's necessary. I know it's an extra blow to know that she may not be able to have more children, but hopefully it won't come to that."

My head whips up. "*More* children?" I ask. "What did you say?"

"How long have you two been married?" Markov gets this uncertain look.

I need to weigh my words carefully before this whole lie about being her husband comes undone. *Then, what would we do?*

"Not long," I say and hold my breath at the same time.

The doctor studies me for a few moments. "Your wife told us she had a child almost three years ago at the end of January. She confirmed that for us when we took her medical history before we gave her the morphine for the pain in prepping her for surgery. Didn't she tell you?" Now the doctor looks skeptical and unsure of who I am in relation to his patient.

I shake my head side-to-side, striving for some kind of outward control, and weigh my words carefully. *Tally had a baby?*

"We had a misunderstanding until recently; and then we worked it out and got married. I didn't know. She never told me. We weren't together for a few years until recently."

The doctor raises his eyebrow and looks at me even more closely. "When did you first meet?"

I nod slowly as this sick feeling overcomes me. "I rescued her from a car accident when she was seventeen. That was the first time I met her. She didn't tell me." I swallow hard, chasing back all these various emotions—anger, joy, and this insurmountable despair that nearly crushes me. I try to damp it all down because the doctor is watching me even more closely now.

"It looks like you have some things to work out." He glances back in Tally's direction one more time. "She'll eventually be fine, but I wouldn't upset her with anything else right now. The surgery is paramount. It's a two to a four-hour procedure. Depending upon how it goes, she'll be sore for at least six weeks, somewhat immobile, and she won't be able to lift anything of considerable weight for a long while. You'll do the vacuuming, for example."

He gets this grim smile. "She'll wake up with a terrible headache and have a lot of physical pain and mental anguish to deal with, but eventually she'll be fine, providing this surgery goes well. I'm sorry. It's terrible that this happened to her."

"Yes." I'm reeling from all he's said and doing a private battle with anger and remorse and guilt. *Tally had a child. Was it mine? Why didn't she tell me?*

"I'm sorry," he says again.

"Yes." I watch them judiciously move Tally onto a gurney and swiftly wheel her away. I stand in the empty room for a long time after she's gone and question if I've done the right thing, as if I even know what that is anymore.

She'll probably hate me for signing the surgical form, authorizing a surgery that may take away her ability to have children. *More* children. *But if it saves her life? Then that's the most important thing, right?*

The anger at her over everything she'd said to me our last time together in San Francisco and at the hospital has fueled me to hate her all these months. But now? That's all gone. *I feel empty. Bereft. Undone.* I struggle to put it all into context now. It's no different than if she had an abortion. Right? Except somewhere out there in the world is a child. Ours? Hers? *Possibly mine?* I can't get past this. And, the anguish over knowing inevitably follows. It carries me through the next several hours while I wait for *my wife's* return from surgery.

In one part of my mind, I stay with the mantra that I can't leave her; while in the other, I console myself with the thought that Nika's pregnant and Nika's baby can replace the one Tally so easily gave up. Yet, later on, it comes to me that it may not work like that. *A child. Tally had a child. She gave it up. It may be mine.* Somewhere out in the world is a child who may be mine that she gave up. And she never told me.

CHAPTER THIRTY-SEVEN

Linc ~ Lies. There are so many.

D R. MICHAEL MARKOV RETURNS AND REPORTS the outcome of Tally's surgery. His *I'm-sorry-she-may-not-be-able-to-have-more-children* speech barely registers. I breathe a sigh of relief that she pulled through the surgery, and that they've stopped the bleeding and now all we can do is wait.

I continue to swim with all the lies—the ones I've told to save Tally's life, and the ones Tally's told me for reasons unknown.

The lies. The lies. They just get bigger and seem to take us both farther from the truth.

The next day I pitch an almost perfect game at Moscow's fine baseball park and finish in seven innings. With Torres relieving me in the eighth, I race back to Tally's bedside before she even realizes I've been gone.

They've kept her sedated for the past few days to allow her body to heal and minimize the swelling on her brain with the concussion. The bruises to her face and legs turn an ugly purple with the outer edges turning this gruesome gangrene green in color. The deep lacerations on her stomach and the front of her legs are all bandaged up. She's being treated with a heavy dose of antibiotics to fight infection. She's an absolute wreck, but I've never seen her look more beautiful.

Right after the game, I convinced Nika to go see her family again. She gave me one of her suspicious pouty faces even as I shoved her back into a waiting taxi and told her to go spend time with her parents. I told her we were leaving within a week, and we have plenty of time.

Lies. There are so many.

Dr. Michael Markov makes his late rounds and stops in to check on Tally one last time. He gives me this curious look, once again. Other than the game and a shower, I've been at Tally's side, waiting for her to wake up. The Moscow Police and I wait for her to wake up.

"She may exhibit some confusion for a few days," Markov says quietly. "We've been watching her closely, just to make sure she doesn't have a brain bleed of any sort. So far, so good. I've ordered the nursing staff to back her off the heavy narcotics, and she'll be waking up in the next few hours or so. She'll be tired. She'll need to be on bed rest for the rest of the week. I'd like to keep her a few more days for observation. But with you here, after that, I don't see why she can't recuperate at home. Then again, she needs to be woken up every few hours to ensure it's nothing more serious. Concussions can be tricky. With a brain injury, it can be nothing, or it can be everything. Do you understand?"

"Yes, I'll watch over her. I'm here. We're staying at The Savoy." I tell this lie as easily as all the others, while Markov slowly nods. My mind also secretly races as to what I just committed to. How can I keep Nika happy and in the dark about all of this and keep a vigilant watch over Tally Landon all at the same time?

"I know. How are you holding up?" Markov asks.

"Good. I've got this. She means everything to me," I say. "She's my wife. I'll take care of her."

"She'll eventually be fine with the right support system around her." Dr. Markov flips the chart closed and stows the file in the slot by the door for the next shift. "We just have to wait and see. She's strong and determined; and she has you." He sighs deep and seems to hesitate. "The police want a statement from her to corroborate what you've told them." He pauses and looks more concerned. "The guy died about an hour ago."

"Oh," I manage to say. "That complicates things, doesn't it?"

I'm too caught up in the lies and too saddened by the blatant unspoken truth that I'm not sorry the guy died. I'm sure my conflicted thoughts show on my face.

Dr. Markov watches me closely again now. "Look, Mr. Presley, this isn't America. They need her statement to clear you. According to the taxi driver, you were the last one in the alley. It's in the papers." He stops for a full minute. "I told them that she'd be well enough to give a statement tomorrow morning. We need to ensure that she does. Technically, you shouldn't even be in the same room with her, but she's your wife, and you're her husband." He gets this steely look and looks at me intently. "She needs to give her statement tomorrow morning, first thing."

"Okay. Tomorrow." I shake his hand. "Thank you. Thank you for doing everything for Tally. I appreciate it."

He reaches into his pocket and hands me a card. "I've got tomorrow off. I'm sure everything will work out fine. Just make sure Tally talks to the detective. Like I said, this isn't America. Just call me if you have any questions. Day or night."

I'm confused by his concern. "Dr. Markov? Why are you here? I mean why did you come back to Moscow? It's way different than San Fran."

"Yeah. Well, my father remembers a far different Moscow then this one. I had all these grand illusions and wanted to return with him, so we'd both be able to see them. The changes. The progress. The freedoms." His smile disappears. "But some things never change." He shakes his head. "I don't know why I stay. He died six months after we got here. I guess I stay to make a difference? Even so, I'm just a pebble causing a brief splash and eventually engulfed by a riptide most of the time I'm afraid." He sighs and heads for the door. "Just make sure she gives her statement. Okay, Linc?"

Dr. Michael Markov leaves. I vaguely hear the click of the hospital door when it shuts closed. *Finality.* I close my eyes and try to breathe and assess what to do next. *How many more lies will I have to tell to make this all work out? For me? For Tally? For both of us?*

For a few hours, I watch over Tally like I've won first prize and must carefully guard my golden human statue. She's weak and worn out when she finally comes around. She vaguely notes my presence, still seems heavily sedated but appears grateful for my company, although she doesn't say much more than *thank you* a few times before she's out again. I position a chair by her hospital bed and set my iPhone with various alarm times, so I can remain vigilant and wake her up every few hours as Dr. Markov recommended. She's groggy and out of sorts, but looks adorable even with the long ugly bruise down one side of her face. She's still too weak to take a shower and although the nurses did their best to clean the blood out of her hair, it's still somewhat matted with it. She won't be happy when she sees that.

She's more golden-blond than a brunette now. "I hate the highlights." I tell her while she sleeps. "I hate the lies, Tally," I say to her, at one point, during the middle of the night. "I hate the lies. I hate how you lie about *everything*."

I'm startled out of my serialized rant when she eventually whispers back, "I know. *I know*, Elvis. I'm sorry."

"Why do you have to make everything so fucking complicated?" I ask.

She laughs softly.

I see her hand move across her face in the dark. She fingers her lips as if assessing the damage.

"Does it hurt? Dr. Markov said you could have an extra painkiller at night if you need it. Do you need it?"

"Noooooooo."

"Let me re-phrase; do you *want* it?" I hold my breath and await her answer. There's so much I want to say, so much I need to say but there are too many questions I want answers to that I can't even begin to ask. I sigh in genuine frustration.

"You've got something to say, Elvis, then go ahead and *say* it." Her voice is hard, laced with contempt. I flinch upon hearing it.

"I should have said something. I shouldn't have let you go like that. I'm a jerk."

"True. True. True," she says softly.

"Why didn't you tell me?"

"Tell you *what?*"

Now she's guarded.

I debate upon upsetting her further but plunge onward because I need to know. "Why didn't you tell me you were pregnant? That you had a child, Tally. We could have—"

"What?" she asks. "I was almost nineteen, but I couldn't do it all— raise a kid, go with a job that barely paid at the time; and I couldn't give up ballet. I made a choice."

"Nineteen? Why did you have it at all?" I'm trying to do the math but it's not coming together for me. If she was nineteen; it certainly wasn't me that fathered her child. *Am I wrong about this?*

"I went for an abortion. I never even told Marla about it, but I freaked out when I got there. After losing Holly…I just couldn't go through with it. And so, I didn't." She turns her head toward me in the semi-dark and looks over at me. She seems to be assessing and weighing her next words carefully. "Besides, it wasn't your problem." Her voice is strong and never wavers as she says this.

I take in air in an attempt to make sense of her response. *The baby wasn't mine.*

"Not my problem," I say, parroting her words.

"Right." I can see her smiling in the dark—the wicked one I remember from the first night we met when she first called me Elvis.

"I wouldn't have cared. I would have—"

"What?" She mocks. "Held my hand? Told me everything was going to be okay? Thrown over your career to help a girl out? Come on, Linc. This is the real world. Bad things happen. We do bad things. Some of us lie so much better than others." She laughs low. "Trust me. I'm telling you…the truth."

She stops and takes an unsteady breath. "It wasn't *your* problem."

Jealousy comes out of nowhere. I practically gag at her words. "Damn you, Tally. Why do you have to fuck every guy who comes along?"

"I like fucking every guy who comes along. That's who I am."

"I don't believe that."

"You don't have to." She sighs and moans a little as she adjusts her broken body beneath the sheets. "I gave her away. I don't even think about her. She's with a nice family, and life goes on."

"You don't even think about *her*."

"Noooooooooo." She draws the word out as if to ensure I know she means it. "I couldn't afford to keep her, and I wasn't the mothering type."

"That's not true. You'd make a great mother."

"You're not hearing me. I don't want to be a mother. I certainly don't want to be tied down. I have a life…*ballet*. There's not room for anything or anyone else…for long. Rob understands." She tacks on the last part like it's an afterthought.

Her mentioning Rob sets me off. "You can't go anywhere for another week. You can't lift anything for at least six more. You may not be able have any more kids. They're not sure. There may be too much scarring. I'm sorry." I don't know what compels me to tell her all of this, but I know somewhere down the line she needs to be told. Plus, there's this cruel part of me that wants to get back at her for all she's just admitted to me—mainly, that the kid wasn't even mine, and she's still with Rob.

"It's okay. I didn't want kids anyway. Neither does Rob. See? It all works out." Her voice doesn't even tremble. It's steady and true.

"It doesn't have to be this way." There's obvious desperation in my tone. I cringe upon hearing it, and I'm glad for the darkness between us. "Tally, I—"

"You moved on." Her voice is soft. "So have I. Everything is the way it's supposed to be," she whispers the last part as if she's grown tired of the conversation. I don't find any consolation in the way she's just said it. "Now about those painkillers, I'll take some of those now."

I don't know what else to say. I'm caught up the obligations of my present life and the persistent thought that keeps invading my psyche that she's still with Rob—this other guy that isn't me. *And what right do I have to her, since I'm with Nika? Getting married and having a baby with Nika?* I shouldn't even be here in this hospital room, alone with her.

Right now? This very second, Nika thinks I'm asleep in our hotel room three blocks away from here. *But here I am. With Tally Landon. Alone with Tally Landon. Fucked up all over again about Tally Landon. When will I ever learn?*

I push back the chair and make my way to the restroom for the painkillers. I drop them in her outstretched hand and give her a glass of water to take them with.

"Elvis?" She keeps her face averted away from me, and I hear her as she takes an unsteady breath in the dark. "I can't remember anything. Did he…?"

"No. They said no." I swallow hard on the lie. But how do I explain semi-detectable but inconclusive?

No. That last word feels like a sword has been swiftly drawn out from my heart. And for some bizarre reason, I can't tell her he's dead, not yet. I'm not sure how she'll react when she finds that out. I'll let the police be the one to tell her that tomorrow, later today. *I can't even think straight.*

"Do you hate me?" she asks.

"No. I could never hate you, Tally. I…I…Tally…" I can't even finish the sentence. Nika's upturned face flashes through my mind. *What the hell am I doing? What can I promise her? She's moved on. Why can't I?*

She doesn't say anything for a long time. There is just this unsteady breathing taking place between us. We both suffer under the heavy weight of all the lies, of the stark reality before us, of the inevitable loss of each other in all of this. Eventually, she turns over on her side away from me. I hear her moan softly.

"My foot?"

"There are multiple broken bones in your foot. They had to cast it," I say dully.

This is the news that causes her to cry. *We're not so different. She and I. She with her ballet. Me with a baseball.* I automatically flex my pitching arm. I can't imagine losing my livelihood—the one thing I'm good at.

"I don't want to be awake." Her voice catches. I grope my way across the bed sheets for her hand as if by holding on to her; I can somehow keep her here. "Sasha's probably going crazy. Where's my cell phone?" she asks after a few minutes.

"I don't know who Sasha is, but you can call her tomorrow. It's the middle of the night. Your cell phone's over by the desk. You can get it later."

"She's my boss. We have to let her know what's happened." She chokes on the last word, and I squeeze her hand.

I listen for her breathing, and it gets steadier as time passes.

There's so much more to say but neither one of us is willing to say it.

"Tomorrow. Okay, tomorrow, we'll call her. It's going to be okay, Tally."

"You think so?" she whispers.

I smile in the dark at her, and she turns over and attempts to smile back. I squeeze her hand, and she squeezes back. "I do."

"Thank you, Elvis. For the rescue. For being here. For always doing the right thing. I wish…" She sits up on her elbows and looks over at me and heavily sighs. "I wish things could be different for us."

"Me, too," I say in answer. "Maybe beginning tomorrow they will be different. Get some sleep, Tally. Tomorrow will be different."

"Tomorrow will be different," she says back to me.

I wake up to the blaring insistent xylophone alarm from my iPhone and hastily shut it off. I dazedly note the room is tomb-silent as I cast my eyes about the filmy darkness, and wonder why it's so dark. I swear I left the light on low by her bedside, but now it's off. I bump my knee alongside the bed as I carelessly traverse over to that side and switch the bedside lamp back on and look around.

It takes only a second to register that the bed is empty. No Tally. A quick survey all around the room tells me she's gone. The room practically indicts me.

Remorse rolls in on me. I should have told her that I still love her. Something.

I brought her a change of clothes and some make-up from her hotel room with me yesterday. Everything I brought is all cleaned out of the hospital closet. The makeup that I'd left on the bathroom counter for her to use is gone. The crutches and the next dose of painkillers the nurse placed at her bedside are missing.

She's missing.

She's gone.

There's no trace of her left, and it's my fault. I glance at the closed hospital door and wonder how long I've been out of it. The clock registers 7:01 a.m.

My eyes come to rest on a note that lies in plain sight on the linoleum floor.

Tally.

It's her handwriting. I'd recognize it anywhere, and the words are exactly the same as before only she's used the hospital's best stationery this time instead of a castoff dry cleaner's receipt.

"Thank you, Elvis."

One of these days I'm actually going to ask her what's she's thanking me for.

Right now?

I sink to the hard floor in a weak attempt to hold myself together and protect my heart from actually breaking.

this much is true

The pain is real—visceral. It burns all the way to my soul.

I can't even be with Tally for more than a few days without losing her again. *What was I thinking?*

CHAPTER THIRTY-EIGHT

Linc ~ I won't give up

No TALLY. AFTER AN EXTENSIVE SEARCH of the hospital on my own, I enlist the hospital staff's help only to reconfirm this. Two hours later, I've paid a whopping ransom of 724,701 rubles, which equates to about twenty-four thousand U.S. dollars in settling Tally's hospital bill. After going through the security tapes at my urgent request, the hospital security staff finally confirms that a young woman wearing a long dark wool coat missing all the front buttons left about 5:13 a.m. this morning from the front hospital entrance by private car. According to the security guard, she loaded up all her things in the trunk, looked away from the camera situated to capture activity at entrance, and appears to have left the premises without being recognized as a patient. Until now.

I doggedly ensure that they know exactly who I am, while the security guard attempts to be helpful and tells me privately the rest of the American dance company members stay at The Savoy while the troupe performs at The Moscow Theater, and I might have some luck on *intel* there. The conversation with Tally vaguely comes back to me. Within a half-hour, after an extensive interrogation of The Savoy's front desk concierge, I'm placing a desperate call to the theater. I finally find myself talking with the director, but it does little to assuage my fears. *"She's gone,"* is about all the director is willing to admit.

Tally's boss, the NYC Ballet artistic director Sasha Belmont, agrees to meet with me in person. I arrive a little after ten in the morning determined to learn as much as I can about Talia Delacourt—the name Tally used at The Savoy Hotel, according to the concierge.

Sasha Belmont appears wary. She's a petite blond that I would guess has seen her thirtieth birthday. She has an edge to her that reminds me of Tally—

determined, dedicated, perhaps even deceiving in this charming *I've-got-this-thing-covered* kind of way, just like Tally. Sasha Belmont looks like she could use a few decent meals, just like Tally.

What is it with these dancers and this unbelievable devotion to all things ballet and nothing else? A few meals, here and there, might actually make them less intense. I smile at my wisdom intent on my charm winning this swan beauty over. Undoubtedly, she knows where Tally is.

So far, she returns that smile, but it doesn't quite reach her big blue eyes. She reminds me of a diminutive Barbie. She's petite but sharp and should not be mistaken as being a fragile China doll. Sasha Belmont answers the majority of my questions with a wave of her small hands, but with very little substance as if I'm just some guy she's promised to spend time with…only later, not now, not ever really, is she actually going to tell me what's going on. It doesn't matter how persuasive I am. She's isn't forthcoming about Tally in any way. Instead, she's protective and closed off.

We've talked about the tonight's performance. I now know Deanna, pronounced Dee-ah-nah according to Sasha, who graciously corrected me when I slaughtered the girl's name, will be performing in Tally's stead because the artistic director Sasha Belmont has deemed it so. I move on to other topics and blatantly trade upon my name and baseball fame, but she remains unmoved, unimpressed. Sasha Belmont doesn't like baseball. She could not care less about who I am. It's obvious her priority is her protégé—Talia Landon Delacourt. She makes all of this abundantly clear within the first twenty minutes of our conversation.

"My fiancée, Nika Vostrikova, will be here soon." It's a lame tactic. I have this vague idea that trading on Nika's famous Russian heritage—known so well here in the city of Moscow—will somehow make a difference to Sasha Belmont.

She tilts her head and looks at me with newfound curiosity. "Nika Vostrikova. The hacker?"

"She does freelance work in computers," I say impatiently. "Wait a minute, you *know* Nika?"

"Does anyone really *know* Nika Vostrikova? We've had drinks a few times with a mutual friend of mine when I was in New York last. She's beautiful." Sasha's looking at me intently now. "She doesn't seem your type."

"I have a *type*?"

She nods and gets this little secret smile, but it doesn't reach her eyes. *No.*

Her secretive smile morphs into this defiant gleam as if she's prepared to toy with me now.

"You're a star baseball player. I imagine the world is at your command these days with a mind-blowing contract to play America's favorite pastime. Mom. Family. Apple Pie. Isn't that how it works?" She shrugs her slim shoulders and smiles again, but then it fades away. "How does Nika fit into all of that with you? She's not your type. She's a taker—a blood-sucking vampire—if we're being honest here. No, not for you, Mr. Lincoln Presley, baseball star."

"We're getting married, having a baby, starting a family. Sorry to disappoint you." I'm getting pissed off. *Is it because she's talking trash about Nika? Or, because on some clairvoyant level she speaks the truth and I don't want to hear it?*

"And *you* told Tally all of that." Her tone is flat, accusatory.

"Yes." I hang my head because I know how it sounds, and I can't defend it right this second. "I didn't know what all was going on with her at the time."

Belmont steeples her hands together and takes a sip of the hot tea that some young dancer has placed in front of her at the café table we share just beyond the theater's main stage. She sits up high and stiff as regal as a queen. She closes her eyes for a moment. I have to avoid rolling mine, even though I'm beyond frustrated by the drama going down at this table that is surely at my expense.

She's my only link to Tally. The last one. I'm desperate. We're wasting precious time. I've already called Kimberley, but she hasn't called me back yet.

"Mr. Presley," she says slowly. "I can assure that she is fine."

"I need to see her."

She shakes her head slowly and tilts it to one side again. This must be a thing with her. It must be her way of softening the blow of her critiques or bad news. *I'm clairvoyant now, too.*

"You can't. She was specific in her instructions. She doesn't want to see you, and she said you'd understand why."

"What did she tell you exactly?" I eye her intently.

"She needed a break. She's been working hard. She wanted some time off. Her ankle was sprained."

"She has a concussion. She can't be left alone. Did she tell you any of *that?*" Now, I'm pissed. I'm sure it shows.

My hand shakes as I attempt to calm down by actually drinking down some of the fine coffee her little diminutive staff member brought to me. The woman can't quite hide her unease with what I've just said. I watch the smallest hint of actual fear travel swiftly across her delicate features. There's a slight frown upon her face as she begins to calculate what Tally must have told her versus what I've said and what she now knows to be true.

Because why would I lie?

That's Tally's trick.

Her eyes shift like a deck of cards, and she looks first to the right and then the left and takes an unsteady shallow breath. "That changes things," she says.

I don't have time for this. I decide it's time to shock this woman into submission. "She was assaulted— almost raped—three days ago on her way back from your luncheon. I just happened to find her, but it was almost too late. He stabbed her twice. She almost died. She would have bled out if I hadn't found her. They had to perform surgery to stop the bleeding and save her life."

Sasha Belmont looks distressed. Her lips press into a firm line. She grips her own coffee cup tightly now. I can see the muscles in her neck tense up as the shock of what happened to Tally settles in on her.

"He must have slammed her into a stone wall, and she hit her head. They performed the emergency surgery because he kicked her so hard that her IUD perforated the uterine wall. She may not be able to have any more children. They had to remove one of her ovaries because it was so badly damaged by the guy's violent assault and he used a knife on her."

I pause and wipe at my face. I'm tired. I'm frustrated with this woman for stalling me like this and in just talking about a possible sexual assault and the damage the guy wielded upon Tally and the fact that she almost died causes me to start shaking all over again. I sigh deep and attempt to get a grip because I'm still intent on appealing to Sasha Belmont's sympathetic side, and I'm beginning to seriously lose it.

"I just want to ensure that Tally is okay. We've known each other a long time, and I was just hoping that you could tell me if you've spoken to her." I'm rambling, and I'm desperate. Sasha Belmont studies me intently. She seems to be holding her breath. I rush on. "I told her she was my wife—to save her life—so they'd perform the surgery. And really, Ms. Belmont, I'm just trying to find her. There are things to say. Things I need to say to Tally."

"How very noble," Sasha Belmont says with a sad, tired smile. "You must love her very much to pretend to be her husband when you're clearly engaged to someone else; and yet, you told her how you were marrying Nika and having a baby and starting a family." Her sarcasm gets stronger with every damning word. "How does that *work* exactly?"

"Like I said, I didn't know what all was going on with her at the time."

"Let me see if I've got this. She'd been stabbed and almost raped by a madman, and you didn't know what all was going on with her?"

In the next moment, she flings her arm toward the stage and uses a few choice Russian words that I happen to recognize.

"And she's sacrificed so much already." This is no more than a whisper, but I hear it.

I nod somewhat confused by what all Tally has sacrificed but attempt to keep myself together by remaining perfectly still as I acquiesce to my own reality and truth.

"I love her." I attempt to control my breathing, but I still sound desperate.

I recognize this moment. It's like the same one I face in a game when I have to get the guy out, and the pitch needs to be perfect; and yet there's this moment when everything's on the line, and I suddenly realize that I have all the control and all the power to blow it or save it.

Blow it or save it. What's it going to be?

I hold my breath while Sasha Belmont seems to take it all in.

"Did you *tell* her how you feel?" She looks completely taken aback.

There will be no more lies from me today. "Not lately."

"Why didn't you tell her?" She shakes her head and then proceeds to answer her own question. "Because of Nika."

"Because of Nika." I hang my head. "Partly. Yes. The timing has never been right for us. Like I said, we go way back. We met. She lied about her age. She was seventeen just graduating from Paly and I was just signing with the Angels. Kimberley Powers, my publicist? She said it would a PR disaster. *Us* being together. I was twenty-two at the time; she was seventeen." I grimace. "It wouldn't look good. We had to wait and let time go by. And before we could work things out between us, the world changed on both of us."

Her expression completely changes. One minute she's looking at me with open hostility and in the next, she looks sympathetic and almost apologetic. "Oh, God. You're Kimberley Powers' client. Her baseball friend. Elliott's brother; aren't you?"

"Yes. You *know* Kimberley?"

Sasha Belmont gets this dazed look. "You could say that. Kimberley is a good friend of mine. She talked about you before…a long time ago. I didn't understand the connection to Tally." She stares at me hard, scrutinizing my face intently. "We offered the contract to Tally because Allaire Tremblay highly recommended her. We wanted to give her another year. Her personal life was…complicated, but Allaire insisted she was ready. We didn't want to lose her to a competitor, which Allaire said we most certainly would. Tally's so talented, gifted. I love her like a little sister. She's so dedicated to the discipline and the choreography in so many ways that other dancers at her level will never achieve. She's everything Allaire Tremblay promised she would be and more." She sighs. "Wow. Small world. I'm sorry. Any friend of Kimberley's and Tally's is a friend of mine." She extends her hand, and I fold it into mine.

"Will you help me find her then? I need to talk to her. There are things to say."

"She's gone." Sasha shakes her head slowly side-to-side and gets this anguished look. "She's not in Moscow anymore. She left this morning. I drove her to the airport myself. Tally was very specific *about you and* on being left alone and leaving Moscow. She said she just needed some rest to give the sprain some time to heal." There's a long silence while conflicted feelings of regret and sadness cross the beautiful dancer's face. "There's really nothing more I can do for you, Mr. Presley," she finally says. "I'm so sorry."

One of her dancers vies for her attention with a small excited wave. Sasha sighs and looks over at me in sympathy. "I'll call her and let her know we've talked. I'll try to talk some sense into her about seeing you, Mr. Presley. But I have to go. If you'll excuse me, my show is going to be a complete disaster if I don't spend some time fixing it with this group of dancers; now that we're without Tally for tonight's opening performance." The dancer gets up and moves away from me so swiftly I'm caught off-guard.

"You won't help me. She's your protégé. She could still be in grave danger with a concussion, and you won't help me find her."

The woman turns back, and her eyes narrow as she looks at me long and hard. "Mr. Presley, I can assure you that Tally is in excellent hands. She told me herself that everything has been taken care of." She frowns, probably trying to remember exactly what Tally said to her. Worry travels across her features. "I'm sorry. I can't help you."

"I'll pay you. Whatever you want. Just tell me where she is."

"You're not listening to me. She was very explicit in her instructions, especially when it came to *you*. She said she wanted to be left alone to recuperate in peace, and that she's going to be fine." She looks more uncertain.

"What if something happens to her? She shouldn't be alone," I say, towering over her by a good twelve inches and still attempt to appeal to her sympathetic side one last time.

Sasha Belmont nervously taps her left foot in rapid succession to some silent eight-count beat. *I've hit a nerve.* She looks conflicted. Obviously, Tally failed to mention her concussion, the assault, the surgery—any of it—other than the cast on her foot for a supposed sprain that she couldn't hide. She tilts her head to one side again. It's almost some kind of tick with this woman— the head tilt. I've decided it must be how she's able to function in her world.

She closes her eyes a moment seemingly seeking some kind of balance. She opens them and glances around the entire stage and grabs my left hand. "Where would you go if you wanted to take a break, recuperate, and attempt to put your life back together, Mr. Presley?"

"What?" I'm confused by her question.

"Think about what I just said and that will tell you all you need to know."

I stand there and helplessly watch her leave. Dancers suddenly rush from all around and surround Sasha Belmont in the middle of the stage. She shouts a few directives as they prepare for tonight's elaborate performance intent on putting the contingency plans into action since their star ballerina won't be performing. I watch the chaos come to order as two different groups of dancers begin to form lines and populate the edge of the massive stage. One of the dancers among them steps out and takes center stage. She's a tall brunette, similar in height and build to Tally. She smiles wide as if she's just unexpectedly won the Olympic gold. *I suppose she has.*

I glance at my watch. *Nika will be back soon. I have to go.*

My body moves toward the door while my mind stays with these dancers. Ballet. I should probably learn to understand it or block it out of my mind completely.

Where would you go if you wanted to start over?

Home.

———————

My cell phone rings as I emerge onto the street just outside of the theater.

"You rang?" Kimberley says with a little laugh when I answer.

"I've got a problem. I just found Tally Landon three days ago; and now, I can't find her."

"Did the statute of limitations on Tally Landon finally run out for you, especially after the damn scene at your cousin's wedding?" I wince at Kimberley's sarcasm. "I can't recall giving you the go-ahead on that one, but I can't recall giving you the go-ahead on Nika Vostrikova either. Aren't you in Moscow? How did the exhibition game go?"

"I pitched almost perfect. Look a lot of bad shit has gone down. I need your help. You're the only one who can help me, besides your friend Sasha Belmont—"

"Sasha's in Moscow?"

"Yes. Look, Kimberley, you have to help me. I need to find Tally. She may have gone back to San Fran. I have to find her. There are things I need to say, and I have to know if she's all right."

"Holy shit. Is this going where I think it's going to go?"

"It's between you and me. No one else. I have to talk to Tally and be honest for once about all of it. Before I tell Nika and end things with her. I mean I'll do the right thing about the baby, but I can't marry her. God. It's a mess. You're the only one I trust. Well, there's Charlie but you know what I mean. I guess she might reach out to Marla. Can you check out her friend Marla Stone? She's with Charlie. That might be the quickest way—"

You're not making sense, Linc. Why would Tally leave Moscow when she's on tour there?"

"She's in trouble and I have to talk to her, tell her how I feel."

"What kind of trouble?"

"She was assaulted by some guy here in Moscow. She was hurt pretty bad. He used a knife. He stabbed her and seriously injured her foot as well. They're not sure if she was sexually assaulted for sure, but she's got a concussion and had to have emergency surgery and have her foot put into a cast. *I signed for all of it, paid for all of it.* They think she's *my wife*. There's just a lot of shit going down, Kimberley. Trust me. She shouldn't be alone. And now, no one will tell me where she's gone. Sasha's hinting that she went home back to San Francisco. I have to find her."

"What? Your wife? You signed for her? She's been hurt? Oh, my God, Linc. Is she okay? Linc?"

"No! We have to find her. Trust me. She shouldn't be on her own."

Now, I'm distracted because the one Russian detective I recognize looks serious and foreign; and he's busy rolling out a pair of handcuffs. In the next thirty seconds, he starts reading me my rights in Russian.

"Hold on. The police are here." My mind clicks. "She didn't give her statement," I say dully to Kimberley.

The harsh reality of the situation begins to close in on me. Markov's words come back to me."She needs to corroborate your story. They need her statement first thing in the morning. She needs to corroborate your story."

But Tally didn't do any of that, and the guy is dead. And she doesn't know that because I didn't tell her.

"She didn't give her statement," I say again.

"Who didn't give a statement?" Kimberley screams into the phone now.

"Tally! And this isn't America," I say, parroting the doctor's words from last night. "Christ, Kimberley, I'm being arrested. Shit, the guy, who attacked Tally, *died* last night. Tally didn't give her statement. I was there. I'm the only eyewitness to what happened, besides Tally. She didn't give her statement."

The detective gives me this apologetic look as he starts to cuff my right hand.

"Holy shit! Okay, I'm on my way. I'll call your coach, your lawyer, your agent. I'll call them! Linc! Linc! Can you hear me? I get it. We'll find her. We have to!"

One of the other detectives slides his finger across the cell phone screen and cuts off the connection to Kimberley.

I close my eyes for a moment in an attempt to get my balance back, but it never happens.

They shove me into the back of one of their police vehicles because apparently it takes four of them to arrest the American who plays baseball for the Los Angeles Angels.

By the time I get my first and only phone call to the States to Marla and Charlie, forty-eight hours have already passed; and everything I've worked for in baseball has already begun to implode.

And that's just the beginning.

CHAPTER THIRTY-NINE

Tally · Other side of the world

THE BAR IS DIMLY LIT AND feels a little austere and shop-worn. The neon sign denoting the establishment's name as *Promissory Note* seems a little behind the times much like its interior. The green velvet looks dated but all the liquor bottles sparkle indicating a recent feather dusting must have taken place. The sun's rays filter through and reach the mirror behind the bar and reflect a little of the outside world, effectively beckoning the nuance and eclectic upper echelon of San Francisco's Alamo Square to come on inside.

It's been a little over a week and a half since the attack, but I still move slowly with the aid of crutches, and attempt to cover up the rising turmoil of what appears to be almost chronic pain at my mid-section at this point. I sidle up to one of the bar stools and slide my ID over to the waiting bartender before he even asks. Pulling my coat a little tighter around my aching frame, I tilt my head to one side, so he won't have time to note the dark bruising on the right side of my face quite so much. The additional painkillers Sasha handed to me as an afterthought, just before I boarded the plane out of Moscow more than a week ago, have all but run out. It seemed to take forever to get back from Russia. It was a long fourteen-hour flight before I finally landed at San Francisco International airport, ten days ago. It only took a little time to find cheapest flight and book passage all the way back to the States; however, when you're not feeling well and your entire life in all kinds of ways, including body and soul, has been violated and effectively torn apart; well, it seems to take for-*fucking*-ever.

Sheer will and terror and Sasha's painkillers in equal, heavy doses—have kept me going. I slept through the last nine days and nights, surviving on sips of water from a cheap hotel glass located at my bedside and a box of Entenmann's cookies. Because when the shit goes down, Entenmann's can serve you in all kinds of ways, in my humble opinion. This is my first official day being up and about in San Francisco, instead of flat in bed, wishing all of me would die. Sasha's extra spending cash helped me get by. I've got enough money to lie low for a little while, before I re-surface in San Fran or New York and ultimately figure out what I'm going to do.

But first, I wanted to see Cara. I had to see Cara. My child. I had to achieve some kind of closure, experience some kind of knowable solace with Cara, especially in light of the all but debilitating news that I may not be able to have any more children. And so, there's the first problem I discovered just thirty minutes ago; Tremblay has moved out. Six months ago. Neighbors had no clue as the whereabouts of the newly-retired ballerina and her little girl. The people Tremblay leased her house to aren't talking other than to say that she moved, and they got a great deal, and the lease is paid through December. *And who knows after that? No one does, apparently.*

The bar, *Promissory Note,* is my last-ditch effort for information about Tremblay's true whereabouts. Right now, it's all I've got to go on. Tremblay used to talk about the *Promissory Note.* She used to order food-to-go from here all the time, usually after working late at the studio; she'd head here. She used to tell us little stories like that, every once in a while, probably out of pure loneliness. And these little bits and pieces of her private life that I somehow remember her telling us are about all that can help me now. I think, at one point, she may have been involved with the guy who works here. I think that guy is the one who studies my face right now as if he might know me. *The bartender.*

I get a little nervous under his scrutiny. My attempt at being nondescript is failing. Then he shrugs and slowly smiles, revealing even white teeth and an easy smile. But he's a guy and by that fact alone, I'm momentarily reminded of my Russian attacker from ten days before. Still, my newly perfected technique in taking in the air through clenched teeth seems to do the trick in warding off both pain and sudden nerves. It eventually calms me outwardly at least. Only the slightest tremble of my left hand reveals the inner turmoil of that horrible memory of Russia that I fear may become permanently branded in my psyche. If I could just have a few waking minutes of respite from remembering that horrible man's face, I'd take it.

Mr. Bartender doesn't seem to notice the hand tremor too much. I suppose I should thank God, but I don't.

"What will it be?" he asks.

Apparently, my downcast state deserves sympathy. I smile ever so slightly.

"Stoli straight up with a lemon twist."

"Hard core," he says with admiration. "Especially for eleven in the morning." He raises a quizzical eyebrow and studies me further.

"I'm still on Moscow time."

He seems to appreciate my casual answer and slides my ID back to me and inadvertently touches my outstretched hand on the bar. My fingers twitch, clearly betraying my distressed mental state, but I force myself to keep smiling. I need information from this guy and the only way I'm going to get it is to build his trust and bide my time with my questions.

"And how were the Russians?"

"Most of them were good to me."

He seems to appreciate my sarcasm. He laughs, pours the clear liquid in a highball glass, and then slides it over.

I think about my mother. Vodka. No smell, very little aftertaste. No wonder she stays with this regimen. My eyes start to sting. *Today, I miss my mother. My Dad. I need to call them. Soon.*

I swipe at my tears with the back of my right hand and feign an interest in the local San Francisco morning program playing on the television located at the far end of the bar in an attempt to ward off the ever-present pain that still tears through me. The bartender eventually moves off, and I make a point of biding my time by doing continual eight-counts in my head and attempting to avoid any kind of deep thought beyond the general, all but persistent focus upon breathing.

It's a long twenty minutes. After performing the subtle circus act of swallowing half a painkiller and drinking down most of the Stoli, my nerves are anesthetized enough to ask him a few direct questions. I'm intent and focused on getting the information that I came for. I signal the bartender's way for another and mentally compose my carefully crafted questions in my head, while he casually pours me a fresh round and continues to study me rather intently.

"I'm looking for someone. She used to live close by. Allaire Tremblay. Do you know her?" I slide over my iPhone, which displays one of the only pictures I could find of her from a few years ago and watch for his initial reaction. He's stoic while he glances through the pictures on my phone. Then he casually studies the pile of letters and photos I slide over his way to look at as well, while I watch him quietly shudder and take a deep breath. *He knows her.*

The letters and photos stopped four months ago. I counted fourteen of them in all on the flight from Moscow. They'd stopped this summer. Four months after our subsequent visit and Marla's wedding.

Did I pay any attention? *No.*

Did I worry? *No.*

Did I realize the power had somehow shifted back to Allaire Tremblay? *No.*

Not until this very day.

Photos. Every one of them was of San Francisco. Every photograph was of Cara sitting on the front step of Allaire's Victorian house at various seasons. There was one photograph of the *Promissory Note,* where little Cara sat at the little café table out front dangling her feet from the high chair. *Summer. The last one.*

It had to mean something. It had to.

"Allaire? Sure. Nice lady. She left about six months ago with the baby and moved out of the city. She said she wanted something different, what with the kid." His glance shifts away, so does his tense. Why?" He gets this guarded look, and then it morphs into disenchantment.

Apparently, he couldn't live up to Allaire's expectations either.

"Well, we lost touch after I went to Moscow. She was my dance teacher, actually, from years ago. She always talked about the food here, and I've never been here before." I make a point of looking around and sweeping my arm around in appreciation of the bar.

Mr. Bartender grins wide, while I do my best to control the tremor in my hand. *Nerves. Pain. It all bursts forth.*

"No, you haven't. I would have remembered you."

He slides the new glass over to me. There's a generous amount of Stoli in there now. I'm not sure how I'm going to get all that down. I'm already feeling the effects from the first round. I haven't eaten anything but Entenmann's cookies in the last ten long days. My stomach growls as if on cue.

"I didn't realize she had a baby." I make my voice casual and force a tight little smile.

"Yeah, a little girl. *Cara.* She named her Cara. She's really cute. A real good baby. Not much of a baby anymore. She'll be three at the end of January, and she's walking everywhere and talking up a storm."

"Cara." I sigh a little in just saying her name but attempt to stay focused on wringing out whatever information I can get from this guy. "Oakland, huh? So she found a job right away, I take it?"

"I didn't say Oakland." He gets this bemused look. "I don't know. You know how it is." He shrugs his wide shoulders. "You think you have it all worked out and then life happens, and nothing works out like it's supposed to."

He seems in need of my approval, so I nod slowly—because it hurts too much to do more than that—and he is so right about everything he's just said.

"She wanted a life out of the city with her little girl. Something more… permanent." He gets this grim face. "That's as much as I know."

So she left him, too.

Defeat settles in. I'm not going to find her. Allaire Tremblay has outsmarted me at every turn. *I got played.*

He turns back to stack of wet glasses he's been drying since I walked in a half-hour ago. I turn my attention to the television in an attempt to keep it together and to figure out my next move and absently wipe at the tears that manage to steal their way down my face occasionally. *I've lost everything. Everyone.*

Anxious for a different answer, I flip through the stack of photos again looking for any clue, any sign. He comes back over and takes the *Promissory Note* photograph from the pile and reads what Allaire's written across the back aloud:

> *Doubt thou the stars are fire;*
> *Doubt that the sun doth move;*
> *Doubt truth to be a liar;*
> *But never doubt I love.*
> *~ William Shakespeare*

"She said you'd come by one day." I watch him reach under the bar and pull out an ivory-colored, letter-sized envelope. Allaire's handwriting is recognizable on the front, even as he holds it away from me, like I need to pass some kind of test first.

"What's your name?"

"Tally. Or the more formal name is actually Talia Landon. Stage name is Talia Delacourt. One of those."

"You're Talia?" he asks, looking a little surprised.

I nod.

"Sam." He extends his hand and I shake it. "Sam Wilde."

He slides the envelope over to me. I slowly open it by sliding a fingernail beneath the flap.

My hands begin to shake because I can only guess as to why Tremblay has decided to fuck with me this way. There's a folded piece of paper inside that matches the fine linen envelope it came in. *Allaire Tremblay* is engraved in gold-embossed script across the top. Now, I'm really afraid. The air in my lungs whooshes away, even before I completely get through reading what she's written.

Talia,

She's happy and doing fine. We both are. The thing is I don't owe you anymore. You've made it. Cara's happy and that's all that matters to me. So, please consider us paid in full.

Allaire

"What's a…promissory note?" My voice trembles more in enunciating every word. "What's…it for, exactly?"

The bartender studies me for a long moment and sighs heavily. "It's like an IOU. It's an old-fashioned concept. It's a note that a debtor keeps until something is paid off. A debt is paid. Why? What did she say?" I hand him the note and begin to shake uncontrollably. "You're Cara's mom?" he asks, incredulous.

All I can do is nod.

The tears come fast now. I can't stop them.

It takes me a while to even begin to get it together. The lunch crowd starts rolling in. I'm still sitting at the bar attempting to compose myself enough so I can leave. Even Sam is in the act. He holds on to another letter-sized envelope with his right hand, and pats mine with the other. Sam is trying to help me get it together so I can actually leave his establishment and basically go back to my hotel and lie on the bed and sleep into forever; because now I really have lost everything. *Everyone.*

Weary. Undone. The noontime news demands my attention all at once because I'm staring at Lincoln Presley's face up on the television screen.

"Turn it up!" I call to Sam.

The news anchor's voice gets louder as Sam turns up the volume. "It's been almost two weeks, since the arrest of all-star baseball pitcher, Lincoln Presley, who has been accused of murder, while he was in Moscow for the Los Angeles Angels exhibition game. According to the Moscow Police, Lincoln Presley is the primary suspect in the mysterious death of Nikolai Balanchine, a vagrant, who was suspected of brutally assaulting Talia Delacourt, a principal ballerina with the New York City Ballet's international tour. Delacourt had been staying in Moscow, Russia, as part of her reprisal of her lead starring role as the *Lilac Fairy* in *Sleeping Beauty* the very role that led to the young ballerina's spectacular rise to fame two years ago. Balanchine later died from his injuries sustained sometime during the attack of Delacourt. The young ballerina star disappeared from a local Moscow hospital and appears to have left Russia without corroborating Presley's story in which the famous baseball player claims to have only assisted the dancer after the brutal attack and, according to his statement, that he never touched Balanchine. According to the Moscow Police, Delacourt did not provide a statement as to what transpired with Balanchine and Lincoln Presley remains their primary suspect in Balanchine's death. The FBI has requested that anyone with knowledge of Talia Delacourt's whereabouts contact the department in relation to the Moscow Police's ongoing investigation into this crime. Sources in Moscow tell us that Lincoln Presley will face a murder charge in connection with the death of Nikolai Balanchine within the next few days. We'll have more on this breaking news story and the fate of the accused baseball star at our six o'clock evening news."

They go to commercial as if nothing matters more than choosing your car insurance premium. Thankfully, Sam turns the volume down.

He looks at me sympathetically for a moment or two while I seek out another painkiller and wash it down with the last of the Stoli.

This can't be happening. If I say it often enough will it become true? That this can't be happening? My mind fractures on one pervasive thought: Oh, but it is.

I close my eyes and only open them again when Sam touches my hand. I barely stop myself from screaming at his unexpected touch.

"That's you," he says in a low voice.

"Yes."

"Who do you want to call?" Sam asks.

"I don't know." My head throbs. I put my face in my hand and try to think.

"They said the FBI." He grimaces and shakes his head. "Not yet," he says mysteriously.

I look up at Sam and eventually nod. "No FBI. Not yet." I sound bleak and I don't attempt to hide it from him now. My cell starts ringing. I can hardly answer it fast enough. My movements have become sluggish within the last five minutes. "No more Stoli. Marla," I say dully. "What happened?"

In the minutes that follow, I let Marla do all the talking, while I solely focus on breathing in and out and attempting to control the pain that thunders through me like a relentless wave. I sip from the glass of water Sam slides my way, and with shaking hands, I take a few more painkillers.

I'm gonna run out. I'm gonna run out. Does it matter if I run out? Does it matter?

Marla's talking and I'm trying to keep up with what all she's saying. I gather that she and Charlie will be here as soon as they can. "Kimberley is already in Moscow. So is his lawyer. We're catching a flight in the next two hours. Do you have any clothes?"

Do I have any clothes? Why are we talking about my clothes?

"No. Not with me. Just what I'm wearing."

"Let me guess. Black T-shirt and jeans," Marla says sweetly, but I can't do more than sigh. "Okay. I'll bring you some. I have a suitcase already packed."

"Can you call my mom and dad?"

"I've called them." She hesitates. I want to ask her why, but the meds and the Stoli are working against me now. It's hard enough already to actually follow what all she's saying to me and forming words fast enough in response proves to be next to impossible. I close my eyes again in an attempt to focus on listening alone but that just makes me dizzy.

"Tally, are you okay?

"No." I laugh a little because it's weird to say the truth out loud. I conclude that the Stoli and the meds are finally working. "Is he okay?"

"I don't know," Marla says with a catch in her voice. "He called us once, a little over a week ago, but he warned us that they probably won't let him call us again. Kimberley thinks he's okay."

"She's great, isn't she?"

"Well yeah," Marla says, sounding confused by my question. "Geez, Tally. We've been so worried about Linc and *you* and what happened. My God. No one knew where you were. Not even Rob."

"Rob wouldn't know," I whisper. "Don't worry. I'm fine. *Really.*" I stop and take in air. "I'm fine. But Tremblay…took Cara." The tears start again. "She's gone, Marla. Cara's gone. But then, everyone's gone."

"Put the bartender on the phone."

"Sam. His name is Sam," I lecture even as I hand Sam my iPhone.

Sam stares at me the whole time he's talking to Marla. "Yeah. Okay. She's a little out of it. About the kid. *This.* She just saw the news. Got it. I'll keep her here."

Sam hands me the cell phone back without a word and gives me this steely *I've-got-this* look. I just nod at him, but eventually I break his intense gaze because I just don't know what to say nor am I able to explain how this last hour became worse than previous two. It's just too hard to actually fathom. I make a point of digging into my bag to pay him for the drinks. I lay down two twenties and a five. "The debt's paid, Sam," I say slowly.

He pushes the money back at me. "You're going to need it. Your friend." He points to the iPhone, reminding me to pick it up. I vaguely hear Marla calling my name. "She's coming for you."

He slides over the thick envelope he's been holding and looks at me intently. I open it with this sick sense of dread. It's stuffed with cash.

"It's from Tremblay."

The consolation in Sam's voice almost makes me start to cry again.

"A payoff for Cara." My head hurts worse in just saying this truth out loud.

Marla keeps talking, but I can't really register what she's saying. He nods.

"There's a hundred grand in there." He leans down against the bar and intently gazes at me. "You're going to need it to help out your friend—the baseball player. You're going to need *all of it*, Tally. Russia isn't a place to mess around in." I wince at his words, having learned this lesson already. "Take it. Tell your friend that you have it because you're going to need it."

"How do you know?"

"I haven't always been a bartender."

My hands shake as I pick up the iPhone again. "Marla? I've settled up the bill with Sam. Tremblay left me…cash." I struggle on the last word and irritably swipe at the fresh tears rolling down my face. *I'm going to be sick.* I struggle to fight off the waves of nausea that swirl through me. "When will you be here?" *Just breathe.* "I could just go to the hotel and pack up my stuff. Change."

"No. No. No. Don't do that. Stay put, Tally. We'll be there in fifteen minutes."

"Where's Elliott?"

"Gina's got him. We're good. He'll be fine."

"I should have been there," I whisper. Now I'm sad because all at once it really bothers me that I missed out on Elliott's birth. Elliott Lincoln Masterson. Six pounds eleven ounces. He was born August 7th right on time; and I missed it, like so many things. "She left me cash for…Cara." I can't help the mournful tone.

"Tally, hang in there," Marla says. "We'll find Cara; but right now we have to concentrate on Linc and on getting to Moscow. Now, eat some food. We'll be there soon. Hang up the phone. Kimberley might try to call you."

"Okay."

Sam brings me a hamburger and tells me to eat the whole thing. He sets down a glass of water as well as a glass of milk and tells me to drink them both.

I decide there's no point in going through the calorie count discussion with him because I can tell he's prepared to win that one. I'm sure he had that same discussion many times with Allaire Tremblay. How I end up within just a few hours knowing so much about this guy is not something I can fully explain.

"Can you at least call Allaire, please?" I swallow hard, pleading with Sam. "And tell her that I *know*."

Sam hangs his head and sighs deep.

He glances up at me and looks angry for a moment, but then it's gone. "She didn't tell me where she was going. She just left. She said good-bye and

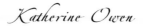

gave me that note for you and the envelope of cash because she knew I'd take care of it. And she just…*left*."

I stare at him for a long while. My head starts to pound even more. Finally, I say, "It's sad, isn't it?"

"What's sad?"

"To lose everything, everyone. To lose the people you care about the most. I mean death is so permanent, and that's one way to lose them. But this?" My voice wavers. "When they just leave you and cut you out of their lives so completely…it ends up being almost the same thing, doesn't it?"

He looks at me for a long time before nodding. "I'm sorry for what that guy did to you."

"Which one?" I grimace and slowly shake my head side-to-side. "It's not half as bad as what I've done to everyone else—Linc, Cara, Marla, Rob, my parents." My voice shakes as I rattle off their names. "The list is so long, Sam."

I can't wait any longer for Kimberley to call, so I just start dialing.

Atonement begins with the first call. He picks up within two rings.

"I'm in trouble," I say to Rob. By the time I've finished telling him what's happened, Rob's on his way to JFK. Knowing Rob, he'll be in Russian airspace long before we hit the tarmac in Moscow.

Marla and Charlie arrive just as I end the call with Rob. After a hurried good-bye to my newfound friend Sam, they help me from each side and get me to their car. For once, I don't bitch at Charlie for driving too fast. I really don't care anymore.

For some reason, I can't feel any of it—fear, sadness, remorse. It's all gone from me now. I think if I allow myself to feel any of these emotions, I might fall down that abyss forever. And I'm burning up—inside and out—and just thinking about the fact that I'm returning to Moscow fills me with all kinds of newfound terror.

CHAPTER FORTY

Linc ~ Either way

HIS ISN'T THE UNITED STATES OF AMERICA. I learn that pretty quickly—within the first few hours of spending time at the Moscow Police station. Russia seems to be still learning the ins and outs of due process and justice. They read me my rights, take my picture and fingerprints, and put me into a jail cell, and then seemed to have lost the key. Two days and nights pass before they let me make a single phone call.

No one talks to me, and they all speak Russian and the one connection to the detective I may have had is permanently severed. Apparently, his pleading my cause, in deference to the others, was construed as being out of line; and he's been taken off the case. One of the other inmates in the cell next door passed me a note explaining in broken English that the note was from the detective himself. '*Sorry*' was all it had said. The guy in the cell next to me is apparently the sole connection I have to the outside world. And that's how it works, here in Moscow.

During those first forty-eight hours, I decide the best call to make would be to Charlie and Marla because surely Tally's best friend could track her down and this whole thing would just go away. Of course, by the time I got those two on the phone everything had started sliding down into this bottomless hellhole that is now my life.

According to Charlie, my coaches were calling; the Angels owner was calling; my father was calling. Charlie told me that Kimberley was doing her best to calm them all down and had already all but enlisted help from the National Guard to get me out of here; however, so far, no one has found Tally, and I'm still sitting here—accused, suspected of murder—in a Russian jail cell in Moscow.

"It doesn't look good," Charlie had said.

"How bad is it?"

"It's all over the news, both locally and nationally. You're the lead story on pretty much every sports page and news broadcast nationwide. Kimberley's handling all of that, and she told me to tell you, just in case you called me first. Your dad's flying in from L.A. this afternoon. We thought it might be best to congregate here in Palo Alto because that's where Marla thinks Tally will show up."

"You haven't found her?" I'd sunk down to the floor and covered my eyes with my forearm. "Shit."

Nine days in, I don't even notice the filth on the floor or complain about the cold and the damp anymore. This place reminds of a cave without fresh water or sunlight or oxygen. And I've begun to wonder just how long I'll actually be able to survive here. After strip-searching me on the third day, they finally let me take a shower under the watchful eyes of some prison guard. Now, I'm wearing this blue jumpsuit that I think they must wash in the harshest detergent possible because I itch everywhere. Dignity flows out of me like a stab wound to my heart that won't stop. Meanwhile, humiliation takes its rightful place and burrows deep inside of me with every breath I manage to take in this place. Just yesterday, they changed tactics and decided to spend the entire day interrogating me all over again. I've begun to wonder if maybe I didn't kill the guy because I said, "No, I didn't do it," so many times that even I am looking for a different answer.

My cellmate next door whistles through his teeth. That's his signal that he's got something for me. So far, these prizes have been the detective's *sorry* note, a razor, an extra slice of bread, and a bottled water. I don't even ask where he gets this stuff because, once he found out I was 'de baseball player', he's done his best to help me out. Again, he whistles and; like Pavlov's dog, I stick my hand through the bars and wait for his next *gift* to drop into my outstretched hand. It's a cell phone. *Holy shit.*

"Thanks, comrade." That's what they say here.

There's a call on hold. I activate the button.

"Hey, Prez." My gut actually clenches at hearing Kimberley's voice.

"Hey," I manage to say without totally breaking down.

I move toward the back of the cell so no one can hear me. As agreed to days ago now, the guy in the next cell will keep watch and whistle when the guard gets close. *This is my life. This is what I do. This is how I survive right now from one moment to the next now.* "How much did this cost you?"

"Oh God, baby, let's just say you're going to need a bigger contract, pronto; or you'll have to start investing heavily on Wall Street when you get back."

I appreciate that she tries to make light of it. Some part of me deep inside must see this faint glimmer of hope; enough so that I actually take a breath and successfully pull myself together for the next couple of minutes. It's been almost ten days. I was beginning to wonder if I was stuck in the place for all eternity. Just holding a cell phone makes me feel somewhat encouraged and normal again. "You found her," I say with a deep, grateful sigh.

"No." She pauses and allows that to sink in.

"Christ, Kimberley, what the fuck do I pay you for? My God, I'm barely hanging in here. Come on, dude, help me out here. They interrogated the shit out of me yesterday; and I felt like I needed to admit to *something* just to get them to stop."

"You didn't, did you?"

"No. Not yet," I snipe. *God damn. I've turned into a complete jerk in as little as nine days. Nine fucking days is all it took to change me from a nice guy throwing a baseball to talking like a regular gangbanger.*

"Okay. Calm down. Listen to me. Okay. *Listen.* Take a breath." Kimberley seems to take one for both of us. "Linc, hang in there. I know it's tough. I am doing everything I can. *This will not stand.* We'll find her. Now I need you to listen. Take a deep breath and listen. You've got to keep your shit together. *You're all you've got.* I'm *here,* and I'm badgering the shit out of them and throwing a lot of money around to get you a cell phone like this, so I can talk to you; but they're playing—pardon the pun—*hardball.*"

"Shit."

"I know."

"Well, what about Nika? She's Russian. She's got her family here. They're affluent. Maybe they can help."

She sighs in notable irritation and quietly says, "Nika bailed. She said you were too hot, and she needed to get out of Moscow before they started poking around into her own affairs. Literally, figuratively. Who the hell knows?"

"Wow." I inhale deep of the stale air, while my mind tries to take in this staggering bit of news. "She *left* me?"

"Come on, Prez. You *knew that* was coming."

"No. No. Not really," I say with a grimace. My eyes sting. I rub at them hard. Then they're more irritated by the God damn soap that I'm forced to use in this place. I suppose I should be happy that they even have soap.

"She was bad news," Kimberley says.

"What about the baby?"

"I don't think there ever *was* a baby. I told you that from the very beginning. And yet, there you were all giddy to marry her. It's my fault for encouraging you to take up with her in the first place, and I'm—"

"The whole Mea Culpa thing isn't helping me very much. Shut the hell up," I say gently.

She laughs for both of us and then sighs. "I got the FBI involved. National treasure, great guy, baseball star, and hero all rolled into one; just know that's all working for you. Just hang in there. I don't want you to worry because we're going to fix this. I promise. And then, we're going to do the biggest press conference mankind has ever seen, and you're going to soar out of here like a rocket into space proudly displaying the American flag along with apple pie in one hand and a baseball in the other."

"I just want to go home. Just sit in some bar in L.A. somewhere and allow you to freely buy me a beer conveniently located near the stadium of the Los Angeles Angels of good ol' Anaheim. I even *miss* L.A.; soon, we'll be able to laugh this whole thing off like it never even happened."

She's silent.

"Kimberley?" I ask with rising fear.

"Let's just get the hell out of Moscow, okay?" She all but chokes on the last word. "I truly believe this will be over, one way or the other, in the next forty-eight hours."

It's ominous the way she says this.

"What do you *know?*" My heart thunders away in my chest. She doesn't sound right. That flippant, fuck-off tone of hers is sorely missing.

"They're going to transfer you to a Russian federal prison until a trial date is set. In two days. That's going to make a cell phone call impossible. And so far? They won't let me in to see you since I'm not a lawyer, and they won't let *him* in, either. Sleeping with someone and even larger amounts of cash may be involved."

"Do what you have to do," I say, attempting levity because the truth she speaks of is too hard to actually fathom. She doesn't laugh. Neither do I. "What are you saying? What are you *really* saying?" I ask.

"They think you did it. If they can't find Tally, they're charging you with the guy's murder."

"I didn't kill him. I didn't touch him. She acted in self-defense; I'm sure of it. I didn't—"

"Listen to me, Linc! None of that matters, okay? These guys aren't looking for the truth. They just need to solve the case, one way or the other; however they see fit. And just know that what's gone on so far is preliminary shit, Linc. It's going to get a whole lot worse, and I need deeper funding to even make a dent into stopping it from happening to you. We're trying to track down Rob Thorn. He's got access to the ready kind of cash; we may need to extricate you from this situation."

I groan at the fucked-up circumstances and just the idea of needing help from Rob Thorn, of all people. "Find Tally," I say bleakly.

"Yeah, working on it. Look, don't freak out on me just yet. Give me two more days."

"Sounds like that's about all I have."

"I'll call you in another twelve hours with more. *Twelve hours*, Linc. Time it. Be ready." Kimberley ends the call, while I dully note the time on the cell phone. I manage to put it on silent, cajole myself to just wait for her call, which will be at exactly four in the morning Moscow time.

Then I attempt to stop my body's uncontrollable shaking and shut my mind off all together; because the truth is I'm falling apart in a way I thought would never happen to me.

Two hours go by.

Finally, I formulate and say a little prayer to God, and since we haven't officially spoken since my mom and Elliott died that takes up quite a bit of my time.

The rest of it I spend on trying to determine what I think love really is and what I actually feel for Tally Landon at this point. Upon deep reflection, I realize that I must be at the edge of life's abyss. This is me. All there is left of me; and yet, I'm looking over and contemplating its meaning on whether to jump or stay. I'm not sure this feeling for Tally Landon is made up of love any more than it is of hate. This must be a kind of purgatory—the in-between place—because these pervasive feelings of rage and passion for Tally are equalized and actually co-mingle together—like fire and water—each ready to extinguish the other. I've come to accept the truth. There may be nothing left for us. It could go either way.

CHAPTER FORTY-ONE

Linc ~The lies we've told

ALMOST TWELVE HOURS LATER AFTER KIMBERLEY'S first phone call, I continue to stare at the ceiling patterns and the shadows being made by this four-by-six-inch window at the top of the wall. This little window serves as the only light source and not much else. It's small enough to put your hand though, but no other part would fit; and yet, I've begun to wonder how many poor souls have tried to escape through that small space just to have the chance to break out of here. To be free.

For the first time in my life, I have an acute understanding of what truly makes a man desperate.

I ate my ration of cold food—bread and potatoes—and drank questionable drinking water, hours ago. It's still quiet. The Moscow jail sleeps, somewhat, at what I discern is nighttime. A half moon shines through that little window and tells me so. It's 3:58 a.m., Moscow time, according to the cell phone. If Kimberley's true to her word, that phone should go off in two minutes. I close my eyes for a brief moment and calculate that the guard came by less than a half-hour ago, and that gives me twenty minutes before I have to start worrying about his next security round. This whole situation is crazy on so many levels that I cannot reconcile it in my mind anymore. *It is what it is. This is all that is left.*

The cell phone flashes at me on silent ring. I sit up straighter and take the call. "Tally's here," Kimberley says without preamble. "We talked briefly with her and Rob on the ride from the airport. Then they met up with her right away in the lobby, and I overheard one of the detectives say something about *interrogating* her." Kimberley voice breaks down at the last part.

"What do you mean they're *interrogating* her? She's just supposed to give a statement."

"That's not what they said." Kimberley sounds scared. "I've got to go. I'll call if I learn more."

"Kimberley?"

She doesn't answer. She's already gone.

I get a reprieve of a mere sixty seconds before the whistling in the next cell starts up. I manage to slip the cell phone in my right hip pocket just before the guard shines a flashlight in my face.

"Presley. Get up. You get to *watch*," the guard says. His English is so broken; it's as if he's practiced it just long enough to scare the hell out of me with the harsh way he's said it.

People snarl and growl in the movies. But here? At the Moscow jail? That's what they do in real life practically every minute of every day.

I'm taken into a room with a two-way mirror that seems to take up one whole wall. In the next room, I see Tally. She sits stiffly in a chair at a weird angle and leans to her right more than her left. Her hair's messed up, and it hangs in wisps around her pale, withdrawn face. There's a thin film of sweat along the top of her forehead as if she has a fever. Even from twenty feet away I can tell that her eyes are bloodshot. She looks like she hasn't slept in days. She's drawn her arm across her left side as if she's in pain. The guard with me smirks as he brazenly gazes over at Tally through the two-way mirror into the next room.

"A nice piece of…how you say? A nice piece of *ass*." He gestures towards Tally. "No?" he asks.

I ignore him, and for doing so, he pushes me down hard into the wooden chair staged next to the window. "Watch," he says in my ear and then steps away from me and starts to laugh. It's a Russian chortle of sorts.

I still attempt to ignore him and remind myself that I'm at least four inches taller than him, even though he has a weapon secured at his belt that he strokes with his right hand every so often. *An intimidating tactic? Most likely. Is it working? A little.*

I'm a baseball player. My day-to-day worries consist of achieving the best stats and the most strikeouts and accruing more wins than losses in baseball and not getting hit by a wayward ball that sometimes flies out toward the pitcher's mound and, invariably, my face. Hell, I do commercial ads for Calvin Klein Underwear in the off-season. I don't shoot people. And they don't shoot me.

I can outrun him. Sure. But can I overtake him? Him and his firearm? Not likely.

Get it together. *Breathe.*

This will all soon be over.

Four Russian guys dressed in a variety of dark suits—ranging from almost charcoal black to pale grey—come into the room and stare at Tally without saying anything to her. All four pairs of eyes convey little sympathy for her. After a few more minutes of complete silence, it dawns on me that none of them must speak English. They must be waiting for someone who does.

The door opens, and the single token female officer enters the room. She stands to one side, as if she will have nothing to do with meeting, but then opens her mouth and speaks in near-perfect English. She is all business, not a time-waster, this one. I flinch at her harsh tone, which cracks like a whip into the silent room. Even Tally seems to startle awake from her stupor. I don't think Tally had yet experienced the gravity of the situation until that very moment when the Russian female cop started talking to her. Tally's mouth is half-open as the woman with dark spiky hair starts to speak to her. This Russian cop is angular and edgy and in motion all the time. I'm reminded of Nika. Nika angry. Nika vindictive. This woman seems to be the same way. I inwardly cringe for Tally.

For her part, Tally seems to have trouble tracking what the woman is saying to her. I watch Tally visibly shudder and take a deep breath and seemingly hold onto it. She closes her eyes for a few seconds as if to steady herself and seek out some kind of balance. The female cop grabs Tally by the chin and yells at her to keep her eyes open and listen. The other cops appear surprised by the woman's unexpected viciousness toward Tally. They shift uncomfortably from their various stoic positions around the room in concerted effort.

I get up from my chair and go toward the window that separates us as if I can somehow get to her. My guard forcibly guides me back to the chair away from the window and Tally.

Meanwhile, this lady cop is all over the place. Tally just stares at her after the woman successfully fires off questions in quick succession not really even waiting for her to answer.

"For the record, what's your name? Age? Where do you live? What business do you have in Moscow? Who's your employer? Why do you think you are here?"

Talia Delacourt. Twenty-one. New York City. I dance for the New York City Ballet Company which is what brought me to Moscow. I'm here to tell you what happened on the afternoon of November 2nd, twelve days ago."

"Talia Delacourt." The woman detective breathes each word. "You're not married to Lincoln Presley then?"

Tally bides her time before answering, processing what must be transpiring. I hold my breath and will her to say *yes*. We have to stick together on the lies. I rack my brain in those ten seconds trying to remember if I told her that

I'd told the hospital staff we were married so she could have the surgery. The guard next to me leans in and studies my face. I try not to flinch at his uninvited scrutiny while at the same time I will Tally to answer.

"Yes, we're married. Lincoln Presley is my husband. We...we keep it a secret because...of our careers."

I take in air slowly at an undetectable rate.

"Lincoln Presley is your husband?" The woman looks incredulous.

"Yes. We're married. Going on three years."

"And you have proof of this?"

"In America. Where we *live*. Yes. Our marriage certificate is in a locked safe back home." Tally gets this little practiced smile. A star's smile.

The Russian woman virtually growls at her. "I want to see those papers."

"Okay. It's a simple phone call. My lawyer can get them for you. I just want to see my husband *now* and ensure he's okay. I want to speak to him *now*."

"Later, comrade." The lady cop abruptly steps back from her and seems to be reassessing the entire situation for a few moments. She gets this vexed look.

Tally looks at her in defiance easily conveying that she won't fall easily. I try not to smile because if this wasn't so fucking real, it would be fascinating entertainment. My anger at Tally seeps away from me all together and; in its rightful place, the love for her surges. I hang my head, ashamed at having ever doubted her.

"I want to see my husband. He had a game with the Angels here in Moscow last week. I missed it. I want to see him. *Now*."

"Later," the woman says. She eyes Tally intently. "Why don't you go through the details of what happened to you the afternoon of November 2nd."

"We, the dance company, for the most part, had a luncheon at Cafe Khachapuri. I left early and decided to walk back to the hotel."

"Why?"

"Linc had baseball practice and I thought a walk would do me some good. I dance all the time. I've hardly seen Moscow at all and hardly spent any quality time with my husband." She carefully slides her chair back from the table and gives the group a cursory look as she gets up slowly, grabs her crutches, and painfully begins to pace the floor. She glances over at the female cop and gets this sad smile. "We were staying at The Savoy under my stage name *Delacourt,* so we could have some much-needed privacy."

Tally smiles wider and inadvertently glances over at the mirror. I hold my breath. She does the same and gets this little crevice between her brow lines and stares harder at the mirror, essentially figuring out it must be two-way.

"Your story, comrade," the lady cop prompts.

"Yes." Tally sighs, wets her lips, and takes a deep breath. "It was early afternoon. I had the next couple of days off, and I thought I'd get some air. I knew Linc was on his way back to the hotel, after a meeting with the team and an early practice, and I just wanted to enjoy a part of Moscow, for once, even if I was on my own."

"Not a wise choice. That neighborhood."

"Yes, well, I didn't know that at the time. It only dawned on me later after I passed that guy that perhaps I should have thought it through better."

"That guy?"

"The guy who attacked me."

"How did you meet?"

"I didn't *meet* him. I passed him along the street after I'd been walking about fifteen minutes when I'd just begun to realize that walking alone wasn't such a good idea. I passed him. He was going the other way. I heard the crunching of his boots along the snow, and I remember thinking, I need to get out of here. About that time, I noticed that the crunching sound from his shoes was getting closer instead of farther away from me. I didn't have any real time to react. He grabbed me by the arms and roughly pulled me into an alley off to my right and pushed me hard up against a stone wall." She stops pacing and subtly grips her side with her right arm. "He hit me so hard that the side of my face slammed against the wall, and I almost blacked out. I'd already started telling myself that I needed to stay conscious if I hoped to survive. Then he brought out the knife and held it to my throat."

"So you felt threatened?" The woman detective gets this disbelieving look and shakes her head.

Tally snorts in answer and her green eyes flash. "He pushed me up against the wall of this alcove and smashed my head into the wall. I almost blacked out from the force of it, and then he whipped out a long knife and held it against my throat. So *yes*, I felt threatened, and that's when I knew I was in serious trouble."

One of the police detectives pours Tally a glass of water. I think that's when the room begins to shift in her favor, except for the Russian female cop asking all the questions. That woman never wavers. She just stands there and fires relentless questions at Tally.

For her part, Tally seems to take note of that, stopping her painful-looking back and forth pacing with the crutches long enough to take a sip of the water being offered. She vaguely smiles all around at them but no one smiles back at her. That's when I realize that she's testing them. She's testing to determine who is sympathetic and who is not. Eventually, she sits back down in the vacant chair designated for her and wipes at her forehead with the back of her arm.

She's so much braver than I've been. All of this has been made perfectly clear to me in the past thirty minutes since the whole interrogation started. I hold my breath just watching this unfold, feeling helpless and ashamed at having ever doubted Tally or thinking I hated her on any level. I begin to shake at my very core, as I listen to Tally listlessly recite and relive the horrible scene from two weeks before. She tells it to them like it's some bad bedtime story, she just happens to know the ending to. Remorse fills me up because of the doubt I experienced earlier about questioning my love of this girl. I run my hands through my hair in growing apprehension as I begin to grasp that what I've been going through is nothing compared to what Tally's been put through.

I'm a jerk.

We're back to that.

I don't even deserve her.

"So, he has a knife to your throat. What did you do?"

"I tried not to panic. I felt woozy, outside of myself. My head hurt like hell. I knew I only had so much time. He unzipped his pants and he took the knife and cut down the center of my clothes—my coat, my blouse, my skirt. It all started to fall away. We ended up on the ground. He was pushing his way inside." She stops talking and then suddenly gasps at the air, pushing her chair back with such force that when she suddenly comes to a stand both the chair and her crutches clatter with a loud crash to the cement floor. "He tried to rape me," she says dully. I watch her as she slowly makes her way to the mirror. It's as if she's staring right at me. "That's when it dawned on me that I'd seen his face. He was going to rape me. He was going to kill me. He called me Talia Delacourt. He knew I was a dancer. He *knew* who I was."

"What?"

She turns to them. "I'd dealt with an obsessed fan last month just after we got here. There'd been a break-in in my hotel room here in Moscow, and before in Rome. The guy knew who I was. That's why…" Tally gets this stunned look. "That's why he stabbed me in the side and in the top of my foot. He *knew* I was a dancer. He was going to rape me and then kill me or at least take away my livelihood and ensure I would never dance again." She turns back to the mirror and to me. "I'm sorry," she says with an imperceptible shake of her head. "Thank you, Elvis," she whispers this like a prayer.

I'm up at the window begging her to forgive me, for doubting her, even as she turns away. But then, the guard puts handcuffs on me in the next. He warns me to shut up and slams me down so hard into the chair again that when my head slams against the back of it, the wood splinters.

Tally moans only once and then she's fiercely pacing the length of the room as if a renewable-energy source has just surged through her body unexpectedly. "He tried to rape me," she says more fiercely. "He was going to kill me but then the knife clattered onto the ground, and I grabbed for it and he wrestled it from me and stabbed me in my side a second time. That's when I started thinking about what exactly I could live with." Her eyes narrow and she looks hard at the lady cop, who eventually has to break her gaze from Tally's. "Even as he drew it out of me and held it to my neck again and I saw all my blood pooling on the stone walkway, I kept thinking: *What can I live with?* Somehow, I wrestled him for the knife, and I stabbed him. He stopped long enough that I was able to push my way out from underneath him. I started to run from him, but he grabbed my ankle and twisted it hard and then stabbed the knife into the top of my foot. And that's when I got really pissed off because now he was just being cruel. I need my feet to dance. I remember turning around and kicking at him with my good foot, but he managed to get up and come after me, and he grabbed my arms again."

She stops for a long moment seemingly caught up in the horror and reliving it all over again. New sweat forms along her hairline. She brushes at it with the back of her hand and begins to make these little gasping sounds as if it's an all but futile search for air of any kind, even as her breath gets shallower. She edges her way so slowly across the floor it's as if she's moving on sheer will, alone. She grabs her midsection and clutches a single crutch with the other, as if she has to physically hold herself together, with this singular effort.

On some existential level, I feel like I'm the one holding her up—by some intrepid force, imagined or otherwise—from the other side of the glass if only because of our intrinsic connection. *And it may not be enough. Panic surges.*

"I pushed him away and he fell. He didn't get back up. I noticed Rebar sticking out of him at a weird angle, and he got this glazed look. I grabbed the stone wall for support and made my way out into the middle of the street. I stopped the first car I saw. A taxi. Miraculously, it was my husband Linc and the taxi driver. They saved my life by taking me to the hospital before I bled to death."

"The taxi driver says Lincoln Presley *your husband* went into the alley."

"He didn't." She vehemently shakes her head side-to-side. "He went to edge of it, but he never went in. He got a look at the guy's face from twenty feet away, but he never left my side because I begged him not to."

"You're lying. You weigh all of a hundred pounds," the Russian woman scoffs. "How could you have pushed a man of that size to the ground?"

"You want to try that theory out?" Tally asks.

She leans the crutches against the table stands firm on her good foot with her hands on her hips now, although I see her secretly flinch with pain. The Russian woman walks over and digs her nails into Tally's forearms. Within two seconds, the woman's on the ground and hits her head hard on the cement floor.

"Anyone else?" Tally asks, rubbing her hands together.

Tally's eyes turn the fierce jade-green again as she stares them down. One of the guys shuffles over, while the woman detective gets up and angrily dusts herself off. He approaches Tally from the front and grabs at her left arm; but within seconds he, too, is on the floor. If they weren't impressed before, they are now. All of them hang their heads and won't look at Tally, except for the Russian woman. She gets this sinister smile, and demands Tally tell the story all over again.

Four more times.

Same story.

The only thing that concerns me is why Tally lied about me going into the alley. *Why lie?* Then, it slowly dawns on me that there's no witness to back up what I did or didn't do in the alley. *She's protecting me with that lie.* She pushed the guy, but her statement doesn't bring into question about what or who killed him if I never went into the alley.

After telling the story in total five times, Tally retreats to the chair they designated for her earlier and hasn't moved since the last retelling. All five leave the room for a supposed conference. Tally stares straight ahead at the blank, yellowed wall in front of her. The guard with me rolls his eyes, and then shuffles out of the room, leaving me alone, too.

It's like we're on different ends of the world.

I'm studying Tally's face looking for any sign of what she might be thinking when I notice the blood beginning to pool on the floor next to her chair. She seems to notice it at about the same time, too. She inhales deep and then kind of sighs as she gets up from the chair, grabs her crutches, and slowly makes her way over to the mirror. She places her palm on it. I do the same from the other side, bleakly noting how her blood stains the mirror on her side.

She's talking low. It takes a few seconds to figure out what she's saying. "I'm sorry, Elvis. I'm so sorry. I really am. I'm sorry about everything." Her eyes fill with tears as she absently wipes at them with her right hand. She attempts to smile and then steps back from the mirror. "I'm sorry for putting you through this. I hope you forgive me someday."

"Nothing to forgive. I love you, Tally," I say, even though she can't hear me. *Such simple words and yet how often have I said them to her? Hardly ever.*

She retakes her place back at the table and places her boot over the pool of blood staining the floor and just stares at the wall.

The guard returns and gestures that I should follow him. I take one look back at Tally sitting there—so forlorn—while her blood still pools beneath the table. Yet I actually smile, consoling myself with the certainty that I'll be able to see her and touch her and tell her, I love her, *in person*, just minutes from now.

We'll finally sort this whole thing and the two of us out. Together.

CHAPTER FORTY-TWO

Linc ~ Hanging by a moment

ELATION CARRIES ME OUT THE DOOR and away from her. Our upcoming reunion doesn't have me looking back because the simple promise of our reconciliation has me moving forward and out the door.

I'll see her in a few minutes. We'll be together soon—minutes from now. We will work this out. We will come together. Finally.

Kimberley's there. One of the officers undoes my handcuffs, while she hands me a stack of clothes and quietly tells me, "*to hurry up and fucking change.*" Only Kimberley Powers could put a finer point on the circumstances more bluntly than anyone else. *Sense of urgency implied.* Another officer thumbs me toward a restroom. I duck inside, wash my face and hands, and marvel at the fine soap that the officers get to use versus their prisoners. I change in a hurry, while my mind swims with endless thoughts of Tally. *I have to get to Tally. We have to stop the bleeding both physically and mentally of her and me. I'll see her in a few minutes, and this thing will be all but over. Our reconciliation will finally happen. Nothing and no one can keep us apart any longer.*

Kimberley meets me in the hallway. She holds up her index finger to her lips as soon as I start to speak. She firmly grabs my arm and leads me toward the front of the police station. We pass the cops waiting around in the outer office. We pass right by the interrogation team at a hurried pace; they still watch me with this recognizable suspicion when I glance their way. Kimberley tells me to ignore them and to keep moving. "Keep fucking moving," she urgently whispers.

The police chief, himself—the cop with the most decorated uniform and endless gold bars and stars bars on his jacket—personally escorts us out of the police station and down the intimidating building's front steps. He briefly shakes my hand and then hurries back up the stairs and into the dark recesses of the front entrance. I'm too stunned by his abrupt escort and my subsequent release to realize what's actually happening.

There are reporters everywhere, holding up their various cameras with flashing white lights and winking red buttons that indicate they're already recording these events. They shout in both Russian and English all around us.

My lawyer, who Kimberley briefly introduces me to as *Ken* something or other, is on one side of me, while Kimberley is on the other. Instead of stopping to address the press, they usher me straight toward a waiting black SUV and push me through the open passenger door without fanfare of any kind.

"No comment," Kimberley says, turning back only once to address the crowd of reporters before she climbs in the car right behind me. Ken gets in from the other side and ominously slams and locks the door.

"Kimberley, what about Tally?" I ask in sudden desperation as I finally realize we're just going to drive away.

"Not right now," she says to me. "Go!" Kimberley shouts to the driver.

We're doing sixty in as many seconds.

"Don't stop," she shouts to the driver above the roar of the vehicle's gunned engine.

Another two minutes sail by before she turns to me.

"You look like shit. Sorry." She frowns. "There's a quasi press conference at the airport with mostly American reporters. Here's a toothbrush. Drink this water. Comb your hair. Chew this gum. Here's your speech. Memorize it. You'll be giving it as soon as we get there."

I stare at the piece of paper and start to read it aloud. "It's been a harrowing experience to be accused of a crime I didn't commit. I'm looking forward to putting all of this behind me and the opportunity to again throw a baseball in the greatest country in the world—the United States of America." I stop and take a breath and hold it for a few minutes to get my temper under control. "I'm *not* saying this."

"Yes. You. Are."

"It doesn't even mention Tally. It makes me sound like a fucking hero."

"You are. It's subtle, but *yes,* that's how we're playing it."

"No," I say with a groan. "I took her to the hospital. She was almost *raped,* Kimberley. The guy attacked her and may have been trying to kill her. He knew who she was. Geez. What happened to her is so much worse than what happened to me in there." I point back toward the receding outline of the Moscow Police headquarters just before it disappears from view. "I have to go back and tell her how sorry I am about everything. I have to tell her how

I feel about *her*. *About us*. I have to win her back. I have to hope that she'll forgive me, despite all of this, and in leaving her right now when she needs me the most."

"No." Kimberley's eyes fill with tears.

I'm taken aback because Kimberley normally doesn't cry, except sometimes when she talks about Elliot. The old fears start to creep in. "Kimberley, I have to get to Tally. You don't know what they can do to her. Turn the car around." Desperation returns.

"You can't be with her, Linc. Not now. Not for a long time. She's Kryptonite for you, Superman. Under these circumstances…she may be accused of a crime before this is done. She'll probably have to go through their courts and clear her name. It will probably be ruled self-defense, but we don't know that for sure. You can't be with her or be near her or even talk to her, until this whole thing blows over. If it ever does," she adds grimly. "And she knows that."

At this point, Ken decides to insert himself in the conversation. "Mr. Presley, my advice is to get you out of the country as quickly as possible before the Moscow Police decide to re-examine your statement."

"I'm paying you five hundred an hour for that opinion?" I don't even attempt to hide my disdain for the guy.

"We're in *Moscow*, Mr. Presley. My rates are quadruple that. We've been here for *seven* days."

I'm not going to get anywhere with Ken. That much is clear. And I owe him a bundle of money already. *Shit.* "Turn the car around!" I roar.

"No," Kimberley says and then cajoles the driver to go even faster.

"Turn the car around!"

"No! She *knows*. I talked to her on the way to the police headquarters. I told her this was how it might go down. She had a pretty good idea of what she might be walking into. I prepared her as much as I could."

"You told her to *lie* about me going into the alley?"

"Well no," Kimberley says, looking confused. "She told me you *didn't* go into the alley. What are you talking about?"

"I went into the alley. *I* went into the alley, and I saw him lying there. I saw his face. He was alive but just barely. I didn't do anything to him, but I saw him. That's how I could identify him to that first detective. Yet when she gave her statement, she said I didn't go into the alley. She was specific about that—"

"Don't say anymore," Ken says.

"So they couldn't hold you." Kimberley holds her head in her hands for a moment and quietly moans. "She *knew* that. She knew that it could ruin your career if you were involved in any way. *She knew.* I told her the Angels were already balking at your contract extension. They're unhappy with how this went down."

"What?" I ask, incredulous. "That I stopped to help a girl, who was in trouble, who, by the way, they think is *my wife?*"

"Yes," she says, but then hastily glances away out the window. A minute goes by, and then she's gazing back at me, looking uneasy all at once. "Don't get me started, Linc. You can't go back. There's nothing you can do. She knows that. I told her the Angels weren't happy with you and might not extend your contract. I was panicked, okay? I didn't know how I was going to tell you that your baseball career might be over."

"Wow. They *are* unhappy," I say. Then, I shake my head in disbelief. "Do you know how that looks to Tally? Leaving her like this? I'm choosing baseball *again.*"

Deeply disappointed with the Angels and somewhat annihilated by the idea that my career may be over, I draw in air and search for courage, although the fears have already begun to roll in on me, one by one, just like Tally and I talked about once. *Falling. Failing. Losing. I feel them all.* My career might be finished. And yet it's nothing compared to the thought of losing Tally forever. I take a fear-releasing breath; and with it comes the staggering realization of how insignificant losing my career baseball is in comparison to losing Tally.

"Do you know how that looks to Tally?" I finally say.

"She knows it wasn't you making that choice."

"And that makes it okay?"

"No." Kimberley sighs. There's a hint of defeat in her eyes. "Look. Rob Thorn is there with her. Marla and Charlie met him at the Moscow airport this morning. I briefly met with her and told her how I thought it might go down so did Ken." Kimberley waves over at my lawyer. "Her own lawyer whom Rob hired on her behalf told her how it might go down. She knew what she was walking into."

"No one can prepare you for the Moscow Police. It's not the States, Kimberley."

We stare at one another for a long thirty seconds. She looks away first but not before I glimpse her uncertainty.

"I have to go back."

She ignores what I've said. "Charlie and Marla are meeting us at the airport. We've chartered a plane. Your dad took care of it and your Uncle Chad and even Rob Thorn. Your trip home is bought and paid for in all the ways that count." She looks unhappy with herself. "Look, you can't help her. If you go back and restate your statement, they'll start suspecting hers. You have to stay out of it. *Listen to me.* It's done. Your part is done. There's nothing else you can do."

"But we're *married*," I say with true feeling because even *I* believe the lies I've told now.

Kimberley just rolls her eyes at me. "You're. Not. Married."

"They think we are. I signed for her surgery. As far as they know, she's my wife, and I'm her husband."

Kimberley sighs big and then gets this vexed look. "In a matter of hours, they'll figure out that wasn't true. We have to get you *out of the country* and back to the States before they actually come up with something legitimate to hold you on—like *lying* about your marital status. Get a grip, Prez."

Kimberley looks out the window again, apparently now intent on studying the Russian landscape that we're passing at the incredible speed of light, and in search of all the right answers. Then she turns and stares at me hard.

"You can't help her. She knows that. She asked for Rob. She *called* Rob. He can help her. Her lawyer can help her. You. Can't. Help. Her."

"Rob never lets her down. She can depend on him, where she's never really been able to depend on me when the chips are down. Kimberley, she is the only thing that matters to me. I can throw a baseball for anybody, any team, anywhere. If I leave Tally this time I will lose her forever and rightly so." I tap the driver's shoulder. "Turn the car around." I look over at Kimberley intently. "You know what that's like…when you really love somebody." She gets this wounded look, and I feel a little bad for unconsciously bringing up Elliott. "Turn the car around," I say again to the driver.

He looks at Kimberley through the rearview mirror. "Turn the car around," she finally says. She gets this little smile when she looks at me. "You really love her."

"I do. I always have." I grab her hand and kiss it. "It's going to be okay, Kimberley."

<hr />

We pull up outside the Moscow Police Headquarters within ten minutes. The reporters are still staked out in their tactical positions, awaiting news of Tally Landon's fate as much as I am. I take a much-needed cleansing breath fully preparing to throw over my career for Tally. *Part of me registers just one thought: That it's about time I took a stand.*

I'm out of the car and jogging up the steps before Kimberley can change her mind about me doing this. Within a few minutes, the reporters have become alerted to the fact that I've returned. A flurry of activity has their microphones set up in front of me to capture every word within a span of five minutes. I borrow a little from Kimberley's prepared speech and center myself. I already know that what I say can make the difference in Tally's release or not. I recognize enough of these reporters. Many are from L.A. and San Francisco. There's enough American representation to ensure this story gets played worldwide; and, for once, I'm grateful that being who I am and my fame might somehow help Tally or hopefully ensure her freedom. The Russians all around us look a little nervous as I address the growing crowd.

"It's been a harrowing experience to be accused of a crime I didn't commit and yet my experience is nothing compared to Talia Delacourt's. She's an accomplished star ballerina, who was violently attacked, just for being in the wrong place at the wrong time and, perhaps, just for being famous. The taxi driver and I just happened along at the right time to help her and save her life by being the ones to get her to a hospital in time." I extend my hand toward the crowd. "Helping Talia Delacourt was the least I could do. I'd do it again, even if it means losing my baseball career over a straightforward misunderstanding and an outright false accusation of a crime I didn't commit." I take a breath. "Now I'm looking forward to putting all that's happened here behind me and knowing that Talia Delacourt is going to be okay is a huge relief. However, right now, she is behind those closed doors telling her story to the Moscow Police and relating the horrible circumstances of that day as the victim of Balanchine's reprehensible violence. I anticipate she'll be released shortly after giving her statement. And I plan to be right here when she is."

The overall crowd begins to murmur at the last part of what I said, and I note a few of Moscow's police officers rush inside the front doors, probably intent on notifying the powers that be as to what I've just said.

"As to my own future, I hope to get back to the States and soon return to throwing a baseball in the greatest country in the world—the United States of America." I stop again and cast my eyes over the crowd of reporters and slowly nod. "Whether that is for the Los Angeles Angels or another Major League Baseball team remains to be seen." Kimberley's in the far background openly glaring at me and practically waving me off. "I'm not the hero here. Talia Delacourt is. She was violently attacked by this Nicholai Balanchine and yet bravely fought him off. He inadvertently died from injuries sustained when he landed on a piece of Rebar sticking up from the ground when Tally defended herself against his attack of her. That's the truth. Truly? All that matters here is that Tally is okay and by some miracle, she'll recover from her serious injuries and Balanchine's reprehensible violence. She did nothing wrong. She's the victim here. She's innocent. We should all be as brave and courageous as Talia. I'm in awe of her. She's is an extraordinary talent, and we should all have a better appreciation for the arts and ballet because of her." I look over at the American reporters I already recognize. "As Americans, we're lucky to have our freedoms and such talents in our midst. I know we all hope that Talia returns back to the States immediately so we can watch all of her fantastic performances. She is gifted. Extraordinary. The real hero—*heroine,* if you will—of this story is Talia herself. She's the bravest, smartest, and the most beautiful woman I've ever known and an incredible dancer, besides. We're lucky to have her. I just hope she knows how much she's loved…by all of us, especially me. Thank you. Now, I'll answer your questions."

"Linc? Brian Addison of the L.A. Times. Can you expand upon your relationship with Ms. Delacourt? There have been rumors that you've been engaged to a Ms. Nika Vostrikova and that this is what brought you to Moscow in the first place. Can you explain your relationship with these two women?"

"Nika and I are friends. We have been since our days at Stanford. She does statistical analysis of my baseball games for me. We were briefly engaged, but that has ended. What brought me to Moscow was the Angels' exhibition game in an effort to share American baseball with more of the world. As for Talia, I've known her for almost four years. We met under extraordinary circumstances and have been struggling to make things work between us while living and working on opposite coasts in the States. She's been in New York with her ballet and traveling and performing in Europe; and I've been on the West Coast throwing a baseball. I can assure you that we will work out those differences, one way or the other, in the very near future. I love her, and I'm going to be with her from now on."

"Follow-up. Are you, in fact, stating here that you won't sign with the Angels again?"

"No, but I haven't seen a contract extension offer from them. They appear to be unhappy with my involvement here in Moscow and with helping Talia when this awful crime was committed against her; however innocent we both are." I shrug. "There's not much I can do about that. It happened. I was wrongly accused of a crime I didn't commit and if the Los Angeles Angels don't see it that way; that's their prerogative. I'm telling the truth. I can throw a baseball anytime, anywhere; and I will."

"Mitchell Watson of the New York Times," says another reporter. "Do you have any interest in pitching for the Yankees?"

The crowd laughs nervously.

I incline my head and grin back at the reporter. "Like I said, I can throw a baseball for anyone—anytime, anywhere—but my immediate future is focused upon Talia. If she's here in Moscow fighting for her freedom, that's where I'll be as well."

The doors ominously swish open behind me. I glance back in time to see the Moscow Police Chief as he walks straight through the line of reporters. "I have a brief statement," he says as he wipes at his forehead. He tries to smile. "Ms. Talia Delacourt has given her statement, which further clarified what happened in these horrible circumstances. She was free to go, and Ms. Delacourt left police headquarters through a private exit about twenty-five minutes ago. We appreciate all the witnesses in this matter." He looks up and over at me. "Mr. Presley is free to go as well." Reporters grab their microphones from where they've been staged by me, while I try not to openly react to what the Police Chief has just revealed.

Kimberley appears beside me. She grabs my arm and steers me away from the crowd. "Keep it together. I know it's hard. We couldn't have anticipated this. I'm so sorry we left."

I nod and attempt to do as she says. *I've lost her.* Tally probably knows I left, and I already know how that looks to her—that all I care about is baseball. Kimberley leads me back to the SUV. I climb in with effort. I'm exhausted. Desolation takes over and practically suffocates me. *I can already feel it. I've lost her. And it's my fault.*

"Rob Thorn called while you were talking to the press. Apparently, a tidy sum has been transferred into their crime victims' fund. The Chief is very happy." She gives me this meaningful look, and it morphs into equal parts of sympathy and *I-told-you-so.*

"What's a tidy sum?" I ask, staring out the car window and seeing nothing.

"A cool six hundred grand."

"So, now she *owes* him. That's how she'll view it. She *owes* him and…I let her down…*again.*"

"Maybe she won't see it that way. I could talk to her. *I will.* I'll talk to her and tell her that you came back insisting on giving your speech, which was awesomely supportive of her by the way."

"Kimberley," I say impatiently. "Don't you see? *I left.* She probably knows that. Rob stayed; Rob paid. She can count on him. She's never been able to count on me."

"What can I say that will make you see this differently?"

"Nothing. There's nothing *you can* say. It's over. We're over. She and I. There's no trust between us. You can't build a relationship without trust; and I blew it." I sigh and lean back against the headrest and close my eyes. "The truth is there's nothing left for me." I open my eyes for a few seconds. "That's the irony, right? I might still have baseball, but the only thing I truly care about is Tally."

"I'll talk to her."

"No offense, but it probably won't matter."

"You're a stand-up guy—the best one I know. *You are.* Maybe, she'll see the press conference and see what you said about her. She'll figure it out. And I'll *talk* to her. Linc, don't give up, please." Her breath hitches. "Please, don't... look like that, Prez. You're going to make me cry."

I just shake my head, while Kimberley gives this same *you're-a-good-guy* speech over and over on the long flight back to L.A. It doesn't help.

I look like a jerk because I left.

I am a jerk.

We're back to that.

I don't even deserve Tally.

CHAPTER FORTY-THREE

Tally ~ Six hundred thousand ways to keep you

TREMENDOUS AMOUNTS OF COLD HARD CASH have a way of turning things around. Six hundred thousand dollars dropped into an untraceable crime victim's fund make a difference.

Rob pays. I'm saved.

And I owe him. And that has to be enough.

My cell phone rings on the nightstand on his side of the bed. Rob hands it to me with a somewhat quizzical look. It's the middle of March. A Sunday. I have the day off before the next round of rehearsals for our next performance that start up again early tomorrow.

"Hello? This is Talia," I say tentatively.

"Well, you are a hard person to track down and, truly, not where I thought you'd be."

"Kimberley?" I ask in surprise. I look over at Rob, and he gives me a smirky smile. It's so endearing, and I need his smile so much right now that I reach out and trace his lips. "What do you want?" I try to sound gracious, but it comes out rather defensive anyway.

"How are you?" she asks.

"I'm fine. Just fine. Gearing up for the next set of rehearsals. I got the lead part and everything. It's nice to be back in the States."

"I'm sure."

"What do you want?"

"I need to talk to you."

"About what?" I ask warily.

"I'd rather not have this conversation over the phone. Can you meet me? How about *Les Miz* after six tonight?"

"Can't we just talk on the phone?"

"No. Like I said I need to see you in person. I have something I need to show you. It's important. So meet me at *Les Miz* at six. *Please*, Tally. It's important."

"Okay, fine," I say.

"Tally, I'm sorry for all that went down in Moscow. I'm really sorry."

"Don't be," I say quietly. "I'm *fine*."

I end the call somewhat upset that she brought up Moscow and somewhat intrigued by what she needs to tell me so badly in person. Rob watches me closely from the other side of the king-sized bed now. I haven't gotten into the sordid details of Moscow with anyone other than Sasha Belmont, who benevolently insisted I rest for a month before returning to the company full-time. I traded heavily on the confusing details of Moscow but only Sasha knows the whole story about me and what transpired in Moscow and about Linc and Cara and Tremblay—all of it. She was speechless for a few minutes after I told her everything, and then she hugged me and started to cry. The feeling was overpowering for both of us, and she readily agreed to keep a promise—to never talk about it with anyone. After Sasha's unexpected reaction, I decided not to share everything that happened to me in Moscow with anyone else, especially Rob. There was no solace in talking about it. There was no solace in thinking about it. I just wanted to forget. And, in my mind, talking about it only brought the horrible memories of all of it back to the surface.

So, I didn't tell Rob about all that happened in Moscow because I didn't want his sympathy, and I couldn't take the devastation that would most certainly appear upon his face if he actually knew everything that went down. The newspaper articles remained vague. I suppose I have Lincoln Presley to thank for some of that and most likely the general language barrier between Russian and English translations caused some of the glossing over parts of this terrible story. Lucky for me, the more salacious parts of my ordeal have been left out. I was attacked—that's the gist of what everyone knows, including my parents and Rob.

Lies. Untruth. We all buy into it because it's just easier.

In the past four months, Rob and I haven't spent any time talking about our future since my bartered-for return. All I know is that bags and bags of Rob's money bought my freedom. I owe Rob. And I want to make it right between us because I owe him. I do.

I carefully lay the cell phone back down on the nightstand, while Rob gets this vexed look. It's funny to me, and I start to laugh. His left brow furrows in contemplation, and I can tell he's trying to figure everything out. "You mentioned Moscow. Who was that? What's going on?"

He looks unsettled at these particular topics of conversation as usual. I roll my eyes, feeling the familiar push-pull from Rob about Linc and Moscow and ballet and us. *If I could just be more like Holly, everything would be fine.*

"It was Kimberley Powers. I don't know what she wants. She's Sasha's publicist for NYC Ballet. I think that's what this is about. I'll just meet with her and see what she needs. I'm sure it's just some publicity stuff for NYC Ballet." I hug my knees to me, gingerly, of course; because my injuries have been slow to heal. I'm wearing one of Rob's dress shirts, a thong I know he likes, and little else. He studies my legs and lightly brushes his fingers along my wounds and the ugly red line along my lower abdomen. I can see on his face all the questions he has for me, but he doesn't ask any.

"Tally." He breathes my name out slowly, tiredly. "Do you think you'll ever get to the point where you actually trust me? Trust anyone?"

I rest my head in his lap and he strokes the side of my face and then runs his fingers through my hair. I finally turn over and look straight up at him. "Can you just give me some time? That's all. I just need some time."

"And then, you'll tell me everything?" he asks, looking hopeful but still a little uneasy.

"Yeah. Then I'll tell you everything."

<hr/>

I push the fear of all there is about Moscow and the heartbreak over Cara and Linc way down. I breathe in deep and hold it for a few moments before opening the door to the bar where I'm to meet Kimberley Powers. I steel myself against the wayward thoughts of Linc. *I'm with Rob. I'm happy. I'm relatively happy. Moscow is over. It's behind me. I've moved on.* For all I know, Linc is married to Nika by now. We've all moved on. I've lost Cara forever. Tremblay is gone, and I have to learn to live with that. My lies have cost me everything. I'm done lying. *There are...so many lessons learned.*

But life goes on, doesn't it? It just does—painfully or otherwise; it just goes on.

Kimberley Powers waits just inside the front door of *Les Miz*. She inclines her head toward me as the maître d leads us to a dining table and watches me judiciously for the next few minutes. I pretend nonchalance, although I'm quaking inside. My mind whirs with the singular thought that this is an extremely bad idea meeting Kimberley Powers in person. *Paranoia runs deep. The woman doesn't miss a thing.*

Kimberley holds her hand in mid-air, but she's stopped talking because I think she must have figured out I'm not listening. "Hey," she says quietly. "Are you okay? You're acting weird. I guess I would be, too, if all that had happened to me. Are you sure you're okay?"

"You're not like setting me up or anything, are you? I mean I know your loyalty is to *him*, but I thought maybe you thought you owed *me*; because... you seriously *do*."

"*Seriously.*" She grins at first and then looks thoughtful. "Yes, I do owe you. Things didn't go the way I thought they would—the way I planned." She shakes her head side-to-side. "He rekindled things with Nika after Marla's wedding, clearly on the rebound from you. And well, Linc has a tendency to, at times, take things too far in his eternal quest to be bound by duty; however gallant, and to do the right thing, sometimes, to his own detriment. His need for a mother, for stability, for a family...not that I believe Nika Vostrikova would have ever fit that bill, on any of level whatsoever, for any of those roles." She stops. "Well, it effectively explains where he's coming from, where he's been. I see bits of Elliot in him—personality-wise; and I'm afraid I end up reacting with my own noteworthy personal experience with the Presley men at the most desperate of times, but it's not always timely on my part."

"I'm not sure I follow," I say slowly, fascinated by her soliloquy on some sadistic level. "Is he with Nika or not?"

"No Nika," she says with a shake of her head. "*Definitely*, no Nika. She bailed on him in Moscow." She looks at me intently.

I lean back from her, frowning and trying to take in this particular newsworthy announcement. I'm about to ask her a follow-up question about Linc and Nika when someone close by utters my name.

"Tally?"

I look up to see Elissa Mantel. My smile falters as the epic sadness of being harshly reminded of both Tremblay and Cara surges through me at this unexpected encounter from my past. "Elissa. Hi."

"What are you doing here?" she asks.

"Elissa, this is Kimberley Powers. She's my publicist. We just met up to go over the events I'm doing for the spring performances. We heard the food is great here; right, Kimberley?" I ask sweetly.

"Right."

Kimberley studies my face a moment longer and then turns her attention to our waitress, Elissa Mantel, who I inadvertently screwed over by awarding the adoption of Cara to Allaire Tremblay. I'm sure she hates me.

For her part, Elissa pushes a tendril of her fine golden blond hair from her face, while confusion briefly passes over her features. But then, it's gone and she gets this tight smile as she whips out her note pad and prepares to take our order. "What can I get you, ladies?" Elissa asks.

Kimberley launches into her drink and food order with a lot of requests for things on the side. Elissa turns to me. Her face impassive and I know the wheels are spinning in her head as to what exactly I might want. "What do you want, Tally?" she finally asks me with a discernible edge to her voice.

"I'd just like a side salad with your house dressing and a Diet Pepsi."

"How's Marla?" Elissa asks.

I'm sure the girl hates my guts. I took away her chance for a baby. I broke her heart and her husband Jamie's, too. Her face seems to convey all of this with just one look.

"She's married. They live in California. They're doing well. She had a baby. A boy named Elliott last summer. I haven't spoken to her in a while. I've been out of town."

"Moscow," she says evenly with a slight nod.

She knows.

I nod back while she reaches for my hand. "It's good to see you. It's terrible what happened to you in Moscow. Nobody deserves that." She sighs. "I'm sorry, Tally."

"It's okay. I'm fine." I force myself to smile. "I'm dancing with the NYC Ballet here now. No more trips abroad. No more foreign countries." Then I give her a pleading look that clearly conveys that *I-don't-talk-about-it.* "I'm sorry, too, about everything."

She nods again. "We've sort of moved on, you know? We're saving up enough money to move back home, and I'm ten weeks pregnant." She fondles her flat stomach.

I focus on breathing and smile ever wider. The heartbreaking possibility of not being able to have another child assails me from out of nowhere. I've put it out of my mind. I haven't even told Rob this yet. I've just moved on. Until now. This moment. *Breathe.*

"Congratulations then about the house, the baby, a new life back home." My throat closes up with fresh pain. I'm sure it shows on my face.

"Congratulations on the NYC Ballet gig…if that's what you want."

Kimberley blatantly stares at me from the other side of the table.

"It's a good gig," I say slowly. "Yes, it's what I want. A lot of sacrifices for it though…" I force myself to smile again.

Elissa gives me this weird knowing look. I know she wants to ask me more about the baby I gave up because, invariably, Marla told her that I gave Cara up for adoption to our dance instructor.

I shake my head ever so slightly, and she writes down my food order instead.

"Well, I'm glad things turned out okay for you, Tally."

"Yes. Me, too. And, for you…with a baby on the way and a life and a new place with Jamie. That's good."

Kimberley is watching this exchange with this unchecked fascination even after Elissa leaves to put in our order. To buy myself some time for the Kimberley Powers' inevitable inquisition, I casually take a sip of my ice water preparing myself for the onslaught of questions and queries. And, not surprisingly, she is way ahead of me. She's amazingly good. She bides her time seemingly to gain my trust, the longer we talk. I have to remind myself, more than once, to keep up my vigilance and be ready for an attack of some kind. Kimberley Power is so smart, so put together that I envy her.

"Your statement…saved him, you know. His career. His contract is up for renewal after this season but now the Angels want to start those negotiations early, but he's open to a trade, if the terms and the team are right. He may sign with the Giants. And the Yankees have shown some interest…" Her voice trails off.

I look at her incredulous. "That's what he wants? The *Yankees?* Why would he want to move to the East Coast?"

"Because you're here."

She studies my face intently for my reaction, but I manage a nonchalant shrug. "Lincoln Presley should not be planning his life around *mine*. I have my own. I'm just trying to move on here and salvage my career out of the flipping fire and move on with *Rob*. We're moving on. *We are.*" I wave my arm around the restaurant for emphasis.

"How's the foot?"

I take in the air and hold it for a moment. "It gives me trouble," I say slowly. "It appears to be chronic. But Sasha *knows*…I'm doing all I can. Physical therapy of every kind. Yoga. It's better." I sound defensive so I just stop talking.

Kimberley nods. "Has she talked to you about San Francisco Ballet? She told me she was going to." She's said this casually like it's just the newest weather report, even though she should know and probably does, that this is career-ending talk. You don't just *leave* the NYC Ballet. *Nobody does.* And yet, Sasha and I have been secretly talking about this very thing for the past several weeks, since Moscow, really. So I have to weigh whether she's guessing or actually knows about Sasha's plans to move to San Francisco to be with Michael.

Sasha met Dr. Michael Markov while we were still in Moscow when she came to visit me right after I had to be re-admitted for a raging infection and return to surgery for a second time to stop more internal bleeding. Yeah, it was another near-death experience for Tally Landon—one last, twist-of-fate performance for the Moscow fans before I could leave Russia and vow to never, ever return.

Funny. Sasha falls in love in Moscow. And I lose the love of my life there. The irony isn't lost on either one of us.

But Rob was there. And I owe Rob. I still do.

I tap the table in a steady rhythm. "Nobody is supposed to know about it yet, especially the NYC Ballet. But I'm considering it. It would be nice to be home. I've only seen my family a couple of times since I moved here. I've missed three Christmases in a row. It'd be amazing to dance for the San Francisco Ballet. They're up and coming. Sasha thinks the dance company is a little more reasonable."

"You mean you might get to have a life?"

"Almost." I laugh and so does she.

After a few minutes, she asks, "Do you think you'll ever go back?"

"Go back? What? To Moscow?" I shake my head side-to-side. "Not a chance in hell of that happening. *Ever.* I hate that city now." My voice is low, so we won't be overheard. "I turned down the European tour. I've paid my dues. More than my fair share. They want to extend my contract, but I want to see what SFB comes up with. Sasha can help me make that happen; hopefully, by some unexpected miracle or twist of fate." I frown. "The thing is you have all these plans, and you hope that things will turn out differently because you sacrifice so much and then *nothing* turns out the way you thought it would…" I force myself to smile. "Just know that if Sasha comes through with an offer, I hope to be able to take it."

"That's what he says about the sacrifices he made, and that nothing turned out the way he planned," Kimberley says with a little sigh.

I can feel her sympathy from all the way across the table between us. Now I'm wary and wondering what her true purpose is, so I glare at her because I refuse to take that particular bait. I'm not talking about Lincoln Presley with Kimberley Powers.

"I don't want to talk about *him*," I say with a dismissive wave of my hand. "Look. I just want to move on. Be off the front pages of the newspapers for a long while and get on with my life. *With Rob.*"

"I can see that," she says thoughtfully. "He wanted that for you, too." She looks conflicted. "But he wanted to make things right for you. He didn't ask me to give you this. I found it one day, when I recently met with him at his place in L.A., I thought you should see it."

She draws her iPhone out of her bag, pulls up a photograph, and slides it over to me. I stare at the image of a bank deposit slip in the amount of six hundred thousand dollars for a long time. It is Robert Garrett Thorn's bank account that received the transfer. *Over four months ago. Right after Moscow.* The deposit slip date—December 3rd—all but slams into me.

"Why would Linc transfer money to Rob's account?"

"He wanted to be the one to buy your freedom, not Rob. When I saw it, I thought you would want to know, especially, when, after a while; it became obvious that Rob never told you, since you didn't reach out to Linc. You have the right to be set free and not feel obligated to a guy, who basically keeps you for six-hundred-thousand different reasons." She frowns. "Rob's a nice guy, but I think he tries too hard. And when he feels threatened he doesn't play fair. Linc always plays fair, sometimes to his detriment. And I'll say it again, because it bears repeating; you have the right to be free. You don't owe Rob. And you don't owe Linc. You *do,* however, owe it to yourself to get what you want and to have a life and to be able to live it as you choose."

"Is this some kind of *payoff?*"

"No! He doesn't even *know* that I found out about this. He just wanted to make it right. He knows that it looks like he chose baseball over you again but allow me to tell you *the whole story.*" She takes a deep breath. "He went back that day in Moscow after they released him. I talked him into leaving the Moscow Police Headquarters. I cajoled him into leaving to catch the flight back, so did his lawyer, but he insisted upon coming back for you only to learn that you were already gone and had left with Rob. He had a press conference. Have you seen it?"

I shake my head. "No. I try to avoid watching the news at all costs now."

Kimberley grabs her iPhone and brings up a video. Seconds later, I'm staring at Linc as he goes on about how great I am and how brave I was and then the camera shifts away from Lincoln Presley to the Moscow Police Chief, who is busy giving his own speech about how fair they'd been and how the witnesses' statements cleared everything up. I wince upon hearing these lies, but the man's words drift away from me as I start to put things together.

"*When* was this?"

"That day—the day you gave your statement to the police--we'd left for the airport and then Linc insisted we go back, and as you can see he gave his own statement to the reporters. Then the police chief came out, and that's when we found out you were already gone. Rob called my cell and told me that you two had left the police station, and that he'd paid six hundred thousand to the crime victim's fund for the chief to ensure your freedom. We knew it might go down that way. I'd told you and Rob that earlier; and, I tried to tell Linc that, too."

She takes a deep breath. "I just want to say how sorry I am and for my role in all of this. I probably contributed to the misunderstandings between the two of you, although Rob Thorn and Nika Vostrikova both seem to be doing their best in their own way to keep the two of you apart at almost…"

She stops talking. I follow her intense gaze toward the restaurant's front entrance, where two familiar faces saunter in together and make their way to a back table. Rob Thorn and Nika Vostrikova don't even glance our way as they quickly move through the bar to their private table. I'm stunned beyond words.

"Well, I guess their hook-up at Marla's wedding was more than a casual thing," Kimberley says softly.

"They were together at Marla's wedding?" I ask listlessly.

She nods. "Look, I know you think I'm the enemy here, but I'm not. I always look out for the best interests of my clients. *All of them.* You're one. Linc's one. I see and hear about things all the time. It's my job to know about them."

"So...you were going to tell me about Rob and Nika?" I glance over at their table again, bizarrely fascinated at learning that my relationship with Rob is on the rocks. This numbing sensation envelops all of me as I watch the two of them together. They seem to share an intimate conversation, laugh at each other's jokes, and obviously don't see anyone else beyond each other. I wince and feel all these conflicting emotions—anger, jealousy, and relief—all at the same time.

"No. I didn't see the point. A lot of stuff went down at Marla's wedding." She looks at me pointedly.

"Right." I nod. "I broke it off with Linc then; and he got together with Nika. Come to think of it; I broke it off with Rob, too. And then there was Moscow." I let the words hang in the air between us.

"Like I said, she left him while he was in jail in Moscow. Nice; huh? It turns out; there was never a baby, and he got tired of her lies. And he loves you. He has always loved you."

"What are you a relationship broker?" I ask in exasperation. Nervous now, I guzzle the remainder of the cocktail in front of me and somewhat slam the glass back down on the Formica and glare at her.

"No," she says wanly. "I *wish.* You two are impossible. *Really.*"

I grab her phone again, replay the press conference, and then re-examine the bank deposit slip.

Then, without my asking her to, Kimberley dutifully sends them as attachments directly to my phone.

"I don't understand any of this at all. Why would Linc send the money? And why didn't Rob tell me?"

"I imagine Rob wanted to keep you in any way he could. But you have to ask yourself...don't you, Tally? Why is that? When did being honest get to be such a hard thing to come by in a relationship?"

"I haven't been exactly truthful in mine," I say with a sigh. Kimberley is being cagey, and I know instinctively she's holding something back from me.

"What do you really want? What does *he* want?" I ask.

"He knows about your baby, and from the things Sasha said to him when he was looking for you...he thinks it might be his. We've all but confirmed it is. It's his, isn't it, Tally? You had a baby girl on the 31st of January, three years ago; and Linc's the father."

I stare at her without answering, but my eyes sting with new tears and I slowly nod.

"Look," Kimberley says gently. "It's my fault for some of the stuff that went down with you two. I'm sure that you felt you had to give up this baby to protect his career and his reputation. He now knows what you sacrificed. We all do. And he just wants to do the right thing for her and for you."

I close my eyes.

"I wasn't expecting that part of the story to ever come out," I whisper under my breath. "And this is not a conversation to have here."

"Why? Because our waitress Elissa knows about this baby, too? Secrets are hard to keep."

I shake my head slowly. "It doesn't change anything. The adoption is iron-clad other than the unlikely event that the adoptive parent dies or something and then custody reverts to me. There's nothing he needs to do, in fact."

"Regardless, he just wants to make it right for you and for the baby—support you with this in some way."

"Wow," I finally say drawing a breath inward. "Just wow. I...I don't what to say. It doesn't work quite like that. First of all, I don't know where they are. The adoptive mother—Allaire Tremblay—has disappeared with Cara." Kimberley winces at this bit of news. "And secondly, well, there is nothing left to say to all of that. Wow. Just wow."

I force myself to smile and then catch my lower lip to between my teeth and bite hard enough to remind myself that I'm beginning to lose it right in front of Kimberley Powers.

She seems to sense I need a minute or two to myself. She gets up abruptly and sashays her way over to the bar, while half the male clientele watches her, except for the two lovebirds at the corner table. They don't even look up. I hear her ask the bartender for two shots of Patron, salt, and limes.

Elissa Mantel picks that particular moment to deliver our food, and then she slips me a piece of paper with her name, address, and phone number.

"Come by sometime. We won't be moving until the end of the summer. We'd love to see you. Be friends."

I'm speechless; all I can do is nod.

"Sorry about Moscow and what happened to you, Tally. No one deserves that. You've worked so hard to achieve all that you have in ballet. We never wished for anything bad like that to happen to you," she says with a slight frown.

"It's okay. Nobody does," I finally say.

Elissa slowly nods. "I'm so sorry, Tally."

"Yes. Thank you. Just know that I'm fine. And I'm sorry that…things didn't work out. It wasn't my intention to hurt the two of you. I'm so sorry."

"I know." Elissa looks curiously over at Kimberley as she makes her way back to the table.

Kimberley laughs and winks at her as she expertly sets down two full shot glasses in front of me, while Elissa gets this relieved smile and hurries off.

Kimberley and I do a couple of shots.

We covertly watch Nika and Rob for the next half-hour and split the tab after anonymously sending over a bottle of champagne for those two just before we leave. Rob Thorn doesn't even look up long enough from Nika Vostrikova's face to know I'm there.

Apathy settles in on me, while this overriding thought begins to beat inside my head. *I'm free.*

I'm really free.

Kimberley says as much to me out on the sidewalk just before she slides into a cab.

I owe nothing to anyone.

I'm free.

To clear my head, I walk the long ten blocks to what I've come to call home. When I finally let myself into Rob's apartment, I take a long, hard look around, realizing that I could probably move my stuff out in a matter of hours because I haven't really put down roots here.

And why is that?

I take a bath, read NYT's entertainment section as well as the sports page where they keep all the baseball stats for Major League Baseball like I've done for the past two years, and slide into bed, undone and exhausted.

It's late when Rob slides into the bed next to me. He strokes my back from behind, and on any other night I would have turned to him and lost myself in his lovemaking. On that front, Rob has proven to be astonishingly therapeutic.

However, tonight, I pretend to be asleep because now there are all these new lies between us. *So many.* And, like an unforeseeable but driving force, they pull us apart. They will not be denied—these lies. The pain of knowing that particular truth tries to suffocate me.

Still, no tears fall.

Eventually, I hear his steady breathing and wonder if tomorrow I'll be brave enough to leave him.

After all, I'm free.

CHAPTER FORTY-FOUR

Tally - This much is still true

"AGAIN," SASHA SAYS AFTER I'VE DONE the jump. I grab at my leg and rub out the sudden stiffness in the thigh muscle and flex the foot that still manages to give me trouble. The scars have almost faded, and I've gone back to my regular uniform of a leotard with a long skirt without the tights. It makes it easier for my partner to hold on to me, and I'm slipping a lot less. Nevertheless, it's not perfect. We all know that. Sasha walks over to me. Her blue eyes don't miss a thing. She watches me massage my leg with renewed interest.

"You okay? Are you sure?"

"I'm fine. It's just tight. Let me stretch it out, and we'll try again."

"We've got a performance in four days, Tally," she says quietly.

There's concern etched all over her face. This is Sasha Belmont's big moment. Her secret sendoff to the NYC Ballet; they just don't know it quite yet. *Romeo and Juliette* is her late spring production from start to finish, and I'm the principal ballerina. It's her moment and mine. We share the spotlight and have been featured on every dance magazine and poster both in New York and Europe willing to do publicity about this highly-anticipated debut since we arrived back from Moscow last November.

"I know. I'll be ready. I *will*. Promise."

She nods and then jumps down from the stage taking her familiar stance with her arms crossed in front of her, while her face remains focused on the stage. The woman misses nothing. I'm reminded of Allaire Tremblay.

It's been a few months since I've openly thought of her. Not remembering proves to be the best way to move on. I've used this technique for just about everyone. *Tremblay. Cara. Linc.* I've put them all out of my mind. I focus solely on the present—dancing again and making things work with Rob for some unknowable reason.

Yes. I have my freedom. The cage door is open, but I still remain inside.

Nika Vostrikova burns permanent scars through all of me, but I ignore this betrayal for some unfathomable reason. I've come to accept that I deserve it. All of this, for the lies I've told. This is all there is. I've told myself this more than a thousand times and convinced myself that this is enough. Rob and I are moving on. *Together.*

"Again," Sasha says as if we never spoke.

We run through the routine four more times. It's after eight o'clock at night when we finish. I wipe at my face with a small hand towel and spend a few minutes talking to Sasha, before I finally notice a guy in a creased blue suit standing over by her and nervously fingering the edge of his suit lapel.

"Ms. Landon? May I speak to you, please?" He looks uncomfortable and I extend my hand and shake his, noting the sweat from his palm. Sasha gives him the once-over but must decide he's harmless because she finally smiles and then struts away, intent on achieving a star performance from the lighting crew as much as she does her dancers.

"My name is Everett Madsen. I'm an attorney for the Tremblay estate."

"The Tremblay estate? What? Why would Allaire Tremblay need an estate?" I lead him farther away from Sasha and the others on stage because it's just too awkward having a conversation with a stranger when all these dancers are within hearing distance. That's when I look up and notice the little girl sitting farther away in one of the last back rows just inside the theater near the aisle. She's kicking her little legs back and forth, unattended, and obviously waiting for someone. She's dressed in a little red dress with white tights and black patent leather shoes. She grips the arm of a tattered teddy bear to her chest as if it is the one last thing in the world she can count on.

"What's going on?" I turn back to Everett Madsen. My hands rest on my hips in a hard stance. I've got no time for games. There's this rushing sound in my ear drums. I instinctively hold out my arms to balance myself, and the little girl comes rushing toward me.

Cara? I haven't seen her in over a year. I automatically calculate she turned three a little over three months ago, but then my mind begins to scatter.

Rob needs me to pick up his dry cleaning. Linc was traded to the Giants. His baseball team leads the division, and he's gotten two out of five in winning starts so far. Not great, but not horrible. Yes. This little girl needs a hug. Look how needy she is for one.

In the next minute, she runs toward me and puts her little arms around the inside of my leg and buries her face in my ballet skirt.

"Cara?" I ask cautiously as if this will make it more real.

She looks up at me and eyes me closely for a few precious seconds and then returns to hug my left leg with her little arms squeezing it tight. Her sadness reaches for me from this faraway place and this unbearable need of her that I buried a long time ago rushes forth. Fresh pain engulfs me all over again. I'm staggered by it. I reach for the back of one of the theater seats to steady myself. I look over at Mr. Madsen.

"What's going on?

He gives me a grave look. "She...doesn't...T-A-L-K," he says spelling out the last word.

"Where's Allaire?" I manage to say. "What's happened?"

He winces. "There was an accident. Her car overturned on an icy road in northern Montana several weeks ago." He gets this anguished look. "Luckily, Cara wasn't hurt, but she had to spend a week in the hospital, and it took a while longer to figure everything out. To find you."

He shrugs his shoulders and gives me an imploring look that tells me quite a bit. He looks tired as if he's been up for weeks. His eyes are watery. The circles beneath them are dark. He clasps his hands together for a moment and then lifts his coat sleeve and wipes at his upper lip. His general nature seems to cry out that he's gotten a lot more in the past several weeks than even he bargained for.

"Her last will and testament that we put together last spring were very specific. You're a hard person to track down." His lips part and he contrives to smile. "It took a while to put together the persona of Talia Delacourt as the one I was looking for. Talia Landon. That's you." I nod slowly, while he gets this determined look. "Anyway, her instructions—her last will and testament—were very specific. She's *yours*, Ms. Landon."

"That's impossible. *This* is impossible."

I flush at my thoughtlessness. A look of disappointment crosses Madsen's features, too. He exhales and gives me a severe look. We're debating this in front of a child. *My child?* I hang my head in shame.

Eventually, I kneel down effectively undoing Cara's unyielding grasp on my leg. I look at her and recognize the sadness in her beautiful grey-blue eyes. *Oh, she's mine all right. And Linc's.*

Her lip quivers and she grips me more forcefully around the neck and holds on to me tighter. I turn my head. I'm immediately smothered by the teddy bear, which she's flung to one side of my face. I get a whiff of her sweet, childish scent as I breathe in both the stuffed bear and this little girl.

"Oh my God," I manage to say with true feeling.

I need all the help I can summon up.

When I eventually look up and over at Everett Madsen, he just beams at me, apparently pleased with the child's stranglehold on me. I give him my best *we'll-be-talking-about-this-later* frown and turn back into Cara.

Then, the tears come for Allaire Tremblay and the little girl she's left behind. *To me.*

God, help us all.

CHAPTER FORTY-FIVE

Tally · Just a fool

SHE HAS A NEVER-ENDING FASCINATION WITH animals. We spend any free time I can carve out from rehearsals and performances at the little petting zoo in Central Park. Her favorite animals this week are the goats. She likes to feed them. Pet them. Kiss them.

Today, Rob grudgingly tags along. I think he's starting to figure out that Cara is this permanent change—for all of us—and we best get on the same page if we're going to be together. We've had this same conversation several times over the past few weeks, since that first night when I brought Cara home with me. I was still reeling with this semi-permanent shock that Tremblay was dead, and I was now officially Cara's mother again. I'd taken the little girl's hand, helped her out of her dress, and rummaged through the little overnight bag that Everett Madsen had managed to put together. I eventually settled upon a Tinker Bell night gown and slipped it over her head with relative ease. A few minutes later, Cara had to show me the overnight pull-up that she was to wear, and I'd helped her put it on after she dutifully tinkled in the toilet and slipped into the guest bed.

I'd just pulled up the covers, when I heard Rob's sudden intake of air from the open doorway. He'd said without preamble, "Who the hell is that?"

My withering glance in his general direction wasn't the last one I would give him over the coming weeks. Our battles—over kids, marriage, commitment, and finances, and the ever silent one being waged about Nika Vostrikova—had just begun.

"She still doesn't talk," he says to me now, while he watches Cara play alongside the other children in the general vicinity of the petting zoo.

"It's part of the trauma. Dr. Layton doesn't know how long it will be before she does. It's a trust issue."

He looks at me sideways. "So…she *is* just like you. Does she have trust issues with me, or you, or both of us?"

The smirky smile is gone. Long gone. It has been gone for the past few months and maybe even before that. We've been thrust into this situation because of a variety of circumstances. NYC Ballet might be one of the most admired throughout the world, but the pay is not that great. It's high in comparison to some parts of the U.S., perhaps, even relatable to San Francisco and the surrounding Silicon Valley where the famous and nouveau riche reside, but a decent salary for a principal ballerina is relative and in comparison to the high cost of living in Manhattan, it's nominal. An apartment in Manhattan costs big bucks. I don't have any. Rob does. The alliance between us has begun to crumble on that point alone. I resent that I need him. He resents that I don't want to need him. The circle of life threatens to strangle us. He's referenced this particular analogy more than once, and I feel it every single damn day. And then, there's the whole Nika Vostrikova betrayal. I keep waiting for him to come clean on that front. He doesn't. But I keep waiting for him to tell me or let me go.

"You should at least tell your parents about Cara."

I turn to look at him more closely, while he continues to avoid my direct gaze and feigns to watch Cara over my shoulder. "That sounds like a threat."

"Maybe it is. I just think you should tell them. Enough with the lies." He gets this stony, defiant look. "And I'm not lying for you anymore."

"You're not lying for me anymore," I say softly. "But are you lying *to* me?"

I inhale, hold my breath for a few seconds, and intently study his face. He looks tired. He finished NYU in three years to please his father, but now he's been busy launching a new business with two of his former classmates from NYU. They're all enthused about this new software they've developed that all three guys believe will change the world. I tune him out every time he talks about it. Well, not every time, I do know that the code they've developed has something to do with security and could change the way people pay for things on-line. He's borrowed another cool three million from his dad, which he constantly assures me is a hardly enough. He and his two partners are determined to secure another twenty million in financing within the next six months, so they can launch this product before some other high-tech start-up gets wind of their idea. Of course, my little ordeal in Moscow set back his timetable. My six-hundred-thousand-dollar ransom came directly out of Rob's personal funds. Of course, Linc reimbursed him for all the right reasons. Of course, Rob doesn't ever tell me that part.

So, of course, there's tension between us.

Of course, there is.

I reach out and tuck a strand of his hair behind his ear. He grabs my left wrist and presses his mouth against it. It's the closest thing to true intimacy we've had since I returned from Moscow, long before Cara arrived, and way after his dalliance with Nika must have begun. He pulls me to him and crushes his lips against mine. There's desperation in both of us.

"Why can't you love me?" he murmurs against the beating pulse at my throat.

"I do."

"Then marry me."

I look up at his troubled face without answering like always. He nods slowly while his disappointment in my continual silence, on this point alone, weighs heavily upon us both.

I'm actually saved from answering him altogether when my cell phone rings. I pull it out of my pocket and stare at the now-familiar number for the San Francisco area code as it comes up on the screen.

"It's Sasha," I say carefully, pulling back from Rob's urgent embrace. I briefly glance at Cara and wave.

Rob gives me one of his best *I'm-so-disappointed-in-you* looks and stomps off in Cara's direction, apparently deciding that the role of daddy might bode well for him with me today. I do admire the guy's fortitude. Rob never seems to quite give up on me. I just wish I could be sure it's because he loves me for me and doesn't just love me because I remind him so much of Holly, or that he wasn't secretly fucking Nika. Yes, there's *that*.

"Sasha?" I ask when I finally answer after the fourth ring. "What's up?"

"You're in! They saw your performance of *Juliette,* and they want to sign you. No audition. Can you be out here by the end of next week?"

She sounds amazingly happy. Envy surges.

Why can't I be happy? Because I have trust issues. Because I've lost most everyone but Cara.

The truth is I've been waiting for this phone call. The cage door just swung wide open. Tremblay left the house in Alamo Square to Cara and, inadvertently, to *me*. It would be a place of our own. We could go there. We could go home. I feel the intense euphoria of freedom surge through me, although it competes directly with the inexplicable sadness I feel in leaving Rob after all we've been through. I've been putting this ending off for weeks. *Months. Years?*

Breathe.

"I'm in," I manage to say.

Sasha squeals with delight. "Awesome. I'm thrilled. This is going to be great. I'll have them FedEx the contract, three years including the NYCB buyout and bonus. Sign it, Tally, and fax it back, and then you can give your notice to NYC Ballet. Just be ready." She sighs.

She's giddy. In love. She and Michael are getting married in a couple of months. She wants me to stand up for her. I said I would. And now, I'll be living there. Living and working in San Francisco with Sasha. This is a dream come true. I smile and allow the happiness in, however fleeting it still might be.

"Yes. Yes. I'm so excited. I can't believe it, really."

"I'll see you in a week or two in San Fran, then. Do you need help with anything? Moving-wise? You can stay with Michael and me until you get settled if you want."

"Thanks that's so nice of you but I'm good. There's Allaire's house in Alamo Square. It's close by SFB, too. We'll be going there." I sigh with a little laugh as the news reverberates with me. "I'm just trying to take it all in. It's all a little overwhelming. Thank you, Sasha. I'm honored to get to work with you in San Fran. It's going to be so great!"

"No need to thank me. You're the talent." She laughs and then gets more serious. "And how's Cara?"

This is why I'm doing this because Sasha understands my need for time off at odd times. She's the best boss I could ever ask for. She's promised me flexibility, the choice parts, and no European tours for a long while. "She's good. Still not talking, but she seems better...more trusting anyway."

"Good. See? She's going to be fine; and you're coming home to your *family*. It's all coming together."

"Not all of it," I say with a trace of apprehension. "I still have to tell Rob."

"I would just like to remind you that you don't *owe* Rob anything."

Sasha knows my whole story. It just came out one day, during one of our many conversations about the possibilities with SFB and moving home and the whys and wherefores of all of that. For all I know, she could have even found out some of the details from Kimberley, too.

As of late, I've avoided Kimberley because of Cara and my inability to decide what to do about Linc and the complications with Rob and his betrayal with Nika. I've been floating in limbo unable to move forward and unwilling to go back. I've just been waiting. The job offer in San Francisco more or less decides it all for me. Linc has a right to know Cara. I owe Linc that much. And that's where I have to start; now that I have a place and a job to go. *Home. I'm going home.*

"Thanks for the reminder," I finally say with a nervous laugh. "I'll see you in a week or two. I've got to go...lots of packing to do and things to take care of." I wince, thinking of Rob.

"I'll get the contract sent over. I can't wait to see you."

"I can't wait to see *you*. San Francisco, here we come."

"Tally, it's going to be okay. *It is*. Everyone has the right to happiness, to get what they want out of life, especially you."

"Thanks for saying that. I want my family to know Cara…Linc, too. *Eventually*. Please don't say anything to anyone about my coming. I have a lot of loose ends to take care of here first."

"No problem. See you soon."

I try to breathe. I pinch the bridge of my nose, and I try to take in what Sasha's just offered me. I look over and discover Rob watching me. I lower my hand to my side and force myself to smile and nod. *Smile and nod*. He gets the old familiar smirky grin and slightly waves back at me, looking only slightly concerned.

Then Cara grabs his hand and pulls him into the den of children. Now all of them want to learn how to blow dandelions away. Rob becomes the pied piper within minutes as six little kids surround him. There are dandelions being scattered everywhere by all of them. I almost feel sorry for the park staff that will be spraying the weed killer later this summer because of Rob Thorn's early efforts to spread the seeds of dandelion love throughout Central Park. Yet, the most amazing sight of all is Cara's upturned face to Rob's and her excited laugh. I can hear all the way over here some twenty feet away. I start to cry. I will miss this. I already miss the way we were at first. I'm sorry for all the lies between us now.

For a needed distraction, I call Marla. We haven't talked in months, but she answers on the second ring. "We're coming home," I say without preamble. I can hear Elliott babbling nonstop in the background. It makes me smile.

"Like coming home *home*? Or, another three-day whirlwind visit?" Marla asks cautiously.

"Coming home. I got a job with the San Francisco Ballet. I want to surprise the family so keep it to yourself. Don't tell Charlie."

"Which really means don't tell Linc," she says.

"Right."

"Hey what's going on there? Where are you?" Marla asks as the crowd noise of squealing kids must register.

I stall, tabulating all the lies I could tell her. It'd be so easy to lie, to deny the existence of Cara. I could pretend I was at the theater. I could pretend I have rehearsal and need to go.

So many lies.

So many have been told.

When will I stop with lies?

"She's here." My voice breaks. "She looks just like me. She has his grey-blue eyes; otherwise, she's the stunning image of me." Marla gasps while I rush on to explain it all. "Tremblay was killed in a car accident a few months ago. She's been with us…she's *with* Rob and me." Now, Marla's crying. I can hear these loud sniffles from her as if she's having trouble catching her breath.

"I'm just so…happy…and sad at the same time because wow; Allaire Tremblay is dead. It's just so hard unbelievable. She was a taskmaster for sure; but she was, well, Allaire Tremblay. And we loved her in a twisted weird kind of way."

"I know," I console. "It's really sad." I grimace knowing what I say next will convey all my hidden angst and fears about my child. "Cara…doesn't talk."

"Cara doesn't talk?"

"No. She was in the car. Tremblay was dead. It took several hours before they found her. They think the trauma was too much for her. Her mother was dead. Well…who she considers her mother to be."

"You haven't told her?" Marla asks.

"I want the timing to be right. And, right now, it's not. We're just…trying to figure it all out."

"So…Linc *obviously* doesn't know," she says gently.

"Not yet. It *is* part of the reason I'm moving back to San Fran. He has the right to be a part of Cara's life."

I've lost track of Cara and Rob. The little group of dandelion-blowers has scattered back to their original play and their ever-watchful parents.

"She's going to be okay. *She is.* I want to enroll her in preschool this fall. Tremblay left her house to Cara, so, inadvertently to me; I think we'll settle there. I'll send you the key. Can you help me get it ready to go? It's been empty for a while, not that I'll have any furniture to fill it, but we'll figure it out. I thought we could paint her room pink and yellow. I've found some pictures of rooms that I think she'll like."

"Sure. I love decorating kids' rooms. Send me the key. I just can't believe you're coming," Marla says with a laugh. "I'm thrilled. But, I can't tell Charlie?"

I laugh at her familiar whine. "Not quite yet, okay? Sasha's sending me the contract, and I need to give notice, pack…and tell Rob."

"Rob's not coming?"

I take a deep breath. "He seems to have taken up with Nika Vostrikova of all people. I saw them together over a month ago."

"What?" Marla sounds completely shocked. "After all she *did* to Linc?"

"What exactly did she *do* to Linc?" I ask coolly.

"She cleaned him out. He'd been keeping his six-million-dollar signing bonus from the Angels in a separate account, and somehow she got access to it and cleaned him out. He's living at the guest house right now. He was going to use that money to buy a house here. He had to sell his car—the Lamborghini. Charlie was heartbroken," she says with a little laugh. "Anyway, he's been struggling to keep things going financially, until year two of his contract kicks in with the Giants, which isn't for a whole...well, *another year*. He doesn't even have a car right now. Charlie was giving him rides to practice on his way to med school and the hospital, but then, your dad loaned him Holly's car. The Jetta? Anyway, I should probably stop talking because it doesn't make him sound very attractive, does it? Just know he's been through a lot, not like you have, but still...it's been tough for him. He's definitely humbled and just trying to keep it all going. His fastball's off, and that's about any sports reporter wants to talk to him about, if they're not still hotly pursuing the sordid details about how he feels about Moscow or the Angels' trading him mid-season." She sighs. "*Sorry.* I'm officially stepping off the soap box. It's just been a nightmare for him. I actually feel sorry for him; he's a good guy after all. I probably shouldn't have said anything; he'd kill me if he knew you knew."

I'm still reeling from what all she's just said about Linc, but, for some inexplicable reason, I decide to take a stab at just some of what she's said. "His fastball's off because he's leaning too far back before releasing the ball; he's losing all that power. He's going to injure himself if he doesn't correct it soon. It started toward the end of last season in the playoffs, probably got mentally reinforced with the whole Moscow fiasco, and now he's just freaked out about it and overcorrecting; I'm sure."

Silence.

Marla's speechless.

I laugh a little before saying, "I suppose you could weave *that* into a conversation with him, without telling him where the sports advice came from, and see if the adjustment I'm talking about improves his fastball."

"*Tally Landon*, have you become a baseball *fan?*" Marla asks.

"Not exactly. *Sometimes.* I check his stats every so often," I say airily, somewhat beholden to sharing one of my little secrets about life here in Manhattan. "There's this guy Sampson Dotson. What a name, right? He runs a newsstand on 8ᵗʰ Street; he keeps track of that stuff for me, and he shows me the reports. We talk baseball when I go there on my way to our diner for coffee or the infrequent burger. Of course, he's a Yankees fan so the conversation is somewhat slanted." I pause. "It's not a big deal."

"No, of course, it's not a *big deal*," Marla says with a little laugh. "Tally. You're the ingenious one and you're coming *home*. I just can't believe it. I'm so happy."

I look over at Rob then, and intently watch him as he plays with Cara with new eyes at all these latest revelations about Nika Vostrikova and what she's done to Linc. I can only wonder if Rob knows about this or not. I sigh deep. "Look, I need to go. I can't talk anymore right now. *Rob's* coming back with Cara in tow. I'll call you later; okay?"

"What? We haven't talked in ages and you're going? You're killin' me, Landon. But *call* me back. *Promise?* We have lots to talk about with this move. And send me the key; don't forget."

"Promise."

"Hey, Tally? I'm so glad you're coming home. I love you."

"I love you, too, Marla Stone Masterson. You're the best friend a girl could ever have. I'll see you *soon*." I end the call and feel completely overwhelmed because talking to Marla makes it real. All of it. Rob. Linc. Lies. Promises. It's all a bit much to take in.

Rob comes over to me, carrying Cara. She rests her little head against his shoulder and plays with his hair. I almost have to turn away from the sweet picture of happiness together they make. Even so, I have to make this right with Linc. Cara is his daughter. I have to try to work it out with Linc and see where we go from here. And, Rob lied. The knight in shining armor had a cause and her name is Nika, not Tally, or even Holly.

"What's up?" Rob asks.

I ignore his question and swallow hard. "I guess dandelion-blowing tires a girl out," I say cautiously. Lost in all these hellish thoughts, I link my arm with his, and we start the trek home. We're about halfway there when I get enough courage to look up at him. "I need to talk to you."

He looks at me intently for a long time but doesn't say anything more. Then the three of us ride the elevator without talking, having adopted Cara's propensity for silence as our own. He doesn't ask me what I want to talk about. Somehow, I think he knows.

Instead, he just lays Cara down on her little twin bed and covers her up with her new favorite blanket. It's the one he brought home from some boutique on the Upper East Side that someone from his work team had suggested he try when he was in search of some upscale kid's clothing.

"It's a security blanket," Rob had said to me when he brought it home for Cara all wrapped up in pink tissue inside a white linen box tied with a large frilly pink ribbon. "It's to help her talk, to remember that when she's feeling sad she has something to hold on to. I bought two of them. One for each of you." He'd brought out a second gift-wrapped box and held it out to me, displaying the increasingly absent smirky smile of his the entire time. I wrapped myself in the pink cotton blanket that night and swore to him that

I'd never take it off. He laughed so hard that tears rolled down his face. And, for a few days, we were okay again.

Now I lie down on the bed and pull the pink blanket over my shoulders and settle in. I look over at Rob, who just watches me from the doorway, looking a little uneasy by the things I've said or haven't said since this afternoon. His arms are folded across his chest. He studies me intently like an astronomer must study the stars. I briefly told him about the phone call with Marla, and he didn't say much. I haven't told him about Sasha's phone call or the job offer.

"Can we just *not* talk, tonight?" he asks. His hands shake as he comes over to the bed.

"Okay." I turn onto my side and feel him as he climbs into bed and nuzzles into me. He seems to breathe a sigh of relief and within minutes, he's asleep, still holding onto me.

It's been a long day.

It's been a long good-bye; probably, since we first got together.

The hours tick by, and I dully note the time on the clock that glows from his side of the bed. It's half-past three in the morning, and I'm still awake.

"I never meant to hurt you," Rob whispers to me in the dark.

"I know." His arms get tighter around me. "I'm sorry I couldn't be Holly."

"I'm sorry I made you feel you had to be. Tally, I love you. I *do*."

I turn into his arms and face him. I reach out and touch his wet face. "I know. I love you, too, but I have to go home. It's been too long since I've been home." My eyes fill with tears. "Sasha offered me a position with her at the San Francisco Ballet. I'm taking it. I want Cara to know my family... and her father." I sigh. "I'm sorry. I'm truly sorry for hurting you and for disappointing you. I wish I could have been more."

"I'm sorry, too. You are *more*; and you never disappointed me. Not really. Not often." He strokes my hair and I can see him frowning in the fading moonlight where it streams through the bedroom window and onto the two of us. "Tally, oh God, Tally. I have something to tell you. Something...I should have told you a while ago. I've done some—"

I put my finger to his lips. "Rob? I really don't want to know. *Please*."

"It's important." He sits up, grasps his knees, and sighs deep. He glances over at me with this look of devastation.

"Is it going to make me want to stay?"

Silence.

"Noooooooooo," he draws the answer out with one long, sad breath.

"Then, don't say it. We've both done and said things that we can't undo."

He inclines his head and looks over at me intently. A single tear rolls down his face. After a few minutes, he sighs and lies back down in the bed. I slide into him. He wraps his arms around me and nuzzles his chin into my shoulder. "I'm so sorry," he says again.

"I know. Me, too."

I don't say anything for a few minutes. I'm conflicted about saying more, but I can't let it end like this because Rob does deserve better. I don't understand all of what is going on with him and the beautiful Russian, but I want to leave with a clear conscience based upon what Marla told me earlier.

"Nika is bad news," I finally say.

His breath hitches. It's a long while before he says, "I know."

There are all kinds of ways to say good-bye. This one, between Rob and me, is definitely one of the hardest. There is plenty of tenderness in his touch and enough remorse in his tone that these two things practically undo all of me and my grandiose plans for leaving at all; because staying with him would be so much easier.

And yet, there's one thing I now recognize, if you don't have trust, you really don't have anything. And so it is with the two of us.

We make a promise to remain friends. It feels hollow even when we say it. So, we say it more than once.

CHAPTER FORTY-SIX

Tally: Back to Wonderland

ONCE WE'RE AT JFK, I CHECK most of our luggage, upgrade to first class, and pull out a credit card to cover it all, despite the fact that I have very little money to my name; budget be damned. The five-hour plane ride is mostly uneventful, although Cara seems to continually pull at my sleeve indicating a need to go potty. We've been working on big girl panties—the pretty ones with Sleeping Beauty on the front—and she's gotten the hang of it in a matter of days. Yet, after the fourth time of this in as many hours, it finally dawns on me that she is just fascinated with the smallness of the space as much as actually needing to go every time. She finally dozes off ninety minutes before we land, and I breathe this sigh of relief and contemplate what will be greeting us on the other end. I came clean with my parents a few nights ago. My mom assured me that hers were happy tears. I cautioned them about overwhelming Cara and asked them to meet us at the house in Alamo Square later. My dad insisted upon leaving a car at the airport for us, but I told him that Marla would be picking us up and had already promised to meet up with us in baggage claim. Marla's been a god-send; because of her, I came properly prepared with Cheerios, crayons, and picture books for Cara.

We're one of the first passengers to exit the plane and now in urgent need of a restroom because Cara really does need to go. It's a good half-hour before we finally show up at Baggage Claim, but I already sent a text to Marla telling her we're running behind. By then, Cara is tired of walking and since the gate agent at JFK talked me into checking the portable baby stroller, I'm struggling with carrying Cara, my purse, as well as her Hello Kitty backpack, which precariously hangs off of my left shoulder, and pulling the carry-on luggage behind us. I am loaded down as they say. *I've got this. This is motherhood. I wouldn't want it any other way.*

Soon enough, I'm studying the Baggage Claim board and trying to remember our flight number when I happen to glance up and see him. His Giants baseball cap is pulled down low over his face, and he's one of the few people wearing sunglasses inside the airport. *The price of fame and being recognized.* He seems to scan the crowd, and it takes him another minute before he sees us. I half-wave at him. He waves back and smiles wide. Somehow, I return it although the sight of him has me practically sinking to the floor because of the bathroom calisthenics earlier, the arduous journey through the airport with my precious cargo, and my libido's radar-like ability to react to Lincoln Presley whenever he is within thirty feet of me.

I'm glad he's here. I'm not completely surprised that Marla ignored my edict for not telling Linc about our homecoming. This will make it easier.

"Claiming baggage?" he asks in this sexy, teasing tone when he reaches us. "I have some. You, too?"

"Plenty of baggage," I say. Determined to somewhat dispel the awkwardness and all the remaining questions between us, I take the lead and step toward him, still holding Cara. She looks at him curiously, but clings to me a little tighter.

"So you're really here and you're really staying," he says.

"Yes." I point to the Baggage Claim sign above us. "As long as you're here to claim me." He laughs with a little uncertainty, and I nod and make a point of removing his sunglasses, so I can see his eyes. I reward him with a knowing smile; put them on the top of my head, where they serve as an instant headband for my long hair which I've worn down especially for him. He seems to know this, and his smile gets wider. If the sunglasses gesture makes him appear to be mine, that is fine by me.

"Cara, this is…Daddy." I smile reassuringly at her to ensure she knows that everything's okay. Then, I look over at him. "Lincoln Presley, this is your daughter…Cara."

I'm sure every child psychologist in the world will have something to say about the way I've just done this, but it seems right as soon as I say it. Linc gets this joyous smile, and it is only seconds before Cara has sized him up enough to hold out her arms. She slides into Linc's open ones, dispelling trust issues for all three of us with her acceptance alone.

"Cara," Linc says softly. "I bet you were a good girl on the plane for Momma; weren't you?"

"I haven't…she doesn't know…about me." Linc looks confused while

Cara appraises me more closely. "She doesn't talk...very much. There was a car accident. She was there when Allaire..." Cara traces my face. I stop and smile at her seeking enough reassurance for both of us. "More on that a little later," I whisper to Linc. "See, kiddo? Daddy's here to pick us up."

"Momma," Cara says, looking uncertain as if she's just trying the word out. It's the first clear word she's uttered since I got her back. My eyes sting. "Momma," she says again with a little nod and then she smiles.

"Yes, Cara, that's Momma," Linc says, taking the lead because I'm unable to finish a sentence coherently at this point. I'm overwhelmed by the truth and just hearing my child utter this single word makes me so happy. I laugh a little and shyly smile over at Cara. "Momma," I say pointing at my heart. "Momma loves you, Cara." She nods and smiles as she catches one of the tears that trail down my face with her little finger. I turn to Linc suddenly in need of his complete forgiveness and saying it out loud. "Linc, I just want to say—"

"Ms. Delacourt? Can I get your autograph? I can't believe it's you. I saw your performance in *Sleeping Beauty* a few years ago when we were in Manhattan. Wow! I can't believe you're here in the airport. This is amazing. *You're* amazing. I want to be a dancer, too."

I turn away from Linc's bemused face and in the direction of the young teenage girl saying this. A blond, willowy child, who looks to be about twelve as well as earnest, dedicated, and willful, greets me. Her request effectively destroys the reunion moment. I quell that particular disappointment and begin to tell the girl all the qualities she'll need to succeed, while I quickly sign the boarding pass that she's proffered for my signature. She gets this look of wonder as she moves off with her parents and waves back at all three of us. Cara even waves.

"I'm going to be dancing for the San Francisco Ballet this fall," I call out. "Come out and see one of the performances if you're in the area and let me know. I'll get you backstage." Her beaming smile tells me I just made her day, maybe her year. *Well, we'll see.*

I turn back to Linc and Cara and discover them watching me in this kind of dazed wonder. Cara's trails her little fingers along the back of Linc's neck. *Lucky girl. I want to do that very thing to him, too.*

My unmasking of the famous baseball player unintentionally initiates a few autograph seekers for him as well. A crowd of at least ten baseball fans begins to form around him. He still holds Cara and begins signing his name with a black Sharpie on whatever item is offered.

I turn back to the conveyor belt of luggage and begin the task of finding ours among the remaining bags. As a world traveler now, I've learned the trick with scarves, and it doesn't take that long to distinguish and assemble our suitcases from everyone else's. I turn and wave at Linc, who slowly extricates himself from the growing fan base after ensuring he's signed every item the fans want signed. Cara smiles and waves back at the crowd while Linc carries her and makes his way over to me and the bags.

"There's a lot of baggage. Sorry. I collected more in Manhattan than I thought possible. Is Marla coming? Charlie? To help us with all of this?"

"Nah…it's just you and me. We thought that would be easier on both of you. But everybody knows you're here…that both of you are here." He grins mischievously and says, "But I'm the only one who gets to claim you."

We share this look—a look that speaks volumes. The past angst and uncertainty between us are quickly extinguished with these palpable feelings of hope and joy that seem to overwhelm us both with every passing minute and that one look. *I feel it. I know Linc does, too.*

He holds out his free hand, and I take it in mine and bring it to my lips. My charm bracelet dangles from my wrist, and he recognizes his gift from years before right away. "I bet you didn't know this is my good-luck charm. I travel with it everywhere. Your bracelet is the first thing I put on for every flight and the last thing I take off after I arrive. See? You've always been with me. You just didn't know it." He sucks in his breath and holds it after my little travel speech. "So, thank you, Elvis." I smile sweetly up at him and pull him closer.

I think he finally understands my notes and what I've always been thanking him for. Because, then? He kisses me and the world watches, and neither one of us cares.

Well, Cara begins to care because she's being squished between us. She pushes on both of us, indicating we should stop.

"Later," he says to me as he steps back.

"Promise?"

"Promise."

⁓⁓⊱⋅⊰⁓⁓

After we've loaded up the back of Charlie and Marla's gigantic SUV, and he's tapped out a brief text message into his iPhone, he slyly glances over at me. "Your mom wanted us to text her as soon as we got the car loaded," he says by way of explanation. "There's a party planned at your newly-remodeled house in Alamo Square, which we—your mom, Marla, and me—oversaw in terms of paint and plaster and general agreements on this is what Tally would want in terms of style." He grins and adds, "Lest there be any doubt about what's going to happen next. I know how you hate surprises, so I'm telling you now. Just act surprised for them all because I'm in good with your parents, especially your mom, and I want to keep it that way." He raises an eyebrow, looking at me quizzically, practically daring me to disagree. All I can do is nod.

He's in good with my parents, especially my mother? Awesome; and really? No surprise there.

This little crevice starts to form in the middle of his forehead. He sighs a little, and it makes me laugh. "I *really* wanted to do this differently. There's this place by San Francisco Bay that I thought would be perfect, but you're not going to want to wait for all of that, are you?"

He doesn't give me a chance to answer before he's reached into the glove box and now holds out an old-fashioned ring box in the palm of his hand. I instantly recognize the ring box from Valentine's Day over a year ago. I swallow hard somewhat unprepared for this moment but having wanted it for so long, I struggle with keeping it together now. He flips open the box revealing the marquis diamond inside. It's unique and absolutely breath-taking.

"It was my mother's ring. I want you to have it. Tally…" His voice breaks down. He starts again. "Talia…Landon, will you marry me?"

My eyes sting. Behind us, ever-patient in her car seat, Cara claps her hands vying for attention in her own sweet girl way. Meanwhile, Linc stares at me deliberately willing me to answer. "Yes. Yes. Yes, Lincoln Presley, I'll marry you."

With a shaking one-handed gesture, he slips the delicate ring onto my left ring finger. It seems apropos that Cara should be our witness. We break our gaze from each other at the same time and look back at our daughter.

"Yes," I say again. "I've always wanted to marry you. *Always*. I love you, Linc."

"There's no comeback to a line like that."

"It's not a line." I smile at the memory of when we first said this to each other.

He frowns. "If I say it back now, it will look like I'm just copying you."

"What are you? In *high school?*"

"Not anymore." He grins. "You?"

"Not anymore."

"I love you, Tally Landon. I love you. I've loved you from the first moment we met; in that first second of looking into your eyes in what must have been the saddest moment of your life, but I knew…it would always be *you*."

My throat gets tight. The banter between us from a few minutes before fades. Cara studies us both; her wide-eyed, childish gaze goes back and forth from Linc to me just taking it all in.

My lips part and I can't help but smile because I'm caught up in the amazing light and utter joy of him and his never-ending love.

He is Wonderland to me.

"Me, too," I finally say. "I already knew on some subconscious level that you meant everything to me even on that day."

We begin our short journey headed north on the 101, which clearly symbolizes the start of our life together. I catch my breath and let it out slowly taking it all in, while Linc concentrates on the road and Cara starts to doze off.

And this is real.

Real, but surreal.

I'm with Lincoln Presley in Charlie and Marla's Escalade, and we're heading north on the 101.

After few minutes of uncertainty, I reach for Cara's little backpack and hand Linc the cashier's check from inside. Rob came clean in six million different ways just last night.

"What's this?" he asks.

"Your life savings. Your signing bonus. She took it from you, and I'm returning it. It's yours. She had no right to it."

I sigh, unable to actually utter Nika's name. I'm not completely cured of all of my fears or insecurities. *No. I'm cured just enough.*

"She invested it in Rob's start-up company, but he can get the funding from somewhere else, not with money she *stole* from you. She…she lied to him, too, about everything."

"I really don't want to talk about Rob Thorn," Linc says getting this stormy look.

"Probably not, but you should know that I know about the six hundred thousand you put in his bank account. Thank you for that. He didn't tell me. About a lot of things. How he'd hooked up with Nika some time ago."

"Tally, I really don't want to talk about Rob Thorn and Nika Vostrikova."

I nod but I steel myself to finish this.

"He asked me at least ten times to marry him, and I accepted one of his proposals because it was easier, and he deserved that much, at the time. But I could never bring myself to marry him because regardless of how things were going between us—good or bad—I still hung onto this thread of hope that things might turn out the way I wanted them to…someday. I kept remembering what my mom said to me once a long time ago about being happy, making mistakes and not being so perfect, and what I wanted to do… *you.*" I laugh. "Sorry that didn't come out right…."

Linc shakes his head and half-smiles. I watch him breathe out slowly, but he still won't look at me. I can only imagine what's racing through his mind about Rob and Nika and us. I'm determined to resolve this issue once and for all.

"Getting your money back was the right thing to do. It has nothing to do with anything else, *with us*. You know it's never been about the money for me, right? I mean Tremblay left me a hundred thousand in cash; and I did my part in augmenting the crime victims' fund in Moscow, too, Elvis; but you were worth every penny." This incredulous look crosses his face when he finally looks over at me, and I smile.

"What?" he asks.

I never told anyone about the hundred grand in cash handed over to ensure Linc's freedom. Only Rob and my lawyer knew about that. It was my one and only condition for giving my statement to the Moscow Police. Clearing Linc was my one and only reason for returning to Moscow.

"You didn't really think they were going to let you walk out of there without a little extortion money thrown their way for freeing a famous American baseball player, did you?"

"Kimberley never told me," he says slowly.

"Kimberley doesn't know about it." I frown. "Tremblay left it for me as some sort of conciliatory payment for Cara after she took her away from me intent on never letting me see her again. I never would have spent the money, but the bartender there—Sam—Allaire's ex-boyfriend? Sam told me I might need it in Moscow, for you; and I most certainly did. Like I said, you were worth every penny. I know Cara would agree. We'll have to save up for her education for Stanford another way, but we've got time. I think we'll figure it out." I smile at him and he finally returns it. "I mean, you know I'm not with you because you're a famous baseball player, right? I'm with you because…you're *it* for me. You always have been," I say this with extraordinary benevolence, and now I know I've blown him away.

He glances at the freeway traffic and then back at me. "Just like I'm not with you because you're now a famous ballerina," he says with a little smile and shakes his head side-to-side. "Why do you come up with the most amazing love stuff, when I'm on the freeway, driving an unfamiliar car with our daughter secured in the backseat, on our way to see your parents and just about everyone else we know? Why can't you say this stuff when we're alone, and I can *do* something about it?"

"It's not about the great S-E-X, either, Elvis, although there will be a follow-up on that particular aspect of our reunion, later. How *late* is everyone staying?" I ask sweetly.

He smirks as he covertly glances into the rearview mirror at Cara.

"She's out. She's sleeping. You can *say* the word. Come on, *say* it for me. You've got to give me something to hang onto for *later*."

"It's easier to spell it. It keeps it superficial and keeps my heart rate from soaring out-of-control even more than it already is."

"Your heart rate is soaring out-of-control?"

"Pretty much. You just asked me to marry you less than a half-hour ago. My pulse is pretty much racing out-of-control from that alone. To say nothing of the fact that we're in a car, on the 101, making our way toward our new home, and the family and friends who pretty much symbolize the beginning of our new life together as a couple and a family of three. Yeah, it's perfect; everything is, but it's a lot to take in."

"Still afraid of falling, failing, and losing, I see," he says.

I'm no longer afraid of falling...in love with you." I smile at my cleverness. "I'm no longer afraid of failing at ballet or as a mother or even a wife because I actually think I'm pretty good at the first two of those things, and the third one is all I've ever wanted to be." He looks at me intently then. "But losing? That one is still a cross I bear. I can't lose you. I can't lose Cara or anyone else I really love."

He grabs my hand and presses it to his lips. "Tally," he says. "It's all working out. We're here. We love each other. This day. Tomorrow. The next day. Six months from now. A year from now. Ten years from now. I'm here. You're here. Cara's here. Together. This is it, baby." He grimaces. "Sorry, I know you hate to be called that."

"Not today. I'll tell you what," I say with a little laugh. "You can call me baby all night long, and I promise to let you know by tomorrow morning how I feel about it."

"Promise?"

"Promise."

<hr />

We've made good time despite the afternoon traffic, and I soon spot the freeway sign for AT&T Park where the Giants play. "So...are you glad you came to play for the Giants? Is that what you wanted?"

He looks over at me intently. "I hedged a bet. I'm glad I'm here because this is where I wanted to play, always have, but that's not why I came back."

He doesn't say anything more, and I'm left to wonder what he means, but I'm not completely sure I want to ask just yet. Still, a few minutes later I try again. "The contract is good. I mean, *eventually*, the contract will be good, from what Marla said..." My voice trails off at his dubious look.

He taps the cashier's check lying across the seat between us. "It's not about the money. It never has been."

"So what did you bet on?"

He takes his time in answering, apparently realizing the importance I must be placing on what he's going to say. I wait, and hold my breath—two, all but impossible, endeavors for me.

"I had to believe—even when it was hopeless, even when it seemed all but impossible and when my world was at its darkest, and I'd begun to fear it might be permanent—that you would come home, Tally. That something or someone would compel you to take a chance and come home. Your parents believed that. Your friends, especially Marla, believed that. All of them told me the same thing: "Hang in there and just wait." So I took a gamble—took the lesser contract offered with the Giants in a mid-season trade and fulfilled my own personal need for returning home—and I blindly hung all of my remaining hopes on you and the remote possibility that someday you, too, would want to come home. To me. And, Tally, the person who believed in that singular hope and lone wish the most—the one that encouraged me when everyone else began to believe it was hopeless—was your mom. She's amazing, bar none. The only two people happier than me that you're actually here are your mom and Marla. Well, there's your dad, Tommy, Charlie, Aunt Gina, Uncle Chad, Sasha, Michael, and even my dad, who's moving back, by the way, simply because you and Cara are going to be *here* with me. Okay, it's true: Everyone is ecstatic that you're here, that you're *both* here. But no one is more elated than I am, actually."

He takes an unsteady breath and dips his head seemingly uncertain at all he's just revealed. He gets this shy smile, as if he can't quite believe what all he's said and what's actually happening here.

Like me, fifteen minutes before.

"But…here you are. *You. Cara.*" He smiles wide. "And your advice about my leaning too far back in my pitching stance was spot-on. My fastball is back to form; thanks to you, Tally Landon."

He dips his head again and rewards me with this little smile of gratitude that could melt snow.

"Are there *any* secrets left? Did Marla tell you *everything* I said?"

"Pretty much. And that's when I was actually able to breathe again—knowing you were coming home. Finally."

A car horn sounds right behind us, breaking up yet another poignant moment. He sighs, looks up at the slowing-moving traffic and begins to merge over to the far-right lane taking the exit that will lead us to Alamo Square and home. At the first stoplight, he fully turns to me.

"You make my life, Tally Landon. Over the past year, I've come to realize that my life has actually never been about *baseball*, but baseball was just all there ever was for me—to count on or to believe in—*before you*." He gets this dazed smile. "It turns out that my real chance in life at true happiness—the risk I had to be willing to take in overcoming all of my other fears in terms of falling, failing and losing—has always been about *you*. Finding you? Saving you?" He shakes his head side-to-side. "Nah…It's always just been about *being with you*. That's all I ever wanted."

The light changes from red to green. He slowly drives the SUV through the side streets; while I sit in stunned silence because I'm so moved by what all he's just said that I can't even properly respond. Instead, I let the tears fall. I need them to, and I allow him to see them. He glances my way, more and more, getting concerned at seeing me cry. About all I'm capable of doing is gripping his hand in mine and kissing it every so often.

"You okay, Tal?" he finally asks.

"If I say it back now, it will just look like I'm copying you," I manage to say.

"What? Are you still in *high school?*" he asks, bringing just enough levity to the moment that I actually laugh.

"Not anymore." I swipe at my face and look at him intently. "It's always been *you*." He smiles wide in answer and slowly nods.

In a daze, wrung out from pure emotion, at this point, I stare out the window out as the neighborhood gets more familiar.

It's truly amazing how profoundly I feel this calling of home, but mostly of Lincoln Presley.

He's always been there for me. Always.

I sigh deeply and attempt to pull it together, but nothing seems to work. I have to touch him. I have to hold his face between my hands and kiss him.

"Elvis," I say softly. "Pull over."

He gets this knowing smile as he edges the SUV into a no-parking zone, puts the car in park, and then just looks over at me with all this barely-contained longing. He's clearly in need of what's going to happen next as much as I am.

I hastily glance at the still sleeping Cara and then gaze back at him. "How is this going to work, exactly?" I ask softly.

In deference to what we both really want to do, I sigh, take his hand, and put it to my lips. He groans softly at my intimate kiss and future promise.

In the next, he fingers the charm bracelet on my wrist. I watch in wonder as he connects the two half-hearts together with the little clasp like he showed me how to do so long ago.

The gesture speaks volumes to both of us.

"Thank you, Elvis," I say, while he visibly shudders.

With a laugh and what feels like the truest of intentions, I adroitly climb into the famous baseball player's lap, hold his handsome face between my hands, and kiss him long and hard. And we share this imprint-worthy moment at a seemingly cosmic level because this much is true: Being together is all we ever wanted.

The End

WITH GRATITUDE

Acknowledgements

WRITING IS SOMETHING THAT I HAVE been doing most of my life, but it has only been the last four years, that the timing has been just right to focus upon it full-time. I've been encouraged by so many: family, friends, colleagues, teachers, and readers, of course. *Thank you, all!*

To my family: I know I'm not easy to live with, and I know the house has been an undeclared disaster zone for the past year and a half while I wrote *This Much Is True*. This is a big *thank you* to all of you for allowing me to do what I love at the expense of serenity and home-cooked meals and all of you having to put up with no more than a quick, cryptic conversation when I'm in the throes of it all. Thank you for loving me anyway. *You do; don't you?*

Katherine Owen

ABOUT THE AUTHOR

Katherine Owen

ATHERINE OWEN IS THE AUTHOR OF the best selling novel, *Seeing Julia*, which won the *Zola Award* and placed first in Romance with the Pacific Northwest Writers Association's literary contest in July 2010. By the end of 2011, Owen had written and released two more novels, *Not To Us* and *When I See You*. *This Much Is True* is her fourth novel and the first in the *Truth In Lies* series. In late August 2014, Owen released her fifth novel and the second book in the series, *The Truth About Air & Water*, which is a continuation of Linc and Tally's story. Owen lives near Seattle with her husband and two children, where she is working on her next novel.

QUESTIONS & ANSWERS

| SPOILERS AHEAD |

This Much Is True

Tell us about your writing process with *This Much Is True*. Where did the story come from?
My writing process is that of a pantser, which means that the story comes to me *organically* as I write it. I've tried outlines, storyboards, rough drafts, outlines *(again)*. However, in the end, as much as I fought the process that is what I am. It's how it works for me. Yet, because I fought the process, this novel took twice as long to complete. You would think, since it was my fourth book, that it would have come easier, but *no*.

The inspiration for this novel came out of an exercise I did for one of my Fiction IV writing classes with *The Writers Studio* about two years ago. That led to the development of the story of Tally (originally she was called Amy), but it evolved to Tally in the later drafts. Lincoln Presley was pretty much set from early on. He was easy to write. He's another accomplished amazing soul with a tragic loss in his past that makes him sympathetic and cosmically connected to the young Tally from the very beginning of the story. Linc is committed to doing the right thing for his father and for his talent, although he is conflicted about it much of the story line. I liked writing about that. It was equally fun to learn so much about baseball and rekindle my love for ballet.

Author Q & A

Why baseball? Why ballet?

I needed a sport that kept them apart much of the time and baseball has these really long seasons. I wanted to illustrate the dedication and sacrifice that comes with being a professional baseball player just as much as a professional dancer. Lastly, I grew up doing ballet from the age of twelve on and made it to toes shoes. Ballet has always fascinated me. Thus, a love story about a ballerina seemed in order.

***This Much Is True* handles some pretty heavy subject manner. How did you get into the mindset to handle writing about such controversial stuff? (SPOILER)**

I was inspired to write a novel where fate and circumstances keep two people apart and the innocent telling of lies by one of them leads to an eventual unraveling of the relationship and virtually keeps them apart. I eventually wrote *This Much Is True* keeping these themes in mind.

Additionally, I think many young women wrestle with the decision of birth control or face decisions related to an unexpected pregnancy. I wrestled with the idea of what Tally should do with this baby. The old Tally would have had an abortion. The new Tally (*changing*) isn't so sure of her decisions. I hope I made it clear in the story that Tally was so affected by her sister's death that she couldn't bring herself to have one, and yet she gives the baby up, which also leads to personal conflict for her and becomes a tough choice.

I wanted to explore the idea of consequences for the decisions we make and what happens to us in (real) life. In this story, Tally naively believes that she'll be able to move on without looking back, but the change in Tally herself over time shows this not to be true. And then there's Moscow. I debated about this part of the story line for a long time, but it kept coming back to me—the price and consequences of fame (a stalker, unintended violence) so I went there and I think it paid off.

So, these were some of the themes I hope I effectively covered with this story. It's a subtle, slower-moving novel. The twists and turns with the plot lines build a little slower with this one in comparison to my other books. I wanted to grow as a writer and literally slow down and take my time in presenting the story, and the character arcs that take place. Love and loss remain ever-present themes, but I hope I conveyed it in a different way this time with this novel. *Discuss.*

Author Q & A

There's a new sub-category out there in the book world called New Adult Fiction. Would you classify *This Much Is True* in that category?

I think *This Much Is True* can play in this arena, but if you're looking for the bad boy with numerous tattoos and lots of racy sex scenes, you'll be disappointed. This story is about two people who find each other, lose each other, and must slowly make their way back to one another. The character arcs for both Tally and Linc are slow in, well, arcing, but they're there. I'm happy with how the story turned out, but this isn't your predictable read. New Adult Fiction centers on characters that are coming of age when they first leave home and experience their first loves. I think *This Much Is True* fits that criteria, but this is a deeper story than most of what I've read in the category. Additionally, there are no vampires, no shape shifters, no bad boys, no tattoos; *This Much Is True* is just a story about love, and loss, and starting over, and how fate intervenes. *You know* my usual stuff.

It's a long novel. Did you contemplate two books?

Yes! I did contemplate breaking the story up. I thought about cutting parts of it out, but in the end, I decided to go with it as is. So, yes, it's long. And *yes, it* could have been two or three books. Lots of authors, these days, do just that. However, I'm not a series gal, and I'm not fond of cliff-hangers. As a reader, I think we lose some of the original enthusiasm for the story line when we have to wait for the full story. Thus, you get Tally and Linc's complete story in one long novel from both of their point-of-views. (Bonus!) *Discuss.*

There are also a few love triangles to this one. What did you do to make those complicated chemistry/interactions work?

I truly enjoyed the character of Rob Thorn. He was another early inspiration for me. I could just *see* him. Here's this guy, who is torn up about losing the love of his life in Holly Landon, and yet he has a thing for Tally Landon. (It is the subtext for much of the story, but it's there. It seems to be the elusive bad twin attraction.) Tally's conflicted over Rob because she both fights and succumbs to being/acting/pretending to be her twin sister Holly some of the time. I didn't want to do the cliché *pick one* Team Rob or Team Linc's scenario. I think it's pretty clear that Tally and Linc belong together, but Rob Thorn adds an interesting element for these two as does Nika Vostrikova. Nika was fun to write. She's the typical insecure girlfriend who does everything in her power to keep her life with Linc and the guy himself in check. She's a minor character but she likes to mess with our heroine, Tally Landon, whenever she gets a chance. I enjoyed writing her as well as Kimberley Powers (again, for those familiar with this character).

Author Q & A

Is there one trait you share with Tally?
Tally is independent and has a passionate dedication to ballet. When I was her age so did I. Thus, we get a story about a ballerina. And most everyone would agree I am highly independent. *Highly.*

When did you know you wanted to be a writer?
As the cliché goes, I have wanted to be a writer for most of my life. I won a poetry contest at the age of fourteen, majored in English and Editorial Journalism in college, and carried the desire and dream to write with me everywhere, until finally, I had the time and the freedom to write novels full-time.

What was your ultimate goal with this novel? (SPOILER)
Truly? I tried to avoid killing anyone off. I got some heat for that in a few of my other novels. I wanted to show loss in a different way with this story line. (Hint: Charlie was saved. I had a whole other story line about him that was really good, but life prevailed (ha!) for all four of them. (Six if we're counting Nika & Rob, and we should, really, right?)) *Still.* A few people had to go in this novel too, but if you've read my other novels, you know how that works. You might not cry as much with this one. *Thus, goal achieved? Let me know.*

What's up next?
I'm busy finishing my fifth novel *Saving Valentines* and another Work-in-progress that I'm dying to get to. Busy. Busy. Busy writing. It never ends.

What else can you share?
As a novelist, (a fictionista as one Twitter follower phrased it) as a writer of contemporary fiction, I tend to write stories that are both edgy and dark—about trust, love, and fate—and how relationships are often tested by all of these things in one way or another.

My novels are often described as emotional roller coasters. If you're in search of the easy-read romance novel, just know that my novels are not those and will leave you reeling half the time. More than one reader has stipulated their own warning about being in need a box of Kleenex tissues when they read my work. I think my heroines and heroes represent today's contemporary women and men and their daily life struggles with love and the pursuit of true happiness. I really do believe that relationships are tested in all kinds of ways by love, trust, and fate, and this continues to inspire my writing.

AFTERWORD

Author Note

*H*ERE'S WHAT I KNOW TO BE true: relationships are tested in all kinds of ways so that's what I love to write about; you can never have enough shoes; you should always pack your make-up in your carry-on; if your glass is half-full, you've got to ask for more; and lastly, go with the adage—never believe your own press—because too much ego or too little doesn't serve you either way.

For future release dates for my novels, go sign up for my newsletter http://bit.ly/KOnewsletter and be one of the first to be notified about my new book releases. For additional information about my novels and general anecdotes about trust, love, and fate, go to my website www.katherineowen.net or "like" my Facebook Author Fan page http://www.facebook.com/katherineowenauthor to get the latest updates.

Thank you for reading *This Much Is True*. If you loved it, tell your friends and please consider leaving a review; and, if not, tell me why. Thank you for reading my work.

Best,

Katherine Owen

TRUTH IN LIES SERIES CONTINUES!

the truth about air & water

truth in lies series, book 2

by Katherine Owen

They share an epic love,
but one moment changes everything.
A life together that seemed certain is shattered.
One learns you never love the same way twice;
the other learns what it means to come home.
You only think you know how this love story goes,
but do you really know how an epic love can end?

Check your online retailer or author's website for buy links www.katherineowen.net The Truth About Air & Water is Available in trade paperback or eBook formats for readers.

CPSIA information can be obtained at www.ICGtesting.com
Printed in the USA
BVOW02s1938200115

384166BV00004B/219/P

9 780983 570769